Olivia

Olivia

Inspired by a True Story

MICHAEL E. BOWERS

LUMINARE PRESS
WWW.LUMINAREPRESS.COM

OLIVIA
Copyright © 2024 by Michael E. Bowers

All rights reserved. This book or any portion thereof may not be reproduced or used in any manner whatsoever without the express written permission of the publisher, except for the use of brief quotations in a book review.

Printed in the United States of America

Luminare Press
442 Charnelton St.
Eugene, OR 97401
www.luminarepress.com

LCCN: 2024902710
ISBN: 979-8-88679-491-5

My wife of 25 years, Diane, was by my side making the decisions needed to keep me alive from day one. She braved the telling of my alternate reality torment and how my brain portrayed her, silently and with a smile. It took me a long time to figure out that she too was traumatized.

Diane had to deal with life and death decisions every step of the way. Every setback (and there were many) she handled with true professionalism on the outside; however, on the inside her world was being torn apart. While I was lost in a different reality, she handled the day-to-day activities of my hospitalization and took care of the household and our son.

Diane is truly a remarkable and strong woman.

CONTENTS

Prologue | 1

CHAPTER 1
Bill Parson (May 1927-1933) | 3

CHAPTER 2
Kimberly Lynn Parson "Kim" | 28

CHAPTER 3
Allen James Schultz (January 1956) | 35

CHAPTER 4
Sweet Sixteen (18 May 1985) | 40

CHAPTER 5
Ciao Bella (Saturday, 29 June 1968) | 65

CHAPTER 6
The Announcement (February 1968) | 78

CHAPTER 7
Mom, Dad, Guess What? | 84

CHAPTER 8
Acapulco Dreams (1984) | 96

CHAPTER 9
Julio "Snowman" Mendez (July 1948) | 104

CHAPTER 10
Cartel de Océano (1962) | 110

CHAPTER 11
Answer My Questions (April 1970) | 114

CHAPTER 12
There's a New Boss (23 September 1969) | 122

CHAPTER 13
Acapulco November 1985 | 126

CHAPTER 14
The Eagle has landed (2 Nov 85) | 136

CHAPTER 15
Two Worlds Collide (3 November 1985) | 143

CHAPTER 16
The Cover-Up | 165

CHAPTER 17
The Conspiracy (5 November 1985) | 182

CHAPTER 18
Wake up (7 November 1985) | 185

CHAPTER 19
Goodbyes (8 November 1985) | 193

CHAPTER 20
Time Heals (3 November 1986) | 198

CHAPTER 21
Living with Memories (10 February 1988) | 201

CHAPTER 22
Shrinks and Drugs (11 February 1988) | 211

CHAPTER 23
The Accomplish (14 April 1989) | 219

CHAPTER 24
Traversing the Web of Lies (12 October 1989) | 226

CHAPTER 25
Back to School (8 January 1990) | 235

CHAPTER 26
Don't Mind Me (23 April 1997) | 239

CHAPTER 27
The Letter (23 June 1997) | 248

CHAPTER 28
The Plan (24 June 1997) | 263

CHAPTER 29
The Locker (12 April 2003) | 269

CHAPTER 30
 The Mailman (3 October 2003) | 275

CHAPTER 31
 The Artifacts (15 June 2007) | 280

CHAPTER 32
 The Artifacts Part 2 (23 August 2007) | 286

CHAPTER 34
 The Last Artifact (3 November 2008) | 319

Epilogue | 329

Acknowledgments | 330

Author Bio | 331

PROLOGUE

"Olivia" is a prequel to the true story "Captured by COVID, Deceit, Conspiracy & Death." It provides context, motivation, and the history of many of the characters.

To understand the people of today, you need to know the stories of those who raised them. Olivia will introduce you to several families that played a part in shaping her life.

Several individuals in this book lived colorful lives, which their language and actions show. This story is derived from true events as experienced by the author.

Warning!!!

"Olivia" contains some harsh language and scenes of rape and murder. The material in this book may not be appropriate for some readers.

CHAPTER 1

Bill Parson
(May 1927-1933)

In the early 1900s, Youngstown, Ohio, was known for its corruption and multitude of illegal establishments. *The Saturday Evening Post dubbed* Youngstown "Crimetown USA" for a good reason. Youngstown was owned by the mob, specifically Mr. Charles Cavallaro, aka *"Cadillac Charlie."* There was illegal gambling, bootlegging, prostitution, and various other crimes, which spurred mob wars between the competing families. This resulted in bodies from all sides piling up. Youngstown is conveniently located between two mafia cities, Cleveland and Pittsburgh. This contributed to Youngstown's unrest but also its prosperity.

William "Bill" Parsons was born in Youngstown in 1916. He was a scrawny little kid, shorter and slimmer than his peers. When he was eleven, his parents abandoned him. Bill said goodbye to them one morning as he headed to school, and by the time he returned, they were gone. Nothing was missing. Their clothes were all there, and the suitcases were still in the hall closet.

Having something like this happen to anyone is horrible, but an eleven-year-old child? Bill was devastated, confused, scared, and felt betrayed by the ones he loved. He hid out in the house as long as he could. Eventually, the authorities came with an eviction notice and found him there alone.

Bill was a bit raucous and didn't do well in orphanages, not because they were bad, but because it wasn't home. The longest he stayed in one place was three weeks; after that, he'd disappear. Eventually, they'd find him and place him in another home. After the fifth time, they stopped looking for him unofficially.

Bill visited shelter after shelter during winter to keep warm, trying to be as inconspicuous as possible. He lived in what most would call the "rough" part of town, where lines for the soup kitchen would wrap around the block. It was hard to get handouts in an area where everyone was deprived. It was the middle of the Great Depression, and even those not living on the streets suffered. For that reason, Bill received empathy and managed to get enough scraps to get by.

Several blocks east of midtown, was a small community that always seemed to be bustling with activity. Bill often ventured there but felt out of place. He had only the clothes on his back that were tattered and torn. His shoes were worn with the soles barely hanging on; he had no socks.

On one such visit, he was walking through town when he passed a busy bus stop. He watched as people got on and off the electric bus. He noticed a mom scolding her daughter because she said out loud, "Mom, that boy stinks." Bill dropped his head and kept walking. He became more observant; sure enough, others talked under their breath and avoided getting close to him. He was like *Pig Pen* from *Charlie Brown*, with a dust cloud that followed him. Unfortunately, it was more than dirt that gave him that nauseous aroma.

Bill couldn't remember the last time he had bathed. It's not like he could dive into the local pond or creek; the water temperature was in the mid-40s, according to a Ms. Know-It-All he overheard blabbering at the diner. He was hungry and really wanted to get away from the townspeople. So, he headed towards the outskirts of town, walking down the tracks looking for homeless camps. The hobos there were known to share their food, as they often needed food themselves. It was like a family; if one person had plenty, they'd share. If he was out, others would share with him.

While searching for a free meal, a freak thunderstorm appeared out of nowhere. Bill was near an open field when the rain came. No shelter was in sight, so he nonchalantly draped his coat over his left shoulder and continued walking down the tracks. It was a strange sight; behind him, the skies were clear, and he could see beams of sunlight streaming down. In front of him, it was dark, with clouds moving at a high rate of speed from his left to his right.

The weather was very inconsistent since it was late spring, more so than in previous years. It would be eighty degrees one day and the next only forty. The plants were confused too; should they bloom or not? The rain, already causing flooding of the nearby stream, was accompanied by thunder and lightning. This wasn't anything new to Bill. He'd been on the streets for some time and had been through worse. He saw a lightning strike in the distance before him, then slowly counted, "One, two, three, four, five, six…" BOOM! The ground vibrated as the thunder roared in the open skies. "Hmm," he thought, "that means the storm is about six miles ahead, and the clouds appear to be moving in the opposite direction I'm walking."

Confident he wasn't in danger, he used this opportunity to rinse the dirt off his body. He placed his drenched coat on the tracks, carefully placing it on the wooden sleeper (aka tie) and rail to avoid getting it muddy. He removed his shirt and used it as a rag to clean his face and upper body. He wrung out the shirt three or four times, noticing the dark water getting lighter each time, then placed it back on. He looked around to verify that no one was nearby, then removed his pants. Standing in his stained, worn, holey underwear, he wiped down his scarred legs. He used the leg of his pants to wipe his butt; however, when he stretched his underwear, they ripped. Not a small rip, but completely from the waistband to the crotch. "Shit!" he exclaimed as he ripped off the rest of his briefs, throwing the scraps into a pile of debris off the tracks. "Regimental it is."

Bill spent three hours looking for the hobo camps. He was confused as to where they might have all gone. The dark clouds had turned into puffs of white cotton balls. The sun shone, and he saw a few deer frolicking in the fields. A rainbow crossed the sky, looking like it touched down on the other side of the tree line. It was so peaceful after a storm; the air smelled better, and the trees seemed to be waving to him.

Bill passed through the east side of town on his way back. It was close to dinner time, and he hadn't even had breakfast or lunch. There were no soup kitchens or shelters here. The sidewalks were packed with people, seemingly hurrying to get somewhere. Bill's legs weren't long enough to keep up without running. He made it past the furniture store but stopped when he arrived at the *Paramount Theater*. He recalled his parents taking him there before they disappeared.

The Paramount Theater was a work of art built in 1918 and formerly known as the Liberty Theater. His parents couldn't stop talking about how prestigious it looked. Bill couldn't remember the movie's name but knew it starred the Marx Brothers. He turned and looked out at the street; the memory of his family brought tears to his young eyes. Bill saw the newly introduced trackless streetcars (buses) that ran by electric lines overhead. He hadn't ridden one yet but had heard others speak of how comfortable they were. He was sure that if his parents were here, he'd be on one right now.

He continued his walk, slowing down when he passed a pastry shop to get a whiff of the confections inside. Bill's clothes were dry, but the evening air and slight breeze gave him a chill. He put his coat on and fastened the two remaining buttons. The aroma of food was in the air, coming from the diner up ahead.

The diner was hopping this evening, busier than he'd seen before. Bill took the alleyway next to the diner and headed to the rear to check their trash for anything edible. He climbed into the large bin and dug through the remnants of someone's dinner. He found a half-grilled cheese sandwich that looked good; he grabbed it and smiled as it was still warm. He turned to climb out and saw two of the largest field rats he'd ever seen. They wanted that sandwich as much as he did and jumped towards him. He screamed and climbed out as fast as he could. "Whew, the things a kid has to go through to get a meal," he thought.

Bill ate the grilled cheese as he walked back towards the Pastry Shop. He wanted to get another whiff of that caramel corn. He became a regular there, passing by slowly, around the same time each day. One day, a family came out eating the mouthwatering popcorn and dropped a few kernels as they walked by. He rushed to pick them up before the stray dogs trolling the streets could get to them. He was in heaven as he took his time, popping one kernel into his mouth and savoring the sweet buttery caramel. He couldn't decide whether to eat the other two pieces now or save them for later. It was now!

Unbeknownst to Bill, two sets of eyes were watching him, curious as to why a child would be unattended on the street. They watched as he practically fought off two strays to get to a measly three morsels of popcorn. They'd seen him before but never paid much attention to him until tonight. They were the owners of the Pastry Shop. A middle-aged couple who arrived in town from Cleveland and opened the shop about five years ago (more tidbits from the Ms. Know-It-All in the diner).

The woman went behind the counter and returned with a full bag of caramel corn and walked out the door towards Bill, who was still floating on cloud nine and didn't see or hear her coming.

Bill was startled when she knelt down. She said, "My name is Joan, and that's my husband James at the door. We're the Johnsons. What's your name?" He almost ran off until he noticed the popcorn. "Are you still hungry?" she asked as she presented the caramel delight to him.

He smiled and said, "My name is Bill." Then, he snatched the popcorn from her hands and started munching as fast as possible. After four or five mouthfuls, he paused and politely said, "Thank you so much, ma'am," then twisted the end of the bag to ensure he didn't lose any and left.

Joan and James stood there and watched as he disappeared into the night. "Did you see his clothes?" she asked James?

"Yes, and I'm glad it's not winter; he'd freeze. I could see his toes hanging out of his left shoe." James replied

Bill came back often and gradually took a liking to the couple. Over time, he explained to them why he was on the streets. He was twelve years old. Bill had been on the streets since shortly after his eleventh birthday, and it was currently well past his twelfth. The Pastry shop owners didn't have kids and felt a need to help this child. They would put a sandwich in a metal tin with his name on it and place it outside each day in case he came by hungry. Once in a while, they'd throw in some sweets.

Bill began staying longer and longer, talking with Joan and James. They were fun people and had good stories from their travels and managing their store. Six months later, Bill was working at the Johnson's pastry shop. It sold other things too, but the people came mostly for the pastries and to partake in what happened when the shades were down.

He really liked Joan and James. They treated him well and looked after him. They gave him a small room in the back to call home. It was heated and had a cot, lamp, and small table. It was perfect. He was even given clean clothes and a brand-new pair of shoes.

James and Joan called him over after closing one night. Joan started, "Bill, we love having you here. You're doing a great job behind the counter. Unfortunately, something unexpected has happened..." She paused and looked over at James.

"What my wife is trying to say, behind her tears, is that you've started to grow on us." James jumped in, trying to smile and hide his emotions at the same time.

Bill was getting nervous; he was sure they would kick him out. "I'm sorry if I've done something to upset you."

"Oh no, dear boy, just the opposite. We wanted to tell you that we are in love with you." Joan cried as she reached down to give Bill a huge hug.

"That's right, son, we love you and wanted to know if you'd like to live with us forever?" James asked, then clarified his question. "Well, at least until you get married," he added with a smile.

Without blinking an eye, Bill said, "YES! I love you too and already feel like this is home."

The Johnsons were not overly religious but did attend church every Sunday. The rest of the week, they did what they had to do to keep the store profitable. This included their side hustle of taking bets on the horses.

One Saturday evening, they came in and presented Bill with a suit and insisted he join them at church, which, of course, he said he would. "I've never been to church," Bill confessed.

"That's ok, son. You just need to be yourself, open your heart and mind, and absorb as much as possible." James said.

"Oh, and mind your language. There's no cursing at church." Joan added.

Bill got most of his sour language from the streets, but the Johnsons were no angels and often swore when they got excited.

Bill woke up late one morning and was confused when he entered the store and saw Joan and James wearing their Sunday clothes. James called him over to the table and softly spoke, "Bill, were you serious when you said you'd like to stay with us permanently?" Bill nodded yes as he looked at Joan sitting across from him. Both Joan and James were smiling.

Joan looked at James and said, "Let me tell him."

She scooted the chair around, making a screeching noise so that she was eye-to-eye with Bill. "Bill, you know we've enjoyed you being here with us, helping in the store and telling us great stories. But you know, it's not what we want."

Bill's eyes started to swell, and a tear snuck out. "You're not going to kick me out, are you?" Bill said with a cracked voice.

"Heavens, no," Joan exclaimed, "We want you here all the time but in a different capacity." Bill looked confused.

James said, "Son, we want to adopt you."

Bill was in a state of shock. James and Joan hugged each other, tears welling up in their eyes. They both looked at Bill as he sat there motionless.

"You want to be my new parents?" he asked.

"Yes," both James and Joan said simultaneously.

Bill started crying, jumped out of the chair, and wrapped his arms around them. "Hell yes," he said.

The Johnsons had hoped that's what he'd say, especially since they had scheduled a meeting with the judge at 9:30 that morning. "Bill, go put on your suit. We're going down to the courthouse," James said excitedly. Within an hour, Bill had a new set of parents.

He had talked about his last name on the way to get the paperwork signed. "Do you mind if I keep my last name? It's the only thing my parents gave me that I have left." Bill uttered softly.

"Of course, you can, and if someday you change your mind, we'd be honored," Joan replied.

Bill was lost until he met the Johnsons. He had no future until he was taken in by this wonderful family that may or may not have had ties with the local underworld.

Bill was very observant and watched as the covert operations were happening. Little by little, he was indoctrinated into the family business. Initially, his job was to watch the door and warn them if anyone he didn't recognize appeared. That was an easy job. He was good at it, but as he aged, he craved more responsibility and clout in the family. His adoptive parents were aware of his desires and were proud to admit that he had matured above his age. By his fifteenth birthday, he collected bets on the horses. By seventeen, he was not only collecting, but he was also managing that portion of the operations. He only stopped because of an incident that changed his life forever.

Bill was specifically responsible for collecting the bets, not the money from the losers; that was Marvin's job. Marvin was a large man who could lift a Ford Coupe with just one hand, or so the rumors went. Marvin's job was to track down and collect from the losers by any means possible. Bill wasn't big or strong enough for this; shit, they would laugh if he came to them demanding money from their losing bets.

Unfortunately, as circumstances would have it, Marvin caught a case of the clap from a whore over at the "Family's" strip club. Marvin practically lived there not only because he was their bouncer but because he also had a thing for a couple of the top attractions. Neither of them knew that he was sleeping with the other. That is, until he got gonorrhea.

Marvin wasn't the sharpest tool in the shed, probably due to the large amounts of alcohol he put down each day or the powder that lined his nostrils. He didn't say a word when the pus started coming out of his dick. Then, when it burned every time he tried to take a piss, he'd drink more to dull the pain. Linda, one of the ladies of the evening, was missing her man and decided to pay him a visit. She knocked on his office door and entered before he could speak. It wouldn't have been intelligible anyway, as Marvin was three sheets to the wind. Linda was pretty lit, too; that's probably why she didn't notice the swelling and disfigurement in his groan area. Linda massaged his enormous manhood until it was hard enough for her to sit on. She was already primed from exhibiting her body to the men in the audience, so she knew it wouldn't take long. Linda looked back at Marvin and saw he was passed out, so she helped herself to his deli meat.

Four days later, on February 2, 1933, she came running back from the doctor and barged into Marvin's office with a shotgun. "How the hell could you give me the Clap?" she yelled.

Marvin was dumbfounded. Shit, he had no recollection of sleeping with her, so he yelled back, "What the fuck are y…" Before he could complete his sentence, she aimed the shotgun, pulled the trigger, and nearly shot off his dick. Marvin fell to the floor, screaming in pain.

The damage had been done. Marvin had buckshot in his lower body. No amount of alcohol or white powder would be able to alleviate this extreme pain. Linda left him there, curled up on the floor. Fortunately, someone heard the gunshot and ran to see what had happened. The doctor would be there shortly and tend to his wounds as best he could.

So, as you can see, Marvin wouldn't be available to collect from the losers for some time. Bill was only supposed to be a one-time fill-in to allow the "family" time to get someone in from Pittsburg. So, they sent him only to the clients they thought would be no problem. By 7 p.m., Bill had only three clients left. He was proud of himself for handling the first eight without issues. When he walked by the deli, he saw one of the losers that was not on his list. His confidence was shooting out his ears, and he thought, *'I'll get this guy to pay up, and the boss will be so impressed with me.'*

Bill waited behind a telephone booth on the corner next to the deli for the deadbeat to exit before confronting him. In his stoutest voice, without so much as a quiver, he walked up to him, shook his finger in the guy's face, and said, "Joseph Fredricks, I'm here to collect what you owe the Boss." Fredricks was over a foot taller than Bill's 5'4" frame and had shoulders twice as wide. Needless to say, he didn't budge. Bill's confidence dropped a couple of notches. Before he could utter another word, a fist barreled towards him, hitting right between the eyes.

The world stopped, or at least slowed down dramatically. Bill stood there as his brain started shutting off bodily functions. He was out cold but still vertical for a few more seconds, and then his stiff body fell like a plank, crashing onto a couple of bikes parked on the sidewalk behind him.

This whole incident was witnessed by a street cop named Bob Jensen, who was initially frisking a homeless man over at the drug store. Seeing Bill hit the ground that hard trumped the homeless guy, so he rushed to assess the situation. As he knelt down to check Bill's condition, he noticed a notepad in his upper pocket with names and dollar amounts, some lined through. That and the large wad of cash in his pockets were a tale-tale sign that the boy was up to no good.

Officer Jensen had a suspicion as to who the kid's guardian was. He wasn't a fan of their operation and was rarely given a golden ticket like this. Jensen ignored the big brute that floored Bill and immediately got him up, informing him that he had more than enough evidence for a conviction. Bill refused to answer any questions, no matter how much Officer Jensen pressured him.

Bill was hauled to the city jail, but not before a quick stop by Mercy Hospital to have his head checked. Bill's head had a goose egg the size of a softball. He also had several cuts from landing hard on the bikes.

Officer Jensen had an ulterior motive for the stop. He would have brought Bill here as a safety precaution, even without visible injuries. It was no secret that Bob had a soft spot for a certain nurse who worked there. He asked the Med Tech behind the check-in counter if Nurse Susan was on duty that evening. He waited anxiously as she looked at the worksheet and saw that she was. "I'll let her know she has a visitor in the Emergency Room lobby."

"No, wait," Bob uttered, "I need to be back in the exam room with my prisoner. Can you have her meet me there?"

Officer Jensen wasn't shy when dealing with criminals, no matter how brutal the crime was, but for some reason, Susan brought out the kid in him. His palms would become sweaty, he'd start to fidget, and his brain would go blank. He'd fall back on crude jokes that no one but him thought were funny. Susan thought this was cute and blushed whenever this happened. She was divorced, loved her job, and adored her patients. However, she had a disdainful taste in her mouth when thinking about her management or even some co-workers. She didn't take much time off to even think about dating and was flattered that Bob was so taken by her. To tell the truth, she thought he was handsome and wouldn't mind going out if he'd ever asked.

The docs had sewn Bill up and given him pain meds to deal with his headache before Susan got the message that Bob was here. As he escorted Bill back to the car, he casually told the Med Tech to cancel the message to Nurse Susan.

After being processed into jail, Bill learned he wouldn't see the judge until the following week. Joan and James had already heard about Bill from sources at the jail. When they arrived, they were told that visiting hours were over and they couldn't see him until morning. "He's a minor," Joan complained, but they didn't care.

The night was long. It's hard to sleep after watching the cockroaches and ants fight over which body part they would feast on. They were formed like small armies, waiting for Bill to close his eyes. Ants on the left near the metal toilet and cockroaches a few feet from the right cell wall. As he moved his head between them, he noticed a set of eyes in the middle, no two sets of …. Fuck there are three rats licking their chops.

A man can only go so long without sleep. Bill was exhausted long before his bout with Evander Holyfield. Plus, he had the ass-kicking meds the doctors gave him. He was fighting an uphill battle. He fought well, but as many humans do, he succumbed; the Sandman would again be victorious. Bill had no idea how long he slept; he woke to loud screaming from some drug addict a couple of cells over. Then, like being shot out of a cannon, Bill recalled the creatures eying their dinner last night and jumped to his feet up on the bed. He checked body parts for whelps, bites, blood, etc., and found nothing. Whew, he dodged a bullet this time.

This wasn't one of those cozy cells you read about in magazines. There were no posters on the wall, no window to see the sunrise or sunset, and no radio. Fortunately, when it got quiet at night, you could hear a radio playing at the guards' stand. It was country music, but Bill didn't care.

As the lights began to flicker on, Bill could see things that weren't visible last night. First and foremost, how small this cell was. He could stand up and touch the walls on each side. There was barely enough room to walk comfortably beside the bed. At the end of the bed was a toilet and mini sink. There were two shelves on the wall opposite the bed, and the cold floor under his feet was made of concrete. The cinder block walls were two-tone, with a greenish paint about halfway, then cream-colored the rest of the way to the ceiling. It hadn't been painted in some time; you could see drawings through the paint (barely) on the upper portion. The previous occupant must have liked large boobs, he thought.

After breakfast, Bill was escorted to what he thought would be an interrogation room. Instead, he found Joan and James with another person waiting for him. Joan immediately stood and wrapped her arms around him until the Guard said, "No physical contact."

"Bill, this is Mr. Hurwitz. He'll be your attorney." James said. Bill looked confused, "Yes, and you can tell him everything." He proceeded to explain how he was collecting the money when he saw Fredricks. He said that Fredricks floored him when asked for the money. When he came to, Officer Bob was standing over him, holding his notebook and the money that was in his pockets.

Hurwitz looked over at the James, then said, "Don't worry, son, we'll take care of everything. Unfortunately, the timing sucks; your initial hearing isn't for four more days. Will you be okay?"

"Of course I will!" Bill said confidently, even though he shook like a leaf last night. "And don't worry. I haven't said a thing to the cops."

James looked at Bill and smiled, "That's the least of our concerns; we would never suspect anything like that about you, son. I'm more disturbed by the message Fredrick's actions sent to others. I need to immediately take action to rectify his stupidity." They talked for a few more minutes until the guard opened the door and announced their time was up. Joan gave 'that mom look' to the guard. He grimaced and turned his head. Joan took Bill in her arms and held him tight. "Don't worry, son, we'll take care of this." The guard turned back around and shook his head. Joan let Bill go, and the guard escorted him back to his cell.

Early the next morning, about an hour before breakfast, Bill woke to the sounds of a commotion a few cells down. Two or more men were fighting. Bill could hear the punches landing but didn't know who was hitting who. There was yelling from the inmates closer to the action and even some who had no idea what was happening. After a few more punches, he heard a loud thud, then silence, followed by a cell door being shut. Bill tried his best to look down the cell block but couldn't see what was happening. A minute or two later, the night guard walked by with blood on his hands and face. He saw Bill and shouted, "What are you looking at? Do you want some of this too?". Fortunately, by this time, more guards were en route, and escalated emotions were subdued.

Bill was around bouncers, collectors, and others of significant size most of his life. He knew what they did, but it was never towards him, so he wasn't worried. Here, it was different. In here, he was alone. Here, he felt vulnerable. In here... *NO!!! There will be no "in here,"* he thought to himself.

When his time came, he faced the judge, who looked down at him from his bench. Bill couldn't muster a single word; however, the judge had no problem. He sentenced Bill to eight years in prison for illegal gambling. Bill turned white, looked at his lawyer in disbelief, and the judge chimed in before he could say anything. "I will give you an option: you can spend eight years in prison, OR you can join the Army. You decide." Bill knew prison wasn't for him and thought the Army wouldn't be that bad. It would be a steady income and maybe help him learn a trade. He again looked at his lawyer, who nodded his head 'yes.'

The Judge said, "OK, what will it be?"

Bill looked up and quietly said, "I'll take the Army."

"What did you say?" snapped the judge, "Speak up so the court can hear your response."

Bill cleared his throat and, in a much more audible tone, said, "I'm sorry, Your Honor, I'll take the Army." The judge informed Bill that he had made the right choice and had 30 days to provide the court documentation to substantiate his enlistment. Standing in the corridor afterward, his attorney said, "They wanted to make an example of you. This deal was the best I could do."

Joan reassured Bill that they also supported the decision as well. "James and I thought about it and figured this would be best for you. It would get you out of Youngstown and the business that got you into this jam. We don't want this life for you."

On Monday, March 27th, 1933, Bill returned to Court with documentation verifying he was now enlisted into the U.S. Army. Six weeks later, on May 15th, a 17-year-old Bill shipped off to boot camp. It was an eye-opening experience; the physical training wasn't too bad, but the psychological aspect was causing him much anguish. Rules, regulations, following orders, and marching in step everywhere he went were mind-boggling. He thought, *"If we're in battle, there's no fucking way we will march in formation. this is stupid."* But he continued to march.

During the last week of Boot Camp is when the soldiers learned what jobs they'd be assigned. Bill had requested a MOS associated with either a mechanic, electrician, or carpenter, anything but an infantry gunner. He didn't realize that in that era, the Army used codes associated loosely with what the men did in civilian life. Bill couldn't tell them he worked for a crime family, so he wrote "Pastry Shop Worker" on his enlistment application. It was no surprise that he was selected to be a cook.

Bill completed Boot Camp and was assigned to an Infantry Division in Fort Riley, Kansas. He and 30 or 40 others received the same Post assignment and waited at the designated pickup for a bus to transport them. It was a long ride to Riley, with few stops to stretch his legs. The Sergeant Major was waiting when they arrived. He gave them a speech, then assigned escorts to show them their quarters and the chow hall. "*This is home*," Bill thought, "*much better than living on the streets or rotting in a cell.*"

Two years later, Bill is well known at Fort Riley, especially within his own Company. You wouldn't believe how much clout a cook has, but Bill wasn't just your average cook; he was phenomenal, especially when making cakes and other pastries. He must have learned a few things hanging out in his parent's pastry shop all those years. One Friday evening, while Bill was cleaning up, the Post Commander, Major General Gerald C. Johnston, stopped by to make a personal request of Bill. When MG Johnston asked if he could make a wedding cake for his daughter's wedding, Bill knew he was in the right profession. MG Johnston called Bill over to the counter, "If you ever need my assistance, don't hesitate to contact me." Then, he handed him a card with his personal number on it.

Bill's cake was the hit of the wedding (as far as food was concerned). It looked as scrumptious as it tasted. Bill put the favor card in his hip pocket for the future. You never know when you might need help from someone with a lot of power.

Bill adjusted to Army life quite well and reenlisted each time his tour was up. He found Army life to be quite comfortable. He knew the rules and followed them most of the time. By the winter of 1949, he was in his final enlistment.

Bill returned home often to see his family and always wore his uniform when meeting up with his old running mates. At 34, he still looked like he was in his early twenties. It must have been the Army life that kept him young. Bill had never married and had no kids, at least none he knew of.

Bill was in the pastry shop during one of his visits when this gorgeous young lady walked in. His eyes nearly popped out of their sockets. He made sure he was the one to take her order and, of course, find out her name. He could tell she was much younger than him, but holy smoke, she was smoking hot. He learned her name was Carol, and she had known about him for a few years. She visited the shop often, and his parents always bragged about him.

After a few ice cream samples he was secretly passing her way, they found themselves sitting at a table near the rear of the shop in deep conversation. Bill asked her age and what she does most days. Carol said, "I'm sixteen and a half years old, a senior in high school, and I graduate in the summer."

Bill thought, "I'm over twice her age at thirty-four, but I can't help myself. I'm head over heels for this girl." He asked her, "Can I come back in the summer and spend more time with you?"

"I would love that." She happily replied. She winked at him as she took her pastries and headed home.

Over the next few months, they wrote each other weekly. They couldn't wait until June when Bill would be back in town. Bill was in his second year of a 3-year term and just one year shy of retirement when he saw Carol again. For the next three weeks, they were inseparable. She would be eighteen in the Fall. They knew they were meant for each other and that Bill would be released from the Army in one year and could return to Youngstown. At the end of Bill's pass, he really didn't want to go back. He wanted to stay there with Carol. After many hugs and kisses, he reluctantly boarded the bus back to base, cursing the Army in his mind.

Bill and Carol continued to write and even talked about marriage in their letters. Two months before Bill's release, his Company was hit with a short-notice deployment to an undisclosed overseas location. This was serious.

Bill's Sergeant Major addressed his platoon: "The Army has issued a *StopGap* message canceling all separations and retirements." There were groans, cursing, and even some crying coming from the men. The Sergeant Major continued, "Each and every man is needed. While I understand this is a shock to many of you, you must look at the big picture. Your Country needs you!" Bill learned he'd be on a ship to unknown territories very soon.

After the disastrous announcement, Bill followed the SGM back to his office. "Bill, I know this is devastating for you. If there was anything I could do, I would." He said.

"I know we'll be deploying soon, but I need a few days of emergency leave before we go so that I can take care of a couple of things." Bill pleaded.

"You've got it. Be back here by Sunday evening." Replied the Sergeant Major.

Bill rushed back to Youngstown. Tired, sleepy, and hungry, he arrived at Carol's house and knocked on the door.

"Oh my god, what are you doing here?" Carol exclaimed, happy to see him.

Bill grabbed Carol and hugged her tight. She could barely breathe. "My retirement has been placed on hold, and I will deploy soon."

Carol cried out, "Nooo…" and continued embracing Bill.

Carol's parents heard the commotion and hurried to the front porch. "What's the matter? Did something happen?" Her dad asked.

After hearing the news, her mom invited Bill inside and asked, "Would you like something to eat? You must be starved after that long trip."

"Yes, ma'am, if you don't mind. A sandwich or anything would be appreciated."

"Sit down at the table. We have leftovers from dinner."

They talked for hours, trying to figure out what to do. "Mom, I can't let him go. We were talking about getting married." Carol cried.

"I know honey," she replied, trying to comfort her, "but he has to go, or the Army will come looking for him. They'd probably throw him in the brig, and you wouldn't see him for a very long time."

Sitting on the backside of the table next to Carol, Bill looked at her parents, "I love your daughter so much. We wanted a large wedding after I left the Army, but now that's in jeopardy." Carol leaned over and laid her head on his shoulder. "I know this isn't something you wanted or expected, but I want to make Carol my wife before I deploy." Bill continued.

Carol raised her head from his shoulder, looked up at him, and smiled while tears were still falling. Her parents sat on the other side of the table and were in a state of shock, sitting there like a couple of corpses with no facial expressions. Then, her dad started to speak. "Bill, I know you love my daughter, but…"

Bill cut him off before he could finish. "Sir, I'm sorry to interrupt, but I need to tell you something. I'm deploying somewhere, and there's a chance that I may not come back. If Carol's my wife, she will get benefits for life or at least until she marries again. This will help with her schooling and medical expenses."

Carol was surprised to hear this from Bill. The last thing she wanted to think about would be him not coming back. She began to cry more.

Her mom and dad had a brief conversation, and then he said, "As I was saying, we know you love each other, and we'd support this idea if Carol is on board." They all looked at Carol and waited for her response.

"I've known from the day I met Bill that I wanted to be his wife. My heart flutters every time he looks at me. I melt inside when he holds me," she said. "He's the only man I would consider spending the rest of my life with."

Her mom and dad smiled and simultaneously said, "Well, let's plan a wedding."

Carol and Bill kissed and then reached over to grab the hands of her parents. "When do you deploy?" asked her mom.

"Monday morning at 0600 hours," Bill responded.

"This Monday?"

"Yes, Ma'am."

"But today is Friday." She came back.

"Yes, Ma'am, and I have to leave Sunday morning to drive back," Bill stated. "That means the 'I do's' need to happen tomorrow. If that's possible."

By 2:00 the next day, they were married. It would have been sooner, but Bill wanted James and Joan to be there. Their honeymoon was a single night in the local motel. All they had were the clothes on their backs. Bill didn't even pack a toothbrush when he left camp. Carol was only a few miles from her house, so she just threw a nightgown into her purse.

"You know this will be my first time tonight?" Carol asked Bill. She had been to first and second base with a guy, but this would be the first time she'd ever gone all the way. She was excited and nervous all at the same time.

"If it makes you feel better, this is my first time too," Bill said.

"Stop the bullshit. I know you've had sex before, you jackass."

"Yes, but it was long before I met you. And besides, this will be our first time together," Bill said as he pulled her closer. Bill was nervous too. He'd never been with a virgin. He didn't want to be too forceful or be perceived as inexperienced. "I brought something to help get rid of the wedding night jitters." He reached over and pulled a bottle of wine out from under his coat.

They laid in bed and talked until the bottle was empty. Bill looked deep into her eyes. He pulled the gown's strap off her left shoulder, never once moving his eyes from hers. He then pulled the strap over her left shoulder and, this time, lowered his head to see the gown slide down over her firm breasts. "You are blessed with the body of an angel," Bill said as he moved his right hand down to her left breast. He was gentle, slowly caressing it.

Carol unbuttoned Bill's shirt, helped him out of it, then started unbuckling his belt. "I've never seen a penis up close before." she shyly said. Bill stood up, helped her with his pants, and watched her eyes as his pants hit the floor. Carol was reluctant to touch it, so Bill took her hand and placed it around his member. "It's so soft and warm." She said as she started to handle it.

"It won't be soft for much longer if you keep that up."

"Do you want me to stop?"

"You must be kidding. Keep doing what you're doing."

While Carol was learning her way around his penis, Bill maneuvered her gown off, then slowly pulled her panties to the floor. They were both naked, their bodies hot with desire. They fell onto the bed and made love all night.

The next morning, they had breakfast at a diner next to the motel, then went back to the room and made love one more time. "You know I don't want to go back," Bill told Carol. "But I have a 12-hour drive."

"I know," Carol said. "Let me wash up, and then we can go." Bill took her back to her parents' house.

"Good morning, Mr. & Mrs. Parsons." Carol's mom said as she opened the door. Her dad was right behind.

"Thank you so much for making this happen," Bill said, shaking her dad's hand, then turned and hugged her mom. "I have to leave so that I'm back before midnight." He continued.

Carol grabbed Bill and hugged him long and hard. Her mom had to pry them apart, "You'd better go. The last thing we want is a criminal in the family." She said with a smile.

Bill and Carol kissed one last time, and then he left for the long drive back to camp. He drove straight through, only stopping for gas. He arrived at his barracks two minutes before midnight, quietly packed his gear, and then laid in his bunk to sleep for a couple of hours.

At 0500, he was up, dressed, and standing in line at the chow hall. He hadn't eaten since breakfast with Carol yesterday. He had a quick meal and boarded the bus that would take him to the ship. He wanted to go AWOL and rush back to Carol's arms. Doing so would most definitely result in a visit to Leavenworth penitentiary, and he recalled what jail experience was, so he boarded the bus.

CHAPTER 2

Kimberly Lynn Parson "Kim"
(6 September 1965)

Kim was a gorgeous young woman with long red hair, which was not the color of the hair she was born with. She had a waist that was pencil thin and a butt that she had been told was built for sex. A white girl with a booty, as she described herself. She was a daddy's girl and, unfortunately, garnered his personality and language. Bill, her dad, may have been in the Army, but he cursed like a sailor. How could he admonish his daughter for following in his footsteps? Kim had a wild side. Like her father, she liked pushing the limit, busting curfew on more than one occasion.

Bill's abrasive temper and language paid off for Kim. She demanded respect at a mere 5-foot 4-inches and wouldn't take any shit off anyone. It may have been her feistiness that attracted Thomas to her.

Kim and her parents enjoyed the Labor Day weekend with relatives. Lots of hamburgers, hot dogs, and beer, which Kim didn't have a taste for. *'One last weekend before the first day of High School,'* she thought. She wasn't nervous;

it was a small town, so she knew practically everyone.

She made the cheerleading squad during summer high school tryouts and was immediately one of the "it" girls. She liked being popular, but not for the same reasons as the other brainless girls. Kim wanted to be in the know about things happening in school as well as in town.

Kim was selective when it came to dating; many suitors asked, but only a couple got as far as a kiss. She had her eye on a senior named Thomas, who played on the baseball team. He was tall, had dark hair, and had an athletic build. She loved his dark blue eyes. She was a freshman but had the body of a senior. This was even more impressive since she had skipped a grade and started high school a year ahead of her peers.

Like her mom, she too was attracted to older men and blushed every time Thomas looked in her direction. Kim wore her dresses just a tad tighter than her dad liked. She called it form fitting. In the mid-60s, girls were getting more promiscuous, but not Kim, she liked the chase. She wasn't in for a quick roll in the hay just to become another feather in some jock's hat. As a matter of fact, she was still a virgin.

Thomas noticed Kim smiling at him and smiled back. He was a bit smitten, and from then on, he looked for her during lunch and when changing classes. After a few days of flirting, he got up the nerve to introduce himself. She was so enticing. She had a smile that would melt the heart of even the most coldhearted man. Her bright eyes and spunky attitude were so unusual for a beautiful, petite girl.

He said, "Hi, I'm Thomas. I've noticed you in the halls and wanted to say hello."

"Okay, not a great first line," she thought. "Hello, I'm Kim, and I've noticed you too." *Great, my response was a regurgitation of what he said. What a dope I must have sounded like.*

I don't think it mattered to either of them. They were both taken aback by each other. Thomas was shy and finding it difficult to synchronize his brain and mouth. Kim found this odd since he was a popular jock.

Kim tried to think of a way she could break the ice. "How many touchdowns did you get last season?"

Thomas smiled and said, "None; I play baseball." Kim's face turned beet red, and they both started laughing. Ice broken!

Thomas and Kim dated all through his senior year. They were inseparable, and one was never without the other. Kim had met his parents, and he had met hers. They were so happy together, but the elephant in the room that has yet to be spoken about is what they will do after he graduates. Thomas came from a middle-class family. He worked hard for everything he had but had no plans after graduation. He was extremely intelligent, even though his grades didn't always show it. Without a scholarship, he would be stuck in Youngstown working in the mills.

Kim was in love but never said anything to him. She was too afraid that he would not return the sentiment, damaging the relationship. She was destined for college. A scholarship? Probably not! She was bright, but her grades were not on her priority list. Her parents (Bill and Carol) had been saving for college since she was born.

Finally, the time came; it was a week before his graduation, and the subject had to be broached. It was on both of their minds, but neither wanted to be the first to bring it up. They looked at each other, eyes watery, and simultaneously started speaking.

Thomas said, "You go first."

"No, not at all. You go first," she replied.

Thomas said, "I really care for you and don't want to lose you after graduation."

You could see a sense of relief come over Kim. He didn't use the word 'love,' but she knew what he meant. She looked at him and replied, "I was worried but afraid to talk about it. I care for you too and want to keep on seeing you. But what would your friends say if you're still dating a High School girl?"

"Fuck 'em," he retorted. "It's my life, and I decide who I want to be with." Wow, Kim rarely heard Thomas cuss, but when he did, he went for it. That was the curse word of choice for Kim and her dad. The F-bomb was used quite frequently in her household.

After graduation, Thomas took a low-paying job while still living at home. He made enough to chip in with his parents' bills and take Kim out on dates. They were getting more and more intimate but had yet to go all the way.

Thomas knew he couldn't provide a good life or raise a family on his meager minimum wage job, so he looked for other opportunities. He saw an ad for an apprentice at the steel mill in the paper. It boasted a starting wage three times what he was making now. He applied the next morning, and two days later, he was notified that the job was his.

Thomas was excited when he got the news. "I need to tell Kim," he thought. His mom and dad were so proud of their young man and planned a special dinner for him that evening. His mom hugged him and whispered, "Be home in time for dinner. I have something special planned." He promised he would and asked to borrow the car to tell Kim in person. His dad was happy to loan him the car.

Thomas was anxious to rush over and surprise Kim with this great news.

Before leaving, Thomas called to make sure Kim would be at home. "I have something to tell you. Will you be home for a while?" he said over the phone. "Sure, what's up?" Kim responded. "I'll tell you in 10 minutes. I'm on my way over," and he hopped in the car and rushed to Kim.

She was sitting in the rocking chair on the front porch when she saw Thomas make the left turn onto Pine Street. He waved as he looked for parking on the street. He found one about a half block down. His excitement was really showing, and Kim had all kinds of scenarios in her mind. Is he going to tell me he loves me? Is he going to ask me to marry him? "OK," she thought, "Bring it down a notch."

Kim lived on a busy street that was somewhat quiet today. Thomas never took his eyes off her. He parked the car, got out, and….

Kim was watching Thomas as he parked. She noticed some teenagers from a few streets over showing off their Chevy Camaro. They floored it as they turned on her street. They didn't see Thomas getting out of his car, and he didn't see them. Kim saw the whole thing unfolding. She yelled and started running towards Thomas, but the car was too fast. Thomas had just shut his car door and never saw the Camaro behind him.

The impact of the Camaro was just below his thighs, sending him cartwheeling into the windshield headfirst. The impact shot Thomas twenty feet into the air and in the direction of Kim, who was still running towards him. The young kid driving the Camaro panicked and hit the gas instead of the brake, then realizing what was happening, stopped the car.

Thomas landed just a few feet in front of Kim with a sound that she will never forget. His body was misconfigured. She saw bones sticking out of his legs. He was bleeding from so many places. She got to him and tried to straighten his body out. Putting his head into her arms, she tried to wake him. "Call an ambulance!" she screamed. His eyes opened slowly; he couldn't speak. He couldn't move. He just looked into her eyes.

Kim was crying and begging him not to leave her. Again, she screamed, "Somebody call an ambulance!" She yelled out his name, "THOMAS, please wake up, I need you. I...." she didn't get to finish her sentence. He had taken his last breath. Kim was bawling. There was a crowd gathering. She could hear a siren in the distance. It was too late. Thomas died without knowing how much she loved him.

The paramedics arrived and tried to peel Kim off Thomas, but after getting a better look, they realized there was nothing they could do. Bob and Carol were by Kim's side and did their best to comfort her. When the police arrived, Kim's parents consoled her, telling her that the paramedics needed to do their job and get the young man off the street. From behind, Bob put his arms between hers and pulled her to her feet. She turned around and wrapped her arms around her dad, both crying as the paramedics put a sheet over Thomas' body.

Thomas' parents were at home preparing a special meal when the police officer knocked on the door. His dad opened the door, but Mom was listening from the kitchen. She was preparing to put the roast into the oven when the police officer said, "I'm so sorry to have to tell you this. Your son, Thomas, was in an accident about an hour ago. He was hit crossing the road. I'm sorry to say that he didn't survive."

His mom screamed, letting go of the roast, and was oblivious to it crashing onto the floor, sending potatoes, carrots, onions, and shards of glass all over the kitchen floor.

"There must be a mistake," she screamed as she ran to the front door.

"It's no mistake, ma'am. His body has been taken to Fernwood Mortuary. You should probably head over there. I can have a minister meet you." She became dizzy and fainted. Fortunately, her husband caught her before she hit the floor. He held her as he tried to process the horrific news.

Kim was alone now. She finished her junior year and was making college plans. She would put her head into her schoolwork and try to forget that awful day when she witnessed her love die in front of her.

CHAPTER 3

Allen James Schultz (January 1956)

Allen grew up poor. He had always dreamed of being someone important; he didn't know what, but he knew he wanted more for himself. During grade school, Allen and his best friend Tim would go to the barber shop where his dad worked, well, owned, and shine shoes for fifty cents. They'd get a quarter each. Of course, saving hadn't been something he was familiar with, so after every shining, he and Tim would hightail it to the store a couple of blocks away. Tim's dad smiled every time they got a customer because he knew what they'd do. One day, he told them about the produce stand next door and how delicious their apples were. They could get several apples for the same price as a candy bar. Allen loved green apples, and after hearing Tim's dad talking about them, he couldn't get them out of his mind.

Allen was a hard worker. When his family moved away, he cut people's lawns on weekends to make a few dollars. When he was sixteen, he went to work in a cotton mill where the hours were sometimes long, and it made high school attendance difficult. Nevertheless, the money was good, especially for a young teenager. But Allen had dreams, and working in a mill for the rest of his life wasn't part of it. When he was eighteen, he had a chance to join the military. It would be his way out. He could get his education and earn a good, respectable living all at the same time. He thought about the Navy but didn't think he'd do well on a ship. What would happen if it sank during some conflict?

He wanted to be on the ground, so he looked at the Army or the Marines. After some research, he realized that his skinny, out-of-shape frame would be too weak for the rugged lifestyle. Besides, he wanted to sleep in a bed at night, not in a foxhole.

Allen had never flown before, but after doing a little research, he found that you didn't have to worry about it unless you were a pilot or aircrew. So, the Air Force it was. He wasted no time heading to the recruiters; he recalled seeing one over near his grandparents' house. He wanted to sign up before something made him change his mind.

Allen had no idea how the process worked. Looking back, he compared the recruiter (SSgt Ross) to a used car salesman. The staff sergeant kept trying to sell him on specific Air Force specialties. Allen wasn't a *Gomer Pyle*. He may have been ignorant about many things, but not this. He held firm about wanting an AFSC related to Information Technology, and it paid off. SSgt Ross signed him up as a Network Management apprentice.

The next step was to pick his length of service. Allen was committed at this point and told the SSgt that he wanted to do six years. For some reason, Ross talked him out of it. with lines like "Just do four years, you may not like it." or "Try it for four years and re-up if you like it." It seemed to make sense, so he agreed and signed the contract.

SSgt Ross failed to tell Allen that he would have gotten two stripes immediately after basic training if he had signed up for six years. Allen didn't know any better and didn't realize what a jerk Ross was until the end of basic. Several members of his flight sewed on Airman 1st Class (A1C) stripes immediately. This infuriated Allen; he wanted six years, but Ross talked him out of it. This would put him at least two years behind them in the promotion cycle.

After a long technical school, Allen shipped off to his permanent base of assignment wearing his first stripe. He was no longer an Airman Basic. He was an Airman. Allen arrived at Maxwell AFB and was assigned to the Network Operation Center (NOC). As an Airman, his duties were limited to basic tasks, the same ones taught to him in tech school. He had a great supervisor/mentor who pushed him and helped him decide on long-term goals. It was this supervisor, Master Sergeant (MSgt) Leon Smith, that shaped him into the man he is today.

Allen had a knack for technology and picked up on it quickly. He was far better than the two-stripers that arrived before him. Smith saw that too and recommended him for Senior Airman Below-The-Zone (BTZ), which he won hands down. MSgt Smith advised Allen to complete his Career Field Education Training Plan (CFETP) sooner versus later. Airmen are not permitted to accomplish off-duty education until they have completed their upgrade training.

Due to time restrictions, completing all tasks for his 5-Level Journeyman certification took another year. Now, he could do as MSgt Smith had advised and pursue a degree in Information Technology. This craving to learn was something new for individuals in his hometown.

They never expected Allen to be more than a simple computer technician.

Allen was at the top of his field and was promoted well ahead of his peers. He could ace the tests with very little effort, or so it seemed to everyone else. Several years later, he had volunteered to spend the holidays at a base in Northern Texas. The Quality Assurance person there wanted to go home and spend the holidays with his family. Allen was happy to lend a hand. He'd be in San Angelo, Texas's cold, snow, and tumbleweeds for two or three months. He had a car but found little to do off base. One of the Captains invited Allen to join him and his family for Thanksgiving dinner, so it wasn't too bad.

Christmas and New Year were lonely; it was cold, and about a foot of snow was on the ground, so he spent most of the time in his room reading cyber security protocols. But even Allen could hit a wall. It was Christmas Day. He had promised himself he wouldn't read any of his cyber or network manuals. He looked outside, and the snow was still there, but at least the wind didn't seem to be blowing too much. Allen put on his cold-weather running gear and did a lap around the base. Goodfellow AFB is not that big, so maybe five or six miles was all he did. After 'A *Christmas Story*' dinner at a fast-food place outside the gate, he was back in his room looking at his computer.

He was on an experimental social media site checking out the different chat rooms. Some had interesting conversations, but mostly just gibberish. He didn't interact with any of them until he saw a chain that piqued his interest. It had to do with internet security and how everyone was taking this new medium for granted. Well, now, this is in Allen's wheel well, so he chimed in and provided a long, technical explanation that rebuked or, in some cases, provided credence to what was being said. Internet security wasn't too popular. Most people were unaware of the need for standards and protocols to keep the internet safe. Allen proposed a hypothesis that would lay the groundwork for new encryption standards. Needless to say, the techno nerds would have nothing of this. Allen had had enough of their petty bickering and left the chat room.

Before calling it a night, he thought he'd hang around for a bit trolling the chat rooms when a message came in for him. This one had nothing to do with the internet. It was a message from a young lady with the username "Red-4Fun"; at least, he hoped it was a young lady. She asked if he wanted to go to a private room to chat. He typed back, "Sure, why not."

CHAPTER 4

Sweet Sixteen (18 May 1985)

"Good morning, luv," Allen whispered to his beautiful wife, who was still halfway asleep. He adored her, even with slobber drooling down her cheek and her long dark hair draping partially over her face. Beauty can be described in many ways, but for Allen, Kim's beauty was inside and out. "Happy Anniversary," he said, wiping her cheeks with the pillowcase.

"Happy Anniversary to you too," she said.

Allen and Kim had been married for sixteen years. They had a beautiful fifteen-year-old daughter, Olivia, and they were madly in love. They both joke when folks ask them how they keep up with the number of years so easily. "Well, our daughter is fifteen and a half, so that means we've been married sixteen years." It always made those hearing it for the first time laugh, but it's true. Laying there in Allen's arms, she began to think back to 1967, her senior year in high school.

(1967) KIM'S FLASHBACK

Kim was hip and up to date on new technology, so when she heard about a new beta app that was just released, she knew it was for her. Her parents would not allow her to have her own computer, so she had to get creative. Christmas was a few weeks away, and she had money saved from her part-time job, so she started discreetly looking for a computer she could afford.

Kim worked downtown at a family-owned law office. It was part of a school program for seniors. It allowed students with enough credits to have part-time jobs in a professional environment. Kim was a receptionist but aspired to be a paralegal or maybe even an attorney one day. There were two attorneys, Mr. Lewinski and Mr. Simon, a paralegal, Mrs. Jennifer Simon (the daughter of the Attorney), and a part-time receptionist who worked the early shift until Kim arrived. She had been with the office for twenty years and was close to retirement. She enjoyed working half days. Everyone in the office was down to earth, easy to talk to, and just pleasant to be around.

"Jennifer," her dad called out, "Can you get me the files for the Olson case?" She was already knee-deep in research for Mr. Lewinski, so she looked over at Kim. "Can you help me out and grab those files, please?" Kim's eyes lit up. She knew about the filing system, but this was the first time she had been asked for assistance. "Of course I will." Before Jennifer could explain to her what to do, she was standing in front of her. "Are these the files that you need?" Jennifer, somewhat shocked at how fast she picked up on this, said, "Yes, it is. Thank you so much. Can you drop those off on my dad's desk?" Jennifer was impressed with Kim and started showing her more of the ropes. Which was great. "This is so much more exciting than answering phones." She told Jennifer.

After a couple of months, she was actually doing paralegal work. It was a small office, and sometimes, they needed things that their sole paralegal, Jennifer, couldn't accomplish in a timely manner, so Kim received on-the-job training. She was smart, aggressive, and a hard worker. Jennifer spoke highly of her to her dad, and she was given a well-deserved raise. Kim was so proud of herself, motivating her to always do her best.

When the time came to get a computer, she was slightly familiar with them. She used one in her office for managing appointments and typing memos as directed by her bosses. When there was a lull in business, she would experiment on the work computer but knew better than to try and access any experimental sites or sites unrelated to anything the lawyers were working on. A couple of blocks from her was a Radio Shack. After work one evening, she went in and asked the salesman, "What type of computers do you have?" The Salesman looked at this young girl and said, "You're a bit young to buy such an expensive device. Is this for you or someone else? Kim was a bit offended by his comments. Was this because of her age or because she was a female? "This is a gift for my parents. I know there are faster and better computers out there, but I probably can't afford one of those."

"I'm impressed," the salesman came back with, "I have a version for the novice wanting to get into computing. It has everything you've described, plus a mouse," he talked as he walked Kim over to the computer section and showed her the one on display. "It's our basic system, and I can let you have it for $499.00." Two things, Kim thought. One, he quoted her the list price on the sticker; two, she had nowhere near that kind of money saved. "I'm sorry, sir, I wasn't expecting it to be that expensive. I'll have to save up more and come back another time. Kim left with her head down. Her dream had been crushed. The next day, she was telling Jennifer about her experience with teary eyes. "I was hoping to get my parents a computer for Christmas, but they are out of my price range." Jennifer felt sorry for her and mentioned this to her dad later that evening.

It was two weeks until Christmas. Kim was off for the holiday break but still working at her office. She worked full-time during her vacation, trying to earn as much as possible. They would be closing down on the eighteenth. Jennifer made sure to talk to Kim first thing that morning. "Kim, what are you doing Friday evening?" hoping her answer would be nothing. Kim thought for a minute, "I don't believe I have anything on Friday. I have family events on Saturday and Sunday, but Friday is free." Jennifer was excited, "I'd like to offer you a personal invitation to the Office Christmas Party this Friday at 7 p.m. The dress is casual, so there is no sense in putting on any fancy clothes. Here's the address." She said as she handed her a sheet of paper. "That's awesome. I can't wait." Kim had the biggest smile on her face. This would be her first office party.

Kim had to come up with an alternate gift for her parent's Christmas present. She thought about maybe a sweater, but that would be too impersonal. What about a weekend get-away somewhere? That would be wonderful for them, and I'd get the house to myself for a couple of days. She went to the travel agency/realtor's office during lunch. "Good morning," Sarah said, "Welcome to Dreams Realty and Travel. How may I help you?" Kim thought for a few seconds, "I'd like to get my parents a weekend get-away for Christmas. Unfortunately, I only have $200.00; what could that get me?" Sara smiled and said, "Well, for one thing, that will get you a lot. Let me see, what about Cleveland?" Kim shook her head no, "I don't think they would like Cleveland. My dad doesn't like the Browns, and I'm sure all the advertising would make it miserable for him."

Sarah looked through her book of destinations and said, "What about Pittsburgh? I can get you a hotel for two nights, coupons for a romantic dinner at the steakhouse across the street, and two tickets to a dinner show. How does that sound?"

"It sounds expensive." Kim blurted out.

"Not at all," Sarah rebutted, "It's only $149.95. You'd have $50 left to spend as you like."

"That would be amazing." Kim puckered up after hearing that. Dad loves the Steelers, and I'm sure Hines Field will be open for tours. "I'll take it as long as they can pick the dates they travel."

"Of course," Sarah said with a smile.

"This was the second thing I've taken care of today. I'll have to tell Mom all about it when I get home. Oh, wait, I can't, it's a gift. It'll have to wait until Christmas. At least I found a gift that I think they will love."

Kim and Jennifer were talking on Thursday morning. "You know how things seem to slow down when you're really looking forward to doing it?" Kim asked Jennifer. "I've been so excited about the party Friday night, but it seems like its taking forever to get here."

"I know exactly what you mean, but don't worry, it'll be worth the wait," Jennifer replied.

Friday was finally here. Kim kept looking at her watch, waiting for quitting time. She wanted to stop at the home goods store and get Jennifer and her parents a nice gift for Christmas. They have been so nice to her that she needed to get something that would express her thanks. What do you get someone who has everything? She racked her mind and wished she could kick herself in the ass for being such a moron and waiting until the last minute. Unfortunately, she had no choice. She had to wait until she got paid.

Kim strolled down the aisles, looking for inspiration. This store was like a mix between the Five & Dime, Woolworth, and Kmart. It had a little bit of everything. Kim turned the corner and walked into a photo/frame section. She immediately saw something that just clicked with her. She took it over to the service counter, where two young ladies were biding their time, "Can you wrap this for me?" she asked with her puppy dog eyes. "Of course, we can," Before Kim could take three breaths, it was wrapped and had a pretty pink bow.

Kim recalled Jennifer telling her not to dress up, but she still wanted to get home, shower, and put something nice on. "Hi, Mom," Kim announced as she headed to her room, "I've got to hurry and clean up. Tonight's the night of the Office Christmas Party, and I don't want to be late. She had laid out her clothes before leaving for work. Well, actually, the night before. She spent two hours deciding what to wear and must have changed her mind a half dozen times.

Kim was like a well-oiled machine. She started undressing as she was walking up the steps. First, her shoes, kicking them off to the side. Then she started unbuttoning her blouse and had it off by the time she got to her bedroom door. Once inside, she lowered her pants, followed by the last article, baby pink panties. She wrapped a towel around her and proceeded to the bathroom. Ten minutes later, she was back in her room, getting primped and pretty while her hair dried, then she dressed in a pair of black slacks and a red blouse with a bit of green. Perfect for Christmas, she thought.

Kim rushed back down the stairs, "Bye, Mom, be home by ten." Seeing her dad, she said, "Hi, Dad, bye, Dad!" Before her dad could respond, she was out the door and headed towards the car her dad let her use. It was a 1962 Ford Galaxy 500, candy apple red, with some power. "Dad *would disown me if he overheard me referring to his car as an IT*," she thought. Kim found the piece of paper with an address on it, thought for a minute about where it might be, and then it hit her. This was not far from town, left at the light and about five miles down the road. She was there in no time, but she was early. The last thing she wanted was to arrive before the other guests or the hosts were ready for her. She was waiting in the car listening to holiday music when a Brenda Lee classic came on. She soon found herself singing along, oblivious to Jennifer, who had walked down to tell her she could come in.

"Rocking around the Christmas Tree, what …." Jennifer wasn't going to interrupt her mid-song, so she waited a few steps behind the car where she couldn't be seen, but Kim could definitely be heard. Jennifer was doing everything she could to not laugh. Then, finally, she broke out in laughter. Kim heard her and lowered her head in shame. Jennifer hugged her when she got out of the car and told her how sweet she sounded.

"I'm so embarrassed," Kim said as they headed up the driveway to the house. "Where's everyone else?" Kim asked, "I don't see any other cars."

Jennifer smiled, grabbed and squeezed Kim's hand. "Everyone is here and waiting inside." Now Kim was really nervous, was she the last one? Did she offend them by sitting in the car so long?

Upon reaching the house, Kim marveled at the artistic masonry and the columns. "This place is beautiful," Kim said, "What is it? A museum?"

Jennifer smiled and humbly said, "No, this is our residence. My parents inherited it from their parents, and maybe someday it will be mine since I'm an only child."

Kim's eyes grew larger as she stepped back and really started taking in this massive home. "Holy shit," she exclaimed, "this house makes ten of mine." Kim's face turned red as she realized what she had said, "I'm so sorry. That slipped out."

"It's okay. I've lived here all my life and am still in awe of its grandeur. Come on, let's go in." Jennifer opened the door into a massive foyer. The floors looked like white marble, and there was a brown circular table in the center, with a beautiful vase of flowers that added color to the room. The ceiling must have been over twenty feet high, with a giant chandelier hanging almost level with the second floor. To her right, she observed a stairway that was solid wood. Later, she found out it was mahogany. The stairs didn't go straight up, but rather a half circle that hugged the wall as it made its way up. It reminded her of the pictures she had seen from the Titanic. "We hardly ever use these stairs," Jennifer interjected. "We must use the ones near the sitting room. Mom says it's too hard to keep that wood shining, so the less traffic, the better. Of course, guests are a different story... What good is it to have something nice if you can't show it off." Jennifer sprouted out.

Hearing footsteps on the marble floor, Jennifer and Kim turned to see this beautiful woman walk in, "You must be Kimberly," she said. "Jennifer has told me so much about you."

"In case you haven't guessed, that's my mom," Jennifer announced.

"So nice to meet you, Mrs. Simon. You are so beautiful, just like your daughter." They both blushed hearing Kim's compliment.

"Please come this way," Mrs. Simon directed, holding her arm out toward the dining room. "You can leave your package on the table next to the fireplace."

"Thank you, ma'am," Kim said as she walked over to the table.

When she walked into the dining room, the beauty of everything was shocking. The floor was marble, like the foyer. There were two China cabinets filled with stunning relics. The wallpaper appeared to be an original artistic design. Without counting, it looked like the dining room table could seat around fourteen guests, but there were only four place settings. One at the table's head, one more on the left side, and two settings on the right. Kim looked at Jennifer and whispered, "I thought you said everyone was here?"

"They are. We only invited you."

"But you said it was a party. I thought everyone would be here." Kim replied

"How many does it take to have a party? I believe just two people could have a party if they were so inclined." Jennifer responded, then transitioned as to the seating arrangements. "We're sitting on the right. Dad will be at the head of the table, and Mom will be on the other side. Your seat is right next to me. We'll remain standing until they both get here. It's impolite to sit unless the entire party is here. These traditions were handed down from generation to generation. It's our role to keep it going." Jennifer explained.

Kim was a little nervous now, "Is there anything else I should know?" She asked Jennifer in a soft voice so as not to be overheard.

"If something comes up, I'll let you know, but don't worry, you're our guest. It's okay if you don't know our culture or traditions.".

Mr. and Mrs. Simon entered the dining room hand in hand through the double doors that lead into the sitting room. He pulled the chair out and assisted his wife to her place at the table, then he walked around the table and did the same for Jennifer. Looking at Kim, he said, "Tonight, you're our guest, not our employee. Here, please take a seat." He pulled out her chair and waited until she was seated before returning to his place at the head of the table.

"This is such a beautiful home. It's like a castle, and you're the King and Queen."

Everyone broke out in laughter, everyone except Kim, that is. "That's the first time I've heard that analogy." Mr. Simon said as he wiped tears from his eyes. "Yes, this is a rather large home, but it's not a castle, and we're not royalty. We have been blessed by our fathers and the fathers before them. We are humble citizens that support our community and try to help those in need," he continued.

Kim felt embarrassed and responded, "I'm so sorry. I didn't mean to insult your family. I have nothing but respect for you…" Kim was cut off before she could finish her sentence.

"Nonsense! You have nothing to apologize for, so relax, and let's enjoy the evening and the feast."

At that cue, the wait staff brought out the first course. "This is the day we celebrate our family and friends," Mr. Simon said as the bread, butter, and soup bowls were placed on the table in front of each individual. Kim started reaching for her utensils when Jennifer softly touched her arm, silently gesturing for her to wait.

"My father must take the first bite before we begin," Jennifer whispered.

Kim decided to watch Jennifer and emulate her for the rest of the meal. Once Mr. Simon took his bite, he smiled, and then Jennifer picked up her spoon and began to eat. Kim followed suit, and as the taste of this heavenly broth hit her taste buds, her eyes almost rolled to the back of her head. The flavors were new to her and awakened her senses. "Jennifer, this soup is to die for. I could eat a whole pot of this." Kim said in between bites.

Once the soup was devoured, the next course made its way to the table. The waiter carried a large platter with what looked to be some type of meat, garnished with carrots, celery, and tomatoes. The aroma of the dish had Kim in dreamland. "If this is anything like the soup, you may have to carry me out of here. This smells so good, what is it?" she whispered to Jennifer.

"It's one of my mom's favorite recipes, another dish handed down through the generations. It's called Holiday Brisket." Kim waited until each individual received their meal, and then when it was time, she used her fork to get a piece of the meat. It was moist and seasoned with more spices she didn't recognize. The brisket melted in her mouth.

After dinner, they sat around the table and talked. Mr. Simon told Kim how impressed he was with her work ethic and performance. "Each year, I host a student of the school's choosing. Each year, I get someone who, with training, can answer the phone and maybe take a message if needed. This year, I did not get that. This year, Miss Kimberly was sent to our office. She has not only been an excellent receptionist but has learned to do so much more. Without any direction from our team, she has picked up on many tasks only a paralegal can do. And, while doing all this extra work, she has not once complained. Miss Kimberly, thank you so much for blessing us with your presence in our office and joining us for dinner tonight." As Mr. Simon finished, one of the servers brought a table and sat it next to Kim. Right behind him was another person carrying a wrapped box, placing it on the table.

"Miss Kimberly," Mr. Simon began, "In this box is a token of our appreciation. Please open it."

"Now?" Kim murmured.

"Yes, please open it now," Mrs. Simon responded.

Kim was excited but also somewhat ashamed. She wasn't expecting a gift. She was happy to have the job and more than pleased with her compensation. She stood over the large box wrapped in holiday colors. As she removed small portions of the paper, she could see partial words, so she removed more and saw the word "Computer." No, this can't be, she thought. Now ripping the paper much faster, she revealed a box from Radio Shack with a new computer inside. Kim started crying. "This is too much; I can't accept this."

Mr. Simon smiled and told her, "Jennifer mentioned that you wanted to get a computer for your parents but hadn't saved enough money. She also mentioned the rude salesperson who wouldn't give you a better deal," he continued "You are very special to us, and especially our daughter. Please accept this gift from our heart to yours."

Kim didn't know if it was against their customs but felt the need to embrace them both. She stood, almost tripping over the chair, then quickly walked to Mr. and Mrs. Simon and gave them a huge hug. "Thank you so much. You don't know how much this will help my family." I also have a gift for you, but after seeing what you gave me, I'm ashamed to give you mine." She sadly said.

"Don't be silly, young lady. You were not obligated to bring any gifts, so whatever it is will be much appreciated." Kim walked over to the table and picked up the package she had purchased. It was about eight inches high and thirty inches long.

"Working with your family this year has been special to me. I have learned so much and now aspire to seek a legal degree. When I saw this gift, I knew in my heart that it was the one. Please accept this with my heartfelt appreciation for everything you've done for me this year," she said as she handed it to Mr. & Mrs. Simon.

"What a beautiful job wrapping," Mrs. Simon said.

"I wish I could take credit for it, but I can't," Kim responded. "This was done by the ladies at the service counter.

They both began to undo the bow and ribbon. They each took a side, meticulously undid the tape, and neatly peeled the paper back. Mrs. Simon held it up facing them, and her eyes began to tear up as she read it aloud. "Some offices have workers; this office has family." "This is very special," Mr. Simon said.

"I know it doesn't compare to the gift you gave me, but I wanted to express how much I've enjoyed being with you each day," Kim explained. "Jennifer has been like a big sister to me. And you, Mr. Simon, have treated me with patience and respect, regardless of whether I mess up or not." They all laughed and then hugged. It was a little awkward, but it felt right.

At the end of the evening, Kim once again expressed her appreciation. Mr. Simon told her, "We'll have the computer delivered and set up for you tomorrow. Give us a call and let us know what time would suffice." He reached for Kim's hand and said, "You are blessed, my child. You will do good things in this world. Have a safe and healthy holiday. We'll see you after the New Year."

Jennifer whispered, "I hope to see you much sooner," then winked and gave Kim a massive hug.

The next day, the computer was delivered and set up. Kim was eager to use it but had to leave for a family Christmas party. She told her mom she would check it out when she got home. Kim had a little knowledge of computers but had never started one from scratch or loaded any programs. This would all be new to her. Kim's mind was on the computer the entire evening. Her cousins would be talking to her, and she'd be in another world, thinking about what programs were loaded, and a ton of other things when her mom put her hand on her shoulder. "Don't you think you should return to this world and stop daydreaming long enough to talk and play with your cousins?"

"Yes, ma'am," Kim responded and began interacting with family until it was time to leave.

About forty-five minutes later, her father yelled into the room where the young adults were gathered, "Kim, grab your things. It's time to head home."

When they got home, Kim ran to her room and changed into her nightgown and returned downstairs, where the computer was waiting for her. It had more features than she expected: a faster modem, more storage, and a printer.

Her mom motioned for her to head upstairs. Kim dispassionately began the process of shutting down the computer. Walking up the stairs, she started thinking about the beta social media program she wanted to look into. Kim thought that tomorrow (Sunday), she would have plenty of time before the last family Christmas party of the year.

Kim was up early the next morning, she signed on to the social media platform and began learning as much as possible. It took her a few days, to begin grasping the concept.

A couple of days before Christmas, Kim was up well past her bedtime doing research and other computer-related things when her mom surprised her. Carol had gotten up for a glass of water and was shocked to see Kim on the computer, especially in a chat room with complete strangers. Kim jumped about two feet into the air when her mom abruptly showed up and startled her.

"What the hell do you think you're doing, young lady," her mom yelled.

"I'm sorry, Mom, I was just doing research on the computer. I'm trying to learn as much as possible about it so I can use it efficiently when I go to college." Kim replied.

Carol refrained from commenting for a few minutes as she pondered Kim's response. "While I appreciate the bull shit answer you gave, I know there's more to it than that."

Kim was stunned. Her mom wanted a better answer than the one she made up. "Mom, I'm sorry, but I need to get smart on computers so that I can rub it in the faces of all those who taunted me in the past. This might be the last chance for me to show them that I'm more than a pretty face." Kim said, over sensationalizing the actual events.

Carol grabbed Kim and held her tight. She said, "Honey, you never need to listen to the words of those struggling while you're working your ass off to do things the right way. They have the opportunity, just as you did, to graduate high school and apply for a degree that best suits them. There is no need for any animosity between you and them at all."

Kim felt a sense of relief as she realized she might be in the clear. Her mom had fallen for her woe is me comment. Now, to seal the deal, "You're right, Mom. I should be able to live my life the way I want, without the interference of others. There is no need for me to feel less because of the words of others."

(1985) Rude Awakening

"What? Did you say something?" Kim woke from her nostalgic dream to see Allen staring at her from the side of the bed.

"Where were you?" he asked. "Your body and expressions were very animated."

"You'll never believe this, but I was dreaming about how we met and all the fun things that happened, like when you invited me to Italy."

"Those were some fun days. We were like rabbits back then," Allen said, smiling at Kim.

"Don't remind me. My body isn't up to those marathons anymore." Kim said, "Now tell me why you really woke me?"

"I'm in the mood to cook and wanted your opinion on what I should make."

"Surprise me." Kim replied, then thought for a minute and said, "Why don't you ask Olivia to come up with an idea? She's growing up pretty fast. We should start adding her into some of our decision-making?"

"So, you're saying that you don't have a clue and either figure it out myself or wake our fifteen-year-old daughter for suggestions," Allen replied sarcastically.

"Go and spend some quality time with your daughter. I want to get back to the dream I was having." Kim said as she rolled over and relaxed her mind and body. She recalled a few old memories, hoping to return to where her dream left off.

Kim began reminiscing about those early years and how she met and continued communicating with Allen. It seemed like every waking moment, they were talking. *'We learned so much about each other, from the types of food we eat to even the most intimate of fantasies,'* she thought. *'We were in love, and honestly, I'm the one that actually proposed to him.'* she chuckled as this always made her laugh. Kim would never keep her feelings locked up again and swore that if the day ever came, she'd be honest with her partner.

A little over sixteen years ago, Allen was in Italy working. He continued writing and calling her. They had yet to meet in person; however, they spent hours talking and learning about each other, which rang up some horrendous phone bills… Kim's consciousness began to fade, and soon, she found herself back in dreamland.

(1968) Back in time

Allen was falling for this girl. It's not like they didn't know each other. They were in constant contact, writing, emailing, and calling. They knew more about each other than most couples living in the same town. He dreamt of the day when he could finally hold her. There was a six-hour time difference between them, and a ten-hour journey from Italy to Ohio. First, a train ride from Pordenone to Venice, then a flight from Venice to JFK, followed by JFK to Cleveland. He had already looked up all the information.

During one of their calls, he informed Kim, "A four-day weekend is coming up. How about I fly to Cleveland so we can finally meet face-to-face." There was an awkward silence on the other end, then a "sure, let's do that" from Kim.

Two weeks later, he landed in Cleveland, took a taxi to the hotel, and waited. He knew she wouldn't arrive until later that evening, so he chilled out in the hotel's bar washing down a chili-cheese burger with a spiced rum and coke. In front of him was a large window, about 6' wide by 4' high, with water on the other side. His first thought was that this must be a fish tank. He was wrong. On the other side of the window was the hotel pool and unbeknownst to hotel guest, they were on full display to the patrons of the bar.

The bartender laughed when he saw Allen dumbfounded by this oddity and said, "You wouldn't believe how many people don't realize there's a window in the pool. Especially late at night when only one or two couples are in the pool." He went on to tell him of the sex shows he's been privy to. Allen thought, "I've got to remember not to bring Kim for a swim."

After eating his burger and fries, he hung out there for a bit, drinking his normal Bacardi and Coke while secretly hoping someone would jump into the pool. An hour later, he headed back to his room. Not much was happening in the pool, and the bar was empty. Kim was due to be there any minute, so he kept watch, looking out his hotel room window. With only pictures to identify her, he was skeptical about what she would look like in real life. One car pulled up, and a young woman got out. It was hard to see her well, but she looked great. Unfortunately, it wasn't Kim. Ten minutes later, another car pulled up, and a single female exited. Allen prayed that wasn't her. It was an hour past her arrival time when Allen thought he'd been stood up.

Looking out the window anticipating her arrival was nerve-wracking, so he walked down to the lobby. As he turned the corner, he saw this gorgeous redhead walk in. She was the most beautiful girl that he could have imagined. He knew immediately that this was her. He walked straight to her and wrapped his arms around her slender frame. Their first kiss must have lasted five minutes. Without saying too many words, he escorted her to his room, where they spent the next several hours making love.

Later that evening, they were back in bed. The next day was more of the same. It was two people getting caught up in the lust that had been kept subdued for too long. Late Sunday, they came up for air, had a nice dinner, then prepared for his departure.

Allen had to fly back early Monday morning so he could be at work Tuesday morning. It was a long flight, getting back late Monday evening. He was exhausted but still had to catch the train from Rome back to Pordenone, where his car was. It was 1 a.m. when he got in bed; knowing he had to be up by 6 a.m. for work.

Two months later, in one of their weekly calls, he asked, "How would you like to come to Italy and spend a few weeks with me?"

Kim immediately said, "Oh shit, are you serious? I would love to."

Allen warned her, "I'll have to work during the days, but would have evenings and weekends to be with you. I live in a commercial district. There are lots of shops, bars, and restaurants to keep you occupied while I'm away."

Kim was on cloud nine; she had always wanted to go to Europe, and besides, she was falling in love with Allen. They set the dates, and Allen purchased the tickets and arranged to meet her in Venice to escort her back to his place about 90 minutes north. There was just one problem: Kim was a minor living at home. She needed her parents' permission before she could go.

Kim was seventeen and in love again, or maybe it was infatuation. Either way, she wanted to visit Allen and be with him. Italy was a dream trip, and Allen could be the one she would spend the rest of her life with. This trip would help her find out, but how would she get her parents' approval? She looked over at the bedside clock. It's 5:23 p.m., which means it's 11:23 p.m. in Italy. Kim wondered if Allen would still be up as she dialed his number.

"Hello."

"I'm so sorry to wake you. I just need your help," Kim nervously said.

"It's ok honey, I'm awake. What's the matter?"

"I'm having a hard time asking my parents if I can come over. I keep hearing my father say, '*I'm only seventeen.*'"

"Have you broached the topic with them? Do they know that I'm in Italy? Do they know that we're in love?" Allen's rapid-fired questioning made her even more upset.

"Allen, please stop with the questions. I'm doing the best that I can." She cried, "I know you've already bought the tickets and all, but I'm afraid I won't be able to come."

Allen tried to calm her down. "Kim, it's going to be okay. The tickets are refundable. Your dad is cool. He's been through a lot. You told me about how he met your mom and had to deal with the age difference. You're the same age as your mom when they got married. I think they will understand."

It was as if a light had just been turned on. "I've never thought about it that way. I think I know what I need to do now. Thank you so much, honey." She said, "I'll talk to them tomorrow and call you tomorrow evening, your time, to let you know how it went." Kim spent the rest of the evening writing notes and practicing her proposal in front of the mirror in her room.

The next morning, she woke early, showered, and put her plan to work. Kim silently went down to the kitchen and made breakfast, finishing just as her mom came down. "Wow," Carol said, "This is a pleasant surprise. What got into you?"

"What's wrong? Can't a girl do something nice for her parents?"

"Of course you can. It's just that I've always been the one that gets breakfast on the table. Don't get me wrong, I'm thrilled. It's just a shock. That's all," Carol said.

Kim smiled and handed her mom a cup of coffee. "It's Hazelnut."

Carol took a sip. "This is delicious, but I doubt your father will drink it. You know he's set in his ways."

"Yes, Mom, I know. Let's give it a try and see what he thinks. I have a pot of regular coffee on as backup."

"What's all the fuss about?" Bill said as he was walking down the stairs into the kitchen. "I could hear you gals chatting for the last twenty minutes; I figured I'd better get down here so I didn't miss out on anything." Bill chuckled.

"Oh, Dad, you always think we're conspiring against you," she said, handing him a cup of coffee. "Have a seat, and I'll bring your breakfast."

Kim fixed him a plate consisting of two eggs over easy, bacon, a cup of grits, and buttered toast. "This looks amazing," Bill said as he took his first sip of coffee. "Oh fuck, what's in this cup?"

"It's hazelnut coffee, Dad. Take a couple more sips before passing judgment."

"You know I don't drink that frou-frou shit. I like my coffee the old-fashioned way. Black!"

"Well then, you'd better finish that up so I can get you a regular cup. I know how you hate to waste."

Bill looked at his smart-ass daughter and started laughing. "What's so funny, Dad?"

"Your dad is laughing because he just realized the apple didn't fall far from the tree." Carol chimed in.

That was it. That was the lead-in she needed to bring up the Italy trip. She waited until her dad finished the frou-frou coffee and got him a fresh regular cup. He was almost done with his breakfast, so now was the time. "Mom, Dad, speaking of the apple and tree, do you mind if we talk about how you and Dad met and fell in love? I recall you telling me that Dad met you in a candy store when you were 16 and he was 34."

"Stop right there," Carol said. "If you're going to tell the story, you need to tell it correctly. I was sixteen and a half, and your dad had just turned 34."

Bill corrected, "And it was a confection store."

"OK, so I may get a few of the details wrong, but bear with me and let me finish. You two were young, and you fell in love. Dad was in the military and headed overseas. You were a high school senior. Look at how your lives turned out. You had me, and I think that was pretty special. You both still love each other." Kim paused to collect her thoughts. She was nowhere near what she had practiced the night before.

"Where's this leading?" Carol asked.

Kim started crying. This definitely wasn't part of the plan. "When I lost Thomas, I didn't think I'd ever fall in love again, but I did. Allen is so good to me. He's in the military, currently stationed in Italy. We talk and write nightly. He wants me to come visit him for a week. I told him I would but needed your blessing. Please, Mom, this will be my chance to find out if my feelings are true. Dad, you have to know how I feel. This is the same shit you and Mom had to deal with." Kim dropped her head to the table and continued to cry.

Carol looked at Bill with sad eyes. Bill looked the same. They both understood, but it was so different now. Carol broke the silence, "Times have changed since we were young. People are different; there are hippies smoking dope in the streets, protestors against the war in Vietnam, and I could name a dozen more things."

"But Mom, it's not different," Kim interrupted.

Carol jumped back in, "Kim, you didn't let me finish. Times, people, and the world in general were different, but love wasn't. You are a very responsible young lady who has had to deal with more in your 17 years than many do in their entire life. Your father and I raised you right. We know you'd never ask us for something this unordinary if it wasn't real, love that is. I believe I can speak for your father when I say that we will give our blessing."

Kim jumped up and went to hug her mom when Bill put a halt to the celebration. "Wait just a damn minute. While your mom may speak for me most of the time, I will speak for myself this time."

Both Carol and Kim were stunned at Bill's outburst.

"This isn't a request to go to the prom or even an overnight party. You're asking us to let you go to another country to be with a man we know very little about. How can we keep you safe over there? How can we ensure he's a standup guy?"

"Dad, you've told me for as long as I can remember that you have connections who can get things done. I know what you did growing up. I know the people you hung out with. Now you're telling me you don't know Allen or how to keep me safe? Really?"

"First, you serve me some nasty-ass-shit coffee, and then you hit me up with this? How am I supposed to act? What am I to think? Maybe you should have skipped all the ass-kissing and just asked. Did you really think you needed to butter us up first?"

"Mom, Dad, I'm confused."

"Kim, that was your dad speaking for himself. This is why I usually speak for him," she said with a smile.

Kim looked at her dad, still confused. "So, are you giving me permission to go, or are you fucking with me?"

"First of all, watch the language…"

"I will if you will," Kim interrupted.

"Fair enough, but remember who pays the bills around here. And the answer is maybe."

"Maybe! What kind of answer is that?" Kim yelled

Bill looked at Carol. "Well, maybe if you get me another cup of that hazel-shit coffee and give me a hug…."

Kim didn't wait for him to finish. She was up and in his arms. "I love you so much, Daddy!" She looked over at her mom, "You know I love you too, don't you?" She noticed her dad holding an empty cup of coffee, turning it back and forth. "Shit, I mean shucks, let me get your coffee."

They laughed and cried and hugged some more.

"One last thing," Bill grunted, "You tell that boy of yours to mind his Ps and Qs, or they might find him at the bottom of a lake with cement shoes."

"Yeah, sure, Dad. I'll get right on that."

Kim awoke from her dream with a smile on her face, startled to see Olivia and Allen standing over her, laughing. "What the hell is so funny?" she asked.

"You should have seen yourself. You were making strange noises and facial expressions. It was hilarious."

Olivia said, still giggling.

"Come honey, breakfast is served," Allen said with a strange face, mimicking Kim's sleep face. Olivia burst out in laughter at the site of her dad.

"You two have your fun. One day, the tables will be turned." Kim said with her stern voice. "Give me two minutes, and I'll be at the table."

After they left, Kim started laughing, imagining the faces she could have been making.

She then began reminiscing about Olivia and how she's grown into a beautiful young lady, inside and out. She was very active in school, track team, and debate club. She was recruited as a cheerleader but refused because she felt it would give her a shallow image. She was modest, putting others' needs before her own, and well respected by her peers and teachers.

Kim snapped out of her trance at the not-so-lovely scream of her daughter, "MOM! YOUR FOOD IS GETTING COLD!"

"Alright, I'm coming," Kim responded. "Don't get your panties all up in your ass."

CHAPTER 5

Ciao Bella
(Saturday, 29 June 1968)

Kim was anxious to call Allen, "Hello," came the voice on the other end of the phone.

"I spoke to my parents today. It was touch and go, but they said YES!"

"Oh my God, that's great; I've made so many plans for us. I'm going to take you to see all the sights, sample the best of Italian cuisine, and even take you to some of the best stores for shopping in Italy. I'm so stoked. I love you so much."

"I love you too," Kim responded. "I'm going to start packing today. I know I have a couple of weeks to go, but I want to be sure I don't forget anything."

Unlike when Allen was at home in Mississippi, phone calls to Italy were much more expensive, so she learned to say what needed to be said and get off the phone. This call was special, so she may have stayed a minute or two extra before saying goodbye.

Allen was in love, and he told Kim each time they talked. She said she was in love with him too. So, one day, while walking by a jewelry store, he purchased an engagement ring. He planned to pop the question at some point during her visit later this month. He was so excited that he had a hard time keeping it hush during their calls.

Kim arrived on a Friday night, 12 July 1968; Allen was waiting for her at baggage claim. "Ciao Bella Kimberly," he shouted when she was in sight. Within seconds, they were in each other's arms. They wasted no time getting her bags and hitting the road. She was in awe by the Italian architecture, at least what she could see in the dark. By the time she got to Allen's place, her adrenaline had subsided; she looked at Allen and said, "I'm sorry honey, but I can barely keep my eyes open. I know you went through a lot of trouble to have a snack waiting, but I'm too tired to eat." Allen smiled and gave her a hug, "It's ok honey, I've made the trip many times and know how it wears on the body. Let's get some rest, and tomorrow, we'll have a proper reunion.

Saturday was beautiful out. He woke to see Kim on the balcony. "You're up early. I figured you'd sleep in."

She replied, "Are you kidding? I'm not going to spend my first day in Italy sleeping. Let's go out and get a cappuccino." Allen could see her excitement, so he hopped in the shower. He bent over to wash his legs and felt a cold hand on his rear. "Ahem, do you want to make some room? I need a shower too," she said with a smile. Allen was up for it--literally.

Kim said, "You didn't think I was going to let you leave the room this morning without a bit of shagging, did you?" Allen was caught off guard but replied, "I wasn't sure but planned to give you a double helping this evening if you had." "I may still hold you to that," she said, blushing.

They spent the day sightseeing, visiting a couple of vineyards, and enjoying the beautiful weather. The food was amazing. Kim put her arms around Allen and whispered in his ear, "I could live here forever." That made Allen smile and reassured him that she loved him. They called it an early evening so they could have some alone time. Kim was naked within 30 seconds of entering his apartment. She crawled into bed and used her sexy voice, "Don't you owe me something?"

"Yes, ma'am," I've been waiting for this moment all day. Let the party begin." Allen didn't have a sexy voice, so his attempt had Kim in tears from laughing.

The next morning, they were heading to Venice. There was very little parking there, so he parked a few exits up, and they took the train the rest of the way. Kim's forehead was glued to the window, taking in all the sights this country had to offer. When they arrived in Venice, it was a short walk down to San Marco Square. They found an outside café near the Cathedral and enjoyed a late breakfast as they watched the town come to life. It was beautiful. The Cathedral was probably the prettiest one she had ever seen. The Bell Tower was to the right of the Cathedral and directly across from where they were sitting. The only thing that wasn't enjoyable was the thousands of pigeons begging for food. As usual, there were more tourists than residents, but watching people was part of the fun.

Allen asked, "How would you like to get a couple of photos from the top of the Bell Tower?"

"What?" she asked with a surprised look on her face. "Do they really allow people to go in there?"

"They sure do. I went up to the top on my last visit. You'd be amazed at how much of Venice you can see from there." Allen replied. They chugged the rest of their cappuccino--thank goodness they had cooled--and walked to the Tower.

The weather was perfect, not a cloud in the sky. When Allen and Kim got to the top of the tower, Kim, looking out over the city, exclaimed, "Well fuck me, this view is to die for!" She realized what she had said and covered her mouth in embarrassment. She didn't realize there was an elderly couple up there, or she wouldn't have used the F-bomb. Allen had his camera out and was taking pictures from the moment they arrived. He caught her excitement and the embarrassment of using foul language in the company of strangers. He would have that one framed.

After the tower, they visited the Bridge of Sighs. Allen put on his tour guide hat and pointed to the structure connecting two buildings, "This bridge connects the interrogation rooms in the Doge's Palace to the new prison. It was built in 1600, and legend is that this was a prisoner's last chance to see the outside world before he was locked away."

Kim asked, "How do you know so much about the bridge?" Allen just smiled and shrugged his shoulders.

The next stop was the Scala Contarini del Bovolo. Again, with his tour guide hat on, he stated, "This is the tallest spiral staircase in Venice. Built in the 1400s, it is a masterpiece of architectural designs, utilizing many styles such as Renaissance, Gothic, and Venetian." Kim once again was impressed by his historical knowledge. Allen asked, "How would you like to go on a gondola ride?"

"Most definitely," she replied. They had been together all day, and she hadn't noticed the bulge in his pants. No, it wasn't an erection. It was the ring. He was going to pop the question on the gondola. How romantic that would be. He had everything planned in his mind. So far, the day was perfect. Let's top it off with an engagement, he thought.

There was a short line for the gondolas, with three young couples in front of them. Allen's hands were starting to sweat. He was a nervous wreck when it was their time to climb down into a gondola. Kim sensed something was wrong, "Are you okay?" she questioned.

"Of course I am. I'm with the woman I love in a gondola in Venice. It can't get any better than this." Their gondola was painted blue on the outside. The inside appeared to be varnished wood and complemented the blue nicely. There were four seats, two facing forward, where Allen and Kim sat, and two facing backward towards the gondola operator. He was dressed traditionally in black pants, a black and white striped shirt, and a traditional gondolier hat.

The gondola operator had a radio playing romantic Italian music. He took them in and out of the canals encompassing the city. Allen and Kim engaged in small talk at first, then silence as they traveled arm in arm. *"Now is the time,"* Allen thought. He reached into his pocket, got on one knee on the bottom of the gondola, and looked up at Kim. "I've never been in love like this before. You bring out the best in me, and I can't bear to think of my life without you. Would you marry me?"

Kim was silent. She took the ring, put it on her finger, stared at it for a minute or so, and looked at Allen, "I'm so sorry, but I can't." she sadly said as she gave the ring back.

Allen felt like a clown. He did all this, and she said no. "How could I have misread our feelings for each other?" he thought. The mood swiftly changed for both of them. She said she'd explain later when she could gather her thoughts. She put her arm around him and laid her head on his shoulder.

Allen was numb inside but stayed strong. He continued the tour of Venice, showing her the glass-making factory, where they watched the craftsman make a vase. He then took her on a boat taxi around the city. Allen boasted, "I bet you didn't know that they have over 100 boat taxis here in Venice." She smiled. "They have larger boats that are like water buses; how about we hop off at the next stop and take the boat bus to Cemetery Island?"

"Sure," Kim replied.

It was getting late, and Allen could see that Kim was exhausted. He had to work the next day, so they headed home after the water bus ride to the island. Before going up for the night, Allen asked, "Would you like to have dinner? With all the excitement, we seemed to have forgotten to eat."

"That sounds nice," Kim replied. She didn't forget to eat; she was hungry but was walking on eggshells after the gondola ride.

They ate at one of Allen's favorite restaurants. The pasta was to die for. After dinner, they stopped at the gelato shop. Allen told the young lady, "Doppi Palline di gelato alla bianco per favore," pointing to himself and Kim. A minute later, she returned with two scoops of vanilla ice cream for each of them.

This is the best Ice cream I've had," Kim said, immediately followed by, "Shit, brain freeze."

Back at Allen's, they made their way up the stairs. Kim said to Allen, "You know I love you, right? You caught me off guard today. I wasn't expecting you to propose. We've only been together in person twice, and while each time was amazing, I fear we need to get to know each other better before marriage. Please don't hate me." The corner of Allen's lips turned upward, "I could never hate you," and they kissed.

The next day or two was awkward, but Allen soon put everything behind him. Work required some long hours, giving Kim time to plan tours to keep her occupied while he was working. This benefited both, as they were both tired when they got home.

After a day of shopping and sightseeing, Kim was ready for a hot bath to soak her tired legs. "Did you forget that not many places here have tubs?" he laughed.

"I did. I guess I'll have to take an extra long hot shower then."

Allen gave her some alone time and then joined her, "I figured I'd better jump in with you before all the hot water is gone."

"I was hoping you would."

The weeks went by fast. It was time for Kim to return home and back to her job if she still had one. She planned the trip so fast that she waited until the last minute to inform her employer that she was taking three weeks' vacation. It's a good thing she's an excellent worker; the job was waiting.

Allen returned to the States a few months later. He was based out of Biloxi, Mississippi. Kim lived in Ohio. That didn't stop them. Every two weeks, they were together. She'd fly down to spend a weekend with him; two weeks later, Allen was flying up to see her. This was costly but worth every penny. When they weren't together, they were on the phone for hours each day.

"Look at the time," Allen commented. "We've been on the phone for almost two hours, and for the last fifteen minutes, neither of us has said a word. Let's call it a night. We can talk more tomorrow."

"What? You don't love me?" Kim exclaimed from the other end of the phone.

"Of course I do, but we've been on the phone for hours, and the last twenty minutes have been total silence." He would appease her and stay on the phone until she said it was time.

Kim was an excellent worker and received a bonus for her effort. The bonus came the same week as her phone bill. $1,232.00. "Holey shit!!! It's going to take my entire bonus to pay this." She had planned to go to Cabo with a friend, but now that's out the window. Amazingly, the calls got shorter.

During one of Kim's visits to the Gulf Coast, she joined Allen for a wine tasting with friends. The conversation was a mix of stupid stories that brought laughter to everyone and world events, which she was totally disengaged from.

They closed the vineyard down, and as Allen paid the bill, she realized they had finished off four bottles of wine. "That's a lot of alcohol," she said as Allen returned. "Is that what we drank tonight?"

"Of course not," Allen replied. "We also had three shots each. Someone at the bar bought a round, so I returned the favor, and then another round appeared."

"You're a dick," she mumbled.

They were heading to a bonfire at one of Allen's friend's houses. Everyone was excited, and some were a bit tipsy. Allen had obtained a glass of water for Kim, "I know you're a bit wasted, but I promised we'd make a quick stop by, then we can go home."

Kim was up and moving around. She chugged the glass of water, "What? Me drunk? You musta thank I can't poled my liquor." She slurred. She had transformed from a quiet young lady in a room where she only knew one person to now being the life of the party.

"Here's some saltines and more water. You need to get something in your stomach."

"Fuck this, I want a cheesebooger," she said.

"I'm sorry honey, the winery is closing down. This is the best I can do for now. There's a burger joint on the way. I'll stop in and get us both something to eat. Then we'll make a quick stop by Sam and Jill's place and hang for just a few before going home."

Kim finished the 2nd glass of water and steadied herself with Allen's arm as they made their way to the car. "That founds like a winber," she said. When the door closed, so did her eyes.

Kim had dozed off, and when she opened her eyes, they were parked at his friend's house. "You wied to me. You promised get to me a cheesebooger."

Allen, trying his best not to laugh, smiled at her. "I did, sweetheart, it's right here. You were sleeping so soundly I didn't want to wake you. I've already eaten mine." She reached for the burger but grabbed nothing but air. Her head wobbling, she tried again. "Here, babe, I'll help you out. Let's get this food in you, say hello to everyone, and then leave. No more drinks for either of us, ok?" Kim had a mouth full of food and just mumbled and shook her head in agreement. The burger hit the spot, and Kim was feeling a little better. It was February in Biloxi, and they were in jeans and t-shirts. Back home, they were dealing with snow and freezing rain. I'm so glad she came here this weekend, he thought.

Allen helped Kim over to the party area. Sam and Jill had made makeshift stools around the fire with tree stumps. Allen led Kim to a couple that were open, and they sat down. Before they could get situated, Sam showed up with two beers. "That's ok, Sam, we're trying to sober up."

"To hell with that," Kim said as she grabbed the beers. Sam almost tripped over one of the logs; he was laughing so hard.

Allen grabbed one of the beers from Kim, "Hey, that's my beer." She protested.

"Nope, it's one for you and one for me." He said. Kim mumbled a few curse slurs, then sat quietly.

Allen looked at her with the wind blowing her hair, the fire shining in her eyes, and thought how lucky he was to have her in his life. Someone had started their car and rolled the windows down so that the music could be shared. Marvin Gaye was playing, and everyone started dancing and singing along. "Don't you know that I heard it through the grapevine? Not much longer would you be mine, honey, honey, yeah." Allen was singing and swaying with the music. He looked at Kim, and she was swaying too. "Shit," she's about to pass out." He grabbed her and the beer before either of them hit the ground.

She found out how low her tolerance was that night, especially when she stood. "Mutha Fucker," she said, "Everything is spinning. I'm going to be sick." After a bout of dry heaving, Allen told her, "It's time I get you home." Kim nodded her head in agreement. It was about a 30-minute drive, and Allen worried she would get sick before they made it home. With his eyes on the road, he asked, "How are you feeling hon?" There was no answer, so he looked and saw that she was sleeping comfortably. Before making it home, he thought getting more food into her stomach would be a good idea. He pulled into a fast-food place and ordered two Whoppers. He shook Kim's shoulder gently, and those sweet, innocent eyes opened.

"I smell food. Where are we? She asked. "We're almost home. I wanted to get some more food in you to help you feel better, and besides, I'm starving."

The last thing she could think about was food, but upon Allen's insistence, she took a small bite of her burger, then another. She must have realized she was hungry too, as she devoured it before Allen could get the wrapper off his. Kim was more coherent by the time Allen pulled into the driveway. "We're home," he announced.

Allen parked, then walked to the passenger side to help Kim out of the car. She was giggly and getting frisky.

"Kim, what's gotten into you?"

"I don't know," she replied, "Are you complaining?"

"Not at all. I'm kind of worked up now anyway."

As they walked into the house, Kim was undressing. First to go was her shoes, and then she stripped off her shirt, exposing a perfect set of breasts. Not too big, firm, and real. Just the way he liked them. Kim hadn't worn a bra since it was a night out, and she wanted to be sexy for her man. What Allen didn't know was that she was commando down bottom too. When she dropped her pants, she was completely naked, her nipples erect, and her vagina looked very inviting.

Kim took care of herself. She used body lotions and kept her legs and vagina shaved, leaving the cutest landing strip. Kim was ready but saw that Allen still had his pants on. "Do you need a little help?" she asked.

"How could I turn down an offer like that?" he responded.

Kim proceeded to get down on her knees and undid his belt. Kissing his belly and rubbing his groin, she undid his pants. She continued caressing his manhood through the pants, unzipping him and watching his pants fall to the floor. Allen was fully erect, and Kim knew what she had to do. She spat on her hand and went to work.

A few minutes later, she could feel Allen throbbing and knew it wouldn't be long before he exploded. She continued to work her magic until the throbbing intensified, and a loud groan came from Allen. The groan wasn't the only thing that came. Bill's knees became weak, and he buckled to the floor. "Now, it's my turn, " he proclaimed after two minutes of recovery. Allen began kissing her thighs, working his way toward the landing strip. He could feel the excitement rising in her body.

Allen thought about how romantic she was with him, taking her time, ensuring each part of his body was not left out. So he did the same. Moving his tongue in a way that gave her chills. Her whole body would tense up, then she screamed, "DON'T STOP!" This excited Allen more and more, giving him incentive to increase his rhythm and make this last as long as he could for her. He felt her body tremble when she came. After a minute or so, with her legs wrapped tightly around his head, she said, "I need you inside me right now."

Allen didn't need to be asked twice. He moved up her body, still lying on the living room floor, and guided his penis into her hot, well-moistened box. She immediately came again. Allen was doing everything he could to hold back. He said, "I'm going to pull out."

"NO, I want to feel you explode inside me." She begged.

"I can't. I'm not wearing a condom." He quickly said.

"It's okay," Kim explained. "I've been counting, and we're good to go. This made Allen pound her harder, knowing he didn't have to pull out. He wanted to fill her up.

"Ask me again," Kim said to Allen.

"Ask you what?" he said, somewhat curious, all the while holding it in as much as possible.

"Ask me what you asked in Italy."

Looking deep into her eyes, he asked, "Are you sure?" She smiled, nodding her head in agreement. Allen, so close to letting loose with his second load, slowed the pace, looked at her with all his love, and said, "Kim, my love, will you marry me?"

Before he could say anything else, she screamed, "Yes, yes, yes. I will definitely marry you!" at the same moment she said yes, Allen exploded into her, filling her with the kind of love only two people crazy about each other could have.

They rolled around on the floor for a couple more sessions before getting up, washing off, and going to bed. They were both so happy. They lay in bed fully embraced until Allen drifted off to sleep. Kim was soon to follow.

CHAPTER 6

The Announcement (February 1968)

It had been several days since Kim and Allen talked. They shared a wild and wonderful weekend, and both of their work schedules would be busy for a few days. It wasn't a concern when the phone didn't ring.

Allen was working 10-hour shifts and then attending classes at night. He was trying to learn as much as he could about the new technology that's currently in design. The government was sponsoring some of the resources on it, so he got to talk with a lot of the experts. He knew this new medium would highly impact the future if the theories panned out.

Kim called Thursday evening. "Hello," Allen squeaked out. "Hi honey, it's me," Kim's soft, sweet voice echoed back. "You sound tired. Is everything okay?"

Still groggy, Allen said, "Yes, babe, I dozed on the couch after class and woke to the phone ringing."

"I'm sorry. Should I let you go?" Kim responded with a disappointing tone.

"Not at all, Love. I needed to wake up. Otherwise, I'd be up all night. It's so good to hear your voice. I've missed you."

Kim had been off work for a few hours and was chilling beside the fireplace with a glass of wine and one of her favorite books. "I need to go and see my grandparents this weekend. Grandma isn't doing well." She sadly said. "I won't be able to come and see you; I hope you understand."

Allen immediately responded with, "Are you kidding me? Of course, you need to see them, we're young and have plenty of time to be together. Be with your grandparents while you can. I hope to meet them the next time I'm up your way."

"That would be great!" Kim exclaimed, "I've been telling them all about you. It would probably be nice to introduce you to them so they don't think you've been a figment of my imagination."

Kim and Allen talked almost nonstop. Every night, they would hook up and talk for hours. They couldn't wait for the next encounter. Allen was already making plans to fly up in two weeks. He missed the red-headed love of his life and wanted to hold her tight.

By the time their lives had settled down, it'd been six weeks since they'd been together. Allen planned to fly up after work on Friday and return on the last flight on Sunday. This would give them two full days to be together. Kim was seventeen, finishing her senior year in high school and working part-time at a legal practice. Her future was planned out in her mind, and her parents were 100% behind her.

Allen arrived late Friday night, took a shuttle to the hotel, and had a few drinks in the hotel bar before heading to his room. The next morning, Kim was supposed to be there around noon. Allen didn't want to sit in his room and wait, so he told Kim that he would be in the hotel bar waiting for her. Kim had met Allen at this hotel a couple of times before, so it wasn't a surprise. She thought this might work better than meeting him in his room.

Kim was due to be there by noon. It was a quarter after when she walked into the bar. Allen immediately jumped off his bar stool and wrapped his arms around her. Their lips finally met, and the passionate kissing began. It was obvious to the two drunks and barfly in the bar that they were in love.

They sat back at the bar. Allen ordered a spiced rum and coke. Waiting for Kim to speak up, Allen looked at the bartender and, in his best Humphrey Bogart impersonation, said, "Hey, hon, can you get a Michelob Ultra for my gal?"

Before she could ask for his ID, Kim spoke up, "Please cancel that beer. I'll just have a glass of water."

Allen looked at Kim and said, "Really? You're going to make me drink alone?"

The waitress brought Allen's drink and sat it on the bar in front of him. "I hope this doesn't mean you've given up drinking."

"Of course not," Kim replied. "I'm just tired from the long week and didn't sleep well last night."

Allen understood all too well. With his numerous travels, even his young body was wearing out. Allen picked up his drink and took a big sip, "Ahhhhh, just what I needed." He took another sip and asked Kim, "Have you eaten?"

"I haven't," Kim responded.

"Want to join me for a late lunch or early dinner at the Italian place near the mall?" Allen proposed.

"Yes, that would be very nice."

Allen finished his drink and laid his money on the counter. The bartender said, "Keep your money. That round was on me."

Allen responded with gratitude and sarcasm, "Thank you, that was much appreciated. Just a word of advice, though—the drink was pretty weak. I could barely taste the rum."

The bartender leaned over and whispered to Kim, "That was straight coke." They both laughed. Kim thanked the bartender as they were leaving. Before they reached the door, the bartender yelled, "Use the money you saved to get some Bogart lessons."

Arriving at the restaurant, Allen chuckled, making small talk, "We picked a good time to eat. This place is usually packed. There's only four cars in the lot, five if you count mine." Kim smiled and nodded.

"Two, Please," Kim said as the hostess greeted them. They followed her to their table. Directly behind them was their waitress carrying a basket of bread and butter. She sat the basket between them and asked, "Do you know what you want, or do you need a little time to look at the menu?"

Allen said, "I'll just have another basket of bread and butter and water." He cracked himself up. Kim, on the other hand, didn't care for his humor.

The waitress rolled her eyes and shook her head slowly from side to side, "I hope you're the funny one in the relationship cuz he's dryer than my grandma, and she's been dead six years."

This cracked Kim up. "Now that's funny, Allen. Pay attention, and you might learn a thing or two." Both of the ladies giggled while Allen was licking his wounds.

Allen looked up at the waitress, who was staring down at him with a pad in one hand and a pen in the other, impatiently tapping it on her pad. "Is funny guy ready to order?"

Kim jumped in with a huge smile on her face, "While 'funny guy' is trying to find his words, I'll go ahead and order. I'll have the seafood pasta with a side salad."

Allen looked up again and said, "I'll have the crow." All three of them busted into laughter then. "Seriously though, I'll have the Angel hair pasta with Carbonara sauce. Add two sausage links. I'll have an iced tea, and my beautiful future ex-fiancé would like more water."

The meal was delicious. They both ate every bite. Allen had just put his last bite in his mouth when the waitress returned and asked if they were ready for the check.

Kim piped up, "Excuse me, what do you have for dessert? I'm in the mood for something sweet." She took the dessert menu from the waitress, peered at it for just a few seconds, and said, "I'll have the White Chocolate Raspberry Cheesecake." Allen smiled and thought, "She must be getting comfortable around me. She usually only eats lite. He couldn't recall the last time she'd ordered dessert. This made him smile inside.

While waiting on the cheesecake, Kim looked at Allen with a serious look on her face. "I really need to talk to you. I was up all night last night, didn't eat a thing yesterday, and have been avoiding my parents as much as possible."

"What's wrong, honey? Is everything all right?"

"I don't know," she snapped. "Remember the last time we were together? That weekend we practically never got out of bed?" Kim began to cry. "The weekend I told you it was safe to cum inside me?" Allen started turning pale. His palms were sweating. He knew where this was leading. "Well, "she continued, "I miscounted."

"What do you mean?"

"I miscounted my cycle. I thought we'd be safe." She was now balling. The other couple in the same area as them was curiously looking over at Kim. "I'm pregnant!" After hearing it out loud, Allen's jaw dropped. He was trying to come up with words to express his feelings but realized he had no idea what his feelings were. Instead of speaking, he went over to her side of the table, knelt down, and gave her a monster hug.

CHAPTER 7

Mom, Dad, Guess What?

Back at the hotel, Allen began remembering their last long weekend together. What was supposed to be an early Valentine's Day celebration became a weekend they would remember for the rest of their lives. They had been drinking with others at a campout. Allen recalled, "It was romantic; there must have been twenty to thirty people there, but I only recall you. You looked so sexy in your Cleveland State shirt and those hip-hugger blue jeans that were painted on—the way your eyes shined in the firelight. I was on top of the world. Then we went back to my place and made love. It was well after midnight, so that would have meant conception was on Sunday, February 2nd, when you said you'd marry me. This will be a story for our grandchildren."

"Enough already," Kim exclaimed. "I'm scared to death, and you're getting all emotional. We've got to figure out a way to tell my parents. And, by the way, my pants were not that tight." Allen thought differently, put both hands up and shrugged. "Well, I guess it'll be a while before you can get into those pants again," he said, laughing so hard that he had momentarily closed his eyes and bent over. As he was rising up, Kim backhanded him across the chest. "What the fuck!" he exclaimed, "Was that too soon?"

"That wasn't one bit funny. You're lucky you only got my backhand." Kim said proudly.

They talked for a while, trying to figure out how this would go down. "How about we take them to their favorite restaurant and break the news to them there?" Kim suggested.

"That sounds nice. Should I wear a bulletproof vest for this meeting?" he chuckled.

"That might not be a bad idea," Kim responded.

Allen's smile quickly turned to panic, "What do you mean? I was only kidding. I mean, I know your dad came from a shady background, but I thought he had calmed down since then…"

Kim was staring right into his eyes as his nervous babbling continued. "Whoa, whoa, whoa, that's enough. Do you want me to get you a tissue? I was only joking, at least for the most part." She said.

"Which part?" he asked, but all he got was a smile and a wink from Kim.

"When do you want to do this?" Allen asked.

"Well, you're flying back tomorrow, and we probably won't see each other up here for three or four more weeks, so I guess there's no time like the present." Allen's eyes were frozen, his forehead beet red and dripping with sweat. "I'll call and see if they can meet us tonight."

"TONIGHT? That's too soon. I'm not prepared. I don't have a gift or a speech written." He tried to sway Kim, but she wasn't having any of it.

"Putting it off will only make it more difficult." She said as she was dialing her mom's number.

"Hi Mom, how are you doing? Allen's in town but flying home tomorrow. Can you and Dad meet us tonight at 7 p.m. at that restaurant you really like? We can talk and have dinner without worrying about who's doing the dishes."

On the other end of the phone, Carol said, "That's because we both know who'd be doing the dishes, and it wouldn't be you, now would it? I'll talk to your dad and call you back. He's out mowing the lawn. Are you going to come home and change before dinner?"

Kim was a bit dismissive when she said, "No, ma'am, I brought clothes with me, so I'll change here."

About 30 minutes later, her phone rings. Allen yells, "I've got it!" and picks up the phone. "Hi, Mom, how are you today?"

"Just great, thanks for asking. Is Kim available?" Carol asked.

Allen responded, "Well, if you can hang on a minute or two, I'll see if she's out of the shower."

"Oh, no, don't bother. Just tell her that her dad and I will meet you at Fischer's Diner at 7 p.m."

"Will do, Mom. See you then."

As Allen hung up the phone, Kim came into the room. "Who was on the phone?"

"It was your mom. She said that they would meet us at the restaurant at 1900 hrs. Are you sure you want to break the news to them tonight?"

"Of course! It has to be when both of us are together. We got into this situation together and will work through it together. What was the name of the restaurant? Oh, never mind, I'll call her back later and get the name.

"Till death do us part," Allen added. It brought a smile to her face. "What are you going to wear?"

"I was going to run to the store and pick up a new dress. I thought you might pick up a nice pair of slacks and a button-up shirt unless you packed one?"

"Are you kidding me? Why would I pack dress clothes? You didn't even tell me about the pregnancy until I got here?"

"I'm just fucking with you. I'm wearing a pair of jeans and a sweater. You can wear anything you like."

"But what if your parents dress up?"

"You need to relax. They are not going to dress up. I can tell you right now what they will be wearing. Dad will be in polyester pants, a button-up shirt, not tucked, white socks, and black shoes. Mom will wear an old dress that she goes shopping in, not one of her Sunday dresses, stockings, and a pair of comfortable shoes."

Allen was amazed she could get that much detail and commented, "I'd bet you a drink that you're wrong, but that wouldn't be fair since you can't drink right now."

"Why don't you jump into the shower and freshen up? I don't want you smelling like a bum tonight."

Allen sniffed his underarms, "You're shitting me again, aren't you?"

"Unfortunately not," Kim replied

It was a 30-minute drive to the restaurant, and Allen wanted to get there early. "I hate being late. I always say, 'If you're not five minutes early, you're late.'"

"Yeah, yeah, yeah, I know. It's a military thing." Kim injected.

They arrived at the restaurant fifteen minutes early and sat in the car discussing how they would break the news to her parents. Allen turned pale, "Your parents just pulled in. They do like me, right?" He looked at Kim; she was frozen in her seat, staring straight ahead, breathing heavily. "Honey, are you okay? Kim?" Allen gets out of the car, runs to the passenger side, and opens the door.

"Kim, relax. Take deep breaths."

"I'm ok," she says as her breathing slows. "I think I had a mini panic attack."

"Here, take this towel and wipe your face. You're sweating." Allen handed her a hand towel he had put in the car this morning. "We should probably start walking in. We don't want to keep them waiting."

"Where did your sudden burst of bravery come from?" she asked.

"It's what I do. I worry about things until it's time to face them, then I put on my big-boy pants and face whatever it is."

"Like your deployments?" Kim asked

"Yes, that's a good example, but there are many more. Here, let me get the door."

They entered the restaurant and saw Bill and Carol at a table in the main room. They both stood as the young couple walked over. "Hi, Mom," Kim said as she gave her a hug. "Hi, Dad, I didn't forget about you." Allen stood there with his hands behind his back in the "Parade" stance. In the military, this is where you put your hands behind your back, your right hand resting in the left, feet about twelve inches apart. Allen is military through and through.

Carol looked over and saw Allen standing awkwardly behind Kim, who was talking to her dad. "Come over here and hug me, young man." He hugged her, and then she kissed him right on the lips. "Don't be alarmed. This is a family of huggers and kissers."

"Ummm, you just caught me off guard. I'll have to remember this next time I meet family."

Bill and Kim laughed at Allen's blushing. "Don't worry, you'll get used to it," Bill said after he caught his breath. If only I had a camera to get that look on your face. Come on over here and sit next to me. And don't worry, I'm not a kisser."

"He's a fucking liar," Kim warned Allen. "Watch your back."

"Honey, watch your language. We're in a public restaurant with your parents."

"Am I embarrassing you?"

"That's a trick question, isn't it? I'm just gonna sit here quietly and have some bread and butter." Now the whole table is laughing.

Kim and Allen planned to wait until after dinner to talk to them. There is no sense in upsetting them and ruining a good meal.

Allen ordered the ribeye with a baked potato and garden salad. Kim ordered salmon with rice and a side salad. She looked at Allen and said, "You seem to have forgotten about our bet?"

Allen looked over at Carol and Bill then dropped his head. "What's the matter, boy?" Bill asked. Carol elbowed him, "Can't you see I'm trying to give Lindsay our order? Quiet down." Carol looked at the adorable waitress and said, "Lindsay, we'll have the meatloaf, mashed potatoes, and okra."

"Both of you want the same thing?" Lindsay asked.

Carol clarified her order. "We'll have one order and two plates. We don't eat a lot." Lindsay smiled, acknowledged Carol's order, and headed to the kitchen to put the order in.

"Now, where were we?" Bill asked.

"What do you mean? We're right here. Are you losing your mind?" Carol smarted off.

"No, smart ass, what were we talking about before Lindsay came over?" He looked over at Allen, who dropped his head.

"What's the matter, boy? Do you think I'm old and feeble and can't remember things?"

"No, sir."

"Then tell me what was going on between you and our daughter that has you losing a bet?" Bill demanded.

"So you heard all of that? Shit, I'd better remember that for next time too," Allen said, stalling as long as he could.

"Allen, you keep avoiding the question. Was it that bad?" Carol asked.

Allen looked over at Kim, who was about to lose it. "Really? Are you enjoying me being roasted on the throne alone?"

"Well Bill…Carol, Kim told me exactly what you'd be wearing tonight, right down to the white socks on Bill and comfortable shoes on you, ma'am." Kim couldn't hold it in any longer and started laughing so hard tears rolled down her cheeks.

"I'm sorry honey, I told them it was ok to harass you." Allen winked and then flipped her off. Kim was quick on the draw and shot the bird back at him. This time, Bill and Carol burst out laughing.

What a great icebreaker. Everyone was having a fantastic time talking, joking, and acting like they'd known each other for years. The food hadn't arrived, but everyone was in a great mood. Kim looked over at Allen and mouthed, "It's time." Before Allen could respond, Kim spoke up.

"Mom…Dad, Allen and I wanted to talk to you. I'm not sure how to start this out…"

"Mr. & Mrs. Parson, not to be blunt, but I proposed to Kim. We're in…"

Carol interrupted, "Yes, we know. Kim told us that you proposed in Italy. She also told us that she said no."

"Yes, ma'am, that's true. But during her last visit to Biloxi, she realized how much she loved me."

"I'm infatuated with this man. We were making love, and I told him to ask me again. I really, really love him."

"Well, you know we love Allen, and you could have left out the part about you two banging out of wedlock. Your mom and I thought this might be why you wanted to have us here tonight. We talked about it and think you two are a great couple. We can start making wedding plans when you're out of school."

Carol leaned over and put her arms around Bill. He turned towards her, and they kissed. "You did good, hon," she told him.

"Dad, thank you so much for your approval. But there's one more thing." Allen gets up and stands behind Kim. "Mom? Dad? I'm pregnant."

There was total silence. Bill stood up and locked eyes with Allen. Bill couldn't muster up anything to say, but if looks could kill, Allen would be six feet under within minutes. Allen knew Bill was using all his restraint not to say or do something that would jeopardize the relationship with his daughter. Carol's jaw dropped. She looked over at Bill, who was still in his frozen mafia pose, then put her head down on the table and cried.

"I'm in shock, Mom! You got pregnant at seventeen too. Dad, you could have gone to jail for statutory rape. And now you're looking down on us when we're just like you two. How can you act like this?"

Kim, hormones in full rage, got up and ran out of the restaurant. Allen was right behind her.

"This didn't go as we planned, huh?" Allen asked Kim.

Kim and Allen held each other tight for what seemed

like an eternity. Suddenly, they heard footsteps coming towards them.

"Are you two alright?" Bill said. "Come on back. The dinner has been served. Come in and eat before it gets cold."

"I don't know that I can eat right now," Kim sobbed. "I'm shaking, hyperventilating, and… I'm just a mess."

"Your mom and I talked. Please come back in and hear us out. Besides, I don't have enough money on me to pay for all the food," Bill joked.

Kim half-smiled and walked over to her dad. They held hands as they headed back inside. Allen walked two paces behind them. When they got to the table, Carol came around and hugged them both. She didn't say a word, and then she went back to her chair.

"Let's enjoy our meal, then we'll finish this talk," Bill said as he sat back down at the table. He reached to his left and grabbed Carol's hand. He then reached to his right and grabbed Kim's hand. Carol and Kim both reached for Allen's hand.

"Let us pray," Bill said as everyone bowed their head. "We are grateful for this blessing of food you have given us, Lord. We are thankful for the health and well-being of this family and how you've given us the gift of reason, compassion, and most of all, love. It is of utmost joy that we also give thanks for the new life that will be entering our world shortly. Finally," Bill pauses and looks up at Allen and Kim. "Finally, we give thanks for the newest member of our family." Kim and Allen squeezed hands and smiled at each other, then bowed their heads again. Bill continued, "Please bless and protect him as he has vowed to protect our country and will soon vow to protect our daughter. It's in your name we pray, Amen."

In unison, Carol, Allen, and Kim all said, "Amen," and the whole table was crying with joy over the change of heart that had happened.

"OK, the official shit is…" Carol elbowed Bill in the gut before he could finish. "Watch your language, you heathen. You were just praying." Bill bent over due to the unexpected blow, "Um, as I was saying, now that the official pregame event has been completed, let's enjoy the meal."

"Yeah, before it gets soggy from all this pansy-ass emotion," Kim said, wiping tears off her cheeks and dabbing her wet eyes with the napkin.

"Oh my goodness," Carol said immediately after Kim's remark. "You are your father's daughter."

"That she is," Allen chimed in as he was slicing into his steak. "Just the way I like it…"

"What? Mooing?" Carol said disgustingly.

The food was still hot and delicious. Carol and Bill finished their meal and watched as Allen devoured the wounded cow on his plate. Kim was about halfway through her meal, struggling to finish the salmon. Her hormones must have been in overdrive. She had never been this emotional before. She was crying one minute and laughing the next. Her anxiety had abated, and a calm had overtaken her body. At that moment, all in the world was right. Until…

"So, Dad, you mentioned we could finish our discussion after dinner," Kim said, noticing the surprised look on everyone's faces.

"Honey, weren't you listening to your dad's prayer?" Allen coaxed her. "I believe he said all that needed to be said then." Bob and Carol shook their heads in agreement.

"Well, not everyone got to speak during his prayer," Kim responded. "I have something I wanted to say."

Everyone got quiet and directed their attention to Kim. Allen was cringing, not knowing what would be coming out of her mouth.

"Today has been an emotional rollercoaster with lots of ups and downs. We had our differences and found a way to make them one. But there is something that I feel I must say." Kim paused to add a touch of drama to the statement. "Mom… Dad…I love you both so much. You have been the best parents I could have hoped for. You raised me to trust in God, love thy neighbor, and show respect to others. I only hope I can be half as good as you with our child." Kim looked at her parents, and the tears started again.

"Can you believe she said all that without a single curse word?" Allen interjected before thinking of the ramifications of his comment.

"Alright, mutha fuckers, let's get this party rolling. Water for everyone!" Kim announced louder than everyone wanted. The family three tables over was all staring at her with disdain in their expressions.

"Wait a minute, little girl," Bill jumped in, "I plan on having a beer."

"You'd better think twice about that buster." Kim stood up and was looking down at her dad. "If I can't drink, nobody drinks, capisce?" They all laughed.

As they got up to leave, Carol whispered to Kim, "Shouldn't we tell Allen that we told you what we would wear tonight?"

"Oh, hell no!" He'll be wondering about this for years to come.

Walking to the car, Bill asked Kim, "Are you riding home with us?"

"Are you kidding? I'm engaged and pregnant. I think I will go back to the hotel with my future husband. Mom, you and I can start planning the wedding tomorrow."

"Take care of my little girl," Bill shouted over to Allen. "I think cement would go well around those leather loafers you have on. Remember, I have connections." He winked at Allen, got in the car, and pulled out. Allen and Kim saw Carol slap Bill across the back of the head as he put it into drive.

CHAPTER 8

Acapulco Dreams (1984)

Allen and Kim spent many a Sunday morning reading the paper, playing games, or watching TV in the living room. It was their decompress day. There were always shows on about buying land in other countries, and as usual, it was just background fodder. They watched the show but never considered moving anywhere outside the country. The military has been doing that ever since they got married.

Allen had finished the paper and started on the comics, the section he always saves for last. He was engulfed with the comics when a show came on about Acapulco, a tourist hot spot on the west coast of Mexico. Allen's eyes perked up since seeing that Elvis movie *"Fun in Acapulco"* in the sixties, he had always wanted to visit. He began watching it, reading the paper only during commercials.

"You usually wait for girls in bathing suits before you put the paper down. You must be really interested in this episode?" Kim said, smiling.

"I've been to South and Central America a few times, and we've both visited a couple of tourist resorts on the eastern side, but I've never been to Acapulco," Allen answered. "Do you remember the Elvis movie that was filmed there?"

"You mean the one where Elvis cliff dives?" Kim asked.

"Yes, and funny how you remember the scene where the guys are all in tight Speedos," he joked. "When diving from a 40 or 80-foot cliff, you need trunks that won't fall off when you hit the water."

Allen and Kim always kidded each other about flirting with someone or watching a cute guy or girl in the drugstore. They were happy and completely trusted each other. The commercial was over; it was back to the program, and Kim knew better than to interrupt him when he was trying to watch something.

TV Announcer: "Acapulco is located on the western side of Mexico, about 235 miles from Mexico City. Only one main highway runs over the Sierra Madre Del Sur Mountains, which can be heavily traveled during peak holiday and weekend hours. The mountain's highest point is Cerro Nube at twelve thousand two hundred feet."

Allen was engrossed with the show. He wondered what life in a tourist spot would be like. Then he thought about driving around the fairgrounds when the fair was in town. It was a traffic madhouse, and he would curse the town for not planning for the influx of visitors.

"Kim, how would you like to go to Acapulco one day? We could travel around and check out some of the small towns in the area and get immersed with the locals."

"That sounds like fun, but somehow, I feel you have ulterior motives."

"Well, watching all these shows has me wondering what it would be like to own property in another country. Not that we'd ever do it, but it would be an adventure to travel down there on vacation and throw in a little investigating. Olivia will be out of school in a few more years. It could be a nice vacation home." Allen tried to convince her. "We could advertise it as a rental for the dates we won't use it… It could pay for itself just in rentals."

"We're not vacation home people," Kim began, "and you know that. We have a little savings but can't afford two homes."

"So is that a NO?" Allen asked with his tail between his legs.

"Hell no, it's a yes! I want to see those skinny men jumping off cliffs wearing those little banana hammocks. Count me in."

"Maybe we'll see some cute girls diving too," Allen added.

While they were discussing Acapulco, another show came on about an alternative resort destination on one of the islands in the Caribbean. He didn't want to be on a small island during a major storm. So he leaned back in his recliner, put his legs back up, and returned to his comics.

"You haven't turned a page in quite some time. Did you fall asleep over there?" Kim asked.

"Sort of, I was daydreaming."

It was almost noon when Allen heard footsteps coming down the stairs. "She lives!" he shouted out to his fifteen-year-old daughter.

"Very funny, Dad. I've been awake for over an hour."

"Wow, a whole hour, huh? Why are you grumpy this morning?"

"School stuff," she said. "They changed my topic for tomorrow's debate, and now I have to start from scratch to prepare myself. To top it off, I have a track meet before my debate."

"It's okay, honey. There will be times in life when you'll become overwhelmed. Try to find a way to relieve your anxiety, then work on your research," Kim offered.

"Olivia?" Kim called out. "Come over here and sit with me for a minute. I know how much you pride yourself on being the best, but sometimes, you put too much pressure on yourself. You've got more intelligence than your dad and I put together. Let's hope this is the hardest obstacle you have to deal with in your life."

"It's not fair, Mom. I had done all my research and prepared my arguments. I was going to use today to practice." Olivia wiped her eyes, stood, and said, "I'm going for a run. I need to clear my mind."

Allen walked over and gave her a hug before she left. After Olivia walked out, he looked at Kim, "Honey, we need a vacation, something that will relax her. I've never seen her have a meltdown like this before. She's getting too stressed out for a teenager."

When Olivia returned from her run, you could tell she was still somber. With her headphones on, she gestured to her parents, acknowledging their presence, and turned and went up the stairs. A few minutes later, they heard the shower running.

"If she doesn't come down right after her shower, I'll go up and talk with her," Carol said timidly, looking over at Allen for approval.

"No, Honey, she needs a little bit of time. We need to give her space and let her figure this out," Allen replied.

A COUPLE OF WEEKS LATER, KIM WALKED IN AND SAW Allen sitting at the kitchen table.

"Whatcha doing?" Kim inquired, noticing Allen looking through travel brochures. "Are you planning a trip?"

"Not really. I was curious, so I stopped by the travel agency and saw Wanda on my way home from work," Allen responded without really telling her what he was doing.

"You seemed to have left off the answer to my question. What are you doing? Are you hiding something from me?"

"No, ma'am, I was thinking about Acapulco at work and thought I could get it out of my system if I knew how much it would cost. The problem is the prices don't look that bad. Especially if we go in the off-season," Allen said emphatically.

"Well, when we win the lottery, or you get a bonus, we can think about it. I don't want us wasting our retirement money on a trip." Carol spoke with a tone of authority, hoping Allen would leave the Acapulco vacation idea back at the travel agency. "By the way, how is Wanda? Has she tried to break up any more homes lately?"

"Come on now, you know she wasn't trying to break us up. We all had a couple of drinks down at Charlie's," Allen reassured Kim.

"It's funny how you keep forgetting that she was all over you that evening. I get up one time to go take a piss and come back and find her in your arms."

"Wow, your version of the story gets wilder each time you tell it," Allen joked, trying to defend himself from this false accusation. "You know what really happened. Half the bar saw it, and several of them came over and backed me up."

"You expect me to believe she was coming over to say hi right when I left to go to the bathroom? And that she tripped over a pickle that had fallen on the floor and landed in your lap?"

"First of all, it wasn't a pickle; it was a dinner roll, and she didn't trip. She stepped on it, and her foot slid out from under her. I just happened to be the one sitting by her when it happened. I heard something and looked behind me just in time to catch her before she hit the ground," Allen explained. "You came out of the lady's room at that moment and let your imagination run wild."

"You can defend her all you want. I know it wasn't an accident. I bet she had schemed for months planning that 'accidental' fall," Kim said in a tone that let Allen know that this topic was closed.

"Well, you don't have to be mad at me. Whether she planned it or not, I was innocent."

"Have you talked to Olivia today?" Allen asked, still worrying about her emotions after the incident on their anniversary.

"Yes, I spoke to her this morning before school. She seemed fine, but it's only been a few weeks since the breakdown. I just hope she understands how much we care."

"Let's just keep our eyes on her for a couple more weeks to make sure she doesn't do anything stupid," Allen replied. "She knows we both love and support her."

A couple of weeks had passed since her meltdown, and Olivia was semi-back to her old self. Kim talked her into a mother-daughter shopping excursion.

After a full day of shopping, Kim looked down at her watch. "Olivia, we need to check out," Kim said while trying to estimate how much she had in the cart.

"What's the hurry, Mom? We've got all day. It's only 5:00 p.m."

"We're meeting your dad for dinner. I'm sorry, I meant to say something earlier, but I was so caught up with shopping with you that it slipped my mind."

"Is this a special occasion, or do you have some bad news to tell me?" Olivia asked, showing concern in her eyes.

"Neither, darling. Your dad felt left out and asked if we could have a family dinner tonight."

"That's so sweet. You have the best husband ever," Olivia said to Kim

"And you have the best dad ever," Kim said, smiling.

They gathered their items and proceeded to the checkout line. "So, where is Dad taking us?"

"He's taking us to an Italian restaurant tonight. Well, actually, we're meeting him there," Kim answered.

Olivia's eyes almost popped out of their sockets when the cash register displayed, with tax, a hefty sum of $438.53. "Mom, that's way too much. Let me put some of my things back."

"Olivia, it's okay. I've been saving some of my discretionary money so that we could have a girl's day out. This has been an awesome day, and I wouldn't have changed a thing."

"Mom, you're the best," Olivia said while giving her a large hug. She held that hug for a couple of minutes, which worried Kim.

"Let's keep this between us, though."

"What?" Olivia asked. "The shopping or the conversations?"

"Let's keep the amount we spent a secret," Kim said, giving Olivia a wink.

"Sure thing, Mom."

They packed the shopping bags in the trunk and drove to the restaurant. "I'm so lucky to have a mom like you."

"Awwwww, thank you, baby girl."

They arrived at Antonio's early. "Let's sit here for a while and talk," Kim said, gesturing towards the bags of clothes in the trunk. "I loved how you looked in the red and black jumpsuit."

Kim was enjoying her alone time with Olivia; the minutes flew by. "So… someone has a very special birthday coming up," Kim announced. "What would you like to do for your sweet sixteen birthday?"

"With everything that's been going on, I really haven't had much time to think about it," She replied. Before Kim could ask additional questions, she saw Allen's car.

"I see your dad's car over in the other lot. We'd better mosey on in and see what he's up to."

"How do you mosey?" Olivia responded with a huge smile and then broke down to heavy laughter.

"Keep it up, young lady. One of these days, you'll have kids to deal with," Kim said with a smirk on her face.

They were almost to the door when Olivia stopped her mom, hugged her, and whispered in her ear. "I love you so much, Mom."

"I love you too, dear. Now let's go and see why your dad is trying to butter us up."

CHAPTER 9

Julio "Snowman" Mendez (July 1948)

Julio "Snowman" Mendez was born in 1932 and was about as cold as they come. He was 6'5", 345 pounds, and not an ounce of fat. He was a monster with a body and the strength that instilled fear in the eyes of anyone who crossed his path. As a kid, he worked on a neighbor's farm about 10km from Palo Gordo. His family was poor, so he had to work for whatever he got. When not on the farm, he meandered around the small towns in the area. There's not much to do in an area mostly consisting of farmland. There were small towns every couple of miles or so, but these towns usually only consisted of a church, which he had to attend whether he wanted to or not, a small store that always stocked the same things, and maybe a small cantina.

It was five to ten kilometers from a town of any decent size; the closer to Highway 95 you get, the more commercial buildings you'll see. Since this is just about the only way to get to Acapulco from Mexico City, this through-way was heavily traveled. Locals took advantage of this and set up roadside stands. In the summer of 1948, when Julio Mendez was fifteen, those roadside stands had evolved into actual buildings.

Julio walked most places; however, he occasionally caught rides with the local farmers. If they saw him on the dirt roads, they'd pull over. He liked going to Palo Gordo. It offered a lot more than just a church and café. There were lots of pretty girls there. Where there were lots of pretty girls, there were boys vying for their attention.

Over time Julio became a staple in Palo Gordo and earned a reputation as a smart-ass kid that didn't take crap from anyone. He didn't like playing games. If Julio liked a girl, he'd go up to her and say so. By his late teens, he had "liked" many girls. Unlike the other boys, Julio had a large muscular frame. He rarely had to fight, as the boys were too intimidated to stand up to him. At eighteen, he earned money as a bouncer at the local cantina. It was here that he was introduced to the Cartel de Océano.

One evening, Julio was smiling at a young lady in the cantina. Her slightly intoxicated male companion didn't take a liking to Julio's attention, especially since his girl was flirting back. He went to Julio, trying to instigate a fight. "Leave my girl alone," he said.

Julio wasn't intimidated and pacified the drunken suitor, telling him, "Listen, Amigo, you need to mind your temper and have a seat; otherwise, I will have to escort you out of here. Then your girl will be left to fend for herself." Julio's greatest talent was his patience. At his young age, he knew how to diffuse most situations. And for those he couldn't, he had the brawn.

The drunk was now getting enraged. He got into Julio's face. "I'm not scared of a punk like you…" before he could finish the sentence, two well-dressed gentlemen took hold of him and took him away. A third gentleman walked over to Julio.

"You handle yourself well. What is your name?" the senior gentleman said.

"Mi Julio Mendez. May I ask your name, señor?"

"Yes, you may," he said with a smile and a slight chuckle. "I'm Juan Diego Garcia. Very nice to meet you."

"Likewise," Julio said as the name finally clicked in his brain. Shit, that was the drug lord, Garcia, he thought.

"I might be able to use someone with your talent in my family," Garcia said, looking him up and down.

"I like making money and am not afraid of hard work," Julio said, trying to promote his talents.

"You continue here, and one day, you'll be ready," Garcia said as he shook Julio's hand and walked out the door.

Garcia watched over Julio and made it a point to visit the cantina every couple of weeks personally. It had been several months since the first encounter. Garcia was at his normal table, but his entourage waited outside this time. Julio looked over at his table, and Garcia motioned him over. "How'd you like to run an errand for me?" Garcia said, eyes still casing the cantina to ensure there were no wondering ears. "I need someone to pick up a package for me in Tierra Colorada."

Julio knew that Tierra Colorada was 15km away and ignorantly said, "Si, I can pick up your package and have it to you tomorrow."

Looking a bit annoyed, Garcia said, "I don't need the package tomorrow. I need it tonight!"

"Si señor Garcia, the problem is I don't get off work until 8 p.m., and it'll take me a couple of hours to ride my bike there and back," Julio replied, feeling embarrassed by this conversation.

"No wheels, huh?" Garcia asked as he reached into his pockets and pulled out a set of keys. "Here, take this car and hurry back. There are instructions on the passenger seat. Be back before my *Sol* gets warm."

Julio looked Garcia in the eyes, gave him a nod, and then rushed out the door. "Shit, I don't know which car this goes to," he said under his breath. Several of his men were outside, obviously pre-informed of this task, and pointed him to the correct car. There was another thing that Julio forgot to tell Garcia. He had never driven a car before.

Julio was as cool as a cucumber. He showed no signs of anxiety as he climbed into the car and adjusted the mirrors and seat. He found the instructions and started to read…

"Hospital Tierra Colorada, Av Vincente Guerrero 71, San Antonio, 399940 Tierra Colorada, Gro., Mexico, Loading dock, 7:30 wait in car."

Julio knew of this hospital. It was already 7:15, so he knew he needed to leave now. Julio put the key in the ignition and turned it to the right. Just because he had never driven didn't mean he didn't know how. He'd watched others over the years and knew the procedures. He put his foot on the brake, put the car in drive, slowly pressed the gas, and let off the brakes. He proceeded down the dirt road at a whopping 10km per hour and turned right onto the main road. There were a lot more cars, which he ignored. He concentrated on the road and getting to the hospital on time. At this rate, he would be lucky to make it by 7:30, so he gave it a little more gas, and the front end almost came off the ground. He pretty much shit himself, or at least he thought he did. Letting off the gas, he slowed to a comfortable speed. Within a few minutes, he saw the signs for the hospital and found his way around back to the loading dock and parked. He checked the time, and it was 7:28. "*Whew, that was close,*" he thought.

Recognizing the car, a gentleman walked over towards him. Julio saw him coming and began rolling down the window. "Garcia," the man said. "Si," Julio responded. He was handed a box about 18 inches wide by 24 inches long. Fairly heavy for its size. Julio placed it in the passenger seat and then nodded to the gentleman as he pulled out. His confidence had improved from the trip over. He was still very cautious, but at least he could keep up with the other cars on the road. He was back by 7:45 p.m., pulled into the drive, parked, then took the package and locked it in the trunk. Not knowing what was in there, he didn't want to take it into the cantina. He walked in just as Garcia took the last swallow of his Sol.

He looks up at Julio, wipes the foam from his mouth, and says, "Sol Cerveza beer gets its water from a lake that's closer to the sun than any other water source in Mexico, thanks to the valleys up in the Sierra Madre del Sur mountains."

"I never knew that, señor Garcia," Julio replied.

"Where's my package?" Garcia asked, curious as to why Julio didn't walk in and sit it down on the table in front of him.

"Señor, I wasn't aware of the package contents and didn't want to jeopardize the cantina or yourself by bringing something that could be illegal and implicating you," Julio explained.

"Good thinking," Garcia said with an impressed look on his face. "Your logic makes sense. Now go get the package and bring it to me."

"Yes, sir." Julio ran to the car and 30 seconds later returned with the package and placed it on the table. He handed Garcia a small pocket knife to open it with.

Garcia laughed at the sight of this puny little toy. Reaching his pants leg, he quickly brandished a knife about twelve inches long, held it up to Julio, and said, "You call that a knife?"

Julio had a lot to learn. He was young and wet behind the ears. *"Give me time,"* he thought to himself, "I'll gain his respect."

Garcia took a couple of swipes at the box with his knife, and the box fell apart. Inside were books. Julio looked puzzled, "Why would he go through all that trouble for a box of books?" he thought.

"You're a bright young man," Garcia started. "I'm impressed with how you handle business and your patience in confrontations. I want you in my family, but you lack education."

"I'm self-taught," Julio came back with. "I can read and write."

"If you want to work for me, you'll need a formal education. Take these books to Nina Sanchez. Her information is in the box. Starting tomorrow, she will be your full-time tutor."

"But sir, I have this job…" Julio started before Garcia cut him off.

"You will continue to work evenings at the Cantina, but during the day, you will study."

"Yes, sir," Julio said, looking at the box and wondering how he'd get it home.

CHAPTER 10

Cartel de Océano (1962)

As a kid, Julio "Snowman" Mendez had to fight for whatever he got. As an adult, his perseverance, hard work, and loyalty were his ticket to getting what he wanted. His predecessor, señor Garcia, had taken a liking to him and took him under his wing. Mendez rose up the ladder pretty quickly. When not carrying out the Cartel's wishes, he was in the gym sculpting his body. He did it the old-fashioned way, not with steroids or any other enhancements.

By the time he was thirty, he was second in command. He was given his own territory to run and didn't waste any time getting the area corralled. He only asked you once. If you blinked, you're dead. The body count was too high to keep track of. His reputation was lauded by the cartel, and feared by everyone else. He had no empathy. He showed no emotion. He was the devil reincarnated.

One evening, he motioned for Juan to come over. "You have something for me, señor Mendez?"

"Yes, I do", Mendez responded. "Get your gear and come with me. We have someone who owes me a lot of money, and I want you to make an example of him."

"Si señor, this ought to be fun." Juan grabbed his tools and followed Mendez out to the car.

Mendez drove Juan down a small dirt road for several miles. Juan was thinking about his hometown in this direction, just a few more miles down the road. They came to an intersection with a church on one corner and a cantina on the other. "You'd think one of those would be putting the other out of business," Juan laughingly said, trying to lighten the mood.

Juan became nervous when Mendez turned left. He began to sweat when he pulled into a garage three blocks later. "What are we doing here?" Juan said, with beads of sweat forming on his forehead. "This is my family's business."

"Yes, I know," Mendez responded, looking Juan in the eyes. "Jesus has been betting with money he doesn't have. He owes me 44,105 pesos. You're to go in there and get this money or bring me back two of his fingers."

"But señor, he's my cousin. Please don't ask me to do this."

"Do you have the money to pay off your cousin's debt?" Mendez asked Juan.

"No, señor, but I will help him get the money for you."

"It's too late for that. Jesus has been given several chances to pay up. Now it's up to you. Either you get the money, or you bring me his fingers."

Juan knew begging Mendez would be useless, so he exited the car and proceeded in. Three of his cousins, his brother and his brother's wife, and two neighbors were in the shop working when Juan walked in.

"Hola," Jesus said as Juan walked in. "It's been too long. What brings you back to town, homie?"

"Do you have any beer?" Juan asked.

"No, cousin, I have some tequila, though," Jesus replied.

"That will be perfect. Bring two glasses with you and meet me out back. We need to talk."

Jesus grabbed a full bottle of tequila and met Juan outback. He poured them both a drink and asked, "What's going on? Are you here on business?"

"Unfortunately, I am," Juan said in a stout voice. "You've put me into a difficult situation. You've been gambling with money you don't have. You owe señor Mendez $2,500, and I'm here to collect."

Jesus was definitely getting nervous but knew he was safe because Juan was family. "Come on, Cuz, you know I'm good for it. Business has been slow, but I promise to pay señor Mendez back as soon as I get the money."

"Jesus, you don't understand. I don't have a choice. I have to return with either the money or your fingers. Please don't force me to take your fingers."

"Cuz, I need more time," Jesus pleaded. "I'm trying to get all the money now."

Juan asked, "How much do you have?" Jesus was quiet. "Tell me how much you have," Juan demanded.

Juan and Jesus were unaware that they were being watched. When Juan got out of the car to come in, Mendez followed, staying out of sight. He'd been watching Juan to see if he had the kahunas to take his cousin's fingers.

Juan pulled out a pouch of tools and pushed Jesus down into a chair. He then slid a table over and placed Jesus' hand on it. "You've put my family and me in danger. Your reckless behavior is a threat to not only my family but your family," Juan said as he opened the pouch and pulled out a small hand-held pair of cable cutters. "You have a choice… pay up or lose two fingers."

"I can't shit you the money," Jesus responded.

"No, but you could have made deals with others so that your debt could be paid. Instead, you wasted the money you were given. I am not going to let my family be punished for your stupidity. This is your last chance. Give me the money."

Jesus was crying, "I don't have the money."

Juan was pissed that his cousin put him and other family members in danger. "Then I'll take your fingers." With two quick motions, he grabbed Jesus's left arm, brought his hand out flat on the table, and then made one swift move using his left hand, which was already holding a meat cleaver. His pinky and ring fingers on his left hand were gone. Jesus screams in pain. No one from inside heard him. Between the machines and radio, it would have been hard to hear six feet from them.

"These fingers have bought you ten days. If you haven't paid by then, I'll be back. Please don't make me come back. One more thing, for being late, $500 has been tacked on to your loan. You now owe $3,000. Your stupidity can get the whole family killed. Get your shit together," Juan admonished as he turned to go back to the car. As Juan walked out the door, Julio rushed back and made it to the car.

CHAPTER 11

Answer My Questions (April 1970)

It was the spring of 1970. Julio was with a couple of young ladies when Garcia walked in. Julio didn't attempt to dress or cover up. He nonchalantly stood up and faced Garcia. "What do I owe this pleasure…" Julio started.

"You are needed in the barn," Garcia stated. "Put your clothes on and get these children out of here."

Julio knew that Garcia didn't approve of his taste for fresh meat. He rejoined the girls and directed them to finish him off. Five minutes later, Julio was dressed and on his way to the barn.

This barn was not a place for farm tools or animals. It was a place where individuals came to talk. Well, actually, they were made to talk. From the outside, it looked like any normal barn in the area. You knew exactly what this place was once you crossed the threshold at the door. The walls were heavily insulated. A chair in the center looked like a patient chair at the dental clinic, with one exception. This chair had restraints. Under these restraints was a mule, someone hired by a rival cartel to smuggle drugs past Garcia.

Two of Garcia's hitmen captured three individuals on Hwy 95 trying to get through Palo Gordo. The vehicle and occupants were brought back to the barn. Inside, they found 30 kilograms of cocaine and 25 kilos of marijuana. The driver and backseat passenger were gagged and hog-tied on the ground to the right. The front seat passenger, the one in charge of this trip, was strapped in the chair. He said his name was Manuel.

Manuel was strapped in tightly. He could see his teammates bound and lying on the floor. He looked around the room and knew this wouldn't be a survivable experience. On the wall to his right, he saw strategically placed tools. They started small and worked their way up, from corkscrews, saws, and knives to chainsaws. Three things that really stood out were a meat cleaver, jumper cables, and chili peppers. He turned his head to his left and saw a cage. The cage baffled him, but there was no time for guessing as he heard footsteps approaching him.

"Hola amigo," greeted Julio. "It seems you and your friends were moving some snow and weed into our territory. That's bad, very bad." Julio walked over to a table set up with what looked like surgical tools. "Normally, I am a very patient man, but tonight, I am infuriated because you interrupted a very pleasant experience."

Manuel was squirming to see what Julio was doing, his eyes bulging and sweat coming from every pore on his body. "I was with two young ladies, and now I'm here with the three of you. I'm not a very happy man." Julio put on a pair of surgical gloves and picked up a scalpel, "You know that you and your friends will not leave here the same way you arrived, correct?" Julio questioned.

Manuel nodded yes very intensely. "The manner in which you leave is up to you. Broken bones, amputated limbs, or ditched in the pit we have out back after Leo finishes with you. Do you understand?" Julio pulled the gag out of Manuel's mouth.

"Si señor, mi comprender," Manuel responded, doing his best to maintain what little poise he had left.

"Ahhhh, Bueno, amigo. This will make it so much easier for all of us," Julio said as he leaned down and got into Manuel's face. "Who do you work for, and where were you delivering the drugs?"

Manuel remained quiet. He knew his boss would kill him and his family if he told Julio anything. "So sorry, señor, we were just asked to deliver the car to Acapulco. Someone was supposed to meet us there and pay us for the car. We don't know any names."

Although Julio wished it would go easily, he knew these men would be dead whether they talked or not. "So, you were just sitting at home, and someone came to you with a request to take their car to Acapulco?" Julia asked.

"Si," Manuel said.

"So, this unknown person came to your home, asked you to take his car to Acapulco, meet someone you don't know in a parking lot, and give him the car for cash," Julio continued.

"Si señor."

"Who were you supposed to give the money to?"

"I don't know," Manuel responded. "I figured they'd contact us again when we got back."

"That's a very good story," Julio began, "But you know we've already talked to your friends, yes?"

"Si," Manuel responded.

"I have been a truthful man to you," Julio began. "However, when you don't tell me the truth, I must show you the repercussions." Julio moved back over to Manuel.

Manuel could see the blade. "Too bad I don't have any anesthesia," Julio said as he moved the knife down to Manuel's ear.

Manuel tensed up. The gag had been placed back in his mouth, so he couldn't speak. He lay there, unable to move, as he felt the blade cut into the side of his head. He tried to scream. He tried to move. Julio was taking his time with the blade. Manuel's ear was halfway off. Blood was pouring onto the floor. Then Julio laid the knife on Manuel's chest and took the dangling ear in his hand. "One more time, who do you work for?"

"No sé," replied Manuel.

Manuel refused to tell him but screamed as Julio ripped his ear off.

Julio asked him again, "Who do you work for?"

Manuel shook his head no.

"Bring me one of the amigos on the floor," Julio calmly ordered.

Two of his hitmen loosened the ropes enough to allow one of Manuel's accomplices to walk. They then escorted him over to Manuel and Julio.

"Is this a friend of yours?" Julio asked.

Manuel shook his head yes.

"Does your friend have a family? A wife? Children? Someone to cry for him when he doesn't come home?"

Manuel shook his head yes feverously.

"Good, then I ask you again, who do you work for?"

Manuel again responded, "No sé."

"That's too bad," Julio said as he began elevating the chair to a semi-vertical position. He then motioned for his hitman to untie his amigo and put him in the cage. "Here, let's turn you a bit so that you can watch your friend."

Once the cage door was locked, a hitman pressed a button that opened a door at the back of the cage. The amigo screamed and tried to climb the fence as a fully grown tiger walked out of the opening. "This is Leo, a pussy cat that hasn't been fed for two days." He's angry and hungry. Your amigo won't be able to escape. Is this what you want?"

Manuel shook his head no, but again, he refused to name Julio.

"So be it then," Julio said, then looked at the hitman and said, "Let him go."

The hitman pushed another button that unlatched a chain that was holding the tiger. Leo wasted no time in racing across the room to the amigo up on the fence. The tiger jumped and must have gone 15 feet in the air before hitting his target. The tiger had the amigo's arm in his mouth as he fell to the floor. The amigo was fighting the best he could but was no match to the strength and agility of the tiger. His screams continued until Leo's massive jaws clamped around his neck, sinking his two-inch razor-sharp teeth into his flesh. Seconds later, the sounds and motions of the amigo were gone.

Manuel was crying. Still bound tightly, he couldn't move his head away from the carnage.

"Manuel, mi amigo, your time is coming to an end," he paused to walk over to the wall, picked a wood saw from its assigned slot, and walked back over to Manuel. "This is not a very sharp saw. Do you see the teeth on the blade? This will not be a pleasant experience. Are you sure you won't talk to me?"

"Si," replied Manuel.

Julio looked at Manuel and said, "You are a brave man, stupid but brave." He placed the saw on his forearm and slowly moved the blade back and forth. Manuel's muffled screams expressed the excruciating pain that he was feeling. Julio had tied a tourniquet around the arm to keep him from bleeding out.

"I'm about to hit bone. If you think this has been painful, just wait," Julio commented, trying to coax Manuel into talking. About halfway through the bone, Manuel passed out from the pain. Julio finished sawing through the bone and stopped. Manuel was no longer breathing. He looked over at his hitmen and pointed to the last of the amigos on the floor. Still bound, gagged, and blindfolded, he only knew of the horrors that occurred by hearing the sounds. They removed the blindfold, removed the gag, and then positioned him so that he could see Manuel with his ear missing and his arm sliced open and dangling. They turned him to see the remains in the cage. The tiger was still gnawing on the bones of his friend.

"¿Qué carajo has hecho?" The amigo screamed out.

"I'll tell you what I've done. I've given plenty of opportunity for your amigos to tell me who you work for, but neither of them wanted to oblige. So now I'm down to you," Julio said, pointing to the remains of both men. "You have the same option. You can leave here alive, or you can join your friends."

"Señor Mendez, you don't understand. If we talk, we may survive here, but our boss will kill us and our families. These two chose to die to protect them."

"How do you know this to be true?" Julio asked.

"My brother-in-law worked for him. Last year, something similar occurred, and he gave up some information to save his life. When he got back, he was slaughtered, but not before witnessing the execution of his children, followed by the rape and slaying of his wife, mi hermana."

"So if this is true and your boss killed your sister and her kids, why do you work for him?" Julio queried

"I have no choice."

"Everybody has a choice."

"No, not me. I know too much. If I tried to leave, he would kill me," the amigo said.

"And your family?" Julio asked.

"No, not my family. My parents died three years ago. My sister was the only one I had left."

"Why are you telling me this?" Julio asked. "You know you shared information that makes you not only valuable to your boss but to me."

"I know. My name is Pedro Gonzales. I will tell you anything you want to know. I prefer not to die, at least not today. In exchange, all I ask for is your protection and the ability to work with you."

"Tell me what you know, and I'll decide if I should keep you around," Julio came back. Deep inside, the heartless bastard felt sorry for Pedro.

Julio, the hitmen, and Pedro moved to a different room in the barn. This room was smaller, cooler, and had a pitcher of ice water sitting on the table. Julio and Pedro sat at the table, and the hitmen sat on chairs in the back of the room near the door. There were no decorations. The walls were bare. A rectangular table with six chairs, three on each side, was in the middle of the room. On top of the table was a recording device. The floor was wood.

Julio poured Pedro a glass of water, turned on the tape machine, and instructed Pedro to tell them everything.

"Mi nombre es Pedro Gonzalez. I work for señor Ernesto Uzeta. He directed me, Manuel, and Jorge to bring drugs to Acapulco. We were to meet with …"

Pedro left out nothing. He talked for almost two hours, explaining the operation, where they got their drugs, and who they were targeting. Julio was impressed with his knowledge and justification for working for Uzeta.

After the confession, Pedro begged to be part of Julio's family, "I've heard nothing but good things about you."

Like the Tin Man, Julio had no heart but felt a bit of compassion for Pedro for some strange reason. He talked to Garcia, and they agreed to bring Pedro on board but keep a close leash on him until he proved himself.

CHAPTER 12

There's a New Boss (23 September 1969)

Later that year, shortly after Mendez's 37th birthday, he inherited the title of Drug Lord. He was now the #1 in one of the largest and most brutal cartels west of Mexico City.

Mendez craved many things—power, tattoos, and young girls, to name a few. They gave him a type of high that no drug could produce. There was only one artist, "Emilio," with whom he trusted his body, and his shop was near the coast. At least once a year, he'd take the one-hour drive down to have new ink added to his frame. This was a struggle for Emilio. You see, while Julio had a large canvas, it was an extremely dark canvas.

"Emilio, my man," Julio greets Emilio with some fancy handshake. "Your artistry is much needed to ink my dream."

"Julio, you're right. I am talented, but even Jesus couldn't heal everybody. I've told you many times that your skin is too dark, so I have to use bright and bold colors. Tell me your dream is apayasa maldito el puta blanca, por favor."

Mendez: "I don't want no fucking whore or clown on my body. No permanente de todos modos. Hahaha," he laughed as he grabbed Emilio and brought him in for a man hug. "Now amigo, consigue tu mierda, and let's get going."

"Sí senior Mendez, I am ready. What is your dream?"

"I want an eagle with his wings spread wide. Now make me proud, or you'll be sweeping streets and cleaning tourist shit for the rest of your life."

"Águila?" Emilio looked up at the sky for inspiration. "Sí, I can do that, you confianza Emilio, bueno? Mi paleta scheme is limitado," Emilio said, hoping he could find the right pallet of colors to make his art beautiful on such a dark canvas.

"Sí, I trust you, but remember the consequences of fucking it up," Mendez responded as he moved over to the chair in the studio near Emilio's equipment.

"Why you want Águila?" Emilio asked while gathering his supplies.

"Mi dream is not your concern, at least not right now," Mendez responded, getting a little frustrated with all the small talk.

Emilio shakes Mendez's shoulder two hours later, "Wake up, señor Mendez. Your eagle is complete." Mendez had dozed off during the tattooing, and it took him a few seconds to get his bearings.

"Get me the mirror. I need to see if Emilio gets paid or if he's bait for the fishermen." Emilio laughs at Mendez's comment.

Mendez moves closer to Emilio, looking down at this puny little man. "Do you think I'm funny? If this Eagle looks like shit, you're turtle bait."

Emilio is proud of his work and readily hands a mirror to Mendez. "I had to change the colors around so my art was vibrant on your dark canvas." Emilio was proud of this particular artwork. He used lots of grey, silver, red, and lots of shadowing, using light colors to define his artwork. Mendez was quiet, taking his time in examining the drawing. He wanted to find every single defect. Every so often, he would grunt, but nothing audible came out. Until... "Do you expect me to like this piece of shit?" Mendez said to Emilio. "The colors are all wrong." Beads of sweat started to roll off Emilio's face. He couldn't understand why Mendez hated it so much. Mendez looked over to his entourage and said, "Take him out back and wait for me."

"No, no, senior Mendez, I can fix anything you don't like," Emilio said as the beads of sweat were being joined by tears rolling down his face. He went from being overjoyed by his artwork to pleading for his life in only a matter of minutes. Two of the thugs escorted him out back, one under each arm. Once out back, one of the thugs instructed Emilio to grab the five-gallon bucket, turn it over, and sit on it facing the wall. Emilio wanted to run, but there were no opportunities. Mendez came out the back door sporting his sunglasses and a skinny cigar.

"Amigo Emilio, you've tatted over 60% of my tattoos, and not once did I have the emotion I do today. I just don't understand how or why," Mendez said, trying to give Emilio justification as to what was about to happen.

"Please señor Mendez, I have..."

"Quiet!" Mendez yelled. "I'm not finished. Don't interrupt me again." Emilio was seated with his knees about two inches from the wall. His body was trembling. Suddenly, the two thugs grabbed him by his arms and stood him up, still facing the wall. Mendez comforted Emilio, "Amigo, it causes me great displeasure to do this. Know that this is no easy task for me. You have a wife and a new baby; however, something has to be done to set an example."

The thugs turned Emilio around, and he was face to face with Mendez. Actually, it was more like face to chest. They were no longer holding his arms. Mendez slowly and articulately, with precise execution of his actions, prepared for the final moments. Emilio was looking straight into Mendez's chest.

"Open your eyes and look at me," Mendez commanded Emilio looked up but could only see a few fingers in his face. He prepared himself to die. Mendez stepped back a couple of feet, allowing Emilio to make out more of what was in front of him. The thugs were gone. It was just the two of them. Emilio started to talk, but Mendez put his large hands over his mouth.

"Amigo Emilio, I am extremely touched by the artistic skills you possess. It is a sign from God. You have a new child now, si?"

"Si," replied Emilio.

"Hold your hands out in front of you, palms up," Mendez ordered.

Emilio did as he was told. He held his hands there for what seemed like minutes before feeling something large being placed into each of them. He brought his hands down and looked to see two large rolls of money.

"You made my dream come true, and for that, I thank you," Mendez said, "Use this money to take care of your family, food, clothes, and other necessities."

Mendez patted Emilio on the back as he walked past him. "Adios, amigo, don't spend it all in one place."

A couple of minutes later, Mendez and his men drove off. Emilio fell to the ground and prayed.

CHAPTER 13

Acapulco November 1985

This was Olivia's first time out of the States, and everything was so new to her. The streets were not pavement like back home. The houses were much different. Olivia thought the colors were very pretty and the roof's clay tiles were very unique. Kim and Allen were in awe just watching her. The taxi left the airport five minutes ago, and their attention was drawn to Olivia instead of the environment outside the cab.

The cab pulled into the Fiesta Americana Hotel. "Your dad heard that this hotel was the best one in Acapulco, with two gigantic pools and the beach just a few yards away."

"And look at all the cute boys," Olivia said.

"We're not here to find you a husband. We're here to have a nice little vacation and check out a few properties," Allen chimed in.

"But Dad, I don't want to go house shopping. I'd rather sleep in and hang by the pool." Olivia said.

After checking into the hotel, Kim announced, "Let's go check out the room, then hit the beach."

"That sounds awesome!" Olivia shouted with excitement.

Allen was responsible for the bulk of the luggage, even though the girls had two to his one. "I'm not sure how you girls managed to stick me with the suitcases. Didn't we agree to keep everything in one suitcase?"

Kim and Olivia looked at each other, smiling, then turned to Allen, "We didn't agree; you did."

Their room was on an upper floor, facing the Ocean. Traveling in November was perfect, as the tourist crowd wasn't as heavy as usual. Good thing he talked with Wanda. It was her advice to travel this time of year. The weather in Acapulco averages in the mid-80s in November. When they left Youngstown, the weather was 43 degrees.

When he got to the room, the first thing he did was set the luggage down and jump onto the bed, landing on his back. "Ahhhhh, this feels so good. I may take a nap before the beach."

The hotel was beautiful, with spacious rooms and comfortable beds. Then they opened the curtains to the balcony, "Holy shit!" Kim blurted out. This view is to die for." They were on the 15th floor, with a room facing the Pacific Ocean. "Honey, we're right on the beach."

Allen looked at Kim and smiled, saying, "I know babe. I did this for you."

"What about me?" Olivia said.

"Of course, you were part of the consideration, but it's your mom who feels the need to be on the beach 24 hours a day. I'm good with just the pool." Allen responded.

The room was more of a suite, with a separate master bedroom. "Where's my room?" Olivia asked.

"Right over there," Allen said, pointing to the sofa bed.

"I guess I shouldn't complain…" Olivia said as she looked out the window to see the beach. "You brought me to this bodacious city."

Kim handed Allen his toiletry bag, "Go take a shower. It might wake you up and give you a burst of energy."

Allen entered the bathroom, turned the shower water on to warm it up, and emptied his toiletry bag, positioning his shaving cream, toothbrush, razor, etc., just like he has it at home. When he checked the water temperature, it was perfect. A hot shower felt good. He had been up since 6 am this morning, with three flights and two long layovers. The girls were able to sleep most of the way.

"How's things going in there?" Kim asked.

"Almost done."

"You know you have two girls out here that need access to the bathroom, don't you?" Olivia chimed in.

Allen was feeling a bit anxious. He wasn't sure why, but his hands were a little shaky. *"Maybe it's the lack of sleep and the extra caffeine he'd had on his journey,"* he thought. "Come on in. I just need to brush my hair and teeth." He continued.

"Hopefully, not with the same brush," Oliva said laughingly.

Kim walked into the bathroom, washed her face, and brushed her hair. Allen finished up what he was doing slightly before Kim. Olivia was right behind Kim and started her beach prep. She closed the door and changed into her bathing suit. When she walked out, Allen's jaw hit the floor. "You're not wearing that. It's too revealing. And by the way, when did you get boobs."

Kim looked at Olivia and told her to wait in the bathroom while she and Allen talked. Olivia was almost in tears as she returned to the confines of the bathroom.

"When did she grow up?" Allen asked Kim.

"She wasn't going to stay little her whole life, you know?" Kim responded.

"I know, but she could have at least waited until she was thirty," Allen said, trying to be funny.

"These walls aren't soundproof," Olivia yelled from the other room. "I'm not waiting until I'm thirty."

"Plug your ears," Allen yelled back. He then asked Kim, "Are you OK with her going out like that?"

"She's almost a woman, honey. You need to find a way to not see her as that ten-year-old little girl. Besides, there is nothing wrong with her bathing suit." Kim said as she removed her cover-up to reveal the same bathing suit. "Do you have a problem with the suit or the person?"

"You're wearing that in public? What if we run into anyone we know?" Bill said.

"Really?" Kim said, giving Allen the stink-eye. Bikinis are in style and trust me, these are more conservative than what you'll see on the beach. Olivia and I went shopping together, and these were on sale. Olivia? Come on out. We're ready to go."

Olivia walked out and stood next to her mom. Allen had always known how beautiful Kim's body was. She was short-ish, pencil-thin waste, with a nice ass and breasts that would make any man's mouth water. And now she's standing next to his baby girl, who's not much of a baby girl anymore. Olivia is a couple of inches taller than her mom and probably not done growing. "You look so much like your mom. And unfortunately, you're filling out like her too." Allen said to Olivia. "I bet you'll be 5ft-10in before you're eighteen," he continued.

"Daaad," said Olivia, embarrassed by the comments. "I'm sixteen years old. I'm supposed to be filling out."

"You're not sixteen yet." Allen fired back

"In TWO DAYS," Olivia snapped. She had the body of a young lady, large breasts, a round and firm rear end, and long legs. The main thing that sets them apart is that Kim is tanned like an Amazonian, while Olivia is extremely white. She's toned, and you can see the muscle definition, but it looks like she's never seen the sun.

"Okay, you two, stop that. We need to get outside while we still have some sunlight," Kim admonished. "After a stroll on the beach, maybe we can find a mom-and-pop restaurant for dinner."

Allen walked over to the two of them and gave them a group hug. "OK, put your cover-ups back on, and let's get to the beach. Are either of you going for a swim?"

"No way, I'm not getting my hair wet. I've spent too much time getting it to look like this," Olivia said.

Walking out the rear entrance to the hotel, they were greeted by two large pools. Directly in front of them was a path to the beach. Kim and Olivia removed their sandals and dug their toes into the warm sand. Many people were on the beach, not crowded but enough to keep your eyes occupied. The girls took their cover-ups off, put them in Kim's beach bag, and walked towards the water. Allen was observing the ladies and the skimpy bathing suits they had on. He was thankful that Kim and Olivia's suits at least covered their asses. "Whatcha looking at, honey?" Kim said to Allen as he almost tripped on a sunbather. "Sorry, ma'am," he said, embarrassed.

"Hahaha, that'll teach you to stare." Kim laughed

"Their butts were hanging out," Allen responded.

"Yes, dear, they are wearing thongs," Kim explained. "Now, aren't you glad our suits are not as revealing?"

Allen would have answered, but a couple of young ladies walked by, and he was too distracted to process what Kim had just said. His attention got a little better after Kim gave him a slap to the back of his head. "Eyes off of their asses before you get a rise that will be hard to hide."

Allen stumbled again, tripping over an imaginary rock on the beach. "I swear something was there." He said. Olivia responded, "Sure, Dad, I'm sure you thought something was there."

Allen tried to maintain his focus as the three of them walked down the beach. Kim was on the side closest to the ocean so that she could walk in the water. Olivia in the middle so that Dad could protect her from the imaginary boogie men, and Allen on the end closest to the sunbathers. People walked both ways on the beach, and occasionally, someone would bump into them. The sun was setting and blinding those coming towards them.

They had only walked about a quarter mile down the beach when Allen noticed Kim, a little distracted, walking further into the water, little by little. Olivia was oblivious to this, as she was still in awe of the crystal-clear water and white sandy beach. Allen looked ahead and saw two men talking. They were standing about five feet into the water, facing in his direction. Then he saw it: their swimwear was barely there. These were almost like the thongs the ladies had on but with a pouch. And one of the men had an extremely large pouch.

Allen didn't say a word. He continued to watch Kim. Her eyes appeared to be directed towards their pouches, and she was walking straight towards them. About five feet from them, Kim found that "imaginary" rock and tripped, landing in the water face first and sending a splash that soaked both men. They knelt down to see if she was alright. When she rolled over, both pouches were a tongue's length away. Kim was speechless, something that never happens. Allen stood there, soaking it in. He would have blackmail fodder for years to come. Olivia ran over and knelt down to see if her mom was alright. After learning she was okay, the gentleman with the large pouch stood up, and now his pouch was within inches of Olivia's face. Allen was getting ready to say something, but it was too late. Olivia looked up and saw it. She froze with her eyes glued to it. Olivia lost her balance and fell backward into the water, soaking her long blonde hair and causing her sunglasses to fall into the ocean. Embarrassed, she searched the water and luckily found them before the next wave came in.

Olivia and Kim both stood up together. Both were extremely embarrassed. Olivia's pale face was so red it looked like she had a sunburn. Kim thanked the gentlemen for their assistance and apologized for getting them wet.

The two men continued their talk as Olivia and Kim walked away. Allen was a few steps behind them. "Did you see that man's package?" Olivia asked quietly.

"How could I miss it?" Kim shockingly said back. "What do you think tripped me," She laughed.

"It was huge. Are they all like that?" Olivia asked.

"I wish," Kim said, accidentally using her outside voice.

"What?" Olivia asked.

"Oh, it was nothing, dear. I just said something like, 'Most men wished theirs were that big.'"

They both laughed as Allen caught up to them. "Well, go ahead," Kim sheepishly said.

"Go ahead and do what?" Allen replied. "I have no idea what you're talking about."

They walked a few more feet when Allen said, "I'll buy you both a bottle of Listerine when we get back to the hotel." Olivia was confused, but Kim understood what Allen was referring to, slapping him on the back of the head for the second time that day.

"They made their way back to the stores parallel to the beach. "There's a nice-looking restaurant," Olivia pointed towards a building about a block away. "Okay, let's go. I'm starving," Allen said convincingly.

"Do you have a brush in your bag?" Olivia asked her mom. "My hair is a mess. It's still wet and filled with sand."

"I sure do," Kim replied. "Let's go straight to the baño when we get there."

"Baño?" Olivia asked confusingly.

"Yes, baño. It means bathroom in Spanish."

The next morning, Allen was the first to wake. Instead of lying in bed, he beat the girls to the shower. Today was a good day. He wasn't tired because he had a great night's sleep. He dreamed he was on the beach wearing dark sunglasses where Kim couldn't see his eyes straying.

Bill didn't really pay attention to the bathroom last night, so he took it all in this morning. The bathroom was nice. It had a large custom shower with mosaic tiles that could fit five or six people and a six-foot vanity with two sinks and lots of counter space for toiletries. It even had a toilet that shoots water up your crack and some of the softest towels he's ever used.

After his shower, he shaved and brushed his teeth and hair. He could hear Olivia the night before joking about not using the same brush for both; this made him smile. When he finished, he turned out the bathroom light before opening the door. He didn't want to wake the girls this early. He could hear snoring or what Kim called 'purring' coming from her side of the bed. He maneuvered around the open sofa bed, looking to ensure Olivia was asleep. Allen stopped in his tracks as he saw her on her side with her knees almost up to her chest. This is the way he remembers her sleeping when she was a toddler. Now she's growing up and out, as he noticed when she had the bikini on. He opened and shut the door quietly, then walked down the hall to the elevator.

Allen was craving a hot cup of coffee. Over near the reception desk, he saw a stand with "café" on it. Hmmm, that must be the coffee. He made a cup, grabbed an English print newspaper, and walked outside to enjoy the beautiful morning. Not many tourists were up at six in the morning except the dedicated ones, the runners, or those who liked hitting the gym first thing. *"Normal people sit and have coffee or sleep in while on vacation,"* he thought.

He looked at his watch: 0730. Kim might be waking up by now. Olivia, she'll sleep till noon if we let her. I'd better order some breakfast and head back up. Allen stopped at the reception desk and ordered breakfast for the room. "I'd like three breakfasts, please. Order number one is for my wife: two eggs sunny side up with limp bacon, fruit, and a cup of decaf coffee. Order number two is for my daughter: pancakes, scrambled eggs, and bacon, with a glass of milk. Order three is for me. I'd like three eggs over easy, hash browns, and sausage. How long do you think it would take?"

"Señor, it may take up to 30 minutes. We've just received six other orders before you."

"Not a problem," Allen replied, "I'll freshen up my coffee and sit down here for a few before heading up."

"We'll let you know when your order is ready for delivery."

"Thank you."

Allen poured a fresh cup of coffee and then went back outside to enjoy the morning air. It had only been about twenty minutes when he was signaled his order was on its way. So, he topped off his coffee and headed upstairs, arriving simultaneously with the breakfast cart. He tipped the waiter and then wheeled the food into the room, where he still heard the purring from the bed. His little princess was practically in the same position as she was when he left.

Allen brought the cart close to the coffee table, walked to the balcony door, and pulled open the curtains to two loud moans, "Dad/honey!"

"Up and at'em!" Allen shouted. "Breakfast is hot, and so is the Acapulco sun." Olivia woofed down her food and announced she needed the bathroom for a few minutes. She picked out a different bikini and closed the door. When Olivia was out of earshot, Allen whispered to Kim, "The car should be delivered to the house tomorrow. I can't wait to see the look on her face when she learns she has a brand new 1985 Camaro."

"Shhhhh," said Kim, "We don't want her to hear us. When do you think we should tell her?"

"It's fine," Allen said, pointing towards the bathroom, "I can hear the shower running. I was thinking we'd take her out to dinner when we get back from looking at properties tomorrow. We could tell her then."

Kim added, "She's going to think we forgot all about getting her a birthday present. I'll let the restaurant know that we'll be there at 7 p.m. and to have a white cake with buttercream frosting ready for us."

The shower sound ceased, and so did the discussion about the car. A few minutes later, you could hear the blow dryer going. "It will take her another 15 to 20 minutes to get ready. Do you mind if I head back to the lobby for another cup of coffee and some fresh air?"

"Not at all," Kim responded, kissing him before he walked out.

CHAPTER 14

The Eagle has landed (2 Nov 85)

Mendez was a determined man. As a boy, he was a rule follower. He worked the fields, got along with everyone, and had a fascinating way of defusing even the hottest situations. He lost all that on his way up the ladder to becoming the kingpin of the *Cartel de Océano*. Many believe his transformation was one of the reasons he made it this far. The kind heart of his youth had turned to stone. Life meant nothing to him.

In July 1984, he ordered his "Flying Eagle," or what most people call a helicóptero. It had been fourteen years since the tattoo, and now he'd have his own whirlybird. For the last four or five years, he had been leasing a helicopter and getting some of his "family" trained. Before he bought his own, he needed to be sure he had enough staff to fly at a moment's notice. It was two months before his custom helo arrived. His Eagle (AKA 1984 Sikorsky S-76) was decked out with all the latest technology. Radar avoidance, police/DEA scanners, sound system, fully stocked bar, TV, etc., you name it, he had it. What Mendez didn't realize was that by adding all the bells and whistles, he'd lose maneuverability and airspeed.

He spent the next six months getting his pilots used to his bird and the landing zones he needed to frequent. No more driving for hours when you can fly in a fraction of the time. Mendez didn't use the Eagle for business only. He was known for his shenanigans onboard. He even got approval from the City Development Board to put a landing pad on top of his club. Money was no object.

One Thursday evening, he had his pilot land at the Club. It was ladies' night, and he wanted to see if any new meat was in town. He loved tourists, but unfortunately, many didn't like him. The local ladies knew him and his power. Some felt it was an honor to be one of his harems. Others avoided him like the plague. Mendez wasn't good-looking. The years were not kind to him. He was a bodybuilder with an upper body that could win almost any competition. But not every young lady was into that kind of thing. That's why he used other methods to get their consent.

Mendez exited the helicopter and walked over to the new rooftop entrance of the club. He walked down one flight of stairs into a hallway by his office. He went down another flight and was at the club's upper level. This is where he liked to sit and watch without anyone really noticing him. There was never any trouble at his clubs, thanks to the dozens of bouncers he placed around the events. He has one strict rule. You only get asked once. After that, you were out of the club, either on your own or with various levels of assistance.

He spots three new faces dancing together. He watched them dance and paid attention to whether or not they had boyfriends there. That wouldn't be a showstopper, but he tries to keep it drama-free since it's his club. When he saw that they were sitting alone, he sent word that he would like to see them and that drinks would be on him that night. They looked up but couldn't see him very well with the lights shining down. But free drinks and with the owner sounded safe enough, so they followed the waitress up the private steps. Mendez had a private bar up top and already had their drinks on the table. Fruit, snacks, and assorted nuts were also on the table. There was even a small private dance floor.

The girls introduced themselves, "Hi, I'm Sofia," the first one introduced herself. She was tall, about 5'10", medium complexion. She had a pierced nose and tongue. Sofia was slim and wearing this tight, poured-on dress that showed her beautiful breasts, all but the nipples.

"Very nice to meet you, Sofia. I'm Julio Mendez."

"Yes, I know," she replied. "I've heard a few people say how powerful you are. I'm honored to meet you."

Her remarks humbled Julio, but before he could engage in further conversation, the second girl stopped by to introduce herself. "Hola," she said, "Mi nombre es Camila. So nice to meet you, señor Mendez."

"Well, Camila, it's very nice to meet you too. What brings you to my club this day?"

"My friends and I were looking for a good party and were told that you have the best." Camila had short dark hair, a gorgeous face, and medium-sized breasts that perfectly complimented her frame. Julio could tell she was educated by how she spoke and carried herself.

Then, finally, the third girl walked over and introduced herself; "Hola, mi nombre es Maria. Gracias for inviting us up here," she said as she twirled her hair and smiled at Julio. He sized her up, looking her up and down, from her feet to the top of her head, paying special attention to her tight jumpsuit and small bra-less breasts clearly visible through her sweat-soaked white shirt.

"Where are you from?" Julio asked.

"We're from Ecuador originally but have been living in Mexico City for the last three years," Maria responded. "We arrived here today, our last stop before we attempt to gain entry into the U.S."

"Do you have travel documents, passports, and picture identification?" Julio asked.

"Yes, we have all of that, but that's boring. We're here to party."

The three girls pulled Julio up on the dance floor to join them. He danced with them for a few songs, then returned to his seat to continue observing. He had another round of drinks brought over for everyone. Maria was grinding on Sofia in the center of the dance floor while Camila did some type of interpretative dance routine in one corner.

Camila looked over at the other two girls and felt left out. She went over and put her arms around Maria, turning her around, and began kissing her. Sofia came around behind Camila and began grinding her while she kissed Maria. Julio was getting worked up just watching the ladies make out on the dance floor. When the song was over, they came back and killed the drinks that were waiting for them.

"You ladies look comfortable together. Have you been friends very long?" Julio asked.

"Yes, we've been together for over five years," Sofia replied.

"Are you married or have boyfriends here in Acapulco?"

"No and no," Sofia answered. "We don't need men; we're together."

"What do you mean?" Julio continued to interrogate Sofia. "Are you dating Maria or Camila?"

"Both," she said, "We're a throuple."

"I'm lost with the new lingo these days; what's a throuple?"

"I'm in love with both Camila and Maria, and they're in love with me. The three of us can't be a couple, so we're a throuple."

"So, you're lesbians?" Julio asked.

"Pretty much, but we have been known to invite a man into our bed for some fun. It's much better than a dildo." A new round of drinks arrived just as Sofia finished her glass.

"Would you ladies like to see my game room?" Julio asked, "It's where the fun really happens."

"Ohhhh, that sounds enticing," Camila said.

Julio's table had already been prepared for him. There were more drinks, a sealed container, and seats to view some of the hottest couples the girls had laid eyes on. They were making out on the dance floor, at their tables, and against the wall, all while moving with the beat of the music. They were all pretty much naked; some had G-strings on, others nothing.

"What is this," Maria asked. "A swinger's club or something?"

"No, ma'am," Julio said. "These people are performers. They provide erotic entertainment for me and my guests. Sit back and enjoy the show."

The ladies were already worked up before coming into this room. Watching the entertainers made them hotter. Sofia pointed to a tall redhead making out with a well-hung stud. She took Maria's hand and pulled her out onto the performance area. Sofia undressed Maria while the show continued, then proceeded to remove her clothes to expose her firm breast and tight little ass. Camila watched them as they played with each other, inching slowly over to the redhead.

"Are you ok with this?" Julio asked Camila.

"Of course. How can you watch them and not get all wet inside? I'll join them soon. But I want to see how this plays out. Will the redhead join them? Will her stud share his massive cock with all of them?" Camila said, caressing her breast with one hand and putting the other down her panties."

While they watched the show together, Julio opened the container with white powder in it. "Would you like a line?" he asked.

"You know it, babe," Camila said, and she moved over and got into the position. She did one line in each nostril and had an immediate rush. "Holy shit, this blow is to die for." She stood up, removed her clothes, and joined the performers, making out with all of them, men and women. She only stayed with each person for a couple of minutes. Long enough to kiss them, feel their bodies, suck their nipples, and caress their gentiles, before ending up with Maria, Sofia, and the redhead. It was a free-for-all with moaning, orgasms, and joyous screams.

Finally, they fell onto the mattress-covered floor in each other's arms and were out for the night. One of the male performers brought over three bottles of water and some blankets.

Julio was sexually frustrated. He could have had any one of them, but something wasn't right. While they were hot, they were not pure or down to earth.

It was 2 am, and Julio was frustrated that things didn't go as he had hoped. Sofia, Maria, and Camila were sleeping nude on the floor next to a couple of the performers. Water bottles were placed next to them, along with light blankets to cover them up. "Wake them up by 6 am and ensure they get home safely." He said to his staff as he walked out of the room with his entourage. The helicopter was ready to go when they got there.

Julio was quiet during the ten-minute ride to his estate. Before exiting, he tapped the pilot on the shoulder and said, "Thank you, mi amigo. Go home and get some rest. We have a busy day tomorrow." The pilot gave a thumbs up and completed shutdown procedures. When he exited, he secured the air vehicle. He knew the night crew would take care of cleaning and refueling.

CHAPTER 15

Two Worlds Collide (3 November 1985)

It was a beautiful Sunday morning. Julio was up by 6 am and headed to his in-home gym. His live-in personal trainer was there and ready to get the day going. "Buenos días, Julio. Are you ready to get started?"

"Sí, amigo mío, ¿Qué me espera hoy? (What's in store for me today)," Julio said, somewhat hoping for a light workout.

"Today is a leg and cardio day. But don't worry, it'll be easy."

"You say that every fucking time," Julio responded, looking a little aggravated. "Let's get going."

After his sixty-minute workout, Julio showered and then made his way to the patio where breakfast and a pitcher of orange juice spiked with a significant amount of 'Don Julio' Tequila were waiting. "Miguel?" Julio called out. "Bring me a pot of coffee, Por favor."

"Sí, señor Méndez," Miguel responded, and within minutes, a hot pot of coffee was on the table.

After breakfast, Julio remained on the patio reading the paper and preparing for his afternoon activities while alternating between the coffee and the Tequila Sunrise. There wasn't a cloud in the sky, humidity was low, and there was a slight breeze. According to the paper, it was supposed to be 82 degrees today.

Julio lived here his whole life. He traveled some but never left Central America. The climate was the same in each of the sites he visited. Nevertheless, he never took it for granted. He appreciated the weather, the phenomenal ocean views, and the lifestyle he chose.

Julio's soft spot never left the estate. Too many people wanted him either dead or incarcerated. So, when he left the confines of his estate, it was serious business. The cartel east of Mexico City was looking to expand and wanted Julio's territory. He'd received several reports of their scouts being in the area. "Let them look," he'd tell his men. "When they act, then we wipe them out." Julio's confidence inspired his men. He always had a plan.

The American Drug Enforcement Agency (DEA) was a different story. He knew he was on their radar but didn't know to what degree. Julio had been shipping crack to the U.S. for years. He had one of the best success rates of all the other cartels, with 75 percent of his products reaching his distributors. Julio knew he was a pain in the ass to the DEA but felt he had covered his ass well enough that there was no evidence that any of the drugs could be traced back to him. He was especially careful since another Mexican Cartel had killed a DEA agent earlier this year. Julio felt safe as their attention would be on the Guadalajara cartel. He knew the DEA had set up a satellite office in Guadalajara and was working with Mexican authorities. It was an hour and a half flight from Guadalajara to Acapulco, but over eleven hours to drive the 933km. There were no direct highways. You had to go to Mexico City, then take Highway 95 to the coast. It was not a pleasant drive.

Special Agent Andrew Thomas was assigned to the Guadalajara field office. He was well aware of Julio "muñeco de nieve" Méndez (the Snowman). He had been tracking his activity for several years and was planning a sting operation to capture him prior to Agent Hernandez's murder back in February. The DEA's priorities changed when Mendez got his helicopter.

Agent Thomas had operatives in Palo Gordo that had established roots and were respected by the local businessmen. One owned a cantina a few miles from Mendez. The other owned a gas station at Hwy 95 and Acapulco – Chilpancingo de los Bravo intersection. They both had families—wives and kids—so everything looked normal to local town folks. The pure nature of both businesses allowed for an easy interchange of information.

Agent Thomas was concerned about Mendez's procurement of the helicopter. He knew this would allow faster transport of drugs to mules in the northern region. The agent had been monitoring Mendez's activities for months and identified one thing—Mendez was a creature of habit. He did the same things on each day of the week. His intel led him to believe Mendez was changing his routine this Sunday. He would personally deliver 35.5 million pesos (about $2 million U.S.) to a sister cartel to carry out executions of government officials.

This was not uncommon in the drug world, but the targets were more prominent and aligned with U.S. policies this time. This would set diplomacy back twenty years if allowed to happen. To ensure Mendez didn't make it to his destination, he had arranged air coverage from a covert military installation in the vicinity. He was ready for Mendez to make his move.

Julio called for his head of security, Alex Perez, to discuss the change in schedule from previous Sundays. "I have a lunch engagement with two kingpins, then we will drive to the Banco de México to make a withdrawal. It's already been coordinated and should only take 10-15 minutes," he said. "From there, we'll return here and prepare to fly to Durango. It'll be a four-hour flight each way. I've arranged a refueling stop at the Aeropuerto Internacional de Guanajuato."

"Gracias, I'll make sure everything is taken care of. I'll personally join you for today's events."

0945 HRS

Mendez meets his driver and security chief, Perez, at the limo and departs for his lunch engagement. He chose a place that was en route to the Acapulco bank. The Palo Gordo bank can't provide the amount of cash needed. Mendez is in the back seat talking with his counterparts in Durango, using his American-made Motorola 8000 X cell phone.

Listening in were DEA officials in Guadalajara.

1100 HRS

Mendez arrives at the restaurant within the Americana Hotel to meet with his business associates in a private room he reserved. Upon entering the restaurant, he received word two members would be late. Mendez walked out to the pool area to view recent updates to the hotel's landscaping. A tall blonde girl walked by before he returned to the meeting room. There are not many blondes in Acapulco, so he was definitely intrigued. She was super fit, swaying her tight ass as she walked to the pool area and laid down in a hotel-provided chair to sun herself.

"Señor Méndez, your guests are here." Perez announced.

"Gracias," Mendez said as he took one last look at the blonde bombshell and headed to his meeting.

Mendez had his agenda in his head. He never wrote anything down. When he arrived in the room, they all stood until he was seated. The doors were closed, and the meeting began.

Forty-five minutes later, Mendez walks out. He stopped by the pool, but the blonde was not there. "Why am I so fixated on this girl," he thought. "Good thing she was gone. I don't have time for this today." He got to his car and proceeded to the bank.

1200 HRS

Mendez entered the bank to make his withdrawal. He was recognized as soon as he walked in and directed to the manager's office. He left 15 minutes later with two suitcases filled with pesos.

1220 HRS

Mendez is back in his limo and making a U-turn to return to his estate. As they near the Americana Hotel, he sees the blonde again. She's with another girl walking down the sidewalk. Without giving much thought to his comment, he told the driver that he wanted her. In a split second, the car pulled over, the security chief jumped out, grabbed the blonde, and pushed her friend to the curb, bashing her head on the concrete. A few seconds later, he and the blonde were in the car and headed east up Highway 95 to Pola Gordo.

0700 Sunday Morning

"What the fuck are you doing up so early?" Kim asks Olivia.

"Well, it is a special day, you know," Olivia responded.

"Come on, Mom! You know what day it is." Olivia came back with a smirk in her tone. Then she began to sing. "I am only sixteen, only sixteen, but you love me soo ohoh. "

"Don't stop, honey. I love Dr. Hook and the Medicine Show."

"Where's dad? I'm sure he knows what today is," Olivia screeched back.

"Your dad is downstairs enjoying his morning coffee and newspaper."

Olivia didn't bother to get dressed. She went down in pajamas, looking for her dad. The lobby was unusually full this morning, and many of the men were staring at her. *"What? You haven't seen a girl in her PJs before?"* she thought. Then she realized she wasn't wearing a bra, and her breasts bounced with each step. Olivia yelled, "Shit!" and everyone turned and looked. *"Fuck, I used my outside voice,"* she thought as she panicked and ran outside. She found her dad at a table next to the door, drinking his coffee and reading the comic section of the paper.

"You know… I always save the comics for last. Something to make me smile after reading all the ugly news," Allen said. "Oh, and did you know you're still in your PJs and obviously not wearing a bra? Are you sure that's wise with all the horn-dawgs around here?" He continued.

"Dad, nobody has even noticed," She lied. "Dad, Mom won't acknowledge what day it is."

"What do you mean, honey? Has she forgotten today is the day that we look at beach properties?"

"Oh fuck, you too?" Olivia replied, then ran back to the elevator—something she probably shouldn't have done braless and in a paper-thin PJ top.

Allen couldn't help but laugh, knowing full well that today was her 16th birthday. He even knew about the bra thing since he was sitting by the door and could see and hear what was happening in the lobby. *"Poor baby, she's gonna be peeved at us now, but can you imagine the surprise she's going to get when she finds out we got her a car?"* he thought.

Since it was her birthday, Allen and Kim agreed they should do a Sunday brunch in the restaurant instead of eating in their room again. Kim had the pleasure of relaying that news to Olivia.

Olivia walks in the door, steaming because no one would give her a "happy birthday" wish. "Olivia?" Kim called out. "Did your dad tell you we're having breakfast in the restaurant this morning?"

"No! He didn't have anything to say."

"Well, why don't you take your shower and get ready? We have reservations for 9:30."

"Yes, ma'am," Olivia replied.

Allen and Kim were already at the table when Olivia came down. "Glad you were able to join us," Allen said. "Why don't you go and make yourself a plate? It's a breakfast buffet, but they have a grill open if you'd like eggs to order or an omelet," he said. Olivia didn't say a word. She just headed to the buffet and loaded her plate. "I'll just have to have my own party today. I'll start by pigging out," She mumbled to herself. She arrived back at the table a little grumpy, wishing she didn't have to go on the day-long house-hunting trip.

"How's your breakfast?" Allen asked both Olivia and Kim.

"Mine is delicious," Kim responded.

Olivia just grunted and displayed a thumbs-up.

"You know we're headed to look at beach property today. I didn't think you'd go wearing your beach wear." Allen joked.

"About that..." Olivia started. "You know I'm not interested in going house hunting. So why can't I stay at the hotel while you're gone? Consider it my birthday present. Yes, I said it. Today is my birthday, so you two can stop playing dumb."

"Wow, your birthday is already here?" Kim answered in a confused tone.

"Yes, and all I want is to stay here. I can enjoy the pool, charge the food to the room, and get better acquainted with Rosita," Olivia pleaded.

"Is that the girl you met at the pool yesterday?" Kim asked.

"Yes, and she speaks English. She wanted to hang out today. Please, please, please?"

"I'm worried, a young bra-less girl hanging around a hotel all alone." Allen jested.

"First of all, that was an accident, and secondly, I have a bra on now. Kind of," Oliva said, referring to her bikini top as a bra.

Kim and Allen looked at each other. Both talked softly so that Olivia couldn't hear them.

"Since you claim that today is your birthday..."

Olivia interrupted, "It is my birthday!"

"Let me finish. Since Olivia claims that today is her birthday, I guess the least we could do is grant her one birthday wish," Allen said, then looked at Kim and nodded.

"We're going to let you spend the day in the hotel. But that means you can't be out shopping or even going to the dress shop across the street. Do you understand?"

"Yes, Ma'am," Kim perked up.

"To clarify, you are grounded to the hotel property only." Allen clarified.

"Yes, sir," Olivia said, then hugged them both.

As they were finishing up breakfast, the real estate agent came in.

"Hola señor and señorita, I'm early, so finish your breakfast. I'll grab a coffee, and you can join me when you're done."

"It just so happens we were just finishing. Give us a minute to get our things, and we'll be right back down," Kim said.

1030 HRS

Olivia stood on the sidewalk as her parents entered the agent's car. "Remember, stay on hotel property," Kim yelled to Olivia.

"I am. This sidewalk is on hotel property," Olivia responded. She blew them a kiss as they drove away. After watching them drive out of sight, Olivia went out and found Rosita by the pool, pulled a chair and side table over, and plopped down in relief. "I'm so glad I could talk my parents into letting me stay here," she said.

Olivia knew she needed sunscreen, or her lily-white skin would be fire truck red when her parents got home. She looked through her bag and didn't see it. "Shit!" she exclaimed. "I left my lotion upstairs. I'll be right back." She ran to the elevator and waited until it got to her floor. She went in, grabbed the lotion, and returned to the pool.

1100 HRS.

Olivia was just in her bikini when she entered the lobby. Her cover-up was draped over the back of her chair. In her rush to return to Rosita, she nearly bumped into a guy at the door to the patio and pool. "Excuse me, sir," she said as she slowed down and walked back over to Rosita. She lay down and began putting the lotion on her body. Rosita helped put lotion on her back, and she returned the favor.

The sun was hot, beaming down on them. Fortunately, the water was their safe haven; they were in the pool every 20-30 minutes cooling off.

Rosita was visiting from another town in Mexico. She was nearly eighteen, had long dark hair, and had a very nice petite figure. "It's almost noon," she said. "Want to get an ice cream?"

"I'm not supposed to leave the hotel property," Olivia responded.

"That's okay. It's attached to the hotel," Rosita added. "We just have to take the sidewalk a half a block down."

"You're on, let's do it," Olivia said excitedly.

They got out, dried off, brushed their hair (it's a process for young girls to get ready to go out in public), fixed their lipstick, and then proceeded to the ice cream shop.

1200 HRS.

Kim and Rosita arrive at the ice cream parlor. Rosita orders a vanilla cone, and Olivia looks for her favorite, pralines and cream. There it is, the very last one. "I'll have two scoops of that one," Olivia said, pointing to the pralines and cream. They sat in the store and ate their ice cream. "This is so good," Olivia said. "Want to start walking back? I'm getting a little cold in the a/c here."

"Sure, let's go."

1220 HRS.

They were about halfway back to the hotel lobby. Olivia had just taken the last bite of her ice cream cone when they heard a car's tires screeching behind them. Before they had time to turn and look, Rosita was being shoved to the ground. A large hand covered Olivia's mouth as she was picked up and thrown into a limo. There was no time to yell; she fought as much as possible, but they were too big. The car had blackout windows, so no one could see that she was being kidnapped. Olivia panicked. She didn't know what to do. They gagged her mouth, tied her hands, and held her down in the back of the limo. She turned her head and saw a monster of a man in the seat across from her.

"I'm sorry to meet you this way, but I'm impulsive and don't have time for the chit-chat you Americans like. So, this was much faster, and I'm sure you'll enjoy the experience." Julio said.

Alex Perez continued to pin her down. Exhausted, she eventually stopped resisting. She was so confused. Her mind was questioning everything. *"What the fuck is happening to me? I'm not supposed to be here. This can't be happening. Please, somebody help me,"* Olivia continued to cry. It was her birthday, and she was hog-tied in the back of a limo, wearing only a bathing suit. "God, please help me," She cried repeatedly.

She hoped they would release her once they found out she was only sixteen. She also wished she had gone with her parents. Her body was shaking. Every negative thought about kidnappings ran through her mind. This made her cry even more. She was no match for these massive men.

Back at the Americano Hotel, a crowd had gathered around a young girl, unconscious and bleeding from a gash in her scalp. "What happened here?" a paramedic asked as he rushed to Rosita's side. The Mexican Policía were there trying to gather evidence. "She was pushed down hard, and the girl she was with was grabbed and thrown into a black limo." A bystander offered.

From the looks of the ground, Rosita had lost a lot of blood. The paramedic stabilized her and loaded her into the ambulance for a short ride to the trauma center. Another Policia vehicle pulled up, and two officers got out, one male and one female. They began questioning the bystanders. The attendant at the ice cream shop was also there and remembered hearing their names, so she provided that to the officers.

Once armed with the girls' names, the male officer entered the hotel while his female partner stayed with Rosita. He asked the receptionist if she knew the parents of two teenage girls, Rosita and Olivia. She wasn't aware of the events going on outside. "Si, Rosita's padres are out by the pool," she said, pointing to the doors. "Olivia's are on a house hunting trip. They are from the States and are here on vacation." The officer took down the information and notified headquarters that an American had been kidnapped. This required a call to the American Embassy.

1345 HRS.

Mendez's limo pulls into his estate. Perez, the man who abducted Olivia, picked her up, carried her to a bedroom, untied her, poured a glass of water, and then locked the door from the outside. Olivia was terrified. *"Are they going to rape me,"* she thought. *'Mom and Dad have no idea what has happened to me. If only they were here to protect me."*

Olivia saw the pitcher of water and the glass next to it. She picked it up and chugged the entire glass. She looked for a way out. The door was locked. The window had security bars. She was trapped.

1400 HRS.

The American Embassy was notified of the kidnapping. The officer described the limo and the man who accosted Olivia.

He reported that the parents were with a realtor looking at properties and were unaware of the kidnapping. Agents were trying to identify the agency and locate the agent.

Rosita's parents were told to meet the ambulance at the trauma center. They ran to their room, gathered their IDs and wallets, and rushed to the hospital. When they arrived, Rosita was having a CAT scan due to her head injury. The doctor said that she was in stable condition and that they were taking pictures of her brain to ensure there were no internal injuries. "Rosita should be back from Radiology in 15 to 20 minutes," he said.

The room had two chairs, a space where the bed should go, and the monitoring machines. The only information Rosita's parents had about the accident was that a girl was kidnapped, and Rosita fell and hit her head. They held each other and prayed for Rosita and the missing girl.

There were police officers in the Emergency Room and a representative from the American Embassy, both wanting a few minutes to question Rosita. They initially spoke with her parents but quickly realized they weren't at the scene and hadn't spoken to their daughter.

Rosita was conscious but very groggy when they brought her back from radiology. Her parents waited as they rolled her bed into place, connecting all the monitors and her BP cup. Rosita began to cry. "They took Olivia," she said. Her parents hugged her, "We know, my love, and the policia will find her. They are here and want to ask you a few questions," her mother said. Rosita nodded her head yes.

The Mexican Policia deferred their questions until after the American Embassy had finished since identifying who took Olivia was extremely time-sensitive. "Good afternoon," the representative greeted her. "I'm glad to see that you're awake and are going to be okay," he continued. "Can you remember anything about the incident?" he asked.

"Very little. It happened so fast," Rosita began. "We had just had ice cream and were returning to the hotel pool. We heard a car's tires screeching behind us. I turned to see what happened and was immediately shoved to the ground. The man was large, very muscular, and dressed in black," she recalled. "I don't remember much after that."

"We have witnesses that said there were two people in the car—the driver and a man wearing a suit in the back," the agent said. "Did you get a look at either of them?"

"I'm so sorry, but I didn't see them," she said, sobbing.

"That's okay, dear. Please tell your parents if you remember anything else." Rosita shook her head in agreement.

The Agent looked at her parents and said, "If she remembers anything else, no matter how small, please call me." Her mom took the card. "We will pray for the other girl and let you know if Rosita can remember any other details."

"Thank you, ma'am," the agent said, then turned and headed out the door.

Kim and Allen talked on their way to the third property. "I'm a little disappointed at how much property costs, especially for the square footage they offer," Kim said.

"I know what you mean. Maybe this one will be more to our liking," Allen responded.

The car stopped, and the realtor announced, "We're here."

Kim and Allen looked confused, and both commented at the same time, "Where's the house?"

"I thought you might say that." He replied with a smile. "There is no house. This is prime land here in Acapulco. You buy the land and can have your dream house built. This way, you get what you want, where you want it. You are currently in the Playa La Mimosa area. We expect this to grow over the next few years."

Kim looked at Allen and asked, "What do you think? I'm digging the idea of living in Mimosa," she said, laughing.

"Let's look around while I ponder the idea," Allen said.

After walking around the lot, Allen had some questions. "How big is the lot that's for sale? How much does it cost? How much do you think it would cost to clear the lot, and how much per square foot does it cost to build here?"

"Those are very good questions. I came prepared with a cheat sheet," the realtor said. "The plot that's for sale is 1.02 acre (44,431 SF), which includes 286 feet of beachfront property; however, the owner would consider breaking it into two half acre (22,215 SF) plots, which would give you roughly 143 feet of beachfront property. It's about $70 U.S. dollars per square foot. If you build a 10,000 SF home, it will cost you $700K. If you are a bit more modest with a 6000 SF home, it would be $420K."

"I like this idea but need to talk to a few people before I decide. Could you give the name of a couple of top-end builders?" Allen asked.

"Sure, I have a sheet here with several names on it. These are all good builders."

"Give us a few minutes to discuss it," Kim said, directing Allen to a shaded area. "I like this area. It's close to town, on the beach, and we can build what we want."

"Can you imagine the look on Olivia's face when she sees this and knows she can help design her room?" Allen smiled and responded, "We have a few days left here. Let's visit a couple of builders and get an idea of costs."

Walking back to the car, they were surprised to see a police car pull up. The officer got out "Are you señor y señorita Schultz?" he said.

"Yes, we are. Is there something wrong?" Allen answered nervously. Kim took his hand and squeezed in anticipation of what might come.

"You should come with me. We had an incident at the Americano Hotel, and your presence is needed." The officer said.

"What kind of incident?" they asked.

"I'm sorry, but that's all they told me. We're only 15 minutes from the hotel, so please hurry."

The realtor said, "Go, we'll talk later."

Allen and Kim got into the back seat of the patrol car. The officer radioed that he had the Schultzs and was en route to the Americana Hotel.

When they arrived, police and Embassy personnel were waiting. "Where's my daughter?" Kim cried out. "Olivia? Olivia?" she screamed.

Alan tried to comfort her. "Let's follow them and see what's going on."

"Good afternoon, Mr. & Mrs. Schultz. I'm Deputy John Wilson from the American Embassy. We have a room this way where we can talk in private."

"What's happening? Where is our daughter?" Kim continued to question.

Allen was in shock. He knew that the police and Embassy wouldn't be here unless something bad had happened. His breathing increased, his body shaking. "This can't be good," he thought. "I need to be strong for Kim."

Unbeknownst to any of them, they were in the same room Julio Mendez had used for his meeting earlier that day.

Deputy Wilson initiated the conversation, speaking matter-of-factly. "At about 1220 this afternoon, there was an incident in front of the hotel. A black limo pulled up; a man exited the front passenger side and accosted Olivia…"

Kim cried out, "No, no, no, god, please, nooo!" Allen held her tightly.

Deputy Wilson continued, "Olivia was walking with her friend Rosita. A man exited the vehicle and pushed Rosita to the ground, knocking her unconscious. He took Olivia against her will, placed her in the back of the Limo, and then sped off. I know this is shocking. If we're going to find your daughter, we need to ask you some questions."

"Yes, please, sir," Allen responded.

"Have you had any dealings with a señor Julio Mendez" or anyone associated with Mendez?" Agent Wilson asked.

"Who is Julio Mendez?" Allen asked. "We've only been here three days; today was the first time we've even left the hotel. I've never heard that name." Allen looked over to Kim, "Have you seen or heard of Julio Mendez?" Kim was still crying and not able to speak. She shook her head no.

"There were several eyewitnesses, and their descriptions of the men in the vehicle and the vehicle itself fit that of señor Mendez. He is a cartel leader from a town about an hour from here. We have reports that he was in town this morning and even at this hotel's restaurant. It's possible that he met your daughter and took a liking to her. This is all speculation at the moment. Nothing has been confirmed."

"I don't know what to say. What would a grown man want with a fifteen-year-old girl?" Allen asked.

"Sixteen," Kim said, still crying, "Today is her sixteenth birthday. She begged to stay at the hotel today instead of joining us. We should have said no… I need a drink. I need some water or something." She cried.

The police officer brought her a bottle of water, "Gracias," Kim said.

"Please tell me what happened this morning and what she was wearing when you left." Deputy Wilson asked.

Kim motioned for Allen to respond. "I was up at 0600, came down for my morning coffee, and to read the paper." I left the girls upstairs to sleep in. I was surprised when Olivia came down a little after 0700 to ask questions about her birthday. We had brunch here around 0930. This is where Olivia begged us to let her hang out here at the hotel with her friend Rosita. Our realtor came and got us at about 1030. When we drove off, she was wearing a pink bikini with a blue coverup. She promised she would stay on hotel property." Allen said.

"Rosita?" Kim thought out loud. "How is Rosita?"

The Police Officer answered, "She is doing well. She was unconscious when they took her to the hospital but has since awakened. Her CAT Scan was negative, so there are no internal injuries. She will probably be in the hospital overnight for observations. Rosita and her parents repeatedly said they were praying for Olivia's safe return."

Deputy Wilson showed them a garment, "Is this the coverup your daughter was wearing?" He handed the item to Kim, who inspected it and then looked at Allen with more tears in her eyes.

"Yes, this is her cover-up. She had this on over her bathing suit."

"We found this by the pool draped over the chair she had been using. Rosita said they walked next door to the ice cream shop at noon. They were on their way back when it happened."

Allen is doing his best not to lose it. He knows why some perverts kidnap young girls but wasn't about to ask that question, not now, not in front of Kim.

1400 HRS.

After drinking the glass of water, Olivia found it hard to keep her eyes open. She sat on the bed and then passed out. Ten minutes later, Julio entered the room. "Ahh, good, she's already out." He acknowledged. He began removing his clothes and laid down beside her. "Don't worry, my child, I will be gentle," Julio told the unconscious Olivia. Without giving it a second thought, he removed her bathing suit and began violating her lifeless body. There was a knock on the door.

"Señor Mendez, the helicopter is ready for your trip. I've loaded your cases and added refreshments."

"Gracias, Manuel. I'll be there in a couple of minutes."

Julio continued his rape, pounding her hard until he orgasmed. "Mmmm, that was good." He complimented the unconscious girl. "I'm going to take you on a trip with me so that we can continue. You'll be a member of the 'Mile High Club' before we get back." Julio quickly dressed, stuck her bathing suit into his coat pocket, then threw her limp, naked body over his shoulders. He took her out to the helicopter and placed her in the back. His pilot and Perez were in the front. Oliva lay naked on the floor.

The pilot provided an update, "Señor Mendez, to avoid radar, we're going to follow the coastline north at a low altitude. This will add about 15 minutes to the journey but should be safer."

"That sounds good," Mendez replied.

They were flying north, about half a mile off the coast.

The weather was beautiful, just as the paper had reported. They had a smooth ride. Mendez looked down at Olivia. He could hear a few sounds, "She's starting to wake up." He happily announced. He had been ogling her perfect little body since they took off and had a rock-hard erection. He removed his jacket, shoes, and pants, got down on his knees, rolled Olivia onto her stomach, pulled her ass up into the air, and began raping her from behind.

1500 HRS.

Agent Thomas had received intel that Mendez was on the move. He notified his air support, and they launched two F-15s to ensure they were set if given the thumbs up. Thomas had received intel of Mendez's actions that day, meeting with other drug kingpins and withdrawing a large sum at the bank. What they didn't relay was that Mendez had kidnapped a young girl and she was in the helicopter.

Agent Thomas was on the phone with his leadership, and they were on the phone with Washington. "Sir, Mendez is flying over water. No collateral damage is expected." Thomas informed his supervisors.

"Hold tight. We're waiting on a decision from the top."

1530 HRS

Back in the Helicopter, Olivia was waking up. She's screaming, "Stop, please stop!"

This only invigorated Mendez. Olivia continued screaming, begging Mendez to stop. He removed his penis and aimed a little higher.

"No, No, No, please, not there." Olivia pleaded. "Please, I'll do anything, just not there. Please stop."

1533 HRS.

Agent Thomas relayed that they were nearing Playa Eréndira.

"It's a GO," came the word from Washington.

Thomas immediately sent the word to the F-15s, and within seconds, they had the helicopter within their crosshairs. "Confirming, we have a go?" Pilot-One asked.

"Roger," you have a "GO," was the reply.

Pilot-One flipped the red tab covering the firing switch. "Missile one has been launched."

Pilot-Two, "We have a direct hit. The target is going down at the following coordinates: 17.92196 -102.22566."

A couple of amphibious rescue vehicles were dispatched to see if there were any survivors. Rescue-One reached the site within five minutes.

"This is Rescue-One. We have engaged with the target and locked on." The rescue lead informed Agent Thomas. "Pilot and co-pilot confirmed exterminated. Occupants in rear compartment…" he paused. "Two passengers in rear confirmed exterminated."

"What?" Thomas asked. "There was only supposed to be one in the back."

"No sir, there appears to be a young girl with Mendez." Rescue-1 said, "I've never seen such a…"

"Mayday, mayday, mayday." Rescue-One transmitted. "Target has shifted, we can't disconnect, taking on water…" then silence.

Two minutes later, "This is Rescue-2. We have one survivor. Divers headed down to rescue the remaining crew."

Five minutes later, "This is Rescue-2. We have two fatalities in Rescue One. Recovery operations are in progress.

Agent Thomas provided guidance, "After you recover bodies from Rescue One, extract the bodies from the Target Vehicle."

Rescue-2, "Yes, sir."

CHAPTER 16

The Cover-Up

Deputy Wilson Informed the Schultzs that they should go to their room and rest. "There's not much we can do here tonight. We have Mendez's estate under surveillance, and the intel we've received indicates he hasn't returned."

"I can't sleep while my baby is out there," Kim cried, her body shaking, just thinking about what might be happening to Olivia. "She's scared, she could be in pain, and it's all my fault. I should have insisted she come with us." Allen wrapped his arms around Kim. He's been quiet, trying to hold it together. He knew that one of them had to remain coherent and able to make rational decisions.

"Mrs. Schultz, this is Dr. Houser. He's been briefed on the situation and would like to have a word with you." Deputy Wilson offered, pointing to the older man in a suit behind him.

"Hello, Mrs. Schultz. I'm extremely sorry to hear about Olivia. Right now, we must believe everything is okay, she's not being harmed, and she will be rescued in the morning. When this happens, you need to be able to care for her." Dr. Houser explained, holding out his hand with a pill dispenser in it. "This is a mild sedative; it will help you get some rest tonight."

"I'm sorry, but I don't like drugs," Kim told the Doctor.

"Honey, this isn't a normal situation. You need to reconsider. I'll be counting on you to be the sane one tomorrow, as I have a feeling I'm going to burst." Allen said.

Kim thought for a minute. She knew Allen had been hiding all of his emotions from her. What he said makes sense. "Okay, Doctor, I'll take them."

"Good, you'll be thankful in the morning. The instructions are on the package. If you need me, my number is on there as well." He handed her the pills, patted her on the shoulders, and said, "Get some rest," and proceeded to leave.

Deputy Wilson told Allen, "You should get some rest as well. We're heading back to the station to keep an eye on events. I will call you if we hear anything."

"Thank you for your assistance today. I'm going to take your advice and take my wife upstairs, and we'll both lie down." Allen shook Deputy Wilson's hand, and the hands of the police officers turned and walked Kim to the elevators.

Deputy Wilson arrived back at the police station and had a message to call the Ambassador at the Embassy. He found an empty office and sat down at the desk. He dialed the number and subconsciously counted the rings. On the fifth ring, a voice answered, "This is Ambassador Taylor."

"Sorry for the late call, sir. This is John Wilson. I just received your message."

"It's been a little crazy around here," Taylor told Wilson, "We have an issue. Are you somewhere you can talk?"

"Yes, sir," Wilson replied.

"It seems Washington gave the order to shoot down Mendez's helicopter. The problem was we had a communication breakdown. The team working on that issue was in the conference room. The team working on the kidnapped girl case was in an office. The two teams never communicated with each other."

"I'm not following, sir. How does the helicopter tie in with my kidnapping?" Thomas asked.

"The helicopter team didn't know about your kidnapping or who your number one suspect was. Señor Mendez was in that helicopter…"

"Oh shit, please don't tell me Olivia was on that aircraft too."

"I wish that was possible. Unfortunately, she was being raped by señor Mendez when the missile took the tail section out. They fell hard into the ocean. There were no survivors. We even lost two men from our rescue team." Taylor informed John.

"The issue we have is that the order to take that target down came from Washington. We can't let it out that the helicopter was shot down. You will tell the Schultz the same thing we will release to the Press." Ambassador Taylor continued, "Señor Mendez's helicopter had mechanical problems and crashed into the Pacific Ocean. He had Olivia Schultz, the young girl who was kidnapped, in the helicopter with him. There were no survivors. I'm going to release it to the press at 0900. Tell the Schultz's in person before they hear about it on the news."

"Yes, sir. I'll stay on script," John told Taylor.

Taylor continued, "The bodies are being brought to the coroner's office for positive identification. Getting them presentable will take a few hours, so hold off until morning to notify Mr. and Mrs. Schultz."

"Yes, sir."

It was a rough night for Deputy Wilson. He laid down but couldn't get the mission he had to perform in the morning out of his head. He wanted to tell Mr. and Mrs. Schultz the truth but was sworn to follow the script. He closed his eyes but was awake every hour like clockwork (pun intended). He finally got up at about 0430 hours, put on a pot of coffee, then took a shower. After getting dressed, he poured his coffee and collected his thoughts. At 0600, he left his apartment for the Americana Hotel.

At 0645, Deputy Wilson knocked on their door. Allen said, "I'll be right there. Give me a minute." He quickly put on a pair of slacks, and Kim put on a house coat. They were both at the door when it opened.

"Good morning, Mr. and Mrs. Schultz. May I come in?"

"Of course, please come in and have a seat," Kim said. Deputy Wilson handed them hot coffee from the shop next to the hotel, with a small bag with condiments.

"Did you find Olivia?" Allen asked. "Is she alright?"

Deputy Wilson cleared his throat, sipped his coffee, and then began… "We confirmed that Mendez and his men kidnapped Olivia."

"Did you find Mendez?" Kim asked.

"After he kidnapped Olivia, he returned to his estate. About an hour later, he was spotted carrying an unresponsive female into a helicopter. We think she may have been drugged. The helicopter took off, and we were able to track it west towards the Pacific, then north in parallel with the coast. They were flying at a low altitude to avoid radar; however, we had already scrambled a reconnaissance aircraft to watch them from a distance."

Allen and Kim were getting antsy and asked, "Are you sure it was Olivia on the helicopter?"

Deputy Wilson took another sip of coffee and continued, "We tracked them for about 150K, then noticed smoke coming from the rear rotor. The helicopter slowed dramatically and then started spinning. It ascended at a rapid rate of speed, hitting the water with great force."

"Please, Deputy Wilson, tell us… was Olivia on that helicopter?" Kim cried out, knowing what the answer was going to be.

"The recon aircraft radioed the crash back to an amphibious rescue team at a clandestine location up the coast. They were at the crash site within five minutes of impact. There were four individuals on that aircraft, three males and one female. None of them survived. I am so terribly sorry to say that the female was positively identified as Olivia Schultz."

"No, no, please God, no… you're wrong. Tell me that you could be wrong," Kim begged. "My baby's birthday was yesterday. Please, please tell me that our baby girl is not gone." Kim was hysterical. Allen was crying, holding Kim, trying to console her. Kim hit the floor despite Allen's presence.

"Honey, let me get you one of the sedatives the doctor gave you," Allen said, wiping his eyes.

"No! I can't be sedated," Kim shouted back. "I need to be able to think. I need to be able to feel."

"I know, Kim. I know. We both do." Allen said. "Deputy Wilson, you said you'd wake us as soon as you knew something. The crash happened hours ago. Why so long before you told us?" Allen asked with a stern voice.

Wilson responded, "The helicopter was severely damaged. Recovering the bodies took hours. Once retrieved, they were taken to a morgue in San Jerónimo de Juárez, about two hours from Acapulco, to make identifications. I was awakened at 0500 with the news. I waited until they checked one last time before coming over here. I wanted to ensure that I provided you the facts."

"I need to see her," Kim announced. "I need to see her now. She can't be alone. She needs me. I need to see her, please," Kim cried. "I need to hold my baby, please."

"There will be a limo at the hotel at 0730 to take us to her," Wilson informed Kim.

Allen, trying to hold it in, couldn't do so any longer. He had been strong for as long as he could. He turned, headed into the bedroom, cried out, "Olivia!" then bawled uncontrollably. After a few minutes, he gathered his composure somewhat and walked back into the room with Kim and Deputy Wilson.

"I'm going downstairs. I'll order breakfast to be sent to the room and wait while you eat and get dressed." Wilson said.

Allen looked at Kim, shaking her head no, "We're not going to be able to eat, not now."

Wilson said, "We have almost two hours of driving. It would help if you ate to get your energy up. Otherwise, you might collapse. I'm at a loss for words right now, but you have to believe this news deeply saddens me. I'll meet you in the lobby at 7:30." Wilson shook Allen's hand and hugged Kim.

When the door shut, Kim ran to Allen. "This isn't real. It can't be real. Please tell me it's a nightmare, and we'll wake up soon." She cried.

Allen had no words for her, so he just held her. "We need to take a shower and get ready so that we can see Olivia." Allen went to shower first. Kim walked into the bedroom, sat on the edge of the bed, and stared straight ahead. She then walked into the bathroom, opened the shower curtain, and said, "All we have are vacation clothes. We can't visit our daughter in the morgue wearing vacation clothes." She shut the curtain and returned to the bedroom.

Kim saw the sedatives on the nightstand. She knew she needed something but didn't want someone else telling her that. She took out one pill, broke it in half, and took it, placing the other half back in the bottle.

Several minutes later, there was a knock on the door. "Room Service," the young steward announced from the other side. Allen opened the door and started to tip the young man when he said, "Not necessary, sir. A man in the lobby paid the check and tip."

Allen and Kim were still getting ready when room service delivered the meal. They were in shock, moving on instinct verses with purpose or meaning. Allen had already showered and dressed. He was sitting on the sofa with the food cart in front of him. He sat there remembering Olivia and that she was sleeping on this sofa the night before. He recalled watching her sleeping and began to tear up again. *"If only I had one more minute with her,"* he thought, "I could hold her and let her know how much I love her.' Allen buried his head into the pillow and cried. He needed the pillow to muffle his pain. He didn't want Kim to hear him.

He looked at the food. It smelled good. He pulled the lid off one of the plates and found a loaded omelet, hash browns, and a bowl of grits with bacon, chives, and pico. Eating took his mind off the pain that was in his heart. Kim came out and saw how red Allen's eyes were and knew he was hurting, even though he continued to pretend to be strong and unemotional. She knew he was doing it for her.

Kim walked over to Allen, sat beside him, and put her arms around him. She held him tightly and whispered, "I love you, Allen. I need you to feel free to show your emotions. Don't worry about being the strong one. You can't hold this in." Allen turned his head so that he was face-to-face with Kim.

"I look at you, and I see Olivia. You and her were so much alike. She had your spunk, your beauty, your personality. I loved her so much. Why did I fuck up and let her stay?" Allen broke down and cried while Kim held him tight. Kim, the one that was out of control, is now the one that is holding things together.

Allen got his shit together and looked at Kim. "You need to eat something. We have a long drive, and there's no telling when we'll get to eat again. I know you may not feel like eating, but I beg you, please have something."

Kim and Allen hugged, and then she uncovered the other plate--steak, eggs over easy, hash browns, and white toast. Allen had an odd thought, *I wish I had opened that one first.* Enjoy your meal, honey. I will freshen up, and then we can go downstairs to meet Deputy Wilson. We have plenty of time. It's only five after seven."

Kim took a couple of bites, then a couple more. When Allen came back from the bathroom, her plate was almost empty. "I'm glad you were able to eat something. I'll take care of putting the dishes back on the cart. You go get freshened up, and then we'll head downstairs." They were both nervous, hoping that Olivia was not the girl on that metal bed.

Kim laid her head on Allen's shoulder during the drive up and fell asleep, only awakening when the car stopped. "The morgue is in the white building straight ahead," Deputy Wilson said, pointing to the entrance.

Allen looked at Kim, "You can stay here if you like. I can go in and see if it's her."

With tears streaming down her face, Kim said, "I need to see my baby girl. Regardless of everything, I need to see her, to apologize for not being there for her, not holding her hand, telling her everything would be ok." Kim then lost it and started crying out loud. Allen grabbed her and held her tight. They cried together.

Deputy Wilson kept his distance, letting Kim and Allen grieve, then said, "We should probably go in now."

Allen looked at Kim and asked, "Are you sure you want to go in and see her like this, or would you prefer to remember her the way she was when we drove away and she was on the sidewalk waving to us?" We have no idea how she will look. I don't want your last memory of Olivia to be of her on the metal slab."

"I need to see my baby," Kim responded. "My eyes will only see the Oliva I birthed, breastfed, and held tightly for 16 years. She needs to know that we are here for her, we love her, and we are sorry we failed to protect her."

Allen exited the car, reached back, and held his hand for Kim to grasp. He helped her up and out of the car. She straightened her outfit, looked at Allen, and said, "Please help me be strong like you."

Deputy Wilson escorted them in to identify the young girl lying under the white sheet. Allen looked at Kim, "Honey, please think about this. Are you sure you want to see her in this condition?" Before Kim could answer, the mortician said, "This young lady has been properly cared for. You will see her as she looked the last time you saw her."

The mortician moved to the head of the table, put his hands on the sheet, and, in slow motion, removed the sheet covering Olivia's face and shoulders.

Allen looked at her beautiful face, laying there so peacefully. You wouldn't know if there was any trauma to her face or upper body by looking at her. Kim was in shock. She desperately wanted this to be someone else's daughter, not hers. But when she saw the beautiful eyes, she immediately knew her worst nightmare had come true. Her baby girl was gone. She started wailing, reached down, grabbed Olivia, and held on to her cold, lifeless body.

There was no indication that Olivia was tortured or raped, thanks to the advice of Deputy Wilson to the mortician. There was no need to add that fact to the death certificate.

Out of nowhere, Kim asked, "Is señor Mendez in here too?"

Deputy Wilson interjected, "Yes, he is, but his body is badly mangled. You should not see him like this."

Kim thanked him for his advice but also instructed him to move over so that she could see the face of the man who kidnapped her little girl.

The mortician began to move the sheet down and over this man's face, unknown to Allen or Kim. The first thing Kim noticed was how huge he was. His face was large, not swollen, but naturally big. There was bruising and abrasions. Stitches were also going from one side of his face to the other. There were no significant signs that he had been in a helicopter crash. Kim wanted to take a knife and gouge out his eyes. She wanted to shred his body apart. But when it came down to it, Kim just cried, put the sheet back over his face, and moved away, mumbling, "This asshole will never do this to another little girl again."

The mortician walked Kim and Deputy Wilson out. Allen lagged behind. When they were out of sight, he pulled the sheet back and released all the anger he had built up. He drew his arm back and buried his fist into Mendez's face with all his might.

Allen arrived at the car in time to hear Deputy Wilson talking to Kim. "The Embassy is working on your travel arrangements so you can leave tomorrow. It may be a day or two before we can get Olivia back."

"I'm not leaving my baby here," Kim cried out. "I'm not leaving until Olivia can go too."

"Ma'am, we'll take good care of Olivia while you make arrangements back home," Wilson said. "The U.S. has strict requirements that have to be followed. We won't be able to get her home until the death certificate has been validated."

"How long will that take?" Allen asked

"As long as there are no unusual findings, then probably the day after tomorrow," Wilson answered.

"We will stay here until Olivia can join us," Allen said as he got into the limo. He looked at Kim, "We need to call your mom and dad when we get back to the hotel."

"I thought the same thing but don't know how to tell them. I still don't understand it myself." Kim hugged Allen. "Please don't let go," she said

The mortician walked back into the morgue and reached for the sheet. "Wait a minute, I already pulled this up," he thought. Looking down, he noticed a new indent in señor Mendez's face, and several stitches were busted open. "I don't blame him," he said, looking at the corpse. "If he hadn't punched you, I would have done it for him."

It was lunchtime when they arrived back at the hotel. The manager was waiting in the lobby. "Mrs. Schultz, I'm so sorry for your loss. Olivia is, umm, was such a lovely young woman." He corrected himself but could see the hurt in her eyes.

"Thank you, señor Lopez. It's so unbelievably hard not having her here by my side," Kim said sadly.

Señor Lopez continued, "I have a small room with a phone that you and Mr. Schultz can use anytime. The staff has been informed that the room is yours as long as you need it." The hospitality room was far enough from the main lobby that hardly any guests were walking around. This would allow Allen and Kim to have some much-needed privacy.

Kim had barely said two words since returning from the morgue. She was extremely depressed, and rightfully so. Allen has never seen this side of her. Señor Lopez escorted her into the room. "Here you go, señora Schultz, please sit here. You will be able to rest more comfortably." Lopez had placed Kim in one of the several contemporary chairs with thick cushions that also reclined. On the end table beside her was a pitcher of ice water and two glasses. In front of her was a coffee table with fruit, sandwiches, and other light food items. There was coffee available on the table next to the door. An aroma in the air drew her attention to the bouquets of flowers surrounding the room.

She just sat in a daze, halfway here, halfway somewhere else. Kim was lost. Her meaning for life was lying in a morgue two hours away.

Deputy Wilson recognized the pain that Kim was internalizing. He tried to distract her, "Ma'am, let me pour you a glass of water." He reached for the pitcher, poured her a glass, and handed it to her. "You should drink some so that you can stay hydrated." He said as her hand reached out for the glass. Wilson noticed her hand trembling as she took a small sip and placed the glass back on the table. Her expression never changed, nor did she speak a word.

Allen walked up to señor Lopez. "Thank you so much for your generosity. We'll need to make a few calls to the States," he paused, feeling overwhelmed. He took a deep breath and continued, "…so many arrangements to make."

"Not to worry, señor Schultz, the calls are on the house."

"My wife needs to rest while I collect the numbers I need. We'll be back in about an hour or so. The room is much appreciated." Allen shook señor Lopez's hand, retrieved Kim, and escorted her back to their room.

Kim was visibly exhausted. "Honey, you haven't had much sleep. Why don't you lie down for a few minutes and rest? I'll get our numbers together, then order room service." Kim nodded in agreement, walked into the bedroom, took the other half of the sedative from the night before, and laid down. She was out almost before her head hit the pillow.

Allen shut the bedroom door, turned the TV on, and switched to an English channel for background noise. He then began the daunting task of finding phone numbers, making a to-do list, and…

Suddenly, the whole world stopped. He set down his notes and stared at the television.

"We'll be back after the break with the latest on señor Julio Mendez's horrific crash," the announcer on the TV reported.

"This has been on the news all day," Allen mumbled. "What if it got picked up on the international channels?" "What if our family and friends learn about Olivia via the news?" Allen sat there waiting for the commercials to end.

"And we're back with the latest from Kingpin Mendez's deadly crash. According to our sources, three men and one woman were on the helicopter when it went down. Witnesses claimed to have heard an explosion before it hit the water. In the background, you see a barge with a crane lifting the helicopter's remains off the ocean floor. Luckily for the salvage crew, the helicopter went down close to the shore." The reporter continued. "And there it is. Wait, that's just the fuselage; the back end of the helicopter is missing and must have been torn off during impact," she continued. "The bodies were extracted sometime after midnight, and we're still waiting for the identification of the victims, who many believe to be Mendez and his entourage."

"Whew, at least one positive thing. They don't know the names. We have time to make the calls before Carol and Bill find out." A knock at the door nearly sent Allen out of his seat. "Crap, what was that?" Then his head cleared, and realizing it was room service, he got up and opened the door.

Kim woke from her nap at the sound of the knock on the door. She continued to lay there looking up at the ceiling while Allen rummaged around in the other room. She didn't want to get up. She didn't want to see anyone. She just wanted to lay there, alone, just her and a fly that had landed on the light globe above the bed. Oblivious to anything outside its world, it just sat there, possibly looking down on Kim and wondering what she was thinking.

The bedroom door opened, and the fly disappeared into another area of the room. "Kim, sweetheart, I have some food in the other room. Why don't you get up and have a bite? You haven't eaten hardly anything all day. We'll go down and call your parents after we eat."

Kim stared blankly as she got up and walked to the bathroom. Allen waited on the sofa until she arrived before beginning to eat. She sat beside him and looked at the food, still blank, with no interest in eating. He handed her the silverware, saying, "You need to eat something, honey. Just have a few bites, please."

She looked down at the mashed potatoes and scooped a spoonful into her mouth. "There you go, have a few more bites. Try the pollo. It's very moist and flavorful." Allen said, trying to coax Kim into eating. She took another bite of the potatoes, then returned to the bedroom, where she laid down, pulled the sheet up over her shoulders, and closed her eyes.

Allen stood there and watched her, imagining the pain that she was suffering. He closed the door and returned to the sofa, taking a few more bites of food before pushing his tray away. *"How do I get Kim back?"* he thought. He looked at the time and realized it was early evening back home. He needed to make the calls. Allen looked in on Kim, who was sleeping soundly, and decided it was best to leave her in bed. He left a note on the coffee table.

Kim, I went downstairs to call home before it gets too late. You get some rest, and after reading this note, please eat more food. You need your strength. I love you, honey.

Allen notified the receptionist that he would be in the Hospitality room for a while if anyone needed him. She smiled and said, "Si señor."

Allen called Bill and Carol to break the news. "Hello?" Carol said as she picked up the phone.

"Hi, Mom. It's me, Allen."

"Hey, son, how are things in Mexico?" She said cheerfully.

"Mom, is Dad there?" he asked.

"Sure, let me get him on the other phone," Carol said, then called Bill.

"Hello," Bill said as he picked up the extension.

"Hi, Dad, I've got some bad news. Can you both sit down?"

"Oh, my!" Carol exclaimed. "Yes, I'm sitting."

"Me too," said Bill.

Allen paused, trying to figure out how to start this off. "Yesterday, while Kim and I were looking at properties, something happened to Olivia." Allen began, "She was walking on the sidewalk in front of the hotel with a female friend when she was abducted."

"Arrrhhh," Carol cried out. "Have they reached out looking for ransom? We can send you money. Tell us how much you need...."

"Mom." Allen interrupted, "it's not like that. She wasn't abducted for money. A very evil man took Olivia because she was a beautiful young girl."

"Have the authorities tracked them down..." Bill started.

"Mom, Dad, please let me finish. Olivia is dead," Allen bluntly said. "She died in a crash after the kidnapping." Allen purposefully didn't go into any details. It would take him too long to explain, and he still needed to understand so many unanswered questions.

Carol screams and drops the phone. Allen hears her crying in the background. Bill hung up the extension and ran to the living room where Carol was to comfort her. "Allen, we are devastated," Bill said, "We can't imagine what you must be going through there. How is Kim?"

"Kim is taking this extremely hard, as expected. She's a mess and will need time and some help to get through this," Allen explained. "I'll provide you with more details later. For now, can you do me a favor and contact the Youngstown Funeral Home and get all the information we'll need to get Olivia back home?"

"Sure, is there anything else?" Bill asked.

"Can you make initial notifications to the family? I'm sure it'll be on the news there by tomorrow. I'd prefer they hear it from you rather than the television."

"Of course," Bill said while comforting Carol.

Allen continued, "They won't release Olivia until after the death certificate has been processed. It could take a couple more days. We're not going to leave her here. So, we'll stay until we can bring Olivia home." Allen gave Bill the number to the hotel so he could contact him when he got the funeral information. "You can call if you need anything from us," Allen said.

"I need to check on Kim, so I'll call you later this evening."

"We're in shock here, son. I'll make the calls and have the information when you call back. We love you. Please hug Kim and tell her we love her."

"I sure will. Talk to you later." Allen hung up the phone and sat in the chair, staring at the walls while the tears that had been bottled up too long began to pour. Allen took the box of tissues from the table and placed them in his lap. Half the box was gone before he could control the waterfall that had been long overdue.

After composing himself, he called the Embassy to see if any new developments were made on Olivia's death certificate. "I'm sorry, Mr. Schultz, the coroner hasn't released the death certificate yet." The public affairs representative stated. "We'll call you at the hotel when we hear something."

"Thank you, ma'am," Allen said before hanging up the phone.

Before making any more calls, Allen decided to walk outside. He wanted to sit near the site where Olivia was abducted. He tried to recreate the scene many times in his head. He looked down at the ice cream shop to his right and the path the car took before nabbing Olivia. He could clearly see the tire marks from where the limo braked. And a few feet away, he saw the marks from where it took off. Something's just not right. Why did Mendez take his daughter? Why did the helicopter crash? There were too many coincidences, and no one could help him put the pieces together.

CHAPTER 17

The Conspiracy (5 November 1985)

Early on the 5th, Deputy Wilson walked into Ambassador Taylor's office. "Good morning, John. So glad you could stop by this morning. Please shut the door and have a seat." Taylor instructed. "How are the Schultzs holding up?"

"About as well as you can guess. Their only child died on her 16th birthday, raped by one of Mexico's top drug Kingpins." Wilson responded, a bit distraught himself. "They are having a really tough time. To be honest, I'm not sure how they are holding it together as much as they have. Mr. Schultz was able to make contact with family back home to break the news before it was all over the media." Wilson paused for a few seconds, visually upset about the ordeal and his role in it. "Here's the information on the funeral home that will be receiving Miss Olivia Schultz," Wilson said as he handed the paperwork to Taylor.

"You're right. It won't be long before the media catches wind that Mendez was with a teenage American girl on the aircraft," Taylor stated. "A beautiful young girl dying in Mexico in a helicopter with a drug lord will be big news there. It could be only a few hours or up to a day, but it'll be all over the news here when it happens. You know that the global networks are going to run with this."

"We have to make sure everything is covered. I need you to confirm that no evidence on the aircraft could indicate that it was shot down," Taylor instructed. "The last thing we needed was this bullshit publicity."

"I'll have my contacts at DoD work to get everyone associated with this mission debriefed and relocated. The two young Airmen that perished will be flown home tomorrow. Their cause of death will be listed as a training accident. The Airman who was injured should be watched since we can't send him out of here just yet. What was his name again?"

"His name is Bowers," Wilson responded.

"What am I missing?" Taylor asked.

"What about the cartel members that were waiting on Mendez? They knew of his targets." Wilson responded.

"Not much we can do about them. Fortunately, they don't know what happened to the helicopter, and let's keep it that way. If that mission were made public, it would be all of our heads."

"I understand," Wilson replied. I'll make sure to cover our tracks. However, I'll need your assistance with Olivia Schultz's death certificate. The coroner's report details damage to her body inconsistent with a crash. Specifically, the fact she was naked, her vagina was ripped, as well as her anus."

Ambassador Taylor placed his head into his hands. "We need to bury this. That news would devastate the Schultz family." Taylor cleared his throat and took a sip of coffee. "Can you imagine how much interest this story would get if that tragedy were made public? Reporters and investigators wouldn't stop digging until everything was out in the open.

As we both know, the 'everything' would be pointing back to Washington."

"I'll see if my contacts at the courthouse can make the original Death Certificate disappear. We want it to list the cause of death as 'Blunt Force Trauma' due to a crash. There's no need to have the image of their daughter's last moments as being raped." Wilson said with a somber tone.

"This needs to happen today," Taylor ordered. "The Schultzs need to take their daughter home as soon as possible. The longer they remain here, the more difficult it will be for them."

"Yes, sir," Wilson said as he retreated from the office and back to his desk to start working on the tasks.

CHAPTER 18

Wake up
(7 November 1985)

Early on the 7th, Wilson got the call to report to Ambassador Taylor's office, 'I've spent the last 45 minutes on the line with the Coroner's Office," Taylor began. "Two copies of the death certificate are on their way here. They should be clean with no mention of the rape."

"I'm sure the Schultzs will be glad to hear that. How were you able to get the information removed from the certificate?" Wilson asked.

"I had to pull a lot of strings to get the data erased from the official autopsy report. That way, there was nothing on the document for the clerk to transcribe to the death certificate," Taylor responded.

"I envy all the connections you have."

"Well, I've been doing this a long time. You make a lot of friends if you treat them right," Taylor boasted.

"Let me know when the certificates arrive. I will call the Schultzs and let them know we will have the documents this morning. I'll also start working on the travel arrangements and get with the airlines to let them know that a coffin will accompany two passengers," Wilson told Taylor.

Deputy Taylor exited the Ambassador's office and hurriedly returned to his desk. He sat down and thought about that poor, innocent young girl. He wiped his eyes and began calling the airlines. But first things first, he thought as he dialed the phone, "Hello, Mr. Schultz, Wilson here. I wanted to let you know that the death certificate is being delivered to our office. I'm working on your travel home for tomorrow morning."

Still on the phone with Wilson, Allen covered the mouthpiece and called out to Kim, "They have the death certificate. We can take Olivia home." She didn't respond. Allen removed his hand from the mouthpiece and said, "I'm sorry, Deputy Wilson, Kim, and I were just talking about this, and I wanted to let her know. Thank you so much for everything you've been doing; we really appreciate it."

"I'm just glad I'm able to assist you and Mrs. Schultz," Wilson said. "As soon as I arrange your travel, I'll stop by the hotel and drop off the documents."

Allen sat on the sofa watching the news while Kim lay in bed. He was happy that the whole kidnapping thing hadn't come up. He walked in to check on Kim. "Good, still sleeping," he thought. I'll run down and read the paper and have a cup of coffee," he said aloud, realizing he was speaking to an empty room.

Allen left a note for Kim, letting her know where he'd be, then took the stairs to the lobby. "I need the exercise," he thought. The coffee was extra strong this morning. "Good, maybe this will wake me up," he continued the conversation with himself. He nodded to the receptionist as he passed, "Good Morning, señorita, you look lovely today," he said.

"Gracie," she replied, smiling at him with lips coated in bright red lipstick and beautiful blue eyes. "Would you like the newspaper?" she asked, not realizing she had lipstick stains on two teeth.

"Yes, thank you very much," He replied.

Allen had become a morning fixture at the hotel, at the same table each day. Always a cup of coffee and a newspaper. Señor Lopez walked by and stopped to say, "Good Morning, señor Schultz. Is there anything I can get you?" he asked.

"No, thank you, but I appreciate you asking," Allen said. "Oh, by the way, we should be leaving tomorrow."

"It will be sad to see you go," Lopez said as he patted Allen on the back and continued on his way.

Allen finished the paper and his second cup of coffee. The resort was beautiful. If only everything weren't so somber. It's hard to see the beauty when your heart and soul are lost. Allen took a few minutes to take in everything in front of him. The exquisite vegetation, from plants to palms, let you know you were in a tropical climate. "You don't see this at home," he thought. All the flowers were blooming; however, he had no idea what they were, only the smell and aesthetics were wonderful. "I don't believe I've seen a cloud in the sky the whole time I've been here," he mumbled to himself.

A family took the table two over from where he sat. They were a fairly young couple. The kids were probably 7 or 8 years old. Allen fell into a daze as he looked at the young girl and thought about Oliva at that age. She was rambunctious, always getting into things, but she was never afraid. She'd be the first one in line at the haunted house, "I'll protect you, Dad," she would say, grabbing my hand and taking me through it. At the end, she would say, "See, Dad, there wasn't anything to be afraid of." Just when he thought he was all cried out, the tears began to flow again.

Allen was still in another state of mind when the young waitress stopped by to see if he needed anything. "Señor, would you like something to eat? More coffee?" she said.

Allen, eyes swollen, face flush, tears streaming, didn't even know she existed. She could see that something was going on with him and put her hand on his shoulder, "Señor, can I get you something?" she said, this time holding out a hand towel.

Allen snapped back into reality, "I'm so sorry. I was just thinking about something and spaced out," he said.

"That's ok, senior. I know what happened, and I am so sorry for your loss. Your daughter was a pleasant sight to have around here. I can't imagine the emptiness you must be experiencing in your heart. Please let me get you something," she begged.

"Okay", he responded. "You can bring me something."

"What would you like?" she asked.

"Surprise me… I trust you," he said, trying to work up a smile.

"Sure thing. I think I know what you need," she said as she returned to the kitchen without writing anything down.

Allen continued to watch the children. At one point, their mom noticed how intensely he focused on them. She called a waitress over and complained. "That guy is creeping us out," she said. "Can you ask him to stop staring at my kids?"

"Ma'am," the waitress said, "that señor's daughter was kidnapped three days ago. He found out yesterday that she had died. He's been like this ever since. He sits at this table, reads his paper, and drinks his coffee. He looks at others but has never said or done anything inappropriate." The waitress explained to her. "Please show him some respect as he grieves the loss of his child."

"I'm so sorry. I didn't know," she came back.

Allen was clueless to the attention. He continued looking straight ahead, where the young girl was in his sight. He wasn't there. He was with family, playing with Olivia. It took several minutes before he snapped out of it. Confused and forgetting that he ordered breakfast, he got up and started to leave. "Wait, señor," the waitress said, "I have your food."

"I'm sorry", Allen apologized. "I've been in a daze and absent-minded lately."

"That's ok," she said, "Have a seat and try this drink."

Allen sat back down and began to eat, each bite getting easier to swallow. He sipped the drink, "This is muy bueno," he said as he took another swallow. The waitress smiled, placed her hand on his shoulder, gave it a light squeeze, and then moved to another table to take their order.

He looked at his watch and thought he'd better check on Kim. He reached into his pocket, pulled out a wad of pesos, and left them on the table. As he stood, the woman and young girl from two tables over came over to him, "Excuse me, señor, I'm so sorry for your loss," she said as she put her arms out and hugged him. "This is my daughter Alexia. She wanted to meet you and say hello."

"That is so sweet. You have a lovely daughter," Allen said as his eyes swelled up with tears.

"Bueno Dias señor," the small child said. She walked over, put her arms around his leg, and squeezed. Allen picked her up and gave her a long hug, tears flowing freely.

"Thank you so much," Allen said. "I really needed that. You are a very kind person." The mom, also crying, picked up her daughter, gave Allen one more hug, and left to meet her husband and son, who were waiting by the door.

Allen followed slowly behind them until he heard "Señor… señor." He turned to see the waitress running after him. "This is too much. Take the money back, por favor."

"No señorita, that is for you. Your kindness has been very appreciated," Allen said as he squeezed her out reached hand closed with the pesos inside. He saw her eyes begin to water and knew he had to leave before it triggered his tears again.

He ran into Deputy Wilson by the elevator. "Going up?" he said, trying to muster up what little humor he had left in him.

"Good morning, Mr. Schultz. I've come to drop off your documents for the flight home tomorrow." Wilson said. "I will be here at 0700 to pick you and Mrs. Schultz up. I've arranged to have the hearse here as well. We will follow 'Olivia' to the airport."

Allen was speechless. He took the documents from Wilson and said, "I have no words to express how I feel…" Allen was getting choked up. "I hope you know we appreciate all you have done."

"Mr. Schultz, I don't feel I've done enough. I, too, have a daughter and can't imagine the pain you and your wife are feeling right now." Deputy Wilson said. "You get some rest today, and I'll see you tomorrow morning. If there is anything you need before then, please give me a call." He waited until the elevator door closed in front of Allen before he walked away.

Back in the room, Kim was still in bed. Allen noticed the pill bottle that once held the sedatives was now empty. He reached over and put his hands on her shoulders, "Kim, wake up, honey," he said as he shook her. "Kim, you need to wake up. Olivia needs you to wake up," he continued.

Her eyes opened slowly, only about halfway. "Honey, Olivia needs you to stay here with me. I need you to stay here with me."

Allen called señor Lopez and asked if he could get the doctor to their room as soon as possible. "Si señor" Lopez said. Fifteen minutes later, the and the doctor arrived. Allen explained what had happened and asked if there was anything he could do.

"Don't worry, señor," he said. "There were only a few sedatives in the bottle, and they were not very strong. I will give her something to help diminish their effects, but you need to get her to eat and drink something. Her body is very weak, which is why the sedatives have a stronger effect. Food will help her."

The doctor looked at señor Lopez and told him something in Spanish. Lopez went to the phone in the living room and made a call. When he returned, he said, "I have ordered some soup for Mrs. Schultz. It will be right up."

The doctor grabbed Allen's arm to get his attention, "You need to get this soup in her. It's filled with everything her body needs to help revive her. After she eats, give her one of these, it will help her become more lucid. If there are any more problems, let me know, and I'll be back," he said as he moved towards the door.

"We have arrangements to leave tomorrow morning at 0700. Will she be able to travel?" Allen asked.

"Si señor, if you get her to eat, she can travel." The doctor replied.

After they left, Allen continued to hold Kim. "Wake up, baby. You need to eat and drink something," he begged. "I know you are lost, but I need you. Mom and Dad need you. Please wake up."

Allen went to the bathroom to get a washcloth. He soaked it in cold water and then placed it on her forehead. Before he could sit beside her, there was a knock on the door. It was the soup. There were also other food items, sandwiches, fruit, and a pitcher of ice water.

"We're taking Olivia home in the morning," Allen said, trying to spark a response from her. "Kim, you need to wake up!" Allen used the ice water to make the washcloth cooler. He continuously wiped her face, hoping the cool rag would help.

An hour had passed since the doctor had left. Kim was breathing normally. She was starting to get a little color back and was making more noises when he tried to wake her. Allen decided to let her continue to rest, and hopefully, the effects of the drugs would wear off soon. It was still early, so he would keep an eye on her.

Allen was mentally exhausted. He positioned the chair in the living room so that he could see directly into the bedroom. He sat down, put his feet on the coffee table, and watched Kim.

CHAPTER 19

Goodbyes
(8 November 1985)

0700 comes early, so Allen packed everything the night before. Kim was still groggy when she finally woke from her drug-induced slumber. She was weak, tired, and malaise. She had no energy or will to get up. In her condition, she wouldn't be able to assist very much, if at all. She felt better after eating the cold soup. Not because she wanted to but because Allen insisted. After ensuring the soup stayed down, he ordered her dinner. Everything was packed when dinner arrived. Kim sat and ate a decent amount from her plate before lying down again. Allen finished his meal, watched TV for about an hour, and then joined her in bed.

By morning, they were both rested, and Kim was physically feeling much better. Emotionally, it was another story. When Deputy Wilson arrived, they were dressed and sitting in the lobby with their luggage.

"Good morning, Mr. & Mrs. Schultz. Olivia is waiting outside and will lead the way to the airport. We will ride in the limo directly behind her." Wilson said. "I have someone that will be getting your luggage, so you can have a seat in the car."

Allen was walking towards the door when he realized he hadn't checked out or paid the bill for their stay. "I need a couple of minutes to take care of the hotel," Allen informed Deputy Wilson.

"No need," Wilson replied. "The Embassy has taken care of everything. Let's get you home so that you can be with family."

Kim saw the hearse when she exited the hotel, and her knees buckled. "Honey, are you ok?" Allen asked, catching her before she hit the sidewalk. Kim had no words but shook her head and used the tissue she carried to dry her eyes. Allen held on to her tightly until they reached the car.

"I'll help you get in first, then go to the other side," Allen informed her. When they were both settled, both vehicles moved slowly through the busy streets until they hit the highway to the airport.

Kim hasn't spoken since leaving the morgue. Her stoic personality has been pretty steady, so when she suddenly sat up straight and slammed her hand down on Allen's arm, he was concerned and a little shocked. "Mom… Dad?" were her first words.

"What about them, honey?"

"We haven't told them about Olivia," she said tearfully.

"It's okay, Kim. I called and talked to them after we returned from the morgue. They helped me make all the arrangements and notified the rest of the family. I called them again last night to let them know when we will arrive," Allen assured her. "The funeral home will have a car at the airport for Olivia. Your mom and dad will be picking us up."

Kim began crying, her first emotion in a couple of days. "How can we go on?" she sobbed, laying her head on his shoulders. "It was my fault…"

Allen stopped her immediately, "It was NOT our fault. It was Mendez's fault. Do not blame yourself, please."

Kim continued to cry. Allen could feel her head, still on his shoulder, shaking "no." He hoped the feeling of guilt would eventually subside.

When they arrived at the airport, the hearse pulled into a private lot and stopped. The limo pulled alongside. Wilson opened Kim's door, "Ma'am, would you like to say anything to Olivia before we prep her for the trip?" Kim was at a loss for words, so Allen said, "Yes, that would be nice, thank you."

They exited the limo and walked to the back of the hearse, where the door was open. Allen helped keep her steady until she had both hands on the coffin, then said, "I'll leave you here by yourself so you can have a private conversation. I'll talk to her afterward." He placed his hands on hers, squeezed slightly, then stepped back several feet so they could be alone. *"She needs this time with Olivia,"* he thought. I pray this will help her.

After a few minutes, he saw Kim lay her head on the coffin. He moved closer and put his left arm around her shoulders. He placed his right hand on the coffin and said a quiet prayer. "Kim," Allen said, "It's time to go. We can talk to her again when we get home." He guided her back to the limo, and they watched the hearse drive slowly away.

They were taken to the VIP entrance of the airport, given their boarding passes, and escorted to the gate. "Thank you so much, Wilson. Your kindness and generosity have helped us endure this painful tragedy." Allen said as he shook his hand. Kim gave him a half hug and waved goodbye as she headed down the gateway.

Several hours later, they landed in Pittsburgh and were met by two government personnel as they deplaned. "Mr. and Mrs. Schultz?" they asked as Allen and Kim exited the boarding door. "Yes," Allen responded. "Please follow us. We'll take you to Olivia." The agent said.

"My parents are waiting for us," Kim said with a concerned tone.

"Yes, ma'am, we have already notified your parents. They will be waiting for you in the private reception room."

They boarded a cart that took them to the reception area. Carol ran to Kim as soon as she saw her, almost getting hit by the cart. "Kim… baby…" she cried. Bill was right behind. It was a very emotional few minutes, loud crying, tears, and two boxes of tissues as the three converged. Allen held back to give her a few moments with Carol and Bill.

Several minutes had passed when one of the Agents came over and said that Olivia was there. Carol turned and saw the coffin on a stand next to the door. She ran to it before the others could process the information. An audible scream could be heard as she threw her body over the coffin. Bill went to console her.

After a short while, they held hands and said a prayer. Both agents bowed their heads out of respect.

Allen had arranged to spend a few days with her parents. It was too soon to take Kim back to their house. She needed time to acclimate to the reality of Olivia being gone.

The funeral was two days later, followed by Olivia's burial in a family plot at the Sunset Hills cemetery. After the services, Kim looked to Allen, "I want to go home." She said, "I want to be in my house."

Allen felt it was too soon; however, he knew there would be no good time for her to return to the house filled with Olivia's memories. Fortunately, he had spoken to Carol before leaving Mexico, and she promised to clean up a few things to make the shock less impactful. Bill came over after the end of the services and asked if they wanted to head back to the house and have a bite to eat.

"Not tonight, Bill. Kim is ready to go home."

"We'll come over too, and then the four of us can say another prayer for Olivia before dinner.

CHAPTER 20

Time Heals
(3 November 1986)

A year had passed since Olivia's death. The saying that time heals is not true. It may mask the pain a little, but it doesn't heal. For Kim, it didn't mask anything. She visited Olivia's grave almost daily. She was so overcome by grief that she quit her job. Her boss told her the job would be open whenever she wanted to return. Kim realized her mental capacity wouldn't allow the concentration needed to perform her job. *"Maybe one day,"* she thought.

Allen's coping mechanism 'is' to work. As long as he kept his brain occupied, there was no time for sorrow. Unbeknownst to him, this would lead to a dramatic event one day.

Kim and Allen were cohabitating. The joyous home life had changed to just existing. Allen noticed that Kim gradually cut ties with all her friends. She never went anywhere and, most of the time, declined when he asked her out. She had let herself go—no spas, salons, or weekly trips to the outlet shops. Allen was worried and continued to hope that time would heal.

"Honey," Allen said to Kim, "I think it would be beneficial if we both see someone."

"For what," she replied.

"We need to speak to someone about the grief we're both dealing with," he said.

"I don't need to talk to someone about grief. I think I know exactly what it is," Kim snapped back.

Allen would broach the topic again every few weeks, only to be shot down. He talked to Bill and Carol, which only made Kim angry, so he let it go.

Allen came home from work one afternoon and saw that Kim's laptop was turned on with a Word document open. It was a poem that read:

> "As people look out at the foliage this time of year, I see them smile at how beautiful the colors are. Don't they realize that this is nature's death?
>
> The luscious colors of orange, red, brown are signs that the once vivid leaves so full of life are now dying. It won't be long until their moist texture dries up, and they fall helplessly to earth.
>
> We never know when our colors will change, but trust me when I say that they will. Looking out and witnessing this passage made me think of my own mortality. Will I peak with beautiful colors, or will I go directly from green to dried up?
>
> Fortunately, I was given insight and have seen what is to come for me. My fall is nearer than some may like. My colors are pale, and my will to continue holding onto the branches is getting weaker.
>
> Still, I look out at the foliage and smile."

Allen screamed for Kim, but there was no answer. He ran upstairs, nothing. She wasn't outside. He noticed her car was gone, so he called Carol to see if she was there. "No honey, she's not here. Maybe she went shopping." Allen got distracted by three knocks at the door.

"I've got to go, Mom. There's someone at the door."

Allen opened the door to find an officer from the Youngstown Sheriff's office. "Mr. Allen Schultz?" he asked.

"Yes... How may I help you?" he replied, then it hit him, "Kim?" he yelled.

"I'm sorry, sir, we found Mrs. Schultz deceased at the Sunset Hills Cemetery," he said.

Allen started wobbling, turned and walked to the sofa, and sat down. The officer followed.

"Sir, we need you to come down to the morgue to positively identify the body."

"Her name is KIM," he replied. "What happened? How did she die?"

"We don't know, sir. There will be an autopsy to determine the cause of death." The officer informed him.

"Today is the anniversary of our daughter's death," Allen said. "She has never gotten over it." Allen continued; we need to make a stop on the way to the Morgue. I need to tell her parents in person."

CHAPTER 21

Living with Memories (10 February 1988)

It's been fifteen months since Kim passed. Allen joined the Baptist Church down the street and has been there every Sunday. He has lunch dates with Bob and Carol at least once a week and was recently promoted at work. The best part of his life is he has a loving wife and daughter at home.

Allen enjoys his daily talks with Kim and Olivia. He has his family back, and life is good. He's back into the same old routine he had three years ago: work, help Olivia with homework, and weekly date nights with Kim.

"Good morning, lovely ladies," Allen said as he walked into the kitchen to the smell of bacon. "Mmmm, that smells delicious, but I will have to pass. I'm running late and need to get to the office. Save it for later, and I can make a bacon sandwich for lunch tomorrow." Allen said.

He rounded the table where Olivia was doing her homework, "What have I told you about waiting until the last minute, young lady?" he asked. She barely looked up. She just kept writing. Allen bent down and kissed her on the top of her head, then walked over to Kim and hugged and kissed her, looking back to see that Olivia hadn't budged from doing her homework.

Many of Allen's co-workers were at both Kim and Olivia's funerals, so his bragging about Olivia getting straight "As" in the break room was very concerning for them. After Allen left, one said, "This isn't right. We need to talk to Mr. Simpson. They walked to the Director's Office and described Allen's strange actions.

Mr. Simpson contacted HR to see who Allen had listed as his emergency point of contact. He was given the name of Bill and Carol Parson.

"Hello?" Bill said, picking up the phone.

"Mr. Parson?" came the voice from the other end.

"Yes, it is. How may I help you?" he said.

"I'm Dan Simpson. Your son-in-law, Allen Schultz, works for me."

"Is everything okay?" Bill asked.

"Well, sir, Allen is acting a bit strange. He's talking like his wife and daughter are still alive." Simpson said. "He has you and your wife listed as the emergency contacts, so I wanted to let you know."

"Thank you for calling. I'll check up on him later today."

Bill was parked in front of the house when Allen arrived home. "Hey, Dad, what brings you over?" Bill said cheerfully.

"I thought I'd come over and visit for a while if you don't mind," Bill replied, constantly observing Allen's actions.

"Of course I don't mind, come on in. I'm sure Kim and Olivia will be excited to see you." Allen said nonchalantly.

Bill was flabbergasted, *'What has happened to him?'* he thought. He was absolutely fine the last time they were together, well, except for the depression that he has been dealing with. Bill walked in and looked around to see if anything was abnormal or out of place.

"Sorry, Dad. It looks like the girls went shopping. How about a beer while we wait on them."

"That would be nice," Bill said, trying to figure out how to bring Allen back to reality. "It looks like you've been losing weight. Have you joined a gym?"

"Nope. Kim has had me on a clean diet with no preservatives or prepared foods. She's been making everything from scratch. Last night, she made a kick-ass chicken dinner. We ended up eating the whole dish."

Bill follows Allen into the kitchen. He noticed the table was set for three. It was the good china that they received as a wedding gift. There were some daisies in a vase center table. Allen opened the fridge and said, "Sorry, Dad, looks like we're out of beer. What do you say we head down to Charlie's and have a couple?"

"That would be perfect, and the first round is on me," Bill answered. He looked in the fridge when Allen had the door open, and it was bare. Every shelf is empty and clean. There are no condiments in the door trays either. *"There's something not right here,"* he thought.

At Charlie's, Allen asked, "What's your preference, bar or table?"

"Normally, I'd prefer to be at the bar, but today, let's sit at a table to talk," Bill said.

"No problem, Dad. Have a seat, and I'll get the beers."

Bill needed to have a plan. How is he going to snap Allen back into reality? Whatever happens, he needs to ensure he doesn't upset him. The last thing he needs is for him to go bat-shit crazy in the bar.

Allen returned with two tall drafts, spilling some of the beer out of one as he sat it down. "Sorry, I'll drink that one," he said.

"So… How's things going these days?" Bill said, breaking the ice.

"Not too bad. Work is good, and home is good. Just living the dream," Allen happily said.

"Son, do you remember the trip to Acapulco a couple of years back?" Bill asked

"I sure do. We'd been planning that for months, then I got sick, and we couldn't go." Allen said. "Good thing I purchased the insurance, or we'd have been out a lot of money."

"Son, you didn't get sick. You, Kim, and Olivia went there."

"That's impossible, Dad. You know we didn't go. Quit bullshitting me," Allen laughed. "We ended up going to Florida once I got to feeling better."

"Yeah, that's right," Bill responded, trying to play along. "You know an old man's memory isn't that great. So, how have the girls been doing? Olivia should be graduating this year, right?"

"That's right, she's already been accepted into Ohio State." She'll be starting in the fall. I'm so proud of her," he continued.

Bill took the last drink from his glass and said, "Well, son, I should be headed home. You know Carol gets worried if I'm out late. She doesn't like me driving when it's dark. These damn eyes need work, like many other parts," he chuckled.

"I'm done too. I'll walk you out."

When Bill arrived home, he called out for Carol. "You need to have a seat," he said as she walked into the living room.

"What's wrong?" Carol asked, "Is he as bad as we thought?"

"No! Much worse…" Bill paused, "He's delusional. He thinks Kim and Olivia are still alive. I brought up the trip to Acapulco, and he denied going. Said it was canceled."

"How can he say that? We have the pictures they sent," Carol responded.

"Trust me, I know. I didn't want him to flip out, so I didn't press him."

"I don't blame you," Carol replied.

"When he opened the fridge, it was bare. Every shelf was in pristine condition. He looks like he's lost about twenty pounds, and when I asked about Olivia, he said that she would be starting at Ohio State in the fall," Bill said in disbelief. "I'm really worried about him."

"I don't want to snoop, but we need professional help. Do you know any psychiatrists?" Carol asked.

"No, but I was thinking about going to the crisis center to ask for their help," Bill said.

"I want to go with you. Let me get my bag."

Due to Youngstown's past reputation for drugs, it wasn't too hard to track down a crisis center. They walked in and were greeted with a smile from the receptionist. "How may I help you?" she asked.

"It's a fairly long story, but the bottom line is that our son-in-law is having damaging hallucinations, and I'm worried for his safety. We need to talk to someone to see how to deal with this before he gets hurt."

"Okay, wait here and let me see if we have someone free," she said. Then she disappeared behind two locked doors. About five minutes later, she returned with the cutest doctor in the place.

"Good afternoon, I'm Doctor Billawitz. Please follow me," he said, pointing to a patient room down the hall. Bill and Carol held hands as they walked down the hospital corridor. As the door closed behind them, the doctor asked how he could be of service.

"We have a rather long story...." Bill and Carol opened up about everything.

"Yes," Dr. Billawitz said, "I recall reading about this a couple of years ago." I'm so sorry for the loss of your daughter and granddaughter," he said.

"Thank you," Carol said. "How can we help Allen? What can we do?"

"Honestly, it sounds like he needs professional assistance, quite possibly in-patient care. If he's not eating, it's only a matter of time before he passes. I recommend bringing him in to see us, and we'll take it from there."

"How long do you think we have?" Bill asked.

"I can't predict, but the sooner the better. If Allen is not eating, that could create a multitude of medical problems. If his delusions worsen, he could be a danger to himself or someone else. I'd bring him in tonight or tomorrow if at all possible."

Allen and Kim agreed and asked, "Can you give us some ideas on getting him here? He thinks everything is fine. He may get a bit agitated if we trick him."

"Give me his number, and I'll use an old trick." The doctor said.

"Hello?" Allen said from the other end of the phone.

"Good evening, is this Mr. Schultz?" the doctor asked.

"Yes, it is. How may I help you."

"I'm Dr. Billawitz from the clinic down on Fourth Street. Would it be possible for you to come down here, please?"

"Why do I need to come there?" he asked.

"We have your mother and father-in-law here, and they are requesting your help," Billawitz said.

"Okay, give me five minutes.

Allen slipped on his shoes and headed out the door. He

was at the clinic within about seven minutes. "Excuse me, ma'am, I was called by a Doctor Billawitz," Allen said.

"Dr. Billawitz is in with another patient right now. Please have a seat," the receptionist responded.

Dr. Billawitz was out within two minutes. "Allen, please come with me," Allen takes him up on the offer and follows him into an exam room.

"Where are Bill and Carol?" Allen asked.

"They are here but in another room." I wanted to talk with you for a short while."

"Why me? I'm fine," Allen replied.

"I'm sure you are. I just need to ask some questions, and then I'll get Bill and Carol.

"OK, shoot," Allen responded.

"Question number one: Are you married, and do you have a child living at home?" Billawitz asked.

"I hope the next question is this easy," Allen replied. "The answer is yes. I have a wife and daughter at home waiting on me."

"Okay, good! Question two: Did you take a family vacation to Acapulco two years ago?"

"Now you're beginning to sound like Bill," Allen said. "He asked me this same question earlier today. I'll give you the same answer. No! We had made plans to go, but I got sick, and we had to cancel." Bill said annoyingly. "Is this why you called me down? I thought Bill or Carol needed me."

Dr. Billawitz pulled a couple of newspapers from his desk drawer and opened it to page one. "You are very well known here, Mr. Schultz. Two years ago, the whole town cried with you at the funeral of Olivia." He said, pointing to the news article on the front page. The headlines read, "Local couple loses their daughter to violence in Acapulco."

"I don't know what you're trying to pull here. That could have been anybody. I'm telling you, Olivia is fine and at home," Allen sounded back with a bit of frustration.

"Mr. Schultz, please read further."

"I don't want to read this fake news article," Allen yelled.

"Sir, it's not fake. You can go to the library, look through the archives, and find the same one," the doctor responded.

"Do you recognize these pictures?"

"Sure, that's Olivia, me, and Kim,"

"Where were they taken?"

"In Florida, on our family vacation. The one we went on after canceling Acapulco," Allen said.

"Look closely, Mr. Schulz. You're at the Acapulco Airport with a sign in the background that reads, 'Welcome to Acapulco.'"

"That's impossible. Someone must have doctored it up."

"Do you remember Nov 3rd of last year?"

"No, not particularly," Allen responded, "Should I?"

"Well, yes, that's the day that Kim died."

"Enough of this bullshit, I don't know what you're up to, but I'm telling you right here and now that my wife and daughter are alive and well and at our house waiting for me to get home."

"Okay, let me just show you one more thing," Billawitz pulls out a picture that Carol gave him (along with the newspaper). "Do you recognize this?" He shows Allen a photo of the headstone that rests above their grave.

"Again, I'll tell you that they are fine. Let's go to my house, and I'll show you."

"That's a great idea," Billawitz said. "Let me get Bill and Carol, and then we can drive over there."

Carol is the first to walk out of the adjoining room, "Mom, what's going on here? Do you all think I'm crazy? Is this a dream or something? We all had dinner together just a couple of weeks ago," Allen pleaded.

Carol was crying, "Allen, sweetheart, Olivia and Kim have passed. We were all at their funeral."

"Mom, that's impossible. I'm telling you they are at home right now."

Bill and the doctor walk into the room, and two other gentlemen join them as well. "Don't be alarmed. I have to travel with my driver and escort. Follow me. The van's out back."

Carol puts her arm around Allen as they walk out back. They share a seat in the back; Bill is next to them, and the doctor is in the second row in front of them. Allen looks around the van and notices that all the windows have bars on them. He knows something is up. He just doesn't understand why.

They pull into the driveway and exit the vehicle in reverse order. "Now, let's put this to bed once and for all," Allen said as he walked to the door. "Honey, I'm home," Allen yelled. There was no response. "Kim? Olivia? Come downstairs and talk to your mom and dad." Nothing but crickets.

"Maybe they are out back," Allen said as he turned to walk to the back door. He went through the entire house, and they couldn't be found. "I'm not crazy," Allen yelled. "They must have gone for a walk or to the mall."

"Isn't it kind of late for two women to be walking to the mall?" Dr. Billawitz asked.

"Maybe we could sit and wait for them?" Allen asked. "I need you to believe me. I need you to see that they are alive."

Carol continued to cry and hold on to Bill.

"Allen," Dr. Billawitz began, "We could wait here an eternity, and they wouldn't come walking through that door. They both passed away."

Allen starts screaming, "They are not dead. You assholes are trying to make me believe they are gone, but they're not! I had breakfast with them this morning. Mom? Dad? Why are you doing this to me?" Allen yells. Carol cries even louder.

Allen's face is turning red. You can see the veins in his neck growing larger. "Allen, it's alright." The doctor tries to comfort him. "This isn't uncommon, especially for someone who has endured two horrific deaths in a short period."

The two escorts stand and move closer behind Allen. "We need to take you with us to help you understand and think clearer," the doctor informed him.

"How many times do I have to tell you I'm fine? I'm not crazy and won't go anywhere with any of you!" Allen was at a loss for words; he was boiling mad and couldn't think straight. He began walking towards the doctor. Before he got there, though, the escorts secured his arms. At the same time, the doctor injected Allen with a powerful sedative that almost immediately rendered him immobile.

CHAPTER 22

Shrinks and Drugs (11 February 1988)

When Allen woke, he was lying on his back, staring at the ceiling. Everything felt different. It was like a blasé feeling of emptiness. Nothing mattered. Nothing excited him. He didn't even care that he was in a strange room with straps around his wrists and ankles. He just looked up at the ceiling.

Eventually, Allen became curious about his surroundings and turned his head to see… nothing? The room was empty except for the bed. It was bright, with white walls, no windows, only a door. He noticed a camera attached to the wall pointed directly at him up in the corner, just below the ceiling. "Good, I'm not alone," he thought.

There was no sense of time. He couldn't tell if he'd been there for minutes, hours, or days. He couldn't tell if it was day or night. He only knew he was in a very bright, white room with no windows.

Allen couldn't move. He couldn't turn over or lift his body. He wondered why he was restrained but didn't care either way. He just wanted to change positions in the bed. Accepting that his immediate fate was to lie on his back, he looked back at the ceiling, thinking of Kim and Olivia.

Allen closed his eyes and pictured being back home holding Kim and watching Olivia being her adorable self. There was an episode of *Married with Children* on the television. It was their favorite comedy, and Allen loved it when Kim did her *Peg Bundy* impersonation.

Allen must have drifted off to sleep until he was awakened by the large metal door being unlocked and opened. "Good morning, Mr. Schultz," came the greeting from a young nurse, now standing next to his bed with her male orderly close behind her. "My name is Stacy. I'm here to administer your morning medications. Doctor Billawitz has you down for injections today but will switch you to oral meds by tomorrow. He should be in to see you later today. I'll be in to check on you at least hourly. You let me know if you need anything, okay?" she said with a valley girl type of tone to her.

"Whoa," Allen thought, "She talks a mile a minute." He couldn't think of anything he needed, nor how he would tell her if he did. He moved his head in acknowledgment and watched her and her bodyguard exit the room, slamming the metal door shut and engaging the locking mechanism. Everything seemed amplified in this small room. Allen didn't care. He just turned his head facing the ceiling, closed his eyes, and was immediately back in his living room with Kim and Olivia.

"Unlike you, Al, a shotgun can go off more than once a month," Kim said, doing one of her best Peg one-liners.

"Mom!" Olivia yelled, "That is totally inappropriate."

"Hahahahahaha," Allen laughed, then grabbed Kim. "Let's take this upstairs, and I bet I can beat that old double-barreled shotgun…"

"Phew…" Olivia interrupted him before he could finish.

"Are you sure this is the conversation you want to have with your very impressionable young daughter in the room?"

"Well, come to think of it, we haven't had the birds and bees talk yet," Allen said, winking at Kim.

Not intimidated by her dad's response, Olivia replied, "I think I should be the one giving you two sick-o's a talk."

Allen and Kim laughed, then jumped on Olivia and rolled around the living room floor, yelling, "The tickle monster is after you." It was just another usual day in the Schultz house.

Allen opened his eyes with a huge smile on his face. He had nothing but great memories. "*I hope they aren't worrying about me.*" he thought. "*I didn't have time to get word to them that I'd be out for a while.*" The medication had him so mellow that even the worrisome thoughts were not upsetting.

Dr. Billawitz knocked on the door, unlocked the mechanism, and opened the loud door to walk in. "Good afternoon," was his greeting to Allen. "I hope you were able to get some sleep and rest. I gave you a sedative that should have made sleeping much easier. If not, let me know so I can look at a different prescription." Allen shook his head in acknowledgment.

"You're probably a little confused about where you're at and why," Dr. Billawitz began. "I know that sometimes things can become overwhelming, especially waking up in a strange place. So, let me fill you in. Last night, per your request, I came to your house to see your daughter and wife. They never materialized. When I began questioning you about it, you became extremely agitated and a threat to yourself and everyone around you, so I called to sedate you on site."

"This isn't the normal routine; I'd prefer you walk in on your own so that we can explain everything as it happened. I know you're confused and probably distrust me and my staff. That is completely normal and understandable. In time, you'll realize we're here to help you."

Allen just laid there and listened, no emotions, no feelings.

"I'll be back to check on you this evening. Until then, the nurse and orderlies will make you comfortable."

When Doctor Billawitz returned to his office, Bill and Carol were waiting on him. "Please come in," he said as he opened the office door. "I've just come from Allen's room, and he is doing as expected."

"When can we see him and explain why we did this?" Carol asked.

"Not for at least three to four weeks," he responded. "We're dealing with a very delicate situation. Allen is suffering from a form of Schizophrenia. Until we can better handle the depth of his affliction, we need to isolate him from outside influences for a short while."

"I don't understand," Bill questioned, "He doesn't seem to be a danger to himself or anyone. He lives in a delusional world, but I can't see where it's affecting anyone."

"Based on what I've seen and been told, Allen does present a danger to himself," Billawitz responded.

"What do you mean?" Kim asked.

"You both mentioned that Allen has lost a lot of weight. You also told me there was no food in the house. Yet, Allen believes he's eating breakfast and dinner at home and taking leftovers to work," Billawitz stated. "Allen believes his wife Kim is cooking for him and that he is eating with Kim and Olivia. Correct?"

"Yes, that's what he told me," Bill answered.

"In Allen's mind, he is eating three meals a day, yet there is no evidence that he's actually had any food. I believe the meals he states he eats are part of his delusion. I've ordered blood work to help determine his nutritional status, which will confirm or disprove my theory." Billawitz added. "We will work with him to get his nutritional behaviors corrected."

"We need to determine the level of Schizophrenia that Allen is experiencing. If it's strictly delusions, we have a good chance of recovery with psychotherapy and antipsychotic medication. If his level…"

"What do you mean by a good chance? Do you think this will worsen or be a lifetime diagnosis?" Carol asked.

"Studies show that patients with only delusions can be treated and have a 50% recovery rate. Antipsychotic medications would be a lifetime requirement to ensure his delusions do not return."

"How long do you think it will take to stabilize Allen so he can come home?" Bill queried.

"That is too hard to tell. It will take a few months before we know what level of medication works best for Allen. His psychotherapy plays a big role as well. Even if we get his medication levels adjusted, without his understanding of why he's taking them, there's a high probability that his condition will return. It is very difficult to treat a delusional disorder. It will take time to gain his trust. His brain believes Kim and Olivia are still alive. He will believe that we are manipulating both him and the facts. Distrust is common. We have to be careful how we approach his specific condition. Allen firmly believes his delusions are real. We can't dispute or correct his beliefs as they are real to him. Doing so will cause him to be frustrated and further agitated. He may even shut everyone out of his life. We will start with short-term goals of gaining his trust and adjusting his medication levels. We will build on these goals."

"How do we let him know we love and miss him?" Carol asked.

"Right now, his mental capabilities are being altered with the antipsychotic drugs. His ability to feel love, loneliness, time, etc., is diminished. He will continue to know who you are but not realize how long it's been since he's seen you," Billawitz explained.

"Can we at least get regular updates on his progress?" Bill asked.

"Yes," Billawitz stated, "I will have Stacy, Allen's nurse, or her aid provide a weekly summary of his condition. I'll call you if there are any significant changes."

Bill was still in a state of disbelief. Carol held back her tears but had a tissue in her hand in case of failure. "Thank you, Doctor," Bill said, then motioned for Carol to stand and join him. They shook Billawitz's hand and left.

Four weeks crept by at a snail's pace. The weekly updates were informative but not really positive. It's been pretty much status quo. Carol blamed herself for him being there. "Bill, I wish we had done something differently. I can't imagine how he's feeling in there. He must hate us by now." Bill comforted her, reassuring her that no other alternatives would make him better.

Dr. Billawitz permitted them to see Allen the following Monday, March 14th. He also provided a reminder, "Remember that Allen has lost some contact with reality. He continues to have hallucinations, seeing and hearing things others do not. The delusions in his brain are real to him. Providing conflicting information will only agitate him."

They arrived promptly at 0900. Bill and Carol were

escorted into a room used for activities and meals. They saw Allen sitting at a table reading a book. "Allen," Carol screamed out. He raised his head and smiled, then stood to greet them as they got closer. "It is so good to see you," Carol said. "How have you been?"

"I'm doing good. The food here's not as good as Kim's cooking, but it's edible," he said. "I've been doing a lot of reading; I find computer technology fascinating."

"What are you reading now?" Bill asked.

"This book is about computer fraud and the damages that can be caused by it. The staff has also subscribed to a couple of technology magazines. Did you know that a man named Steve Jobs is revolutionizing the computer industry? I can see that computers are not your thing, so I won't blab on about them." Allen said apologetically.

"How have you two been doing?" Allen asked.

"It's been difficult at home. Bill is as ornery as ever, so I get no rest," Carol said with a smile. "Actually, things are getting back to normal. We go out to dinner, watch high school sports, maybe a movie now and then. You know, standard old folk things," Allen smiled.

Bill and Carol would see Allen twice a month for the next several months, each time with basically the same conversations. Dr. Billawitz had no end date in sight. "I'm sorry, but Allen's not responding to therapy," he stated. "We've been looking at newer medications to see if these will help. It's a very time-consuming process, weaning him off one med, then introducing his body to a different one."

Several months later in April 1989, there was a breakthrough. Allen was responding to the meds and treatment. "Good morning, Allen," Billawitz said. "How are you feeling today?"

"Actually, I'm feeling pretty good," he said. "I've been studying computers and information technology and have found a new passion."

"That's great news. I'm glad to see you with this much enthusiasm," Billawitz said. "I read the notes from your therapy session yesterday. It seems you've been discussing Acapulco lately."

"Yes," he said as his tone shifted from enthused to sadness. "I started remembering things, especially our time there."

"That's good that you can remember and deal with everything that happened," Billawitz said, trying to ease into the conversation. The alarm sounded for a patient emergency before they could get into a healthy discussion. "I'm sorry, Allen, I must go now. I'll be back as soon as I can." Dr. Billawitz said as he rushed out the door.

CHAPTER 23

The Accomplish (14 April 1989)

Allen has been keeping a secret from the doctor. He's been palming his medication. Then, once he's in the clear, he throws the pills in the toilet. Since stopping the meds, Allen's head has been clearer, and he can think, rationalize, and understand complex issues, which has really paid off while reading his technology literature. The thing that he thinks about most is Olivia and Acapulco. With a clear mind, he realizes that Oliva and Kim have passed. He also realized that there were clues that he missed and started second-guessing the events.

Allen continued to hear the commotion going on in the activity room. He laid down, looking at the ceiling, his mind deeply involved with the events as he knew them. Why was the Embassy so helpful? How did the helicopter really go down? What was the cause listed in the accident report? Why was the hotel so accommodating? Something was going on that he was too blind to see. So many questions, and now that he has a clear head and a quiet place to think and plan, he begins to lay out a course for obtaining the truth surrounding the events of 3 November 1985.

Allen has always been an intelligent man. He knows the steps he needs to follow, so now he just needs to get access to a computer or other means of communication to submit his request for information. Deep in thought, he was startled when he heard a knock on the door, followed by the clanging of the latch and door.

"What a pleasant surprise," Allen said as Stacy entered the room.

"What's that supposed to mean?" Stacy responded.

"Well, I was expecting Dr. Billawitz, but you are a much better alternative," Allen said with a smile.

Allen enjoyed Stacy's company. She was sweet and not too bad on the eyes, either. She had shoulder-length blond hair, stood about 5 feet, 9 inches, and had a very fit body. You can see the tone in her arms.

"The medications must be really helping," she said. "You are laughing and making jokes. I like that."

"Please keep this between us. I don't want to be released just yet," Allen begged. "I have things I need to plan, and I don't need the distractions of the real world… at least not yet."

"You know I'm supposed to tell Dr. Billawitz everything, right?" Stacy admonished. "What is it that's so important that you'd rather be committed than free?"

Allen knows what he says next could jeopardize his plans, but he realizes he needs an ally on the inside. He doesn't want anyone else to know that he's looking into something that could have profound political implications.

"Stacy, we've known each other for some time, mostly with me drugged and unable to think or speak clearly. I need to know that you will hear me out before you make any decisions. I need you to trust me," Allen pleaded with her.

"I'm a bit confused," she started. "I've had many patients try to bamboozle me into helping them with one scheme or another over the years. I didn't help them, so what makes your request any different."

"My name is Allen James Schultz. I was born on 18 January 1950. Today is Friday, April 14th. Your taxes are due on Monday, April 17th. Shall I continue?" Allen asked.

"Ok, I see that you're very coherent. But what is the secret that you need my help with."

"This will take a bit, so please sit on the bed next to me."

Stacy looks at him with a suspicious smile. "Is all of this just so you can get me into bed?" she asked.

"Some day maybe, but not today." He replied. "I'm not sure how much you know about my history, so I will give you a brief recap. I was married to Kim Parson. We had a daughter, Olivia. I talked them into a family vacation to Acapulco, where my daughter was kidnapped and killed. My wife never got over it and committed suicide a year later."

Stacy looked shocked, "You remember all of this? You don't believe that Olivia and Kim are alive and at home waiting for you?" she asked.

"I've been palming my meds for the last three weeks and becoming more coherent each day. And, yes, I realize my family is gone," he said sadly. "I also realize that many things that happened in Mexico don't seem right."

"What do you mean?" Stacy asked

"I've used the last couple of weeks to replay the events that happened in Acapulco over and over in my mind. Many things don't add up."

"How so?"

"That's all I can tell you until I get your word that this information will remain between the two of us."

"I want to believe you, but I need to know more and also what you want me to do before I make a decision," she responded.

"All I need you to do is to mail a couple of letters for me."

"Keep going," she said.

Allen pondered his impulse to tell her everything. If he does and his theory that it's a government cover-up, she could be in danger.

"I believe that the events surrounding my daughter's death didn't happen the way I was led to believe. If I tell you more, it could put you in danger, as you'd be the only one who knows what I'm doing."

"So, all you need is for me to mail a couple of letters for you?"

"Forms, actually. I need you to mail a couple of FOIA forms to government agencies requesting the release of information surrounding specific events." Allen gave her the information without being specific.

"And how will my mailing the FOIA forms put me in danger?" she asked.

"That's all I want to say for now. If you agree to assist me, I can tell you more, but the less you know, the better."

"Let me think about it, and I'll let you know tomorrow."

"Please promise me you won't mention our conversation to anyone," Allen begged.

Stacy looked at him and said, "I promise."

When Stacy returned to her desk, she thought about what Allen had said. Could there be any truth to his beliefs, or is he still suffering from delusions, she thought. She read through his files, and when she got home, she started looking for old news stories. The ones that came up in the U.S. were pretty bland and didn't contain much information. However, she found an article about señor Mendez's crash with more details and theories that provided some creed to Allen's beliefs. Now she's interested as to what could have happened.

The next morning, she walked into Allen's room and said, "Okay, I'll mail the forms for you, but first, I want to know the rest of the story. I promise that this conversation will never leave this room."

Stacy kept her word. She mailed the two Freedom of Information Act (FOIA) requests; unfortunately, they both came back disapproved. She sent a request to the Forward Operating Base (FOB), but it was denied again like the others. "If there were nothing to hide, I would expect to at least get something back, even if it was redacted," Allen said to Stacy.

Although there was no record, he recalls Deputy Wilson telling him that the rescue vehicle was following the helicopter. Why would you do this unless you expected something to happen?

"I haven't been completely honest with you," Stacy began, "I went home after your initial request for my assistance and researched all I could about the Acapulco accident. A couple of articles from international writers laid grounds for suspicion on the helicopter crash."

"What do you mean?" Allen asked.

"One article referenced witnesses that swear there was an explosion; then the helicopter fell to the ocean in two pieces."

"That contradicts the information I was given and what was printed in the U.S. papers. Was there anything else?" Allen asked.

"Yes, the witnesses said there were two rescue vehicles, and the second one was pulling bodies out of the first one.

They also heard two jets fly over immediately after the crash. I printed the articles but didn't want to bring them in here. It would raise a lot of questions if found," Stacy said.

"I agree, you did the right thing."

Allen prepared one last letter addressed to the American Embassy, c/o Deputy Ambassador John Wilson, Acapulco, Mexico.

> *John,*
>
> *A lot of things have happened since we last talked. Kim could never stop blaming herself for Olivia's death. She took her own life on the second anniversary of Olivia's passing. I've been struggling with mental issues due to these traumatic events.*
>
> *I desperately need to speak to you concerning señor Mendez and the kidnapping and murder of Olivia. I have questions that I believe you can help me find the answers to.*
>
> *You know how to reach me. Please help me understand everything.*
>
>
>
> *v/r*
>
> *Allen Schultz*
>
>

Stacy read the letter before sealing the envelope. "Do you think he'll respond?" Stacy asked.

"I don't know. I hope so. I felt like he wanted to tell us more than what he did. It was like he knew more. We were too distraught to question his actions. He went out of his way to help us out. Now, I'm wondering if it was out of guilt." Allen said.

"I think it's time that I go home. I need more resources if I'm going to get the answers I seek." Allen said to Stacy, placing his hands on her shoulders, "Thank you so much for everything you've done for me. From day one, I could tell what a sensitive and genuine person you are. After you mail this, I have two final requests."

"And what would these requests require of me?" she inquired.

"First, I'd like you to help me convince Dr. Billawitz that I have all my faculties and should be considered for discharge."

"Okay, that shouldn't be too difficult. What's the other request?" Stacy asked.

"Over the last year, you've been kind, generous, and caring to me. You never once talked down to me or made me feel less than human. My last request is that you have dinner with me within thirty days of my discharge." Allen proposed.

"You're asking me out on a date?" Stacy questioned him.

"No, not yet. I know it would be unethical for you to go out with a patient; however, when I'm no longer a patient, I'd like the opportunity to see you again."

"First things first. Let me get the envelope in the mail and talk with Billawitz."

CHAPTER 24

Traversing the Web of Lies (12 October 1989)

Allen was discharged on Tuesday, 12 October 1989. After several sessions with Dr. Billawitz and the kind words from Stacy, it was hard to find a reason to keep him. Neither he nor Stacy let on that he'd been well for quite some time.

Allen returned to the home that he shared with Kim and Olivia. Carol was gracious enough to handle the upkeep, including hiring a lawn maintenance company. Allen paid the house and cars off with the money from their insurance policy. The car they bought for Olivia's 16th birthday still sits in the garage with a giant bow and happy birthday decals all over it.

He invited Stacy for dinner a couple of weeks after his discharge, and she accepted. They hooked up several times, but Stacy knew she'd always be second to Kim and Olivia. She also knew that he was too wrapped up in finding out what really happened that he would be unable to focus on anything else... well, except anything that dealt with computers, networks, and something called "the Cloud."

Stacy was nervous but knew what she had to do. "Allen, we've been seeing each other for a couple of months, and

I really, really like you. We had a very nice time during the holidays; I joined you at Kim's parents' house for Thanksgiving. It was just the two of us for Christmas, but we watched movies you and Olivia used to watch every Christmas," Stacy started, worried that he might get upset with what followed. "I'm a bit selfish. I need to know that I have you, all of you. I want 100% of your attention when we're together. I'm starting to get feelings for you and am afraid we'll never be the couple I dream of."

Allen was sitting at the table with a cup of coffee and a slice of lemon cake, trying to take in everything Stacy said. "I understand," Allen said, knowing the next words would seem cold. He took a sip of coffee while trying to organize his thoughts, burning his lip in the process. "You don't deserve to be second to anyone. You're an amazing woman with great looks and a brain too. You're the perfect woman for someone. Unfortunately, I don't think I can be that someone right now. Stacy, I have feelings for you as well. I've had them from the moment we first met, but I'm still in love with my wife and need to find out what really happened in Mexico," Allen finished.

Stacy silently wept as Allen explained things to her. It wasn't a surprise, but she still hated to hear it. *"Allen is a good guy and doesn't want to lead me on,"* she thought. Stacy also knew that she would never be enough for him. Flooded with emotions, she walked over to Allen, placed her arms around him, and softly cried on his shoulders.

Allen did his best to comfort her. "While I'm in no shape for a long-term relationship, I would be devastated if we couldn't continue to be friends. I need you in my life," Allen whispered in her ear as he held her tight to his body.

Stacy looked up at Allen, gave him a long, passionate kiss, wiped her eyes, and headed for the door. "I'll call in a couple of weeks to check up on you. Maybe we could get coffee or something," she said.

Allen just looked at her. Standing there like a statue, he watched her walk away. "That would be very nice," he said. "I can't wait." Stacy turned back towards Allen when she got to the door. She blew him a kiss, and then she was gone. Allen spent the rest of the morning and up until evening sitting in his living room, staring into space. "I'm alone again." He said out loud to the picture of both Olivia and Kim.

Sitting there alone gave him time to think. *"How can I get the truth from these people?"* he thought. Allen knew that he needed more leverage if there was any chance of him getting the information he wanted.

He hadn't heard from Deputy Ambassador Wilson and figured he'd been blown off. If he wanted people to take him seriously, he would need to become a threat to them. Staring at the crack in the ceiling, he remembered when paint chips had fallen on Olivia one afternoon. She refused to sit at that spot from then on. Allen smiled at the memory.

Allen made a list of everything he could remember from his time in Acapulco. In his log, he wrote down every conversation he had with Deputy Wilson, Agent Thomas, and even señor Lopez. He started compiling all the documents he had from that time. He noticed that Olivia's death certificate had someone's name he didn't recognize. He couldn't remember the guy's name at the morgue, only that it wasn't the name on the certificate.

Allen looked at his watch. *"Hmm,"* he thought, *"if it's 1923 hrs here, that would make it 1723 hrs there."* He started digging for señor Lopez, the hotel manager's phone number. "*Ah, here it is,*" he thought. "*Now, let's get this investigation underway.*"

"Buenas tardes, Americano Hotel," came the voice from the other end of the line.

"May I speak to señor Lopez, por favor?" Allen asked.

"Si señor, un momento por favor."

A male voice came a few minutes later: "Hola, this is señor Lopez."

"Señor Lopez, this is Allen Schultz. I'm not sure if you remember, but my wife, daughter, and I were there a while back."

"Mr. Schultz, yes, I remember you well. How are you and your wife?"

"I'm doing okay. Unfortunately, my wife Kim passed away a little while back." Allen responded.

"I'm so sorry to hear that," señor Lopez said. "Is there anything I can do for you?"

"I'm glad you asked," Allen said. "I need to know what really happened that day. Can you help me out?"

"Si señor, what do you need," Lopez asked.

"I need the name and contact information for the coroner who did Olivia's autopsy. You know, the one who was there the day we went there to identify her. I'd also need someone who could help translate. Is that possible?" Allen asked.

"Si señor, call me back in one hour, and I should have what you need."

Allen thanked Lopez and hung up the phone. He looked at his watch, mentally noted when to call back, and took a long overdue bathroom break. Allen was biting his nails, watching the minute hand slowly circle his watch face. Finally, it was time.

When Allen called back, señor Lopez gave him all the information he had requested. Then he said, "señor Schultz, would you like to talk with him now?" Lopez asked.

"Yes! Yes, please," Allen said immediately.

"Una momento, por favor, while I get señor Cruz on the line." Allen could hear dialing and other noises coming from Lopez's end. Once señor Cruz was on the line, they talked for about 45 minutes. Allen broke down when he found out Olivia was raped. He was also told that she had burn marks on parts of her body. Cruz informed him that Olivia was deceased prior to hitting the ocean, as there was no water in her lungs. Cruz said he would send Allen a copy of the death certificate.

Allen was having a hard time maintaining his composure and understanding this new information. "*Why didn't Wilson say anything about this? He had to have known. Why would they cover this up?*" Allen had a million thoughts running through his mind. He knew he needed to find out more. He was elated when he found business cards for Agent Thomas and Deputy Ambassador Wilson buried in the piles of paperwork.

"Hola, Deputy Ambassador Wilson's office. How may I help you?" came the sweet voice from the end of the line. Allen noticed her perfect diction, even with the heavy Spanish accent.

"Hola," Allen said. "I need to speak with Deputy Wilson, please."

"Yes, sir, one minute while I transfer your call."

"Hello, this is Deputy Wilson. How can I help you?"

"John? This is Allen Schultz. How are you this afternoon?" Allen asked, trying to be sociable. "It's been a long time."

"Allen, so good to hear from you. How have you and

Kim been these last couple of years?" He asked.

"Well, not so good," Allen began. "Kim could never get over Olivia's death. She died about three years ago."

"I'm so sorry to hear that. She was a good woman."

"That's not why I called... well... it is part of the reason." Allen stammered as he tried to formulate thoughts into words. "As I go through all the paperwork, I'm finding things I wasn't aware of, or maybe I was aware of but had forgotten. Either way, I have questions to ask if you have a few minutes."

"Of course, I have time, fire away," Wilson said.

"John, I always felt that you were sincere in all of our interactions. I also felt like there was more to the story that you wanted to get out but couldn't. I was thinking about something you said the day you broke the news to us about Olivia's death."

"I was sincere in every way. And I'm sorry if you feel I misled you," Wilson responded.

"You said that a rescue vessel was following behind the helicopter. Why would there be a need for a rescue vessel unless they expected an incident with an imminent threat?" Allen asked.

"Hmmm, I don't recall my words back then or why I would say that," Wilson responded.

"I'm sure you read both the US News and the International news sources," Allen said with a more serious tone. "I've done some research and found several details from the local and international papers that have been conveniently left out of the U.S. papers."

Deputy Wilson was getting a bit agitated; Allen could hear it in his tone. "Yes, we've seen some of the things written by the local reporters, but you have to understand that, unlike the US, these reporters are not very credible," Wilson warned.

"I understand that could be the case for some data, but I've got several facts from multiple sources. Such as witnesses to the helicopter crash." Several people stated there was an explosion, then saw the helicopter fall to the ocean in two pieces, the front cabin, and the tail section," Allen pointed out.

"To the naked eye, I can understand why they may have thought that happened, but the helicopter broke apart after hitting the ocean, and all occupants died from either impact or drowning," Wilson retaliated.

"John, I'm an educated man who has had a lot of time to piece things together. I wouldn't be calling if I didn't have substantial evidence to contradict your comments." Allen replied with frustration in his voice.

"Allen, I'm sure you believe the information you have is accurate, and I would love to talk to you more about it; however, I have a meeting in two minutes and will need to run. I appreciate your call and concerns; hopefully, we can discuss this further," Wilson said as he hung up the phone, not giving Allen a chance to respond.

Before Allen could say anything, he heard a dial tone. *"Crap,"* he thought. *"He knows more than he's letting on."* Allen made a few notes from the phone call, then got up to get a beer out of the fridge. As he returned to the living room, the phone began ringing.

"Hello?"

"Allen, this is John Wilson. Can we talk for a few minutes?"

"Sure, but what about your meeting."

"There was no meeting. It's just something that's said when we need to get off the phone. I wanted to call you from my private number, one that's not being recorded." Wilson confided.

"I'm speechless," Allen responded.

"Allen, I can't tell you everything, and I'll deny telling you what I'm about to say. The actions that night were the result of a government top secret operation. Certain agencies were tracking the helicopter but had no idea that Olivia was on board. We knew that Olivia was on board but had no idea that a military operation was in progress." Wilson said apologetically. "This whole incident is classified Top Secret. I could go to jail for saying what I have," Wilson explained.

"Why? Or better yet, how did my daughter get caught up in a drug cartel and military operation? There has to be more to this story," Allen said, more confused now than when he started.

"I'm sorry, Allen, I've said too much already," Wilson replied.

I know that Olivia didn't die from drowning. I also know that she was dead before she hit the water. Her body had burn marks on it, leading the coroner to believe the aircraft had an explosion of some sort. I also know that she was raped," Allen said, burying his face into his hands.

"I will keep an eye out for credible information and pass it on. I'm planning a trip to the States sometime in the next few months. If you like, I'll swing by and take you out for drinks," Wilson said.

"Of course I would," Allen responded.

"There's one more thing I need to tell you," Wilson began, "You can't raise any red flags. People in high places are following this, and if word got out that someone outside of the operation knows something, it could be bad. Be careful who you tell this to, as it would also put their lives in danger."

Allen agreed to put his search for the truth on hold until after Wilson came to visit. He would have formulated a new list of questions for him by then.

Ambassador Wilson never came. He tried calling and leaving messages, but nothing worked.

CHAPTER 25

Back to School (8 January 1990)

Allen wanted to sign up for night classes at Youngstown State University but decided to go all in once he got there. Instead of one or two classes, he became a full-time student. He wanted to know as much about computers and the varying hardware as he could. His first semester of classes would begin on 8 January and end on 4 May 1990.

On January 8, Allen sat in his car with a hot cup of coffee. He thought back to the day he registered, *"What the fuck was I thinking? I'm not going to survive with a sixteen-credit workload."* His eagerness to learn may have bit him in the ass. On Monday, Wednesday, and Friday, he had Information Technology in the morning, followed by Computer Networking in the afternoon. On Tuesday and Thursday, he had Computer Science in the morning and Database Development in the afternoon.

It was the first day of class, and Allen couldn't sleep, so he got up early, ate, made a pot of coffee, and finished two cups while he was shaving and getting ready. He poured the rest of the pot into his thermos, packed his books, and off he went. He had a primo parking spot. He sipped his coffee and looked at his watch: 0645 hours. Class doesn't start until

0800, "I've got time to review my books before I head in." It was like this most mornings. Allen was a creature of habit.

Allen's interest in technology made the classes fun. He breezed through the lessons and homework and finished the semester with a 3.85 GPA. He had a little bit of time off before his next semester, so he made a point to visit with Bill and Carol. Summer classes would begin soon, followed by fall. He kept himself busy, and the time flew by.

He finished his final semester in the Fall of 1992 and wasted no time getting his application in for graduate school. He followed that by getting his Ph.D. Seven years had passed since the first day of school, and he was already recognized for his analytical mind.

His commencement ceremony was in two weeks; Allen invited Stacy, Carol, and Bill. He had not been as close to Stacy as he wanted. Their monthly lunches continued for a couple of years but then slowly dwindled to once or twice a year. He had hoped this would be a good time to reconnect. He knew it was his fault, first with the constant distraction of wanting to know what happened in Mexico, then schoolwork and all of its demands. He had little time to himself.

On the day of the event, he waited at the stadium entrance for everyone to show up. Carol and Bill were the first to arrive. Allen escorted them to a private reception area that he and a couple of other graduates had arranged. "I'm so glad you could make it," Allen said to them.

"We wouldn't have missed this for the world," Bill replied.

Carol added, "You're like a son to us. Seeing how focused you've been these last few years is a blessing. This is your day in the spotlight, and we wanted to be here to witness it."

"I'm waiting on another guest, so I'd better return to the entrance," Allen said hurriedly, and then off he went.

Allen had been back at the gate for about 7 or 8 minutes when he spotted Stacy. "*Wow,*" he thought, "*She's more beautiful now than ever.*" As she got closer, he noticed a man walking with her. 'What? She brought a date to my commencement?' he wondered. He approached her and said, "I'm so glad you could make it. Because of you, I dedicated the last few years here."

Stacy smiled and said, "Do we call you Doctor now?" She hugged him. Allen didn't want to let go but still wondered about the gentleman with her.

"So, who is your plus one?" looking at the nice-looking man beside her.

"This my husband, Alex," Stacy said, "Alex, this is Allen."

"You're the infamous Allen," Alex said, "You wouldn't believe how much she goes on and on about you.

Allen was still in shock. Why didn't she tell me about him? Why would she let me learn of it on my graduation day? "I'm sorry," Allen said, a bit self-conscious about the long delay in his response, "My mind sorted went on hiatus. I didn't realize Stacy had gotten married."

Alex was speaking, but Allen couldn't focus on what he was saying. Instead, he watched Stacy, who was standing behind Alex. She could tell he was confused and hurt. She mouthed, "I'm sorry." Allen nodded.

"I'm so glad you both could make it. I have a private reception area, so please follow me." He turned and began walking towards the tent. When he arrived, he began introducing them, "Mom, this is…"

"You don't have to introduce that woman. Come here, Stacy, and give me a hug. It's been ages since I've seen you." They embraced and said a few quiet words before letting each other go.

"Carol," Stacy began, "This is my husband, Alex."

"Nice to meet you, Alex. You've found yourself a remarkable woman in this girl right here."

While Alex was trapped talking with Carol, Allen escorted Stacy over to the refreshments. "I'm not supposed to have alcohol, so be careful. Some of these drinks may taste funny." Allen warned.

"I'm so sorry. I should have called you and told you about Alex. I wasn't going to bring him, but he got upset thinking I still had a thing for you, so I had to bring him," Stacy said.

"So, do you?" Allen asked.

"Do I what?" she questioned.

"Do you still have a thing for me?"

Before she could answer, Alex rejoined them. "Wow, your mom is so sweet. She has such amazing stories," Alex said.

"Yeah, sometimes she gets on a roll and…"

The loudspeaker interrupted Allen: "All graduates, please report to the assembly area."

"I'm sorry, I have to go. Maybe we can talk after the ceremony." Allen said. "Do you know where your seats are?"

"You go," Stacy said, "We'll be able to find our seats." Allen blew her a kiss and ran off. Stacy and Alex walked over to Bill and Carol. "Shall we head to our seats?" Stacy asked.

CHAPTER 26

Don't Mind Me (23 April 1997)

Allen's knowledge of how computers operate, programming, code, etc., was just what the industry sought. Unfortunately for them, Allen wasn't interested in working for another business. He had bigger fish to fry. So, he bypassed all the job offers and found a research team looking for a qualified programmer. It's not the position he wanted, but at least he has his foot in the door.

Allen rose quickly to the top. He was placed in charge of the Data Analytics team. In his spare time, he worked on Artificial Intelligence (AI). He had presented his theories to a couple of people, but they felt his ideas were too farfetched. No one wanted to embark on a journey that was surely destined for failure.

Allen believed that he could create a virtual world inhabited by humans with the right technology. He started very small, designing a world around a hamster cage. He brought his programming to life by projecting it to the area around the cage. He added an exercise wheel, followed by a couple of other hamsters. Over time, the original hamster accepted the AI companions. He even used the AI wheel, or at least he thought he was using it.

Allen gradually expanded his experiment, making it larger and more complex. He brought larger animals, like rabbits, cats, and small dogs. He had a CCTV system set up so that he could watch the alternate world without physically being there in the building. He could study the AI from afar, take notes, and implement his notes the following day.

A year or so had passed, and progress was slow…, but there was progress. Allen felt he was far enough along to bring in the military and a couple of Defense Department personnel and their contractors for a demonstration. For Allen, it wasn't about making money. It was about making history.

When the day came, Allen had everything set. He'd run through the scenario a dozen times. He was ready. "Good morning ladies and gentlemen. I hope your Wednesday morning has been pleasant so far. Please come into the viewing area. We have coffee and doughnuts. Help yourself." The chairs were set up in a quarter-moon configuration. Allen wanted to be able to see everyone. The back wall was bare. It didn't really need anything. It was built with local rocks and then covered with polyurethane.

To the group's left was a six-foot-tall wooden Indian with real feathers on his headdress. Next to the Indian was an antique roll-top desk with the same wood as the Indian. On the ceiling was a six-foot skylight that amplified the sound of falling rain.

Once everyone was seated, Allen walked over in front of the group, stood silently, looked around the room, and then back at them. "Have you ever wondered how far you can stretch reality? What would make you question the things before you?" he began. "At what point do you question if reality is real? Do you believe it's possible to create an alternate reality all around you? How would you know?"

Everyone was looking at each other, wondering why they were there. One of the gentlemen had had enough. "Is this going to be some type of Houdini act you're putting on?"

"Not at all. Everything you hear and see here today is real, at least to your brain," Allen responded.

"I've heard enough. You promised groundbreaking technology that will change the way leaders think. This is nothing but a circus sideshow." He got up and walked to the door with two others.

"Before you go, let me give you an example…" Allen started.

"No, thank you. I've heard enough," he said as he walked around the corner to the door. "Where's the door? I could swear it was here." The other two agreed.

"How did you move the door? This has to be some type of illusion."

"This was just a minuscule example of what I want to show you today. Please have a seat and let me continue; I guarantee you won't be disappointed," Allen continued.

"Does everyone hear the rain pinging down on the skylight above?" Allen asked. He looked around, and everyone was nodding their head yes. Has anyone wondered why it would be raining when the sun was shining when you walked in?"

"That could be as simple as hooking up a sprinkler on the roof," one of the men yelled.

"That's correct, but have any of you wondered how I have a skylight on the first floor of a seven-floor building?" Allen asked.

They all shook their head, then looked back up to see if they could figure it out. "It's gone," one of them shouted. "It was there just a couple of minutes ago."

"Let me finish my presentation, and I'll explain everything," Allen pleaded. He had piqued their curiosity. "The powers of observation are very important for many people. Can anyone tell me something about the wall behind you without looking?"

"It's a stone wall," one yelled out.

"The stones are shiny as if they have been polished or shellacked," another one said.

Allen puts his hand on his chin, then asks, "Do the rest of you agree with their observations?" They shook their heads yes.

"Well, why don't you turn around and take a look?" Allen directed.

"Where did it go?" a young lady from the Air Force asked. "What happened to the wall?"

"Another example of what I'm talking about," Allen said. "Why don't you…" Allen was in mid-sentence when a young naked woman came running through the door screaming, "Please help, he's after me." A USAF Captain ran towards her. A Major ran towards the door to stop whatever threat the woman was running from.

The Captain took off his jacket and was getting ready to wrap the woman when a large man burst through the partially opened door, knocking the Major to the ground and firing one fatal shot to the chest. He then pointed the gun at the naked lady and said, "Take this bitch," and then pumped out three rounds before the others could stop him. The lady fell to the floor, gasping for air. One of the bullets must have pierced her lungs.

The Captain and three visitors tried their best, but there was too much blood. One of the other bullets must have hit an artery. One was putting direct pressure on the wounds.

One was managing her airway. The other was prepped to start CPR if needed. Someone from the viewing room yelled out that he had called the police.

"She's gone." Came the tearful words from the lady prepped to do CPR. Blood was coming from her nose and ears. Allen walked over and checked her out. He removed a sheet covering an antique chair and put it over the young lady's blood-soaked body.

The gunman had been subdued, tied up, and placed in the closet. When the police arrived, they had everyone move back into the viewing room and be seated. The paramedics came rushing in and went over to the body on the floor, pulled the sheet off her, and stood up pissed. "Whose idea of a joke was this?"

Everyone looked at the body under the sheet. "She's gone!" someone yelled. Instead, it was the wooden Indian statue.

The Captain informed the police that his wingman was shot and killed. He then said, "The killer is tied up and locked in the closet." But when the police opened the closet door, they were shocked when they saw a petite young lady bound and gagged.

"Don't you think this is overkill? That's a lot of rope for this young lady," the officer said.

"What do you mean by "young lady?" We put a very stout man in there."

Everyone had gathered at the door and observed the lady coming out of the closet, puzzled at the chain of events. "I don't understand. I saw him put a man in there," the Captain said.

The police officer informed everyone to return to the viewing room and have a seat. "We're going to need to ask you a few questions."

They were in shock as they turned to walk back to the viewing room. It looked like an old warehouse with crates, cobwebs, etc. "What happened to everything?" a young lady asked.

They turned back towards Allen and noticed the police, paramedics, and the girl were gone. Two of them ran out to see if they could catch the officers before they left. They were nowhere to be found.

When the two heroes returned, they were not alone. The Major was with them, confused and disoriented. Allen asked for everyone to be seated.

"What you think you saw here today never happened. There was no shooting, no naked lady, no coffee and doughnuts. If you could please indulge me for a few minutes, I'd like to play back what happened. The audience got quiet, with their eyes glued to the two large screens that were being lowered from the ceiling. Each screen with four video insets to give eight views of what happened.

"This is you when you entered the studio this morning. You can see a few of you helping yourself to coffee and doughnuts. I believe one of you thought you burnt your lip."

"This can't be real. It's showing us alright, but everything else is wrong," the young lady said.

"Again, please bear with me as I fast forward to when you think you saw a killing," Allen said.

"What do you mean? We all saw that young lady run in here. We saw her fall to the floor."

"Look up at monitors," Allen instructed, "This is all of you running to aid or hide."

"It looks like we're performing medical procedures on thin air," the Captain said.

"No one was injured today. Everything you thought you saw was in your mind. I've discovered a way to change reality, placing one or a hundred and one people into a scenario of my choosing..." Allen was cut off by one of his guests.

"Where did the coffee and doughnuts go?" he asked.

"They were part of the illusion," Allen said.

"That's impossible. I ate one of the doughnuts and recall how strong the coffee was. They were real."

"I'm afraid not," Allen said. "The technology I've built can make you think you have food and drink and signal the brain with any flavor, texture, or taste."

"The implications of my theory, er, my work, could be far-reaching. Can you imagine how the prison system would be if you could control what the inmates think, see and hear? The rehabilitation methods could be limitless."

"What about on the battlefield?" Allen continued. "Can you imagine the implications if you can control the thoughts of your enemy?"

"You've got our attention Mr. Schultz," came a voice from the back. It was one of the Department of Defense (DoD) executives. "I'd like to suggest a ten-minute pause before you continue. My associates and I would like to have a few words with you before you go much further."

"That's a great idea. Everyone, please take ten minutes. You'll find real doughnuts in the kitchen, as well as freshly brewed coffee."

"Can we go somewhere and speak privately?" the DoD Exec said quietly.

Allen led the four of them to an empty office. "So, gentlemen, what do you think of my project?"

"That's just it; your project has us really thinking, and frankly, it worries us," General Steuben replied. This is Deputy Secretary of Defense, the Honorable Russel McComb, and I believe he has a few words for you.

"Mr. Schultz, I am truly amazed by what you have demonstrated today. I agree with your comments 100 percent. This technology can change the course of war. It could also change the course of the world if this got out to one of our adversaries." McComb continued. "I don't know how you made this happen, and frankly, I'm hoping no one but you knows at this point."

Getting worried about where this conversation is going, Allen replied, "Sir, this technology has been years in the making. My associates at the department know of it but not how it works. At least not down to the minuscular level."

"That's good," Hon McCombs said, "I'd like you to return to the viewing room and open the floor up for questions, followed by concluding the demonstration. Afterward, we'll talk some more." Mr. McCombs said. "Try not to be obvious about the ending. Make it seem like a normal spot to close this event out.

"Yes, Sir," Allen replied and then walked back into the room with the rest of the attendees. "Welcome back. I hope you had a chance to freshen up and grab some coffee and doughnuts." Everyone smiled, then looked around to make sure nothing else was happening.

"Hahahaha," Allen laughed out loud. "I'm glad you're on your toes. Unfortunately, there are no more events planned for today. For the next 30 or 40 minutes, I'd like to have an open forum where you can ask me questions. I will answer as much as I can, but don't expect me to divulge any secrets about how I made this happen," Allen said with a big smile on his face.

Several members of the audience were talking among themselves, then a young man stood up. "Sir, what you've shown here today is unbelievable. We can only imagine the amount of research you've put into this. My question has to do with motivation. Your invention has the ability to negatively impact entire continents of people. If it got into the wrong hands, the world could be held hostage to its powers. What motivated you to pursue a technology this powerful?"

Allen thought about it for a few minutes. Does he tell them the truth about how he wants to use it to find out what happened to his daughter or to seek revenge for those behind her death? "That's a very good question. I wasn't expecting a philosophical question today," Allen opened. "Can you imagine how many criminals we could get off the street with this? You bring a couple in for questioning and then totally immerse them into a psychological session of questioning. Their brains would be acting at up to ten times its normal rate. In a matter of minutes, you'll have them confessing to things you never could imagine. Giving you anything you want." There would be no more torture, no marks, no physical pain. That's just the tip of the iceberg, but it was the tip that got me interested in this technology."

Allen answered several more questions and then announced that the time was up for today. "Remember, you all signed a NDA upon arrival. This event must remain a secret until it has maturated to its intended state."

Everyone left except the DoD entourage. "Well, now, I'm sure you have a few more things you want to tell me, so go for it," Allen said, poking the bear right in the belly.

"I have only one request." Mr. McComb said. "I need you to cease all further development of this technology until I have spoken with the JCS."

"JCS?" Allen questioned.

"The Joint Chiefs of Staff," General Steuben responded. Allen agreed, and they proceeded to leave. '*Good thing I had my fingers crossed.*' Allen thought.

CHAPTER 27

The Letter
(23 June 1997)

A couple of months had passed since the very successful demonstration. There were several follow-up messages from the attendees, not including the DoD. Only vague responses were given.

Allen had achieved validation. The DoD's reaction was all it took. Now, it was time to go dark.

He decided to move his experiment to a more isolated location and cut ties with the research company he worked for. This was his plan all along, as he'd been procuring the equipment he needed for a couple of years. The move would allow him to continue his research unrestricted, with no oversight.

Sitting at his desk, a montage of photos started appearing on his laptop's screen saver. He began to reminisce about a time when he enjoyed living—when laughter was common. Then, a picture of Olivia popped up. It reminded him of why he started this line of research in the first place.

Before he could continue his trip down memory lane, the phone rang. "Hello," Allen answered.

"Hi, hon, are you busy tonight?" came a voice Allen knew all too well.

"Not at all, Mom. What do you have in mind?"

"Bill picked up three steaks at the Giant Eagle and wanted to know if you'd like to join us for dinner," Carol said

"Well, it has been ages since we've grilled out. So yes, I'd love to come over tonight. What time?"

"Why don't you get here around 5 p.m.? I'll have a pitcher of Margaritas ready. You and Bill can chill and grill, as he calls it."

"That sounds like a plan. What do you need me to bring?"

"Nothing at all, hon. We have everything, including dessert."

"Fantastic, Mom. I'll see you around five."

This ought to be fun. I like hanging out with Bill. He's such a trip. I'll pick up a few drinks to supplement the margaritas with. I might also grab another dessert just to poke a jab at Mom.

As he settled back down at his desk, the laptop's pictures were still rotating, reminding him of what he was thinking. He started this research to get to the truth about what happened in Mexico. If he could deploy his technology in a certain area, he would be able to seek out those that were involved. He could question them without them knowing what he was doing. It all came down to the names he had on his list—Agent Thomas, Deputy Wilson, señor Lopez, and, of course, Ambassador Taylor.

It's been quite some time since Allen had attempted to contact Deputy Ambassador Wilson. The last few attempts have netted him no leads. It seems Taylor has moved on from this position and now resides in a small town in Utah. There's been no word on Wilson or where he might have moved on.

The phone rang again. "Hello?"

"It's me again. I'm sorry to keep bothering you. Can you bring a bottle of tequila with you? I just checked, and we're all out."

"Sure thing, Mom. See you in a couple of hours."

Allen hung up the phone, then stood and made his way to the bathroom. As he took a leak, he heard the neighbor's dog barking. He glanced at his watch. "Yep, that must be Harry, the mailman. Wonder what great news he brings today." Allen sarcastically pondered out loud. A quick shake or two, flush, zip, and he's ready to get the mail.

"Harry must hate me today. There must be five pounds of mail for me alone," he thought. Allen proceeded back to his desk, plopped the stack of bills, letters, and advertising on the desk in front of him, and began sorting. Bills in the pile on the left, letters on the pile in front of him, and advertisements go straight to the trash bin. *"It's not a technical system,"* he thought, but it sure makes life easier. Then he came across a manila envelope from the American Embassy. For some reason, he had a flash of anxiety. Looking at the envelope and thinking about what it might contain made him panic. He set the envelope down on the right side of the desk and stared at it for a couple of minutes. He couldn't bring himself to open it.

Allen took a deep breath, went to the fridge to grab a beer, and returned to the desk. The damn envelope was still there, staring at him. He pretended to ignore it and went back to sorting the mail, occasionally getting a glance of it out of the corner of his eye. Finally, everything was where it needed to reside. He started with the bills, opening each and looking at the information inside. He'd write the amount and date due on the outside of the envelope, then do the same for the next one, and so on.

He looked to his right, and the envelope was still there. Nothing good is going to be in there. If I open it now, it will ruin my entire evening. If I open it tonight, I never get to sleep. He placed it back down and went through the rest of the pile. Once done, it was just the two of them. Allen got up, walked around the house several times, then returned to the desk. It was calling him. "Okay, I'll open you," Allen shouted at the envelope.

Allen slowly stuck his finger in-between the flap and the sticky portion and ripped the envelope open at the seam. He peered inside and saw several sheets of paper. He brought out the first one. It was an official notice of the death of Deputy Ambassador Wilson, with his obituary at the bottom. Reading on, he noticed the date of death was a few years back. "Why am I getting this now?" he wondered.

He pulled out the next page. It was a log of all Allen's phone calls and messages, with a paragraph at the bottom that read. "We're deeply sorry for the extreme delay in providing you answers to the questions in your correspondence. Our intention was to forward them directly to Deputy Wilson; however, they never made it. When the package was returned, an intern mistakenly filed it, where it has sat for several years.

Allen brought out the rest of the pages, including an envelope that was addressed to him, with Deputy Wilson's return address. He opened it to reveal a handwritten letter dated a few days after their last conversation.

Dear Mr. Schultz,

My apologies for not getting back to you sooner. It's been a little hectic down here. After our conversation, the coroner you spoke with turned up missing. There was an envelope in his procession that contained Olivia's death certificate. It was turned over to the Embassy, where I was able to secure it for you. It would only be speculation, so I'll refrain from my thoughts on what happened.

This whole incident has led me to rethink my role in life. What happened to your daughter was horrific and could have been prevented. Unfortunately, that information is classified at this time, so I can't delve into it.

Another U.S. Agency called out the rescue vessels you referred to. Two crew members died on the first one trying to recover the bodies. There was one survivor who is still on Active Duty. The names of the individuals on the other vessel were not disclosed.

I intended to relay all the details during our discussion after Olivia passed; however, due to the sensitivity of the data, I was directed to provide only the basic info. My deepest apologies.

While I can't discuss the events that happened, I can give you information that will aid in your search for answers. There are four agencies you should be in contact with once the declassification of the information has been declared. The documents I saw had a Declassify date of 1 October 2000. I know that's still a ways off. But, once it's declassified, you can request the documents via the Freedom of Information Act (FOIA).

Send separate requests to the Justice Department, to the attention of Foreign Affairs, the CIA, the DEA, and the American Embassy here in Acapulco. Ask for the release of *data surrounding the 1-10 October 1985 events. Use the CODE NAME: "Snowman" in your request.*

I pray you stay safe and continue on your path to mental stability. I will contact you again if anything comes up on this end.

Sincerely,
John Wilson

After reading the letter, Allen emptied the envelope. Out came a few more pages of notes and a sealed envelope with "To the attention of Mr. Allen Schultz" written outside. Allen's heart rate increased; beads of sweat started to form on his forehead. *"If this is the death certificate, do I really want to know how she died? Can I handle it?"* Allen was confused. He wanted to know but was worried that it would be more than he could handle.

He sat it down and started reading the other pages of notes that Wilson had sent. Allen couldn't focus. The uncertainty of what the death certificate and autopsy might reveal was overwhelming. He wanted to know what his baby girl endured. "What am I doing? It's been twelve years, and I've been ok not knowing. Do I really need to know?" Allen said out loud while looking at a picture of Kim.

Then Allen heard Kim's voice, "Knowing what is in that report could be the motivation to get to the bottom of Olivia's death. Or, it could be what was originally explained to us. Either way, you cannot live with yourself if you don't open it. Don't open it alone. You'll want someone with you, maybe with a medical background, to help you with the jargon."

"Stacy!" Allen yelled out, "She's the one that knows me, knows my story, and knows medical lingo, but I can't call her. It's been years since my graduation, the last time I saw her." Allen was having a one-sided conversation with Kim's photograph, pacing back and forth on the hardwood floors, with the sound of his footsteps getting louder and louder.

"I need a beer," Allen said to the picture frame. "First things first," he thought as he walked into the bathroom to take a leak. Allen looked at his in the mirror as he was washing his hands. *"Who is this guy?"* he thought. *"I look like my dad."* Allen was right. The last couple of years have been rough on his body. "I can't think about it anymore." Allen walked to the fridge, grabbed a beer, and then sat down on the other side of the room, as far away from the envelope as possible. Then the phone rang.

"Oh Shit!" he exclaimed. "Hello, mom, I'm so sorry. I got tied up and completely lost track of time."

"That's okay, son, just get your scrawny butt over here."

"Yes, ma'am"

"And don't forget the tequila."

"Thanks for the reminder. I'm leaving the house now." Allen rushed to get a couple of things. He found a nearly full bottle of Jose Cuervo in his cabinet. *"Great, I don't have to make a stop,"* he thought. He grabbed his keys and wallet off the counter, looked at the envelope, then turned and left the house, locking the door behind him.

"Well, it's about time you showed up." Bill nipped at Allen. "You've seriously cut into my drinking time. Now I've got to multi-task and cook too," Bill said laughingly. You just move over and let a young man show you how to cook a steak properly. Allen pulled a bottle of seasoning out of his pants pocket, then tenderizing salt from the other. "Close your eyes, Bill. You can't see my secret recipe." They both laughed.

After dinner, they sat around the fire pit. They enjoyed the evening, getting caught up on everything that was going on in both of their lives. "So, I had some tests done over at Mercy Health," Bill began. "Nothing serious, but Carol here is such a worry wart."

"What do you mean by nothing serious?" Carol yelled. "They found three clogged arteries."

"I know, I know!" Bill yelled back. "But they weren't 100% clogged. The docs said there was no need to get emergency surgery done right away, but that sometime in the future, he may need to put a stent or two in."

"Pop, why didn't you tell me this before dinner?" Allen said

"Because I knew if I did, you'd be trimming off the fat from my ribeye, and we both know that's the best part," Bill said, chuckling.

"Do you need some help with the dishes?" Allen yelled into the house.

"No, son, you enjoy the evening air, and I'll knock these out. Bill, you need to come in and take your medicine."

"Geez," said Bill. "I tell her one little thing, and suddenly, she's babying me. See if I tell her next time."

"Go take your meds, pop. I need to do a couple of things on my phone anyway."

"Will do, boy," he replied, "I may stop off at the outhouse on my way back."

Allen was alone at the fire pit, remembering the package he received that afternoon. He looked at his phone, scrolled down his list of contacts, and then stopped when he got to the name "Stacy." Maybe I'll send her a text message instead of a call.

Allen looked at the phone, trying to make up his mind. Finally, he began typing and didn't stop for several minutes. "Stacy, I apologize for the lateness of my text. I didn't know who else I could talk to. Today, I got a package from the embassy in Acapulco. One of the things inside was the death certificate and autopsy report I had asked for years ago. I couldn't bring myself to open it. I know I'm asking a lot, but would you be available sometime tomorrow to be there with me when I open it? I'll understand if you can't make it." Allen was going to sit on it for a while and reread it to make sure it sounded okay, but accidentally hit send instead of save.

Within thirty seconds, his phone pinged. It was Stacy. She replied, "Yes, of course I can be there. How about 0800? I'll stop and get coffee on the way."

"Thank you so much," Allen wrote back. That was a huge relief. Allen was so afraid she'd say no or that she was busy.

"Are you ready for some more dessert," Carol shouted out to Allen.

"No thanks, Mom, I'm probably going to head home. It's been a long and stressful day, and I'm beat."

On the way home, Allen stopped at Giant Eagle and picked up some groceries. He also picked up some flowers to brighten the place.

The next morning, Allen was up at 0600. He had shit, showered, and shaved by 0630 and had breakfast done by 0745. He recalled that Stacy likes to be early. "If you're on time, you're late." She always said. Sure enough, at 0753, there was a knock on the door. And there she stood, more beautiful than ever.

"Are you going to open the door or make me stand out here with two piping hot cups of coffee in my hands?" She said.

"I'm sorry, I was just mesmerized by the sight of you," Allen bashfully said. "Come in, please."

"What's that smell?" Stacy asked

"Oh, that must be the flowers."

"No, I smell food, jackass. You weren't supposed to cook for me."

"Well, too late now. Come on in and eat, and I'll get you up to speed on things before we open Capone's vault."

"I just hope this vault isn't empty," Stacy snickered back.

They sat down at the table directly across from each other. "Oh my God, you cooked enough food for six," said Stacy.

She was pretty much right. He made a half dozen scrambled eggs, a pound of bacon, a huge bowl of hash browns, toast, and assorted pastries. Allen held most of the conversation. He told her about the package and the letter from Wilson. He talked about his work and that he was working on a project that could be revolutionary. He wouldn't tell her what it was about, "If I tell you, I'd have to kill you." Allen said with a fake evil look on his face.

"You don't have it in you," Stacy said, laughing.

"She may be right, but at least I kept the conversation going. The last thing I wanted her to do was to talk about her life and how she and Alex were so happy, blah, blah, blah. I want this visit to just be about us." Allen thought.

"So, where's this mysterious envelope?" Stacy asked. "I'm ready to get my sleuth hat on. Detective Stacy at your ser….." She didn't finish her sentence. She saw the pain in Allen's eyes. He was terrified to read the contents, and here she was making jokes. "I'm sorry, Allen. I wasn't even thinking." She went over and put her arms around him.

"That's okay. I'm probably overreacting," Allen replied. He wanted to say, "Please stay here with your arms around me," but he didn't.

"Let's rip the bandage off and get it over with. I'll be here to help you deal with whatever comes up," Stacy assured him. "Even if it takes all night."

Allen's mind went somewhere it shouldn't, thinking, hoping, wishing she would stay the night… *"Snap out of it, you perverted jerk,"* he chastised himself for thinking inappropriate thoughts when he should be thinking about Olivia.

"I keep losing you," Stacy said. "One minute, I see a sparkle in your eyes; the next, it is doom and gloom. Do you want to talk about it?"

"Someday, but not right now." Allen softly said, touching her shoulder, "If you're ready, let's get started."

They walked over to the desk where the envelope had sat patiently for the last twelve hours. Allen had placed an extra chair by the desk in preparation for her participation. He pointed to the stack of pages he had already gone through and waited patiently for Stacy to read each one. Finally, it was down to the one remaining envelope. She picked it up and held it out in front of her. "It's time," she said, "We both know that regardless of what it says, it's going to be hard to read. This was your daughter. No parent should lose their child, especially the way you did."

Allen was shaking. He took the envelope from her hands and stared at it for a bit. Looking up at Stacy, he said, "Thank you again for being here." Like he does with all envelopes he opens, he went to one end, stuck his finger under the sealed flap, and neatly ripped the end open at the seam. He looked inside and maneuvered the death certificate out, took another deep breath, wiped his sweaty hands, and then unfolded it. Stacy watched as he read over the form.

"Well?" Stacy said with a puzzled look on her face. "What does it say?"

"Pretty much what I expected. Cause of death is listed as blunt force trauma." After talking with the coroner, he knew this would be the determination. "The coroner told me there was no water in her lungs, meaning she was dead before she hit the water."

He handed the document over to Stacy and then proceeded to remove the autopsy report. He unfolded it, and tears started to swell in his eyes. He read every word. Every description of the multitude of injuries she had from her ordeal—burns over 40% of her body, open fracture on both legs, and tears to both the vagina and anus…

Allen dropped the document. His tremors got worse. The tears were flowing a steady stream. Stacy picked up the report and read it. "Oh my God, she was brutally raped," she said without realizing she used her outside voice. "He penetrated her vagina and…" she stopped before saying it, then looked at Allen. "I'm so sorry, Allen. I didn't know." She continued to read. There were hand prints on her buttocks and back, consistent with someone slapping her really hard. Traces of fentanyl and etomidate were found in her system.

"Allen, the drugs found in her were knock-out drugs. The kind that leaves you unconscious. There's a good chance she never knew what happened to her," Stacy said, trying to comfort him. "I pray she was unconscious the whole time."

The notes say that the victim was brought in with no clothes or shoes. Why did they feel to put that in here? Stacy looks at Allen. He's turned as pale as a ghost. He's not shaking anymore. He's just sitting there with a blank look on his face. Stacy is doing everything in her power to be strong, but she makes the mistake of looking at the picture of Olivia on his desk and lost it. "How could someone do this to that poor child?" she said while bawling out of control.

"Allen stood, walked over to the sofa, sat, took his shoes off, and laid down. His worst nightmare had come true. "Mendez had defiled his baby girl. Her birthday present was torture. While I was out happily looking at property. I should have demanded she come with us. No, I should have never taken them down there in the first place. He couldn't stop the images from appearing in his head. Every possible scenario, every gruesome injury, played over and over in his mind." Allen couldn't stop thinking these horrid thoughts.

Stacy was able to compose herself. She went over and laid down with Allen. He had his wish; she was lying with him. Unfortunately, he was someplace else. It didn't even register that she was lying in his arms. They lay there for hours. Finally, Stacy got up, went to the bathroom, and then went to the kitchen to munch on leftover bacon and hash browns. She drank a glass of water, checked on Allen, and found a bed to crash on.

Allen woke to complete darkness. He looked at his watch, "*Shit, it's 3 a.m. How long have I been sleeping?*" He didn't see Stacy. "*She must have gone home while I was asleep,*" he thought. Standing, he noticed a crick in his neck from the sofa. He headed to bed, moving his head far to the right, then the left, trying to get the crick out. He quickly stopped at the bathroom, and while in mid-stream, he heard his neck pop. When he got to his bedroom, it was pitch black. He undressed and climbed into bed. Within minutes, he was fast asleep.

The summer sun came up early. The bright beams pierced through his thin bedroom curtains, turning the blackness into light. He lay there awake, still in the same position when he climbed into bed. "I'm starving," he thought. "I haven't eaten since breakfast yesterday. Good thing there were plenty of leftovers."

The sun was warming the room, so he removed the covers and laid there thinking about yesterday. He was thankful that Stacy came over and hoped she'd made it home safely. He was deep in thought when he felt something moving in the bed. He turned in time to see Stacy opening her eyes. "What the fuck…." Allen screamed.

"Nice to see you too," Stacy said, covering her mouth.

"You caught me by surprise. I wasn't expecting to have a sleepover."

"I had forgotten how nice it was to wake up next to you," Allen said.

"Well, from the look of your erection, I'd say at least part of you remembered."

"Shit, I'm sorry, I forgot I was naked."

"You seem to be forgetting a lot lately," she laughed. "Besides, it's nothing I haven't seen before. Although, it has been a few years."

Allen jumped out of bed, put the pants on the floor from yesterday back on, and disappeared into the living room. Stacy came running behind him, wearing one of his t-shirts and a pair of thong panties.

"Why did you run out so fast?" she asked.

Allen's brain was in a fog. He couldn't stop looking at her standing there. "All I thought about from the time you arrived was you and I in bed. At least until we opened the envelope," he explained. "You're a married woman…" Allen paused, thinking about what he just said, "Shit, Alex must be worried sick. He's going to be angry as hell with me. You should call and explain. I'll help."

Stacy smiled, "You don't have anything to worry about. Alex and I divorced a long time ago."

"I'm sorry, I didn't know," Allen apologized.

"Well, you would know if you hadn't been ghosting me for the last few years," Stacy said with a stern look. She took Allen's hand and said, "Come with me," leading him back to the bedroom.

CHAPTER 28

The Plan
(24 June 1997)

Allen was all smiles when he emerged from the bedroom. Stacy went straight to the shower. About fifteen minutes later, she joined him in the living room-office combination. He was sitting at his desk, looking over the paperwork from yesterday. She stood next to him, wearing nothing but a towel. He looked up at her, "You're such a beautiful woman. With your wet hair, pure face, and mesmerizing eyes. You make me happy again."

Stacy bent down and kissed him, looked at the piles of documents, and then said, "You have to do something. They can't get away with this."

"I have a plan," he said. "I've been working on something for years and am so close to perfecting it. Once I get it laid out, I'll just have to implement it."

"Don't keep me in the dark. Tell me about this technology you've created."

"I've figured out how to manipulate reality," Allen began. "Through the use of Wi-Fi and strategically placed equipment, I can send ultra high-frequency signals that can't be heard, but the brains can receive and process. I'm working on being able to direct these signals to specific individuals or groups instead of everyone. However, it's still a ways out."

"This is like a plot from a sci-fi movie," Stacy interjected.

"I know it sounds far-fetched, but I assure you, this will work. I gave a small demonstration to the government and a few military contractors a few months back, and they were in awe. The DoD directed me to halt my research, fearing what could happen if it fell into the wrong hands. After that, I moved my operations to a remote area where they couldn't regulate me."

"Holy shit," Kim shouted out. "How will this get the assholes in Mexico to come clean?"

Allen thought about it for a few minutes, then said, "If I can get the right people in a room, I can use this to control what their brains will see, hear, feel, smell, etc. I'm still a few years away from deploying it, but theoretically, it's a sound plan. The information here on my desk is the key."

"How so?" Stacy asked.

"Wilson's letter gave me the path. In two years, I'll be able to get the documents via a FOIA request. I've got names, dates, and agencies responsible for covering up Olivia's murder. I know that there were two Air Force amphibious vessels in the area. Most military operations have video and audio feeds. I'll submit a FOIA request for them too."

"Are you sure you'll be able to get everything ready by the time the FOIA documents get here?" Stacy curiously asked.

"I don't know, but I do know that I now have direction, a clear path, and the resources to make it happen," Allen explained as he looked out the window. "It's beautiful out. How would you like to go for a quick walk?"

"That sounds great, let me change, and I'll be ready."

Allen held the door open for Stacy. As he was pulling it shut, he heard the phone ring. "Aren't you going to answer it?" she asked.

"No, it's gonna be something work-related or a prank call."

"What if it isn't? What if it is something serious?" She replied.

Okay, I'll answer it," Allen replied, sounding a little annoyed. "Hello, how may I help you?"

"Allen?" came a crying woman on the other end. "This is Mom. Bill passed away."

"What? How? When?" Allen bombarded the questions one right after the other.

"Can you come over, please?"

"Yes, Mom, I'll be right there."

"Stacy, I've got to run. Bill died."

"I'm coming with you," Stacy answered back.

When they arrived, there wasn't much they could do except comfort Carol, who was sitting on the sofa crying. "Why does everyone I love have to die?" she cried. Allen sat down and put his arms around her.

"It's God's will. He has a special plan for them," Allen softly answered. Then he squeezed Carol a little tighter.

Stacy gathered Carol's clothes, toiletries, and a few other things and returned to the living room. "I've packed a few things for you. You're going to stay at my house tonight." Both Allen and Carol looked up, surprised.

"What do you mean?" Carol asked

"You need to be away from here for a couple of days. Allen has too much going on at his place, so it's best if you come and stay with me," Stacy replied. Allen smiled at her, knowing that she was right about his place and grateful that she volunteered her place without hesitation.

They met the family three days later at their church for Bill's funeral. He had a beautiful funeral with a military Honor Guard's Twenty-One Gun Salute. Allen and Stacy placed themselves on each side of Carol for physical and emotional support. A little over two weeks later, the autopsy report stated that Bill died of a heart attack due to clogged arteries. He had lied to Carol about the severity of his health; he didn't want her to worry.

Over the next few weeks, Allen spent his free time helping Carol. She wanted to stay in the house as long as possible. It was paid off, so the finances were right. It just needed some TLC to get it modernized. "Mom, you know we need to go through the attic and basement and get rid of things. There is no telling what type of retrofits this house will need once a contractor starts cutting into it. The more we have out of the way, the better."

"I know, son, it's going to be hard parting with his things."

"Mom, you don't have to get rid of everything. Don't worry, I'll help."

Over the next four months, he was there almost every evening, helping move boxes, sort memories, and anything else Carol needed. One night, they were working in the attic when Casey Kasem's Top 40 for October 1979 began playing in the background. "Come on, Mom, we need to finish before he gets to the number one song."

Kasem's first introduction was the number 40th song of the week, "Tusk" by Fleetwood Mac. Allen's head was getting into the beat. He was moving and shaking with the music. "I love this song, Mom. How can it be at #40?"

Carol sort of did the Shag with a mix of the Sprinkler as she went by. "There you go, now we're talking." Allen got up and danced with her for the rest of the song.

"I needed that," Carol said, "I'm so glad I have you in my life."

They continued sorting through the various boxes until Allen saw an Army foot locker at the bottom of a stack of boxes. "Is that what I think it is?"

"Well, it is if you think it's Bill's Army stuff," Carol replied.

They both went through the locker, filled with old uniforms, orders, tons of paperwork, and other odds and ends. "This is amazing. Everything is still in great shape," Allen commented.

"I guess I don't have much use for that anymore," Carol said depressingly. "You can take that to the Salvation Army with the other boxes if you don't mind."

"Can I have it?" Allen asked. "I love military things and would be honored to go through this someday."

"Of course, son, anything you want here, please take it," she said with drooping eyes. "I think I'm done tonight. I'm worn out."

"But mom, we're only up to number 20, "Loving, Touching Squeezing" by Journey."

"We've spent enough time up here this week. You go home and get some rest, and we'll tackle the rest of this in a day or two.

"Sure thing, Mom. Is there anything I can get you before I leave?"

"Yes, you can get me a nice warm hug, then go and call that sweet girlfriend of yours. I bet you haven't seen Stacy in weeks."

"With pleasure, and for your information, I saw her last night and again this morning," Allen said with a smile and a wink of his right eye.

He took the locker and put it into his car, then came back for one last hug. "Love you, Mom. Call if you need anything."

It would be years before Allen opened the locker again.

CHAPTER 29

The Locker
(12 April 2003)

It had been a long week, and Allen had his first Saturday off with no plans in what seemed like an eternity. Bill's foot locker had been stored away in Bill and Carol's attic for decades and then another five years of being used as a dust collector before Allen decided to do a thorough inspection of what was inside. He started by sorting and folding the old uniforms, then the dreaded task of reading each of the documents and sorting them by date and type.

He was amazed by all the accolades Bill had received during his career. There was one, from early on, that Allen really took an interest in. It was an official letter from Major General Gerald Johnston thanking him for saving his daughter's wedding. "If you ever need anything, all you have to do is ask," was handwritten at the bottom. The letter was dated 21 July 1935.

"*I'm sure the General has long since passed, but what if he has a descendent associated with the Military,*" Allen thought. "*Maybe they could help me through the red tape and push my FOIA request through.*" It had been over two years since he submitted his first Freedom of Information Act request, each being rejected numerous times.

Allen set aside everything else and went to his desk. *Maybe I can find out more about Gen Johnston on the internet.* He started with a broad search that netted him over a hundred names. He added the date of the letter and his branch of service, and the list was narrowed to about a dozen.

Over the next year, Allen would reach out to over a hundred individuals, trying to find descendants of Gen Johnston. He would write one of the names on his list. A few weeks later, the envelope would come back with either a forwarding address or a letter stating that no one at that address had heard of Gen Johnston.

Several summers later, Allen was lying in bed reading the paper when the neighbor's dog started his crazy barking again. "Harry's here," Stacy said.

Allen rolled over and kissed her. "I'll run out and get the mail when I finish the paper."

"I'm craving a cup of coffee," Stacy said as she climbed out of bed. Allen watched her naked body walk around the bed and out the bedroom door. He thought about how firm her ass was and that her body hadn't changed in all the years he's known her. About fifteen minutes later, she returned with two cups. "I placed the mail on the kitchen table."

Allen said, "Thanks, Luv," and returned to reading. He made it all the way to the Comics section before realizing that Stacy left and returned to the bedroom in the nude. "How the fuck did you get the mail bare ass naked?" he asked.

"Wouldn't you like to know," she responded. "Harry wanted me to tell you that you're a lucky guy. Poor fella, I yelled good morning, and he fell over. Most of the mail came out of his bag."

Allen was blank-faced. "*She's fucking with me. She has to be fucking with me.*" he thought. Pretending not to be jealous, he said, "You should have helped him gather up his mail."

"Oh, I did. He was so appreciative that he gave me a long hug. I think he was even crying a little," she said. "He probably had a boner too. By the way, he was hunched over as he walked away."

Allen didn't know if he should be pissed or impressed. Either way, the whole scenario had him worked up. "Come here, you little whore," he summoned. Two hours later, he emerged from the bedroom, took a quick shower, then proceeded into the kitchen to make breakfast. Stacy had fallen back to sleep, so he sat at the table with his eggs, bacon, toast, and a fresh cup of coffee. He noticed the stack of mail on the table that his naked wife had fetched earlier. He began reading through it as he ate.

Near the bottom of the stack was a handwritten address with an APO return address. He knew this meant it was from a military installation overseas. He shoved an entire strip of bacon in his mouth, then opened the letter. It was from a relative of General Johnston. Allen almost choked on his bacon.

February 27, 2003
Dear Mr. Schultz,
Please excuse the delayed response to your inquiry concerning my grandfather, General Gerald Johnston. Your letter had been sent around the world a couple of times before it found me. The wedding that your dad saved was my mother and father's. Growing up, I had heard them talk about an issue with the bakery and how your dad volunteered to bake them a cake the night before. My mom would say it turned out more beautiful and delicious than the cake they had originally ordered.

They had many fond memories of that day. It seemed like every anniversary, they'd recant the story of how mom's dad (Gen Johnston) found you. They are in their mid-70s and currently living in an assisted living facility. I would happily honor my grandfather's obligation if it's within my ability.

You briefly described how you lost your daughter and wife in your letter. First of all, my condolences on such a horrific story. You also mentioned something about FOIA requests that you needed help with. I'm not sure how I can help you, but if you send me more information and copies of the FOIAs, that will let me know which direction I need to go. My deployed address is in the sender block at the top. I will be here for four more months.

I look forward to hearing from you.

Tim
Timothy M. Preston, Lt. Colonel, USAF

Allen was ecstatic. It was a shot in the dark, but at least there was hope that his requests for information would be listened to this time. He was busy rifling through papers, getting together the documents he needed to send to Lt. Col. Preston, when Stacy walked in still naked. "I smell bacon," she said.

"I left you a plate on the stove." She walked in, poured herself a cup of coffee, grabbed her plate, then walked over to the table. "You know it's closer to lunch than breakfast, right?" She informed Allen while pointing down to the food on the plate.

Allen ignored her question and then stated, "Did you know your left tit is bigger than your right one?"

"You're an asshole. My tits are the same size."

"OK, if you say so." Allen egged her on. "Oh, and by the way, thanks for dry-humping Harry. It brought me some luck. In today's mail was a response to one of my inquiries."

"The ones you sent a few years back?" Stacy wondered.

"Yes, long story short, it's his grandson. He's in the military as well. He has offered to help. I'm putting together a few documents to send," Allen replied while studying Stacy's boobs.

Seeing where Allen's eyes were glued to, Stacy threw her fork down on the table, got up, and started to leave the room. "Where are you headed, honey?" Allen said, almost cracking up.

"To the bathroom to see what makes you think my boobs are lopsided," she angrily replied. Ten minutes later, she returned to the table wearing a T-shirt and panties. "Have I told you lately that you're an asshole?" she asked.

"Well, if you want a second opinion, you can ask Harry in the morning," Allen said nonchalantly. He had seen her housecoat draped over the sofa earlier that morning, so he knew she didn't go out there naked. Allen stood, pulled her chair out, cupped her arms, and pulled her up to him. He looked directly into her eyes.

"Stacy, I love you!"

Stacy was in shock. Throughout their relationship, he's never used the "L" word, and now, right out of the blue, he throws this on her?

"Where did that come from?" she asked.

"I know. I should have said it many moons ago, but I couldn't. I felt guilty for falling in love with another woman. I swore to Kim that she was my one and only, but I lied…" He paused a moment, then continued, "Does this make me a horrible person?"

"Not at all, and if Kim loved you as much as you loved her, I'm sure she'd want you to be happy. Are you happy?" Stacy asked.

"I am," he said.

"Now, ask me if I'm happy." Stacy came back.

"Well, are you?"

"Hell no! I've waited a long damn time for you to tell me you love me. I pictured a romantic restaurant, a stroll through the park, or during the heat of passion. But no, you say it as I sit at the kitchen table, stuffing my face with bacon."

Stacy stuffs the last strip of bacon into her mouth and storms out, turning before completely out of sight and says, "I love you too, asshole." She smiles and then closes the bathroom door. A minute or so later, he hears the shower running.

Allen finished getting the documents together and placed them in a large manila folder. "I'm going to make a quick run to the post office. When I get back, we should go out and do something," he yelled into the bathroom.

"Sounds good," she said from the shower.

CHAPTER 30

The Mailman (3 October 2003)

Allen hadn't heard from Lt. Col. Preston in quite some time; the weeks had turned into months, but nothing. "Maybe it was too much to ask of him," Allen thought. So many people had dismissed him in his attempt to learn the truth. Maybe this was one more.

Allen was feeling depressed. He had resolved that this would be another one of those false dreams. He still held a thread of hope that a miracle would happen one day, and he'd finally get the artifacts he had requested.

One Friday morning in October, while washing his car, he saw Harry, the sixty-something-year-old mailman, making his rounds. He was about three houses away when Allen called for Stacy. "Stacy, can you come out and help me with the car?"

"What kind of help do you need," she asked from an open window.

"Um…" Crap, I hadn't planned for that response. "I need you to help me check the lights." Whew, I pulled that one out of my ass, he thought.

"Sure thing, give me a minute, and I'll be out."

Stacy came out wearing her short shorts and a white

tank. Allen saw Harry headed to his neighbor's house, so he sprayed the car down again before she arrived next to him, then set the hose down.

"Come here, beautiful, and give me a hug. You look so hot today. Actually, you look like you've been sweating," he said.

"I just finished cleaning the kitchen and taking the trash out. Then I made two trips up the stairs because I forgot what I wanted the first time, so yeah, I've worked up a sweat," she replied, a little annoyed, as she hugged him.

Allen got a little frisky with her, keeping one eye peeled on Harry's whereabouts. Just as he saw him leaving the neighbor's house, he turned Stacy around and bent her over the car, pretending to hump her from behind. "What the hell are you doing? Your car is soaking wet."

"I'm sorry, babe, I was just playing around," Allen said as Harry neared. "I want you to stand in front of the car and verify when I turn my lights and signals on. Piece of cake, right?"

They were standing in front of the car when Harry made his way to their mailbox. "Good morning," Harry said.

Stacy and Allen turned around and said, "Hey, Harry," almost simultaneously. Harry's eyes almost popped out of his head, his mail bag got tangled in his legs, and he toppled over.

"Harry, are you okay?" Stacy asked as she went over to help him up.

"Uhhhh... yes, ma'am," Harry said, his eyes peeled on her chest.

"Let us help you get your mail back in your bag," Allen said after stifling his laughter and walking over.

It only took a couple of minutes to get Harry on his way again. He kept looking back and almost bit the dust again.

"What got into him?" Stacy asked.

Allen used his eyes to point down to her breasts, clearly visible from her see-through wet T-shirt. "You asshole!!! You planned this the whole time, didn't you?" Stacy said, reaching for the hose.

"Wait just a minute," Allen said, but she wouldn't listen. As she picked up the hose pipe and pointed it towards Allen, a voice came from behind her.

"Excuse me," came a voice, startling Stacy. She turned real fast to see Harry standing about two feet in front of her. She forgot all about the water hose for several seconds until the water started bouncing off of Harry and back onto her.

"I'm so sorry, Harry, you startled me," Stacy said.

"I was a bit distracted before and forgot to give you the mail," Harry said while staring at Stacy's freshly wet chest.

Noticing what he was looking at, Stacy put her arm across her chest and used the other to collect the mail from Harry. "Have a great day, Harry." She said as she took the mail and turned her back towards him.

Harry waved at Allen and gave him the thumbs up, mouthing, "You're a lucky man."

"I know, Harry. I know."

Stacy strutted in front of Allen as she made her way to the front door. "You're a dick," she said as she passed. Allen couldn't hold it in any longer and burst out laughing, following her into the house. "I thought you needed to check your lights," she said.

"Naw, I did that last week," he said. "Just wanted to see if Harry could give me more good news. The last time he saw you naked, I got a package from Lt. Col. Preston."

"That was a joke," she yelled back. "I had my house coat on and made up the part about him falling. How am I going to face that little old man again?"

"You'll do just fine. He'll be your fan until eternity, as long as he doesn't tell his wife." Allen laughed. "As for the other event, you got what you deserved. You portrayed your encounter with Harry as real; however, I knew better since I had seen your housecoat on the sofa that morning."

Stacy starts sorting the mail and finds a package from Lt. Col. Preston. "Well, you're one lucky son-of-a-bitch," she said. "Here's an envelope from Preston."

Allen stopped what he was doing and reached for the envelope. He opened it in the same way he has in the past. Inside was a simple two-paragraph note from Lt. Col. Preston.

25 Sept 03

Dear Mr. Schultz,

I received your package and was shocked by all the details. I visited the websites you included and even some that you didn't. I called my mom and dad, and they will assist me in obtaining copies of the items you'd like. My dad has a lot more connections in the DEA than I do.

    The delay in response was needed to research your issues and get the right people involved. I also returned from deployment and had a lot of things on my plate. Please be patient with me as I continue to pursue the information you want.

v/r
Tim

"Did you provide your phone number and email address on your last correspondence?" Stacy asked.

"You know, I'm not real sure," Allen said with a confused look. "I probably left that off. I was in such a hurry to get the response back to him that I bet I forgot."

"Well, it would make getting in touch so much easier," she said.

"I'm going to reply to his letter with a quick acknowledgment of receipt and include my phone number and email," Allen said and immediately started writing. He wanted to let Preston know he had encountered endless dead ends and red tape while trying to get to the truth. He told Preston everything except for the information that Deputy Ambassador Wilson had sent him. He wanted to keep that close hold until he got to know Preston a little bit better.

"Let me review your letter before you seal the envelope," Stacy urged.

"Yes, ma'am, I appreciate the offer. It's good to have a second pair of eyes on it."

CHAPTER 31

The Artifacts (15 June 2007)

Allen had become accustomed to the long waits between messages, so he would mail and forget. *"No sense worrying about something I can't change,"* Allen would say. Stacy has been a huge influence on him, bringing back his old self, joking, and cutting up. He is generally a great person to be around.

It was two months after he sent his email and phone number before Lt. Col. Tim Preston got back in touch. There was no news; however, the contact helped let him know that Preston was still working on it. Over the next four years, Allen and Tim talked or emailed almost weekly. They were even on a first-name basis.

The first break was when Tim informed Allen that he had obtained information about the rescue vehicles and the occupants. It was a small step, but at least it was a step up and not back. Tim said that he learned that the amphibious vehicles had video feeds of the incident and was working to get those released.

The next break came when he learned that the DEA had been investigating Mendez for over six years and was following him the day his helicopter went down. Tim's dad was key in finding that information. He continued working with his contacts to get all the data he could on the incident. The main roadblock is that many of those around back then have either passed away or moved on to other sites.

On Thursday, 14 Jun 07, Allen and Stacy were out later than usual. They were not super NBA fans; however, they were at the pub, and game four of the NBA finals was on, so they watched. They got caught up in the action and stayed until the end. The San Antonio Spurs squeaked out a win, beating the Cleveland Cavaliers 83-82 and sweeping the series four games to none. While they wouldn't mind seeing the home-state team win, they were just happy to see a good game.

Friday morning was rough. Allen's head was still spinning. He felt nauseous if he sat up, but he had no choice. There was something in him that wanted out, and it wanted out right then. It's amazing how fast the body can move when you're about to projectile vomit. He made it to the bathroom just in time. He didn't even turn the light on. He flipped up the lid and, "Oh shit, I'm never drinking again," he whispered to himself. Then another urge came… He tried to catch his breath, but there was no time. It was one projectile after the other until nothing was left inside him. Allen collapsed on the cold bathroom tile floor, *"This is what I need,"* he thought.

Allen woke up cold. He wasn't sure how long he'd been out. He felt some clothes behind him and tried to pull them towards him to use as cover. "What the fuck!" came a scream that echoed in his head. "Quit pulling on me. I'm sick and just want to lay here." It was Stacy. She must have been here the whole time. After puking and getting a nap, he wanted to try and get back to bed. He made it to his knees and then tried to help Stacy. She wasn't budging. Allen made it to the bed, head still spinning. He removed the comforter and took it back to cover her partially naked body. Allen returned, fell into bed, pulled the sheet and blanket over him, and was out within seconds.

He opened his eyes sometime later, still groggy but feeling better than he did a few hours earlier. He saw Stacy was back in bed, minus the comforter, but he didn't want to wake her. Allen was thirsty. He was dehydrated from all the fluid loss overnight. He managed to stand and make his way downstairs. After chugging his glass of water, he sat on the sofa and stared out the window.

"Last night was rough," he thought. "I'm too old to be partying like that." He saw his neighbor, Larry, checking his mail out the window. Larry is a talker, and the last thing he wanted to do was get into a conversation with anyone. Once Larry returned to his house, Allen gingerly walked out to grab his mail. The sun was bright; he wanted to get back inside as soon as possible. The brightness was giving him a headache.

He set the mail down on his desk, made a pot of coffee, made four spicy hot sausage patties, and then scrambled some eggs. The coffee finished just as the eggs were coming out of the pan. He quickly washed the pan and put it back in the cabinet. Allen took his food and coffee to his desk, where he ate and sorted the mail. The mail was mostly bills and advertisements; however, a letter from Tim was mixed in.

Allen sat it down, finished his breakfast, refreshed his coffee, and opened the envelope.

2 June 2007

Allen,
I've spent the last few weeks finalizing things. I now know what you must have been dealing with. The information you seek is

highly sensitive, and most agencies don't want to give it up. I showed them the approved FOIA request, so they had no choice.

The DEA will be sending you information concerning the Julio Mendez investigation. The Embassy will be doing the same. From what I understand, both agencies were involved, but didn't know that the other was also involved. They will also provide information on the amphibious rescue vehicles and their crew.

Unfortunately, they wouldn't give the information to me since the FOIA came from you. They will be mailing the data via registered mail, so hopefully, a few days after you get this letter, the packages will start showing up. I don't know how many will come, but you should receive something from each agency.

I hope the information you seek will be in the packages and that you find peace. I've been happy to assist you with this endeavor and look forward to hearing the outcome of your journey.

Your friend,
Tim

Allen was excited with anticipation of what might be coming his way. Almost immediately, he was feeling better. He made Stacy a plate and a cup of coffee, then sat on the bed beside her. "Wakey, wakey," he said, placing his hand on her shoulder. "I have some food here for you. I also have a glass of water and a cup of coffee. You need to eat something, honey."

"Go away. I don't want to get up," she groggily said. "What time is it?

Allen looked at his watch and said, "It's 3:15 in the afternoon."

"Oh shit, I need to get up," Stacy said as she tried to sit up, "But not right now. My head is spinning."

"Here, eat something. It'll help you recover. Also, drink as much water as possible before you start on the coffee." Allen knows all too well how she's feeling. "I'm going to shower. Please eat and drink."

Stacy picked up a sausage patty and took a bite. The heat from the patty had her reaching for the water. *"Asshole didn't tell me that he made the hot sausage,"* she thought as she continued to eat it. By the time Allen finished his shower, she had cleaned her plate.

"I see you made a happy plate." He said.

"Yes, thank you. I feel a little better but just want to lay here for a bit."

"Sure thing, honey. You get some rest; I'm going to run a couple of errands. Call if you need anything." Allen kissed her on the forehead, placing a couple of pills on the nightstand, "Take these aspirins before you go back to sleep. I love you." Then he left.

In expectation of what might come, Allen felt the need to go to his lab and make notes of what he might need to make this work. He began setting up his equipment. After a short while, he glanced at the clock on the wall next to the water cooler. "Crap, I've been here two hours; Stacy is going to be pissed," he said out loud. He picked up his phone and called.

"Hey babe, how are you feeling?" Allen asked.

"Like crap," she said with a weak voice. "Where are you?"

"I'm sorry, hon. I stopped by the lab and started setting my equipment up and lost track of time," Allen apologetically responded. "It's a little after six. I'm going to power down my computers and head home. Is there anything you need?"

"How about some chicken noodle soup? I'm afraid to eat anything solid right now. The sausage and eggs didn't sit well on my stomach."

"Of course, I'll pick up a few things on the way home. Give me fifteen minutes to close things up here, and I'll be on my way. Love you, babe."

Allen rushed to get everything powered down and secured. He knew that Bob Evans had good soup, so he called and placed an order for the soup and a Turkey dinner for himself, then locked up the lab.

CHAPTER 32

The Artifacts Part 2 (23 August 2007)

Several weeks passed before the first shipment arrived. Allen was sitting at his desk reading techno magazines while Stacy was in the shower. It was a quiet morning, and the article entranced him. Boom, boom, boom, came three heavy knocks on the door, startling Allen and causing his magazine to fly up in the air.

Allen opened the door, "Harry? What are you doing back here? You delivered our mail over an hour ago?"

"I have a couple of boxes that require a signature. I usually wait until my route is done before delivering the larger parcels," Harry explained.

Allen helped Harry with the boxes. "Can I get you a cup of coffee?" he asked.

"Umm, I've never had a resident ask me that before. If you're sure you don't mind, I'd love one." Harry replied. "I have two more stops, and I'm done for the day." Harry finished, looking around to see if Allen's beautiful wife was around.

"Not a problem at all. Have a seat, and I'll get you a cup."

Harry walked into the living room. A couple of chairs were on the far wall, and a sofa to the right. He sat in one of the chairs and was distracted by their artwork when he heard Stacy coming.

"Who was at the d…. Arrrrrrggggggghhhhh!" she screamed as she entered the living room and found herself buck-naked, standing before Harry. Almost immediately after her scream, Harry let out one.

Allen came running in, "What's going on in here?" he asked.

"Umm, your wife didn't know I was here, and I believe I startled her," Harry said. "She left rather quickly."

Allen handed Harry his coffee and then went to check on Stacy. "Are you ok, honey? I heard you scream."

Stacy was visibly shaken. She was sitting on the bed, still wrapped in her bath towel. "No, I'm not okay. I came out of the bathroom, still drying my hair with the towel, when I walked in and saw Harry in our living room. What the fuck was he doing here?" She asked.

"He delivered a couple of boxes, and I asked if he'd like a cup of coffee," Allen explained.

"He saw me naked. I gave Harry the full Monty." Stacy said with an angry tone.

"No wonder Harry was shaking when I came out of the kitchen. You almost gave him a heart attack."

"You don't understand. This is progressively getting worse. First, the bathrobe, then the wet T-shirt, and now this. Harry's seen more of me than my gynecologist."

Allen tried to comfort her, holding back laughter at her GYN comment, "There is some good news…" he stopped when she looked at him with a stare that could only mean nothing was good about this situation. "The good news is that Harry delivered two boxes of artifacts. I haven't had a chance to open them or even see who they're from. Would you like to join me so we can find out together?"

Stacy was still upset about Harry but felt close to Allen when he asked her to share this important event. "Sure, I'd love to," she said. "As long as you promise me Harry is not in the house."

"I promise," Allen replied while second-guessing his answer. He rushed into the living room as she was getting dressed. "Whew, good news, Harry's gone," he whispered. He picked up one of the boxes and moved it closer to the sofa, noticing a full coffee cup on the end table. "Hmmm, Harry must have left in a hurry." Allen took the coffee cup into the kitchen, then placed one of the boxes on the coffee table and the other on the floor next to it. "Hmm, this one is from the American Embassy in Acapulco," he said, talking to himself. He looked at the other box and couldn't find a return address. "That's strange," he said, still using his outer voice.

"What's strange?" Stacy said as she entered the room. "And who were you talking to?"

"The box from the Embassy is on the table; the one on the floor doesn't have a return address, which I thought was strange."

Allen used his pocket knife to cut through the packing tape. Inside, he found neatly organized files with dividers:

Section 1: The Schultz family
Section 2: The Kidnapping
Section 3: Señor Lopez (Hotel Americana Manager)
Section 4: Mendez Surveillance
Section 5: Helicopter Incident
Section 6: The Morgue
Section 7: Miscellaneous

"Crap, it will take days to go through all this," Allen said.

"Isn't this a good thing? You wanted all the documents, so now we need to be patient and start reading. While you're going through the papers, I'll create a spreadsheet so we can track key items," Stacy said eagerly, ready to start.

"You're right, as always," Allen said as he picked up the first folder. "This one should be easy. It's a folder about us."

SECTION 1: THE SCHULTZ FAMILY

As he went through each page, it was plain that the Embassy had done background checks on all three of them. There was a report on Kim, Olivia, and him. As he skimmed over the documents, there wasn't anything unusual. He knew there wouldn't be. He didn't have any skeletons in his closet.

"You can put down section one; it's no concern to us. It was only background checks and a brief synopsis basically stating that we were clean."

"Got it," Stacy said. "Now, this is teamwork work," she continued.

SECTION 2: THE KIDNAPPING

This folder would take a lot longer than the hour he spent on section one. There are a lot more papers that he would need to read. The first folder contained the police reports. He began reading and then started having flashbacks. "I need to take a break. This is getting too intense," he said as he got up to go into the kitchen.

Stacy followed him, "Why don't we both take a break and grab a bite to eat? It's nearly noon, and we haven't eaten today," she said.

"Let's go out to eat. I think a little time away would be good. How about the Blue Wolf Tavern? We haven't been there in a while. What do you say?" Allen asked.

"That sounds great. I love their Cowboys." Stacy said.

"I'll bet you do, but don't you usually bite off more than you can chew?" Allen responded.

The Blue Wolf wasn't crowded, so they were seated immediately. Allen ordered a sweetened iced tea, and Stacy got a diet soda. "Watching your weight for that cowboy?" Allen snickered.

"Are you jealous?" Stacy asked. They both just laughed. No words were needed.

The drinks arrived rather quickly. Neither Allen nor Stacy had a chance to open the menus. The waiter asked if they needed more time. "No, not at all. I think we both know what we'd like," Stacy answered.

"Fine, ma'am, what would you like today?" the waiter asked.

"I want a Cowboy…" She glanced over at Allen and smiled.

"And how would you like that cooked?" the waiter asked.

"Medium rare, with a loaded baked potato and a side salad with blue cheese dressing," Stacy ordered.

"Sir, may I take your order?"

"Yes, I'll have what she's having, only I'd like extra onions on the salad and Thousand Island dressing," Allen replied.

After lunch, they sat and talked. "What got you upset while reading the documents?" Stacy asked.

"It was difficult. I was reading the police report, and everything started flashing back into my mind. I wasn't prepared for that," Allen responded. "I need to do a better job of preparing myself. It's going to be hard, but it's something I have to do."

"You know I'll be there with you. I love you," said Stacy as she reached for his hand.

"Ahhh hahaha," Allen laughed. "That's the first time you've told me you loved me without the word asshole following it." Even Stacy found humor in his untimely remark. "Okay, asshole, I'll give you that one."

When they returned home, Allen said, "Okay, let's give this another try."

"Are you sure you're ready for it?" she asked.

"Not really, but the pages aren't going to read themselves."

"Section 2, here we go again," Allen thought as he picked up the police report he read earlier. He found witness testimonies in it, each very similar to the other. The car slammed on its brakes, and two men got out. One grabbed Olivia, and the other pushed Rosita to the curb, followed by the car speeding away. "*They are all alike*," he thought, "I need to find one that has obvious evidence in it."

In another report, they are interviewing the reception desk attendant. She identified the man in the picture they showed her. "Si, that is señor Mendez," said the frightened receptionist.

"Are you sure?" asked the investigator.

"Si, he was here earlier this morning for a meeting with other men like him."

"What do you mean, 'like him'?" they asked.

"Mal," she replied. "They were all evil men that did the same work as señor Mendez."

She knew the names of a couple of the men, but that was it. "La chica? El señor Mendez golpeo a la chica." It was translated as, "The girl? Señor Mendez bumped the girl." They asked her when this happened. "This morning, about 10:05. She came through those doors (pointing to the main lobby doors and Mendez bumped into her. He followed her to the pool, stood there for a minute, then left."

"Stacy," Allen called out. "They never mentioned that Mendez was at the hotel earlier that day and had a chance run-in with Olivia. Can you add this to the database?" he asked, handing her the report.

He read through a few more documents, but nothing stood out. "I guess it's time to move to the next section," he said to himself loud enough that Stacy thought he was talking to her.

SECTION 3: Señor Lopez

Allen was curious about why they would have a file on the hotel manager and was shocked to see several documents. The first one was a background paper. He was born in a small farm town on the outskirts of Acapulco. His parents died when he was thirteen. He had no siblings and attended a private school for boys, tuition covered by an anonymous donor. 'That's strange,' he thought as he noted this in the database. It said he graduated at the top of his class and received a scholarship to a local university, majoring in hospitality management and English language. "That explains why he's in the hotel industry," he thought, "but why is this relevant?"

The next file explained a little more. It was an investigation into Lopez's sponsorship. "Hmmm, they want to determine who was bankrolling his education and living expenses," Allen said out loud.

"What are you talking about?" Stacy came back at him as she continued to fine-tune the database. She added special columns that could be sorted, including document number, page, names, descriptions, locations, etc.

"I'm sorry, hon. I sometimes talk to myself." Allen responded. "It looks like the DEA was working with the

Mexican officials to connect the dots on Lopez. This is getting interesting."

"You don't believe Lopez was involved with any of this, do you?"

"I had no reason to believe he was involved until I read this." Allen took a long pause. "Shit," he shouted. "I called and talked to Lopez while trying to get in touch with the coroner. Instead of giving me his number, he called and connected me. He listened as the coroner gave me information contradicting what I was told. He said he'd mail me a copy of his original autopsy report. I never received it. He was murdered within a few days of our call."

"This doesn't make sense. Mendez was dead. Who would want to squelch this information?" Stacy asked.

"I don't know, but this is definitely unusual," Allen said. "Be sure to add this to the database."

Allen continued to read through the documents, "It's amazing how many secrets this guy had," he thought. The next few pages were insignificant; however, the following section proved very interesting.

SECTION 4: Mendez

The first document in the file was titled 'Surveillance Report.' The DEA had been investigating Mendez for over a year. The report described his travels, meetings, and a trail of death that seemed to follow him around. Unfortunately, according to the report, they couldn't directly connect him to the crimes. He was very smart and always had an alibi or a fall guy. However, the mundane meetings he had added up. He used the Hotel Americana for many of those meetings. There were descriptions of Mendez and Lopez regularly talking.

Allen's attention to detail just got a little more focused. In twelve months, Mendez held meetings at the hotel at least monthly and sometimes twice a month. A review of the hotel's ledgers didn't account for these meetings. Further investigations identified Lopez's parents as associates of Mendez, whom a rival cartel killed. The report suggests that Mendez was the financier of Lopez's education. Allen highlighted several lines for Stacy to log.

"Are you getting thirsty?" Stacy asked.

"Ummm, what?" Allen, confused with the question, responded.

"You've been so entailed with your reading that I'm sure you didn't realize we've been at this for four hours straight. I figured you'd need a break," she said.

"Yes, a break would be nice. I'm not really hungry after that huge lunch, but maybe a drink and a sandwich would be nice." Allen then suggested, "I know I swore off alcohol after our last bender, but how would you like to go to the pub for a drink and an appetizer? We can discuss everything we've found so far."

"You had me at alcohol," she responded.

"You two look much better than the last time I saw you," the bartender joked.

"Thanks for noticing, Max," Stacy responded. "I wish I could say the same about you."

"Ouch, that hurts," Max said, gesturing to his heart. "What can I get you?"

"I'll have a Captain and Coke, and Stacy will have an Ultra," Allen said, looking over at Stacy for her approval. They both picked up a menu and began looking for something lite.

Max brought the drinks and placed them on a coaster in front of them. "Would you like to order something to eat?"

he asked. "The Philly Cheesesteaks are really good today."

"Thanks, but I'll have a Ruben with extra Thousand Island on the side. It comes with fries, correct?" Allen asked

"That's correct; it comes with fries and a pickle. What would you like, Stacy?"

"Hmmm, I was going to get a Ruben as well, but now you have me craving a Cheesesteak," Stacy replied. "You said they were good; you'd better be right. Put extra onions and peppers on it."

"I had one myself about an hour ago, I assure you… it's delicious," Max said, rubbing his belly as he walked to the kitchen to put the order in.

"What do you think about everything you learned today?" Stacy asked curiously.

"I'm perplexed. How could I have been so blind? I actually liked señor Lopez. He went out of his way to accommodate us after Olivia's abduction. How could I have misjudged him? I'm only halfway through with his section of documents, so hopefully, there will be more details about his involvement," Allen commented. "What's your take on everything?"

"First, I wouldn't blame yourself. It looks like these guys have been crooked most of their lives, so they've had a lot of practice putting on two faces," she said. "Let's relax tonight, and we'll get a fresh start in the morning."

"I planned that trip. I picked the hotel. It was my idea to go and look for houses. I allowed Olivia to remain at the hotel all alone. It's my fault this happened." Allen said, then killed the rest of his drink. He looked over at Max and raised his glass, indicating he wanted another.

"Honey, it was sheer coincidence that this happened," Stacy said, trying to comfort him. "It wasn't your fault."

Max put Allen's second drink down in front of him and removed the old glass. Allen took a large gulp, getting choked on it, "Whoa, what the fuck, Max! Warn me when you pour the alcohol in after the mixer. Whew, that was a head rush."

Max just laughed and walked away, saying, "That's what the little red stick in your drink is for."

Stacy looked around to ensure no one was watching, then slid her hand down Allen's thigh. His eyes brightened as she moved it closer and closer to his penis. Allen was getting excited by her actions and sat back a little, making it much easier for her to get there. They were both looking down at what was happening. "You know we have a room in the back if you need it," Max said, "but if it's an audience you're looking for, please continue."

"Really, Max? Can't a couple play around under the bar in here," Allen yelled, followed by hysterical laughter from him and Stacy. He looked over at her and mouthed, "Thank you."

"Maybe we can finish this when we get home," Stacy said.

Allen put her hand on his erect manhood, "He's ready when you are." Allen threw a few bills onto the bar, and they left. He couldn't get home fast enough.

The next morning, Stacy woke early and decided to make breakfast. She was excited that she'd be able to surprise Allen, as he's the cook in the house. She tip-toed out of the bedroom, closing the door behind her. "Okay, let's see what we have in the fridge. Shit, there are two eggs, and that's it. No bacon or hash browns." She said softly, getting upset that her plan was foiled. She looked in the pantry and found a box of oatmeal. "Well, this will have to do."

Allen was thrilled with the thought and even smiled as he ate the oatmeal. "Thank you for the breakfast. It was great. If you don't mind, I'm going to take my coffee and get started on the files," he said, without hinting that he doesn't like oatmeal.

The Mendez file was still open from last night. He picked up the folder and proceeded to read the next document. This one didn't make sense, at least not at first. It was a listing of his meetings and the individuals at those meetings. They must have had a mole that documented the exchange. It talked about meetings with other cartels. There were insinuations that a hit would be on for several people, not just their competitors, but high-ranking government officials. Mendez was upset that the Mexican authorities were cracking down on his turf. He needed a hit, and it needed to send a message. "Wow," Allen said out loud. Still in the kitchen, Stacy came out and asked what he found. "You're not going to believe this, but Mendez was planning an assassination of high-level government officials."

"You're kidding me. With all that going on, how did he have time to plan a kidnapping?" Stacy came back.

"I'm not sure, but I hope the more I read, the more it will say."

Allen went back to reading the documents. Before, he was mostly skimming, but now, it's every word. He was three or four pages in when the neighbor's dog started barking. "Harry's here," Allen shouted. "Can you grab the mail?"

"What the fuck?" Stacy came back. "What are you trying to do, piss me off, or give Harry a heart attack."

"Shit, I'm sorry, I totally wasn't thinking," Allen said as he got up and went to the mailbox. "Hey Harry, how's it hanging?" he yelled. Harry ignored him. "Harry, turn around and say hello," he called out. The mailman turned, confused, and looked at Allen. "You're not Harry!" he said.

"No, I'm Patrick, but most folks call me Pat," he said.

"What happened to Harry? Is he okay?" Allen retorted.

"Harry had a problem with some swinger couple on his route and decided to retire. We all begged him to switch routes, but Harry (or should I say his wife) wouldn't have anything to do with it. His retirement party will be next week."

"Well Pat, I'm Allen. It's nice to meet you. I'm sorry to see Harry go. He's been a fixture here for years. Do you know if the neighborhood is doing anything for him?"

"I'm not sure, but I'll ask," Pat replied.

Allen returned to the house with nothing but junk mail. "So, how's Harry?" Stacy asked. "I bet he was in a hurry to get away from this house. Or was he looking for an excuse to come in?" She wasn't into exhibitionism, but her ego was fueled by the way Harry looked at her.

"Sorry honey, Harry's gone," said Allen

"No! Don't tell me he died," Stacy said, almost in tears.

"Not at all, honey. Harry (or Harry's wife) decided it was time for him to retire. Something to do with a swinger couple on his route. I wonder who that could be?" Allen said with a smile. "Before you get sad, Harry's been talking about retiring for the last two years."

Allen went back to work on the Mendez files, looking for anything that could connect this investigation to Olivia. Mendez's last meeting, well next to the last meeting, discussed delivering three million dollars to get the ball rolling. There was to be another meeting before the transfer happened. "That must be the one at the hotel the day we were there," Allen said softly.

The rest of the documents in that file were pretty benign. Allen finished up and moved to the next Section.

SECTION 5: The Helicopter Incident

Allen had butterflies in his stomach when he reached this section. He hoped it would be full of details but not graphic. It took several minutes and two beers before he could begin. The first few pages recapped the meetings with Mendez and other cartel members. Then, it got to the document dated 3 November 1985. Intel had Mendez at a cartel meeting at the Fiesta Americana Hotel, where he announced that the money would be delivered that evening. It went on to say that several agents were following him until he made an abrupt stop, where he took a young female with blonde hair by force. The surveillance team had to keep going so as not to be detected. They turned around to see if they could intervene, but it was too late, as now Mendez was headed in the opposite direction, coming straight at them. Traffic, narrow roads, and lack of opportunities prevented them from pursuing their visual surveillance. Mendez was too far ahead of them, and there was no way to get caught up. Upon arriving at Mendez's villa, they verified that his car was there; no occupants were seen.

Forty-five minutes after arrival, they observed the helicopter pilot doing pre-checks and starting the engines. Several security personnel walked Mendez to the helicopter, some carrying briefcases identical to the ones from the bank. The men completely surrounded Mendez, making it extremely difficult to obtain an unobstructed view. They observed someone throwing a large object into the back of the helicopter, then saw Mendez climb into the vehicle and close the door. The helicopter took off five minutes later with three people on board. The Pilot and his security chief Perez were up front, and Mendez was in the back. The men who had accompanied him to the helicopter stood with empty hands as the helicopter flew away. The conclusion of these reports indicated Mendez had the money on board and was en route to pay off the cartel for the assassinations.

The targets were high-level, pro-American politicians; their loss would set back diplomacy between the U.S. and Mexico for decades. The DEA was directed to stop this action by whatever means necessary. "They were directed by who?" Allen stated out loud again.

"What are you talking about this time?" Stacy asked.

"The document states that the DEA was directed to stop Mendez by whatever means possible. But it doesn't say who did the directing," said Allen as he tried to piece things together. "The DEA works for the Justice Department, and they work for the U.S. Attorney General. But it doesn't identify the entity that actually pulled the trigger."

Allen handed Stacy the document, "Can you log the highlighted areas?"

"You got it, babe," she replied

The next file was a report on the amphibious response vehicle. The first document was a coversheet that stated: 'This record is protected by the Health Insurance Portability and Accountability Act (HIPPA). "What the hell is this?" Allen said out loud, then upon seeing Stacy's head turn, he explained what he was referring to.

Stacy, being a medical professional, knew about HIPPA. "It's a relatively new Congressional Act that came out sometime last year. It's been a headache to implement. The intent is to protect patient privacy," she continued, "and… it's not subject to FOIA requests."

Allen was frustrated. He feared that anything of importance within the file would be redacted. He flipped the coversheet over and started reading the first report. It was an encapsulated account of the Amphibious Rescue Vehicle (ARV) mission. The location of the base the vehicle came from was "*redacted due to security concerns,*" said a handwritten note on the page.

The narrative started, "ARV-3302 departed home port at 1535 hours to provide expeditious search and recovery capability to a Top Secret (agencies redacted) operation." The agencies involved were redacted, per another handwritten note. "ARV-3302 was manned by three USAF rescue personnel. Two USAF F-16s intercepted the target at coordinates *(redacted)*. Once word was received from *(redacted)*, the pilots were given the green light to engage.

"Oh my God," Allen said as he stood and covered his face.

"What's wrong, honey," Stacy asked with concern.

"Our own government murdered Olivia," Allen said, tears forming in his eyes. "So this is why they lied to me all these years? The assholes shot her down."

"I'm so sorry. That's a bit different than a mechanical failure," Stacy said, trying to comfort him, "To be honest, it was probably better to go this way than the horror of falling to earth after the tail section fell off, as they originally told you." She walked over and gave him a hug and a peck on the lips.

"This explains what the coroner meant when he said she was deceased prior to hitting the water," Allen interjected, then went back to reading the report.

"Target was in two pieces at a depth of 50 feet. Upon observation of the cabin section, ARV-3302 radioed that there were four bodies and no survivors. Approximately 2 minutes after that transmission, ARV-3302 suffered a catastrophic event. The two front-seat USAF members (names redacted) were mortally wounded. The rear technician *(name redacted)* suffered serious injuries and was transported to *(redacted)* where he was treated for his injuries."

"Wow," Allen said. "I wasn't expecting this much information. Even with all the redactions, I'm getting a better picture of what happened…" he paused for a moment. "This also brings up a lot more questions."

He continued to read the report. It spoke of recovering Olivia's body and those of Mendez and his posse. There was a section on the recovery of the helicopter parts; however, the location of their disposition was redacted. Four or five pages later, he came across another shocker.

"What the fuck?" Allen cried out. "They have videos of the initial contact with the helicopter and the recovery of the bodies."

"It says there's a transcript of the videos attached to this report…" Stacy stopped Allen.

"It's time to take a break and let what you've already read sink in before you continue. The better you can comprehend the information, the more you'll understand what is being said." Stacy said, trying to provide some bullshit jargon to make him take a break.

"You're right. This was a lot to take in." Allen conceded.

"How about we go see a movie?" Stacy asked, really craving popcorn more than watching the movie. "Where's the paper? I'll look and see what's playing?"

Allen handed her the paper, then turned and walked towards the bathroom, "I'll be a few minutes, so if you need to go, tell me now."

"I'm fine."

"OK, then pick something nice." Allen walked into the bathroom, shut the door, and immediately yelled, "No chick-flicks!"

Stacy thumbed through the paper, looking for the Entertainment Section, when she came across an article about the Minneapolis bridge collapse and started reading it. *"I can't imagine being on an interstate highway driving to work or my parents' house and… BOOM, the road underneath you is gone, and you're falling into the Mississippi River. Those poor people,"* she thought.

She was so caught up in the article that she didn't hear the muffled sound of the toilet flushing. "So, what are we seeing?" Allen asked, heading into the bedroom to change.

"Shit! I forgot to find a movie," she said under her breath. Stacy quickly found the ads and saw one listed that she remembered from a commercial. "The Bourne Ultimatum!" she yelled.

Allen walked back into the bathroom, fixed his hair, and applied a handful of Old Spice to his face. "Great, I've been waiting for this one to come out. We should have rented the last one to refresh our memory of how it ended," Allen said, a little excited.

"Whew, I dodged a bullet on this one." she thought.

"What time does it start?" he asked.

"If we hurry, we can make the 6:00 p.m. showing," she replied, running into the bedroom to change. "

The movie ended around 8 p.m., and they walked out talking about the movie and its special effects. When they reached the lobby, Stacy broke off from Allen to visit the lady's room. When she returned, she saw Allen still in line at the concession stand, waiting for a refill of his popcorn to munch on later. Stacy heard someone call her name, so she turned and saw two individuals smiling and walking her way. It was Ron and Nancy, a couple they had known for years. "What movie did you come to see?" Stacy asked.

"I wanted to get wet watching my dream man, Matt Damon, but this old lug is literally dying to see Halloween," Nancy said disgustedly.

"Halloween? It's only August. What are you thinking, Ron?" Stacy chided him. "You should think about pleasing your wife and letting her get all hot and bothered watching Matt. Shit, it may benefit you when you get home," she continued.

Allen returned from the amusement park line to the concession stand with a full bucket of popcorn to hear them talking about the movie. "Don't let them get to you, Ron. It's not a chick flick. It's an action-packed movie that has eye candy for the women-folk."

Ron looked over at Nancy. "Well, would you prefer to see…." Nancy interrupted him before he could finish.

"Yes, I would," she said, then gave Allen a hug.

"Wait a minute, young lady, I'm the one taking you to the movie. Don't be getting all flirty with the friends," Ron said.

"Give me a break, old man," she came back. "It's not like they're walking around with upside-down pineapples or something."

They all laughed, even Allen, and he had no idea what the pineapple reference was all about. "Enjoy the movie," he said. "Unfortunately, we need to head home. I have a lot on my plate right now."

"Give me a call and let me know what you thought about the movie," Stacy said as they walked away, then turned and said, "Take care of your man when you get home." You could hear laughter down the hall to the theaters.

Allen immediately sat his bucket of popcorn down next to the box of artifacts, went to the kitchen to grab a beer, and then anchored himself between the popcorn and the box.

He opened the file he was on prior to leaving and picked up where he left off. There were many things about the helicopter parts they recovered and the salvage of the amphibious vehicle. It appeared they made sure there was no sign of the U.S. presence before they finished up. He skimmed through the next few pages, looking for anything that may have been important, but found none. He might have been more focused on those pages if not for the fact that they were the only thing between him and the transcript.

Allen stretched his back, filled his hand with the extra buttery popcorn, and munched on it for a minute or two. He followed that by chugging almost half his beer, belching, and then returning to the documents. He took a deep breath and said, "Well, here I go. This should be interesting."

This file was more redacted than the others. I'm sure it had to do with code names, equipment references, etc. Nothing indicated why they were there, only that they were to meet up with USAF air support and be in the vicinity if needed. In fact, there wasn't much chatter at all. There would be lines that gave a time, then nothing but 'silence' for several minutes before more information was shed.

"ARV-3302 in position" were the first words uttered by the rescue vehicle.

Allen assumed that the command post was the entity they were talking with. "Continue on current course of *(redacted)* at a speed of *(redacted)* and prepare for hostile encounter."

"Copy current course and speed, prepping for contact," was their response to the command center. "Mike, are trauma kits one and two ready?"

"Check," was his immediate response.

"Terry, take the helm."

"Yes sir," Terry replied

There was silence for a few more minutes. Allen wondered what could have been going on at that time. His mind wondered, as they probably had no idea what was in store for them, or did they? He continued to read.

"Command 1 to ARV-3302."

"3302 copy."

"Proceed to coordinates *(redacted)*. Monitor channel *(redacted)* for chatter."

"Copy, proceed to *(redacted)* and monitor channel *(redacted)*. The ARV changed course and headed to the coordinates provided. Through their headsets, they could hear the chatter between two entities that Allen deduced were the DEA and the F-16 pilots.

"Target in sight."

"It's a go," came the word from the command post.

"Confirming that it's a go."

"Roger, you have a go."

"Missile one has been launched," Pilot 1 radioed.

Pilot 2, "We have a direct hit. Target is going down at the following coordinates: *(redacted)*."

"Command post to ARV-3302. Proceed to *(redacted)* and access situation.

"3302 copy. En route."

According to the transcript, it was about five minutes before they arrived at the downed helicopter. "3302 to command. We have arrived at the site."

"3302, we're unable to pull up the video feed."

"Copy, we spotted two large sections of the AV. We're at the cabin section. The two occupants in the front of the AV are deceased. Two occupants in the back are...." There was a pause as he saw the two in the back and was overcome. As were the others in the ARV.

"3302, confirm number of occupants."

"Sir, there are four occupants. Two males in the front and one male and one female in the back." Everyone in 3302 was silent as if they knew the young girl wasn't supposed to be there.

The report indicated a long delay before the command post responded. "3302, begin recovery operations."

"Copy, beginning recovery," followed by "Mayday, Mayday..."

The narrative indicated a catastrophic event occurred, crippling the ARV.

"ARV 3314, do you have 3302 in sight?"

"Roger, divers dispatched," followed by, "Pulling one soul out of the water, two in the SRV are deceased."

"Copy 3314. Get our guys first, then proceed with recovery of AV occupants. Air support en route to assist with recovery and disposition efforts."

Allen read and reread the last two pages of the report. What happened to the ARV, and what did the surviving member see? "*I need to get a hold of the video recording,*" he thought.

Stacy was busy cataloging the pages as quickly as he handed them to her. "Can I break in? I want to send an email to Tim Preston."

"It's getting late. I'm going to be shutting down soon." She said. "Let me finish this last page, and the computer is all yours."

Allen went for another beer, ate some popcorn, and then relaxed as he waited for Stacy to finish.

"Goodnight, honey. Don't stay up too late," Stacy said as she kissed him on the forehead."

Allen looked up from his typing and blew her a kiss, "I just want to send this email out before I forget what I want to say."

The next morning, Stacy awoke to find a vacant spot on his side of the bed. She found him on the sofa with an empty bucket of popcorn and two drained beer cans. "Wake up, honey, and go to bed."

"Huh, what... Hmmm, what time is it?" he asked, dazed and confused.

"It's about 9 a.m. Get in the bed and get some good sleep. I will go to the grocery store after I shower, so you should have it nice and quiet here."

Without saying a word, Allen got up and attempted to kiss her on the lips but got her nose instead, turned, and walked towards the bedroom. Stacy followed him to make sure he made it to bed.

SECTION 6: The Morgue

Stacy returned about two hours later. She had two bags in her arms and was trying to unlock the door simultaneously. Suddenly, the door flew open, surprising her. "Welcome home. I was beginning to worry about you," Allen said with a smile.

"You worry about me? It should be me worrying about you," she replied with a snarl. "You didn't come to bed, then I find you cheating on me with two beers and a bucket of popcorn."

"Very funny," Allen said as he smacked her on the ass as she walked by.

"That's not fair. My arms are full, and I can't defend myself. If you have that much energy, why don't you get the rest of the groceries while I put these away?"

Without hesitation, he jogged out to the car and back two times with all the bags. "What now, Princess?"

"I stopped by Mom's to drop off a few supplies. I invited her to dinner tomorrow night; I hope that's alright."

"Of course it is. I've been slacking on visiting her since these boxes showed up."

"Yep, I know all about it. She may have mentioned it once or twice," Stacy laughed. "Not to change the subject, but why didn't you come to bed last night?"

"I spent so much time trying to write a one-paragraph email to Tim that I lost track of time."

"Did you get your paragraph done?" Stacy asked.

"Yes, about three pages later," Allen said, shaking his head. "There was so much I wanted to say and couldn't find a way to condense it." He continued, "By the time I finished, I was wound up, so I acquired another beverage and went back to work on the files. I finished section five and then sat on the couch with my popcorn. I didn't want to start the next section before bed, so I sort of spaced on the sofa."

Stacy noticed that Allen seemed somber this morning. "Are you okay, sweetheart?" she asked.

"Did you know that it's going on twenty-two years since Olivia died?"

Stacy didn't know what to say. She wanted to comfort him but was at a loss for words.

"I need to get to the bottom of this. I believe that she will have peace if those involved are held accountable. Every year that goes by is an indicator that I'm running out of time," he said.

Allen went to the kitchen and poured a glass of milk, yanked a banana out of the bunch, then went to his spot between the box of artifacts and now empty bucket of popcorn. "I have my lunch right here, so I'm ready to knock out these last two sections."

Stacy had a few more pages from last night to catalog, so she went to the computer and returned to work. It was hard, even for her, and she didn't know Olivia. She looked over at Allen. He was going through the autopsy report that was in the files. He had already read one but wanted to ensure no discrepancies between the two.

Allen looked over at Stacy, amazed by her beauty, even in one of his t-shirts, no bra and gym shorts. Sitting at the desk, the window behind her accentuated her perfect body. She caught him staring at her, "Did I grow horns or something?" she asked.

"Not at all, my love. I'm just basking in your beauty. I'm sure I don't tell you often enough, but I sure do love you." Allen said in a voice that was definitely sincere. "I don't know what I would do without you."

Stacy, taken back by his impromptu compliment, got up and removed her shirt, dropped her pants, and pulled Allen by his arms into the bedroom. "Don't say a word. You owe me for not being next to me when I woke up this morning," she chided him with a look of lust and excitement.

"Yes, ma'am…" was all he could get out before she threw him on the bed and jumped on top." Their sex life was as thrilling as the day they met.

"Don't try and resist. It'll only make me delay your pleasure," she said as she removed his clothes.

Allen didn't resist. He lay there, amazed by her sensuality.

It was over an hour later when they emerged from the bedroom. Allen had placed his shorts and t-shirt back on. Stacy wore only a T-shirt. Each returned to their respective places and picked up where they left off as if the last hour was a figment of their imagination.

Allen finished the autopsy report and informed Stacy that it was the same as the last one. He was glad that it didn't have anything new. "I don't know how it could have gotten worse," he thought. Of course, this was accompanied by the flashbacks he had before. Images of Olivia suffering at the hands of that monster—how her innocence was taken from her at such a young age and by such force. She would never know the love that her mother and he shared or what he has now with Stacy.

"You're staring at me again," Stacy said with a sexy smile. "Are you ready for round two?"

"Are you kidding? I'm still recovering from round one! Besides, I haven't had a real meal today."

"You seemed to have eaten fine a little while ago," she said, pointing down to her now-exposed nether region.

"Stop that… Are you trying to kill me?" he said. There's nothing he'd like more than to return to the bedroom, but he wanted to finish this box of files today. "You know how I work, right? I set goals and try to live up to them; otherwise, the boxes would be here for months waiting on me."

"I understand. You keep reading those files. I'm going back to the bedroom for some private time." Stacy said as she lifted her t-shirt once again.

The next file he looked at had to do with the internal investigation that took place shortly after the coroner disappeared. It spoke of uncharacteristic behavior that had occurred within a few days of the crash. One witness report described men coming in and threatening the coroner to change his report. He wasn't sure but thought they were Americans. They wanted the autopsies of all the occupants altered to remove any mention of severe burns or fragments from an unknown source. It also wanted the removal of brutal findings concerning the young girl.

"I can understand why they would want to cover up what happened to Mendez and his men, but why hide everything they did to Olivia," Allen thought to himself. Allen was so intensely focused on the reports he didn't hear the bedroom door open or see Stacy return to the desk. He continued reading while Stacy watched, amazed at how he could block out everything around him.

When the witness was asked what type of data they wanted removed from the girl, he responded, "Everything related to the sexual assault." He said, "More like labs that wouldn't normally be included anyway in an autopsy of an aircraft accident victim."

"Due to the nature of her injuries, we ran labs on the vaginal fluids that were obtained. These reports came back as semen from Julio Mendez," the witness said. When asked if any others were found in her, he replied, "No, only Mendez."

This brought a small sense of relief to Allen. *"At least it was only one of them,"* he thought.

"Your lines went away," Stacy commented.

Allen, still unaware of her presence, was startled. "How long have you been there, and what lines are you talking about?" he asked.

"Just a couple of minutes, and I was talking about the lines on your forehead. They've been there all day, and suddenly they're gone?"

Allen shrugged his shoulders and then continued to read. There were two other witness reports, but nothing significant or that he hadn't already seen was mentioned. The final document within this section was an invoice for the work the morgue's employees had done, from the autopsies to the cover-up. The U.S. Government paid for it. An addendum instructed the local government to send all costs associated with Olivia's transportation to the U.S. Embassy.

"It looks like they were trying to cover up the military involvement with the downing of the helicopter," Allen said. "Maybe they were admitting guilt in the crash by paying for everything associated with our visit." He highlighted a few paragraphs and gave the file to Stacy.

"Before I start on this folder, let's get something to eat," Stacy said. "This way, you'll be fresh."

Allen, back in his somber mood, replied, "I agree. You pick the place this time, but nothing too heavy, if you don't mind."

"I agree. It's a little late for a large meal. What about Chinese?" she offered. "It's a buffet. You can eat as little or as much as you want. It'll be faster than a normal sit-down restaurant."

"Mmmmmm, that sounds good," Allen replied. Stacy pulled on a pair of jeans and a thick shirt and barely beat Allen to the door. "After you, Muh Lady," he said.

SECTION 7: Miscellaneous

"So much for a light dinner," Stacy said, walking past Allen, who was holding the front door open for her.

"It's hard when you have all that delicious food in front of you," Allen said, holding his stomach. "Besides, it was your idea to go there. I'm gonna have a seat and let my stomach process its contents while I'm reading."

Allen reached into the box and pulled out the last section. It was one folder that contained six documents. It looked like the internal affairs agent put it together.

The first page was a personal message from the agent.

Dear Mr. Schultz,
It saddens me to be sending you these files. I was in college when these events occurred and only

learned of the Mendez operation when you submitted your FOIAs.

During my investigation, I found numerous inconsistencies between communications with you and other agencies.

I wanted to respond sooner, but I needed to investigate your allegations. It was heartbreaking to read about your loss. It drove me to dig deeper and make sure those involved were held accountable.

Several policies have changed since this incident to hopefully prevent others from suffering as you have. Inter-agency communications and protocols are now in place.

While I truly believe that some of the actions were taken to save you from the devastating details of your daughter's ordeal, how they went about it was wrong.

Please accept my apologies for the actions that happened, and be assured that I left no stone unturned in providing you with the enclosed information. Should you have any questions, please contact me using the card enclosed in this file.

Sincerely

Kimberly L. Hammond
Special Agent, DEA Internal Affairs

"I'm impressed that she took the time to write this and provide her contact information." Allen thought as he rummaged through the box to find it. He was even more pleased when he saw that she had given her mobile phone and email address. "Stacy, look at this," Allen said as he handed her Hammond's letter.

The next page was a partial transcript from Ambassador Taylor's deposition before his departure. "We did not know that the DEA was investigating Mendez and planning to make a hit. We were following him because of the kidnapping of an American girl. We knew that Miss Schultz was on board, and we were tracking her."

"It was my call to withhold information from Mr. Schultz. I have a daughter. Losing her would be horrible. Knowing what happened to Olivia would have caused him and his wife more pain." Taylor stated. "I directed Deputy Wilson to tell them the helicopter had a catastrophic malfunction which caused it to crash. I also negotiated with the coroner to leave the rape information out of the report. Mendez was dead. There was no need to put the family through more pain than necessary," Taylor continued. "Deputy Wilson didn't agree with me but carried out my orders."

"If I had an inkling that the DEA was involved, I would have provided data that may have stopped them from engaging with Mendez's helicopter. I still have nightmares thinking about what that poor little girl went through."

"Why did Deputy Wilson resign his post?" was a question listed on the report, but it didn't state who asked it.

"Wilson was a good kid. He was young and energetic but didn't have thick enough skin to do this job. He was so distraught that he couldn't function. I covered for him as long as I could."

When asked about the coroner's disappearance, Taylor stated that he had nothing to do with that. "I cooperated with the local authorities and our own agencies. No one at the Embassy had a clue as to what happened."

"What about after the Schultzs left town? Why did you continue the charade?" were the next questions listed.

"I'm sorry, I can't talk about that," Taylor stated. "That's classified information, and I can only talk to people with the proper clearance and a need-to-know," he finished.

Taylor insisted that the direction came from high up and that the entity responsible was untouchable.

The next interview was conducted by someone at the DEA regarding señor Jose Lopez, the Manager of the Americana Hotel in Acapulco. Allen had read all about him and Mendez earlier, so he skimmed through most of the file and concentrated on the summary paragraph.

When asked why he didn't charge the Schultzs for their stay and provided food at no charge, he answered, "They were a nice family that had a major tragedy. I felt it was my duty to pay for their accommodations using private funds."

"Is that so?" the agent retorted. "Since you've been the manager here, there has been a long line of 'tragedies,'" the agent said, using the first two fingers on each hand to make air quotes. "How many of those did the hotel pay for?" The report stated that Lopez was quiet and didn't speak for several minutes.

"It happened on my property…to Americans, on my sidewalk. And I saw señor Mendez say something to the girl and then follow her. I felt responsible," Lopez confessed.

"Is it that you felt responsible, or were you afraid of being sued by the Americans?" Lopez didn't answer.

Allen looked through the rest of the documents, but nothing important stood out. There was hardly anything to pass over to Stacy, who was reading other files while waiting for more data to log.

The remaining box was from the Drug Enforcement Agency (DEA). It was smaller and not as heavy as the one from the Embassy. He opened it and found a stack of papers, not the neatly chronicled files the Embassy had sent. He picked up a handful of pages and glanced over them. They were not in order. There was no rhyme or reason to the mess. "Stacy, can you give me a hand here?"

"Sure, luv. What do you need?"

"Can you help me sort through this crap?" Allen said, frustrated with the lack of consideration.

The rest of the day was spent putting the files in order, first by date, then by subject. It was obvious that the DEA didn't like being asked for their files. Ultimately, there wasn't much new information in the box. Since he only asked for a specific period of time, there was no context to some of the files. He did pick up the jargon when it got to the helicopter incident. But again, nothing he could use.

Allen was tired. "I'm glad we went through the Embassy box first," he said, "Otherwise, I might have given up if these were the only thing I had seen."

It was getting late, and Allen was burnt out. "I'm ready for bed," Allen said as he made his way to the bathroom.

"Me too," was Stacy's response.

They both brushed their teeth and then climbed into bed. Within minutes of turning the lights off, the phone rang. "Who the hell would be calling at this hour?" Stacy asked.

Allen looked at the number. "It's Mom," he said as he simultaneously answered the phone and turned on the nightstand light. "Mom, is everything ok?" he started… There was silence on the other end. "Mom? Are you okay?" Allen heard nothing except the sound of the phone on the other end falling to the floor. He hung up, called 911, dressed, and headed out the door with Stacy by his side.

When he arrived at her residence, the ambulance and police were already there. He raced into the driveway, slammed on the brakes, and was out of the car before the pistons could come to a complete stop. "Go honey, I'll be right behind you," Stacy said as he ran to the house, only to be stopped by one of the police officers. Stacy caught up as Allen was explaining that he was the one who had called 911 and needed to get in and see if Mom was okay.

The officer was young and a bit crass, "The resident was found deceased," he said. "No one can go in right now."

Allen was devastated. There was no one else. "Kim, Olivia, Bill, and now Carol," he said with tears streaming down his cheeks. "Mom was the only one left—the only immediate family of Kim and Olivia. No one else understands their importance in this world," he said.

The days turned into weeks, then months. Allen had drifted into a depressed state, having to plan a family member's funeral once again. Carol didn't have much family around; Allen and Stacy were the closest to her. Even though she was Kim's replacement, she loved Stacy as a daughter.

It took weeks to take care of her affairs. When the will was read, Allen discovered he was the sole benefactor. He spent the next few months cleaning out the house, donating most of its belongings to friends and family and then to Goodwill and the Salvation Army. He didn't need anything. None of the family wanted the house, so he sold it, giving the proceeds to a local charity.

Allen felt lost. Although he had Stacy, the rest of his family was gone.

CHAPTER 34

The Last Artifact (3 November 2008)

"Do you believe there's a God?" Allen asked Stacy.

"What? Uhm mm, of course, I do," she responded, caught off guard and freaked out that he went from total silence to such a philosophical question. She hoped there was nothing dark going on inside his head. "I may not go to church as I used to, but I still believe. Is there something going on that I should know about?"

"Do you believe in heaven and hell?" he asked, totally ignoring Stacy's response.

"Can you tell me what's going on? We've never discussed our religious beliefs, so I'm a bit taken aback by this line of questioning. But yes, I believe there is a heaven and a hell," Stacy stated, getting more concerned that something was going on with him.

"So, when you die, where does your soul go? Does it stay with your body or transition to another realm?" he asked, digging deeper into the weeds of this topic.

Stacy thought for a minute, then said, "Well, I suppose if you're a believer, your soul would go to a beautiful place where it would remain until the coming of Christ."

"So you believe that when you die, your body is irreverent to what happens to your soul, thoughts, and mind? You believe they leave the body and stay in limbo, whether in a hospital bed, a coffin, or an urn?" he pressed.

"I guess so," she responded.

"I do too. I believe the mind/soul departs the body and goes to a place to reward them for their good life or punish them for a life of deceit and peril," he said in a somewhat somber tone. "Our bodies don't transition with us. I think our bodies are how we remember or want them to be. And the pleasures we receive in Heaven are spiritual, not physically felt. The same holds true for hell. I believe that if your soul goes to hell, you are placed in a loop of scenarios meant to torture you mentally for eternity. There's is no physical pain, as your body didn't transition with you."

"Allen, you're scaring me. Why are you bringing this up? Did something happen?" Stacy begged him.

"It's the anniversary of…." Allen began. Stacy cut him off before he could finish the sentence.

"Oh shit, I'm so sorry, honey. It totally slipped my mind."

"It's been twenty-three years, and I have yet to get vengeance for Olivia. Could her soul be out there in limbo, waiting on me to end this?"

"Oh honey, please don't think like that. I'm sure Olivia's soul is in Heaven, and she's looking down on you right now." Stacy said.

"I just have this feeling like she's in some place somewhere between Heaven and Hell and can't move on. How can I find out? Why does this haunt me?" he asked.

"I don't know," Stacy said, "but we can stop by the church tomorrow and talk with the pastor."

Allen gets up and walks towards the door, "Let's go for a walk. I need a change of scenery. We can talk while walking."

Stacy was in no position to say no, so she joined him at the door.

"I've been thinking," he began, "it's been too long. I've lost everyone connected to Kim and Olivia. I'm fifty-eight years old. This investigation has to come to an end. I need closure! Olivia needs closure!" he said. "I'm going to get to the bottom of this before anyone else dies, even if it's the last thing I do."

Stacy looked at him, deeply concerned, and asked, "What are the next steps?"

Allen didn't respond immediately. He appeared to be in another world. He continued to look forward, eyes glossed over, chin slightly down, and arms that appeared to be rigid and vibrating. Just when she was about to say something, Allen broke his silence.

"I need to continue my work. I must dedicate all my time to finding the truth. I don't believe I'll find any relief until I'm satisfied that I've done all I can," he said. "I've been burying my emotions too long, pretending to be on a crusade for justice. It's not about justice. It's about the truth, suffering, and revenge. I can't go on living like this." Allen looked over at Stacy and saw despair in her expression. He realized she was hurting and maybe a bit scared by his revelation. He moved to her, placing his arms around her. "I'm going back to the lab to check over my equipment. I need to evaluate my equipment and processes to ensure I'm on the right path. I need to work on this until I have everything figured out."

"How will this get you what you need?" Stacy asked.

Again, still rambling and not answering Stacy's question, he said, "At some point, I need to make the setup smaller.

I need to figure out how to increase power input as well as make my signal stronger." He glanced at Stacy. "Once I get the bugs out, I will systematically visit everyone associated with this case. I'll have my equipment set up and ready to go with the click of a remote. If they talk to me willingly, I won't activate the device. If they refuse to talk, or worse, give me false information to pacify my needs, I'll press the remote switch and take them into one of many prefabricated scenarios. It won't take much to get them talking.

"You won't torture them, will you?" Stacy asked.

"Of course not," Allen responded. "My scenarios are benign. For example, if I'm talking with a military member, I can arrange for a General Officer to walk in and order them to speak to me."

"That's good," Stacy commented, "I was afraid you would be doing something illegal or dangerous."

"The legality of this is still questionable. To date, there isn't anything like this on the market. As far as danger, well, there's always a chance of danger, but I'll do my best to keep it minimal. Then, when I find out the one responsible, I will make them suffer."

Stacy knew Allen was kind and caring and couldn't picture hurting someone purposefully. She hopes that he never has to.

Allen spent the next few years pretty much a recluse. His only contact was Stacy, who was doing her best to support him.

It was close to Christmas, and Allen was finishing breakfast when Patrick knocked on the door. "Come on in, Pat. I'll get you a cup of coffee."

"I'd love to, but I have a few more stops; you know how it is around Christmas," he said.

"I do know. That's why I'm asking you for a cup of coffee. It's cold outside, and you need to warm up to avoid getting sick. It's the neighborly thing to do."

"Since you put it that way, I don't mind if I do," Pat replied.

Allen directed Pat to the sofa, then went into the bedroom to let Stacy know Pat was there. He'd learned from his mistake a couple of years back. He made Pat a large black coffee with two Sweet'N Lows, just as he liked. He returned to the combination living room and office and gave him the cup. "Pat, I want you to know how much we appreciate all that you do. You're out there every day, rain or shine. You bring us good news and bad. You keep us informed…" Allen continued with his praise of Pat. Stacy joined them just in time to concur with everything Allen was saying. She walked over to the desk, picked up an envelope with Pat's name on it, and brought it to Allen.

"Pat, we want to wish you a Merry Christmas and hope you can spend some time with your family this year," he then handed Pat the envelope.

"What's this?" Pat asked.

"It's just a small token of our appreciation. We love having you here for your occasional coffee breaks." Stacy interjected.

Pat opened the envelope and found a crisp $100 bill. "No, this is too much. I can't accept this," he said.

"No, it's not, and yes, you will," Allen came back. "You're a good man, and we can afford it."

Pat stood and shook Allen's hand, almost in tears. He went to shake Stacy's, and she pushed his hand away, wrapping her arms around him. "I'm a hugger, not a shaker," she said.

Pat finished his java, thanked them again for the coffee and gift, and walked out. Halfway down the sidewalk, he felt a package in his coat pocket. He turned to walk back, seeing Allen and Stacy standing at the open door. "Did you forget something?" Allen asked. Pat shook his head in embarrassment, then handed Allen the small package before returning to the sidewalk to continue his route. "Thanks, Pat, Merry Christmas." Pat turned and waved, not missing a step.

Allen was opening the small package as he and Stacy walked back in. It was a priority package that contained a thumb drive from Mrs. Kimberly Hammond, the DEA Internal Affairs lady. Allen quickly plugged it into his computer and opened up the drive. There was only one file, a video from the first vehicle to reach the wreckage.

Allen sat there staring at the opened folder on his screen. His hands were shaking, fingers moving nervously; Stacy saw that his respiration had increased and placed her hands on his, trying to calm him down, "Honey, you're not ready for this..." She paused as Allen seemed determined to overcome his anxiety and clicked play despite her concerns.

As the video began playing, Allen clinched his left hand, rubbing it with his right, then switching hands. He was second-guessing his decision to view the video but wouldn't stop. The video encompassed his entire monitor, showing two views simultaneously. On the left side of his screen was the inside of the cabin, from the front to the back. On the right side, the image showed a wide-angle view of everything in front of the vessel. He could see the facial reactions of the three crew members as they reached the helicopter.

Allen paused the video to better see the men on the screen. The two in front seemed older than the one in the back. Something stood out with the young airman, so he tried to zoom in on him to read his name tag; unfortunately, the controls didn't support that function. The names appeared blurred out anyway, so he gave up and resumed watching the video.

The camera scanned the areas outside the wreckage before panning up to the front of the vehicle. It was graphic, showing things that Allen wished he could un-see. Whoever controlled the external camera was meticulously canvassing the wreckage, starting at the front of the helicopter and slowly panning the cabin section. For the most part, the structure of the helicopter was still intact. The pilot and co-pilot were seated, and the visuals were horrific. Body parts were misconfigured, missing, or barely intact, a fact corroborated by the accompanying audio recording of the crew narrating what the camera was showing to the command center. The camera was moving at a sloth's pace, so there was plenty of time to see every detail. The view of the US crew showed them as stoic, with no reaction to the carnage. They appeared to be documenting the events as they were happening. As the camera zoomed in on the body to the pilot's left, Allen froze it. *That's not the co-pilot. That's Perez, Mendez's chief of security.*

The camera then moved slowly towards the back of the cabin. Allen took a deep breath as the camera gradually started pulling in the images of Olivia. At first, it was only her blond hair waving in the water, then the top of her scalp appeared. Allen saw a gash on her forehead, with what looked like blood seeping from the wound into the water. "Don't look at this!" Stacy yelled. She had been behind him, watching and listening. "You can't do this to yourself. These images will haunt you for the rest of your life."

"You don't understand. I need to know," Allen replied.

"NO, YOU DON'T!" Stacy shouted. "I've seen the horrors of accidents where bodies are torn apart. It's very hard to lose those images. Fortunately, I've never had to see a loved one. Trust me, you're not ready for this."

Allen looked at the frozen video; on the left was Olivia's face, eyes wide open. You can see the pain in her expression. When he looked at the other feed, the crew that had been so stoic earlier was now in a state of shock. They were seeing something that truly upset them.

"Honey, I'm going to watch it. I'd prefer you be here with me, but if you can't, I'll understand." Before she could respond, Allen hit play on the video, and it continued its slow panning through the back of the cabin with Olivia's image in full view. Allen gasped when it passed over her upper torso, and he saw that her bathing suit wasn't there. There were open wounds with more seepage. He looked at the other scene and heard the crew describing the scene to the command center. As the camera slowly panned, he heard the crew radioing, "Mayday, Mayday…" Then, there was total silence, and everything went black.

Stacy sighed in relief and wiped tears from her eyes, throwing the moist tissue into a pile on the desk, thankful that Allen couldn't see the rest of Olivia's body or Mendez's next to her. Allen was about to turn the video off when some after-the-fact graphics appeared, depicting the names of the deceased crew and the sole survivor, Senior Airman Mike Bowers. "I know him!" Allen exclaimed. "I thought he looked familiar. Why would he have kept this from me all these years?"

This lit a fire that had been stagnant inside him. He knew what he had to do. Allen spent the next several years preparing for the ultimate revenge, even more personal since he found out his friend had betrayed him.

Ten years had passed. Allen, now sixty-eight years old, was ready to go. There had been other opportunities in the past, but due to Bowers' work travels, he had to keep postponing it. Then, the COVID pandemic hit, and no one was traveling. With everyone on lockdown, this would be easy, or at least so he thought. He realized years ago that he couldn't do this on his own, so he began a strategic search for assistance. Allen amassed friends and associates over the years and a couple of contacts associated with Bowers. He knew he could count on them to help him carry out his revenge for a price.

Little did he know the world was changing. The pandemic had altered many lives. The plan must be fluid, as constant change would be inevitable. He was ready. His equipment was ready. He looked over to Stacy and gave her a nod, ran his hands through his hair, and then, like in a scene from '*The Shining*,' Allen mimicked '*Jack Nicholson*' when he said… "*It's show time!*"

THE BEGINNING

EPILOGUE

Allen was able to alter his plans, but due to the COVID-19 pandemic, it required constant modifications. Time and money weren't a problem before; however, time was running out for him. This could be his last chance to exercise revenge on the remaining individual that he felt was a part of the cover-up.

To make this work, he needed to get Mike back to Central America, where it all began. He needed to coerce others to assist.

Stacy wanted to help, but now in her early sixties and failing health, she was left in Youngstown while Allen set the wheels in motion.

Not all stories have a happy ending; some have no ending. This story is just beginning, at least for Mike. Allen's years of planning were ready to come to fruition.

To see how this all ends, read "Captured by COVID, Deceit, Conspiracy, and Death – A True Story" by Michael E. Bowers.

ACKNOWLEDGMENTS

The success of "Captured by COVID, Deceit, Conspiracy & Death – A True Story" inspired this book. Some of the individuals needed to have their stories told. The nonfiction story of my ordeal in 2021 laid the groundwork for this book.

My friends and family stood by my side when I couldn't stand and provided the support, friendship, and kindness needed to get me to where I am today.

This book wouldn't have been possible without the ICU team at Soin Medical Center. They kept me alive against all odds. Those dedicated doctors and nurses are truly amazing.

AUTHOR BIO

MR. BOWERS is an award-winning author that used his first hand experience to write *Captured By COVID, Deceit, Conspiracy & Death – A True Story*. The images are still very real, and he used this to write his novel "Oliva"

His military background helped develop the characters, but it was his experience with critical care psychosis that made this book possible.

Critical Care Psychosis is real and experienced every day by patients on their death bed. I would have never believed it possible if I hadn't experienced it firsthand.

The next time you visit a friend or loved one in a coma in the hospital, don't assume they are just sleeping. Their brain is still active and could be putting them through hell.

Some individuals in this book were derived from real experiences detailed in Captured by COVID. This book gives some of the main characters, especially Allen and Olivia, a fictional background. "Olivia" describes the motivation that made one kind, caring husband and father seek revenge at all costs towards those involved with his family's demise.

Made in United States
North Haven, CT
26 February 2025